Sacred Wilderness

AMERICAN INDIAN STUDIES SERIES

Gordon Henry, *Series Editor*

Shedding Skins: Four Sioux Poets
Edited by Adrian C. Louis | 978-0-87013-823-2

Writing Home: Indigenous Narratives of Resistance
Michael D. Wilson | 978-0-87013-818-8

National Monuments
Heid E. Erdrich | 978-0-87013-848-5

The Indian Who Bombed Berlin and Other Stories
Ralph Salisbury | 978-0-87013-847-8

Facing the Future: The Indian Child Welfare Act at 30
Edited by Matthew L. M. Fletcher, Wenona T. Singel, and Kathryn E. Fort | 978-0-87013-860-7

Dragonfly Dance
Denise K. Lajimodiere | 978-0-87013-982-6

Ogimawkwe Mitigwaki (*Queen of the Woods*)
Simon Pokagon | 978-0-87013-987-1

Plain of Jars and Other Stories
Geary Hobson | 978-0-87013-998-7

Document of Expectations
Devon Abbott Mihesua | 978-1-61186-011-5

Centering Anishinaabeg Studies: Understanding the World through Stories
Edited by Jill Doerfler, Niigaanwewidam James Sinclair, and Heidi Kiiwetinepinesiik Stark | 978-1-61186-067-2

Follow the Blackbirds
Gwen Nell Westerman | 978-1-61186-092-4

Bawaajimo: *A Dialect of Dreams in Anishinaabe Language and Literature*
Margaret Noodin | 978-1-61186-105-1

Sacred Wilderness
Susan Power | 978-1-61186-111-2

Sacred Wilderness

Susan Power

Michigan State University Press | *East Lansing*

∞ The paper used in this publication meets the minimum requirements of ANSI/NISO Z39.48-1992 (R 1997) (Permanence of Paper).

Michigan State University Press
East Lansing, Michigan 48823-5245

Printed and bound in the United States of America.

20 19 18 17 16 15 14 1 2 3 4 5 6 7 8 9 10

LIBRARY OF CONGRESS CATALOGING-IN-PUBLICATION DATA
Power, Susan, 1961– Sacred wilderness / Susan Power.
pages cm.—(American Indian Studies Series)
"This is a Clan Mother story for the 21st century"—T.p. verso.
ISBN 978-1-61186-111-2 (paper : alk. paper)—ISBN 978-1-60917-401-9 (ebook)
1. Indians of North America—Fiction. I. Title.
PS3566.O83578S23 2013
813'.54—dc23
2013012253

Book design and composition by Charlie Sharp, Sharp Des!gns, Lansing, Michigan
Cover design by David Drummond, Salamander Design, www.salamanderhill.com
Cover image is detail from *Bear Medicine* ©2000 Andrea Carlson, and is used with permission.

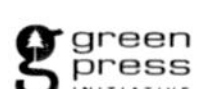

Michigan State University Press is a member of the Green Press Initiative and is committed to developing and encouraging ecologically responsible publishing practices. For more information about the Green Press Initiative and the use of recycled paper in book publishing, please visit *www.greenpressinitiative.org.*

Visit Michigan State University Press at *www.msupress.org*

For my mother, Susan Kelly Power,

who made the journey with me—

longer, farther, deeper.

Contents

The Visitation of Gladys Swan

The city of Saint Paul was named for a man of extremes, Paul of Tarsus, the Pharisee who became a Christian martyr. His Cathedral rises majestically near the mouth of Summit Avenue—the Victorian-era jewel that runs from east to west through the city like a river of material abundance. Mansions stare at one another across the wide road, some of them red-bricked and haughty, some of them a fairy-tale dream of wood lace trim and turrets.

Gladys had never lived in such a fancy neighborhood. She'd spent most of her life on a reservation in northern Minnesota and later years in a small Minneapolis apartment. But she wasn't unduly impressed by the display of wealth. She viewed the avenue from the passenger seat of her daughter's car and saw the generous lots and governor's mansion through her grandfather's eyes. She could just imagine his reaction: "Look at you, Noozis. Now you really *are* Queen of the Heavens, moving into some Minnesota castle! Watch out—they always say rich people are crazy. Me, I wouldn't know for sure since I never knew any, so give them a chance. But don't take any nonsense off them. Remember, you are Ojibwe, Anishinaabe, and that means you are good enough for anyone. You are one of the Original People." She smiled to recall his warm voice, always crackling with mischief, and his habit

of making a judgment and then backtracking a bit as if he could mend the trail he'd just broken.

"Your great-great-Grandpa would've been crazy about you," she told her granddaughter, Ava, who was buckled into the back seat, holding a squirming bundle in her small lap. She had just turned five, a summer-baby Leo with thick black hair that laid down flat and shiny like the mane of a horse. She had warm brown eyes, round as the moon when she was happy, and wore glasses with rectangular frames that made her look grown up.

"The Great One," Ava said in a dreamy voice. This ancestor was one of her favorite characters in Gladys's stories, though she couldn't quite pronounce all the "greats" of his title, clumped so closely together, so she shortened it to the brief honorific.

"See, just you calling him that would've made him puff up with satisfaction and then brag on it to everybody. A good man, he was. A smart man."

A muffled sound of misery—part moan and part growl—filled the small car.

"How're you doing back there?" Gladys's daughter, Binah, checked the rearview mirror to glance at Ava.

"Fine. He's just scared. Don't be scared, Zhigaag. No one's gonna hurt you." Ava crooned to the unhappy cat in what she considered to be a mother's voice.

"He better not scratch her. I don't know why I let her hold him." Binah noticed the impatience of the driver in the Hummer behind her, riding the tail of her car, so she reduced her speed in response.

"He won't," Ava protested. "He's all wrapped up like a mummy in the towel and can't move his hands."

"You should have a carrier, Mama," Binah told Gladys in a clipped voice that sounded to the older woman like scissors. Gladys shrugged, unperturbed, but Ava jumped to her defense.

"He doesn't like carriers. Grandma told you. Makes him feel like he's in jail."

"So a straitjacket's better?" Binah rumbled under her breath. Now she sounds like the cat, Gladys thought.

Ava was singing to Zhigaag in a soft, soothing voice: "Giizhenaamin, Zhigaag. Giizhenaamin, Zhigaag."

"How can she love that cat when he never lets her touch him?"

Gladys shrugged again. She knew her daughter was angry with her for other reasons and was trying to pick a fight. Better not to engage. Her daughter was in

a mood where she was just like one of those exploding firecrackers that can take off your hand if you hold it too long. But Ava was fearless and charged ahead in defense of her grandmother and the cat.

"He does let me pet him when he feels like it. He just doesn't usually feel like it. He's Grandma's cat. He's a one-person person," she said with great dignity, like an ancient sage.

Binah snorted. "He's not a person, he's a cat."

"Yes, he is," Ava said urgently, distressed. "He's both. And you're hurting his feelings. Don't listen to her, Zhigaag. You *are* a person, I know it."

"I smell your influence all over this," Binah hissed at Gladys.

"Probably," was all she said.

They'd reached Ramsey Hill, and for a few moments it looked as if they would drive straight into the sprawling University Club perched at the top of the hill, where F. Scott Fitzgerald had tossed back frothy champagne and danced in optimistic wildness. Then a curving lane appeared, and Binah nosed the car to the left, ready to turn.

"There's Lookout Park," Gladys spoke on impulse. "Let's pull over there. I want to see that bird."

"What? What bird?" Binah turned left, following Summit Avenue as it curved past the hill and continued on—the mansions would only get larger from this point.

"Stop here."

Despite Binah's irritation she did as her mother requested and parked near a wedge of grass that overlooked the expanse containing downtown Saint Paul, Lowertown, and the High Bridge that stretched across the Mississippi River.

Ava struggled to unbuckle herself and still keep hold of the wriggling cat. "I'll take him for a while," Gladys told her. "You've done a good job with this rascal." She opened the back door and reached for the cat who was barely visible in the mound of beach towel. His black-masked face looked fearful. As soon as he saw Gladys he cried as if his heart were breaking.

"Oh, hush," she said with tender affection. "So dramatic. No one's torturing you. You're just fine." Zhigaag seemed to sense that further protest was useless, so he closed his eyes and fell asleep in her arms. Gladys led the others to a sign that told the story of Lookout Point and explained the presence of a bronze eagle, poised at the edge of the hill, its wings beginning to open.

"This is the eagle that once stood atop a building in New York City," she told

her granddaughter as she read the plaque. "The New York Life Building. So, this isn't one of ours, a Minnesota eagle, this is one that flew all the way from Iroquois country."

"Iroquois?" Ava asked, wrinkling her brow in concentration and pushing her stylish glasses further up the bridge of her nose.

"Yes. They're the Six Nations Confederacy—that means six tribes came together and agreed to be allies and stop fighting."

"This is a Mama eagle," Ava said in a determined voice, sounding like a school teacher. "See, she's guarding her babies from that big snake."

Ava looked to her mother for confirmation. Binah shrugged. Undiscouraged, Ava made a wringing motion with her hands as if she herself were battling the snake. Victory. She pressed her palms against the stone pedestal and stared at the eagle's face with awe. "Could we offer her some tobacco?" she whispered, as if she didn't want the bird to hear in case the answer was "no."

"Of course," Gladys said. "Just what I was thinking. You read my mind, Noozis."

Binah snorted, which woke Zhigaag. He sent a warning noise in her direction. "Oh, pipe down," she told him. "Mama, why on earth are you offering tobacco to a statue? It isn't alive. It's a man-made object, no, a white-made object that perched over a commercial enterprise which no doubt ripped off a lot of people in its day."

Gladys sighed. She kissed Zhigaag's forehead, where the black mask edged against blinding white fur. "Everything is alive. Everything is moving. Don't even scientists say that? Haven't they figured out what we knew all along? They call it 'matter,' the tiny, wiggling movement of matter. So, I say, all matter matters! How's that?" She looked to Ava, and the girl nodded with great solemnity.

"Fine." Binah pulled a pouch of fragrant tobacco from her purse and held it open. Ava reached in and extracted a small pinch. She held the tobacco in her palm and closed her eyes in prayer.

"What are you praying, Noozis?" Gladys asked, after waiting a respectful minute in silence.

"I'm praying that if this eagle talks to other ones here in Minnesota, she'll tell them that we don't want them to starve, but please leave Zhigaag alone when he's outside."

"Good thinking. May I add something?" Ava nodded. "I'd like to welcome this eagle to the territory of the Ojibwe and Dakota people. Well, given where we're standing right now, I should reverse that order. Okay. Dakota and Ojibwe

territory. We're glad you were saved when they pulled down your building and hope you like our view here. All the trees. Please watch out for us since you can see so much farther than we can. May we share some of your remarkable vision."

Ava waited until she was certain her grandmother had finished speaking, then she placed the tobacco at the base of the statue. A sudden gust of wind curled around their legs, but the clump of tobacco remained intact, as if the small flakes were magnetic filings.

"It's been accepted," Gladys said, and the three trooped back to the car.

Two weeks earlier, Gladys had received a call from the director of the Native American Journalists Association, a young Ojibwe writer named Marcus. He sounded sheepish, reluctant to say why he was calling. After a few exchanges of pleasantries he sighed, took a sip of coffee, and got to the point: "Gladys, here's the deal. There's some society lady who's been calling all the Indian organizations in town—the Indian Center, even Birchbark Books—saying she's looking for an Indian housekeeper. I know, I know—" he hurried along as if anticipating an eruption from the older woman. "God, she's so hopelessly politically incorrect you almost got to wonder if it's an act, some kind of schtick put on by a writer for *The Onion*. Anyway, we've taken a few calls from her, and she's annoying my assistant. Fern's about ready to take that lady *out*. So I thought I'd pass the message along. Not that you'd be interested. Just trying to get this woman off our backs. Says she lives over in Saint Paul, on Summit Ave, and could offer a spacious carriage house to whoever. Oh, and she's looking for an Indian because supposedly she's part Mohawk. Well, you know how that is," he finished, skeptically.

Gladys heard him sigh again, this time in relief, and take another sip of coffee. The brief silence made him nervous, so he rushed to fill it. "The Indians around here, geez, you know how we are, pushed to the last nerve with ignorant crap like this. Oh, sorry, my bad."

Gladys rescued the young writer with a warm chuckle. "Don't worry. You've come to the right place. I've been a little antsy lately, feeling there's something I should be doing, but what? I'm sure she means well, this lady, just doesn't know how to go about things. Lost in a time warp! Maybe she's lonesome for Indians. What's her name, anyway?"

"Candace. Candace Jenssen."

"A good Mohawk name," Gladys said with gravity. The two erupted in laughter, and Marcus spit coffee all over his desk blotter that was really a calendar from 1997, twelve years earlier.

"Shit, I got to clean this up. Oops, sorry. I'm a potty mouth today."

"Don't worry, Marcus, you take care. Oh, but what's her number?"

When Gladys phoned her daughters, Binah and Grace, to tell them she was going to be a housekeeper living in a carriage house on Summit Avenue, their reactions were typically different.

Grace had said: "Well, if you really want to do this, Mama, at least you'll be closer to us. We don't see you enough. Wait 'til I tell Dylan, he'll be so excited!"

Grace was a visual artist who specialized in landscape paintings that were constructed of a swarming galaxy of minutiae—small objects and creatures that swirled together to create the impression of a single, larger view. She lived now in an artists' cooperative in Saint Paul with her thirteen-year-old son, Dylan, who was still, even at this fractious age of growing pains and abject self-consciousness, an unabashed fan of his grandmother.

Binah, on the other hand, had torn into a blistering lecture upon hearing her mother's news, the kind that made Gladys retreat into what she thought of as "Peanuts mode." She'd always loved how the Peanuts gang of kids—Lucy, Linus, and Charlie Brown—never heard what adults were saying beyond a tinny hash of noise: "*wha wha wha wha wha wha.*"

Well, she listened to her daughter's outrage for a while: "Do you really want to be reduced to some kind of throwback stereotype from the Dark Ages? Honestly! A maid for some rich lady in a mansion? Beyond the ludicrousness of her search for an ethnic specimen to do her dirty work, there's this to consider. You're seventy-four years old. Have you thought how much work it will be to clean a massive house? You could keel over and then what would we do?"

As Binah made her points seven different ways, Gladys was singing, silently, in the recording studio of her mind. "We all live in a YELLOW SUBMARINE . . ." she was belting into a microphone, headset covering her ears, her girls singing backup with gusto and cheer just as they had when they were little.

"Mama? Mama? Are you listening to me?" Binah's question brought Gladys back to her kitchen where she sat at the scarred wooden table where so much news had been aired—confessions made, apologies offered, tears shed, jokes performed. She patted the table and wetted her finger to press away an errant crumb.

"Yes, my girl, I hear you," she said with disciplined patience, for Binah's tears

were there, too, soaked into the table. "I know you're worried for me and I'm lucky to have girls who care what happens. All I can say is that I am *meant* to do this. I can feel it. There's work and then there's *work*. This lady doesn't need a maid so much as something else. I have to go figure out what that is."

Binah was quiet for several beats, and Gladys knew her daughter was pacing angrily, chewing on her cuticles which she'd made ragged in recent months. Binah sighed, an exhalation so deep she nearly snagged the edge of a flood of tears, pooled in her chest, her heart, vast enough to wash everyone right off the map. Gladys heard her check the pain before it gushed away from her. "The only thing that could possibly make this worse would be if you were African-American. You know that horrible cliché of the ever-loving arms of Black women, Black Mamas; perennially in service to their white charges, be they children or so-called adults. As if they have no life of their own, no dreams or problems of their own as important as what happens to their beloved white employers. Ugh! That's my final word on all this, Mama. Ugh!"

Binah missed the house where Gladys would be working and living, drove right past it, so she continued on to the end of Summit Avenue and turned around in the Cathedral parking lot. This time she found the place—an imposing red-bricked structure with leaded windows, tucked into the corner of Summit and Western. Binah parked the car and turned off the motor, then sat quietly, hands in her lap, staring straight ahead as if hypnotized.

Gladys was able to look at her daughter for the first time in months. Binah was so angry these days it was hard to see past the frustration and scorn that snapped around her like a live wire. She looked older than forty-eight; silver strands of wiry hair raked through her dark brown waves, and her eyes were an empty black as if the spark of pleasure that once lit them had been snuffed out. She was always the beautiful one. The dramatic arch of her eyebrows and long lashes, her regal nose and teasing lips that curled on one side, made people watch her when she passed them, then remain transfixed by the waterfall of hair that spilled down her back past the waist of her jeans. The loveliness was still there, just dimmed with shadows. Gladys could see her daughter's pulse jumping in her neck, beating out a fast, unhappy rhythm. Without thinking, Gladys reached out and gently touched Binah there with her finger. Binah flinched.

"You're all keyed-up," Gladys said. "I can see your heart racing." For one

moment Binah looked ready to fall into her mother's arms, but she cleared her throat instead and grabbed the steering wheel with long dark fingers.

"I'm stressed about this decision of yours," was all she said. Then she shook herself as if she'd passed through a cold spot that caught her unawares. She turned to face her mother. "Answer me this. You feel you have some business here, with this woman. Okay, let's say she needs some existential help. Who doesn't? What makes her so fortunate, no, so *worthy* of your aid? You know as well as I do that there are kids dying on the rez every day. They need help. They need guidance. Why the—" Binah glanced into the rearview mirror and, seeing Ava, caught herself just in time. "*Bleep* does some rich wannabe who could purchase a legion of therapists merit a second of your time and energy? Explain it to me, please!"

Silence fell heavily in the car and seemed to stop time. Gladys refused to answer until her daughter's breathing slowed and became regular again.

"I'm sorry this is so hard for you," she finally said. She attempted to make eye contact with Binah, but her daughter stared at the steering wheel. "I don't know what it is about this person, this position, that pulls me. I was taught to trust my instincts, the guidance that comes from deep inside, and I'm not going to stop now. It's my map, and I have to follow it. Be careful about thinking you know someone from looking at the front lawn of their house. You don't know this person's story. Everyone's story matters, I always taught you that. If yours matters, then so does hers. And that's that."

Binah sighed and stretched her hands, cracked her knuckles to fill the silence.

"Are we here?" Ava suddenly asked from the backseat.

"We sure are," Gladys told her. "Let's go see what your grandma is getting herself into."

They pulled out the few items Gladys had brought with her, primarily supplies for the cat, and easily carried the load between them. For all Binah's ferocious talk, she appeared daunted when it came to mounting the manor's stone steps, guarded by two stone lions perched at the top. Their mouths were open as if they considered growling, depending upon the conduct of those who approached.

"Look, Zhigaag, your relatives!" Ava crowed, pointing at the dignified statues with her small lips in imitation of her grandmother's favorite gesture. Zhigaag recognized his name and looked down at her from Gladys's firm grasp, but his eyes were gold disks, dilated with nerves, and he didn't seem at all interested in his proud cousins.

Binah gave her daughter an encouraging smile though Ava didn't seem the

This is a Clan Mother story
for the twenty-first century.

Sacred Wilderness

least bit nervous, and the two followed Gladys who charged up the stairs without hesitation. She was about to ring the bell when the door opened.

A woman stood before her, smiling nervously. Is this Candace? Gladys wondered. She looks younger than I thought she was.

"Oh, I'm *pleased* you're here!" the woman gushed with a warmth almost embarrassing it was so nakedly sincere. "Candace, I'm Candace," she said when no one moved.

"Oh, okay. You looked like such a young little thing, I wasn't sure," Gladys told her.

Candace blushed and ushered everyone in, or tried to. Binah stood rigidly on the landing—an elegant stone porch—and would not budge.

"We're just dropping her off," she said to the air, without looking at Candace or anyone. She set down the luggage with an angry thump.

"Please, you must come in. There's fresh lemonade and a raspberry torte, and I'd love to give you a tour so you can assure yourself your mother's in a good place."

Gladys heard a low growl and wasn't certain if it came from her cat, her daughter, or the fussy stone lions. Zhigaag apparently, for Ava peeked at him and gently, respectfully, stroked his head with a finger which he couldn't evade, wrapped as he was.

"Ah, this is the famous Ojibwe-speaking cat," Candace said. "Or should I say, Ojibwe-comprehending? I take it he doesn't launch into actual speech?" She smiled down at Ava.

"You'd be surprised," the little girl said in a knowing way, lifting her eyebrows significantly as if to indicate there was no end to the miracles of this cat.

"Why don't we put him in the solarium for now? He can enjoy the view—a lot of birds back there, flowers and sunlight. We can bring him to the carriage house apartment later." She moved to lead the way, but no one followed. Binah was still resisting entry.

"I don't think my girls can join us today," Gladys said. She looked at Binah to confirm this statement and Binah glared, her eyes cold and hard, sharp like black spikes.

"That's such a shame," Candace said with genuine disappointment. "I think you'd enjoy the Indian Art Room."

"The art's segregated?!" Binah hissed, suddenly very animate, a new irritation unlocking her limbs. "Oh, I can't *believe* this, Mama, you've *got* to be kidding me! How can you stay here? Let's turn around and just go back."

Now it was the mother's turn to stare, and Binah was no match for Gladys when she finally came to the end of her generous patience.

"Okay, okay. *I'm* going. You can handle this insanity on your own." Binah stuck out her hand and Ava grasped it reluctantly, eager to view the fascinating castle before her.

Candace hadn't heard this exchange; she had stepped further into the hall to allow Gladys to confer with her daughter in private. Candace pretended to examine her slender hands and their perfect manicure that was careful to look like no manicure at all. Gladys kissed her granddaughter and lowered Zhigaag so Ava could whisper an earnest message into his twitching ear. Then Binah marched her daughter back to the car and made the motor spit a little before she swept them away from the land of well-tended lawns and mansions and small forests of trees huddled at the edges of rich lots.

"Now, was this your daughter who teaches at the U?" Candace inquired politely, apparently oblivious to any discord.

"That's right. In American Indian Studies."

"Oh, she *has* to see my little museum then, one of these days."

"One of these days," Gladys murmured, thinking of how many mountains would have to move before her daughter made that particular expedition.

"Well, at least *you're* here!" Candace said.

Zhigaag was taken to the sun room and set free of the towel. He hunkered down in a suspicious crouch, and the women decided to have refreshments right there, so he could be comforted by the presence of Gladys.

"He's really stunning," Candace remarked when she could see his jet black mask and robe swept over brilliant white paws and chin. He wore a pattern of diamonds within diamonds on his back that clearly marked him as rare. "What does his name mean?"

"Poor thing, he deserves better but when I found him he was a tiny kitten, huddled against a curb, all ears and bones. He had something wrong with his insides, intestines, that made him smell real bad 'til we got it sorted out. Because of that and his color, I just called him 'Skunk.' Then he learned it and it was too late to change."

"Sounds much nicer in Ojibwe," Candace murmured, suddenly shy.

Gladys watched how carefully she ate a sliver of torte, forking microscopic morsels that Gladys doubted were substantial enough to form a taste. She'd guessed wrong about the woman's age; she was fifty-four but looked like a girl, so small-framed and flexible she could be a gymnast, well, a tall one. She carried herself in such a nimble, youthful way and was so slender, she appeared to take up little space when actually she stood several inches higher than Gladys. She had summer freckles scattered across her nose and cheeks, and gray eyes that drew Gladys's attention, they were so unusual. They flickered from silver-white to steel gray, to a warm color that was almost blue. Eyes that changed with every nuance of mood.

"I like your hair, it reminds me of that flapper," Gladys said, so used to mothering girls who appreciated it when you noticed the trouble they took with their looks.

"Really? Thank you. It's something new. You nailed it—I went in with a photograph of Louise Brooks and said, 'This is what I want,' though keeping my color." Her hair was dark brown with streaks of red highlights that gave her a kind of sunset halo. The cut was short at the nape, exposing her creamy neck, and fell in wings on either side of her face like stylish curtains.

Gladys asked if she had children. Twin boys, both of them working on JD-MBA degrees at Harvard. "Lethal competition between them, yet they're inseparable," Candace sighed, and Gladys couldn't make out whether she was proud or disappointed. So she just nodded her head.

Candace didn't sit still but kept bouncing a leg or shifting in her chair. Gladys knew the woman was anxious to show her the place. "I'll just give you the abridged version," Candace said, once the tour commenced. "The main rooms as opposed to every nook and cranny. Oh, and I hope I made it clear that you don't have to worry about maintaining all of this." Candace indicated the house with a graceful sweep of her hand. "I have a crew that comes in each week to do a proper scrub down. But I wanted someone on hand to maybe help with the cooking and the light daily touch-ups."

They were standing in the spacious foyer, and before setting off to view the rest of the place Gladys noted the modest tableau made by her own possessions—how they huddled together in the vestibule as if prepared to make a run for it as soon as she wasn't looking. She'd brought a suitcase, her purse, Zhigaag's litter box that was really like a small cave (Ava approved of it; "he likes his privacy," she'd said), and a shopping bag containing Zhigaag's favorite cat food. Gladys wrenched herself from that oasis of comfort and glanced around the entrance hall. She appreciated the gleaming wood floors, buffed until they looked like amber.

"I change things up every few years, but right now I went with Shelly at Real

Designs for the ground floor. I love the Italian influence she brought to the place. Murano glass lighting, of course, and the furniture from Milan. God, don't you love that pomegranate suede?" She was pointing to a group of plush armchairs that somehow managed to look both cozy and regal. Gladys nodded and followed along, losing count of how many bedrooms and bathrooms there were, each one its own masterpiece of design and decoration.

Gladys noted that Candace was more confident now, enumerating her things, opening an occasional drawer to exhibit a level of organization Gladys didn't realize existed in the world. Socks folded and separated by color, nestled like jewels in a drawer with dividers, rubber bands kept in an expensive jar, linen stacked with such precision it looked like a machine had done the work. She could hear her grandfather's voice, commenting on all this order: "Noozis, be careful now. It isn't natural to live like this. Oh, there's an order when you lead a simple life, your few things in their one neat place. But this is something else."

The kitchen was palatial, dazzling. A copper island the size of a car gleamed before her. Silken maple cabinets extended from floor to ceiling, and black granite counters topped every surface for what seemed to be miles.

"My dream kitchen," Candace breathed, and pointed to the backsplash which she said was constructed of ancient Roman glass. Gladys couldn't imagine food in this glistening church. Steam and oil, crumbs and spills, charred pans and licked spoons. "Cooking in here is an epiphany," Candace said, and looked to Gladys for a reaction.

"It's real pretty," she finally commented. "And very clean."

Candace's face showed disappointment. In one quick moment Gladys saw the nervous energy leave the woman, and she nearly reached out a hand to steady her because Candace looked limp as a guitar string once it breaks. "Am I ridiculous or what?" Candace said, her voice trembling between laughter and tears. "I know this is probably all wrong, dragging you hither and yon through the miles of this place as if I'm showing off. I'm not, I'm really not meaning to do that. Show off. I want to bring you in and make my home your home."

Gladys was so startled by this sudden declaration and plunge in mood she wasn't sure what to say, so she patted the woman's arm in support. Candace immediately brightened as if Gladys had flicked a switch in her.

They skipped the art room for the moment because Zhigaag was crying so urgently he could be heard throughout an entire level of the house. So they grabbed the luggage in the hall, and he and Gladys were ushered outside and walked to another building on the property which had once housed carriages and now contained cars. Stone lions again, this time flanking the entrance to the stairway leading to a second-floor apartment. These ones were smaller and less fierce. More curious than anything. Zhigaag hissed at one, and when he received no response his confidence seemed to return, and he struggled until Gladys set him down and let him trot up the stairs ahead of her.

The apartment was so luxurious Gladys had a difficult time imagining herself living there. The den had a loveseat and sofa made of velvety, plum-colored suede and a flat-screen television mounted on the wall. The bed was king-sized, draped in silky sheets that reminded her of an Indian woman's sari, and what looked to be a hundred pillows were arranged on it in a complicated, puzzle-like design. There were granite counters in the bathroom, a smoked glass sink somehow lit from below, and a jacuzzi bathtub set in an expanse of rose tile.

"This place was the boys' playhouse back in the day, then party central during high school and college. But they're so rarely here anymore, and then not for long, I thought it was time to make use of it again. I hope you like it. We can make adjustments if needed."

Candace looked almost crushed by Gladys's reserve. The older woman roused herself to offer compliments and assure her that this would be just grand. But when Candace left to allow Gladys and the cat the chance to settle into their space, Gladys dropped into the loveseat and shook her head.

"Now I know why we're here, Zhigaag. Oh, that poor lady." Zhigaag watched her with intense devotion and jumped in her lap so smoothly it was like water had just poured into her arms. "We have to help her, Zhigaag. You hear me? You're in this, too. No one should have to live this way."

The next morning Gladys woke up when the sun was still a red yolk, moving out of darkness into a new day. She washed her face and looked in the bathroom mirror, smiled at herself, flattered by the lighting. "This makes me look pretty good," she told Zhigaag, who was mesmerized by her morning ablutions. "Maybe it's one of those magic mirrors and I'm going to get all vain." She laughed, never one to worry much about beauty regimes. She had the same figure she'd always had—neither slender nor heavy, what she would have described as unremarkable and strong. She had thick gray hair she wore off her face, held in smooth place by beaded combs and then woven into neat braids. Her nose was narrow and small, what some would call "fine," and her lips the lush dark color and texture of the shells of Brazil nuts. But her eyes were what drew people—a vivid coppery green that was somehow a joyful reminder of spring.

After her usual, and necessary, cup of coffee and slice of dry toast she went out into the morning and stood in the backyard admiring the lilac shrubs and purple butterfly bush used to obscure the fence surrounding the property. A lacebark elm provided generous shade and seemed so comfortably solid compared to its neighbor, a slender redbud tree. Bright flowers burst joyfully from each side—poppies and veronicas, Russian sage, coneflowers and daylilies. Gladys spoke to each group and gently stroked a fat little bumblebee that drowsed on a petal, drunk with pollen.

She felt a sudden presence at her side. "There you are! Good morning. I'm sorry you haven't met Barry, he's so busy right now, the hectic life of a corporate attorney, but tonight for sure. Had breakfast yet?" Before she could answer, Candace tugged her into the house and the room off the foyer in the eastern end of the mansion. This was the Indian Art Museum.

Candace paused dramatically before opening the elegant double doors of inlaid wood that formed a pattern of open fans. Her hands rested on the knobs as she looked back at Gladys and smiled with touching pleasure. She pulled the doors open and entered lightly, nearly dancing on the warm golden floors. Gladys followed her and then halted abruptly when the energy of the room hit her. In childhood she'd fallen once from a tree and knocked the wind from her body for several frightening moments. She felt the same way now—socked, gaping, airless, even a little afraid. Directly ahead of her, fixed to the eastern wall of the room, was an Iroquois Medicine Mask. He was made of rich basswood and painted red, his face twisted on one side in a powerful grimace not to be ignored. He had long black horsehair and bright copper eyes that flashed at Gladys with strong emotion. She knew that if she touched one she'd be jolted as if lightning-struck. Waves of anger surged from the Face, enough to form a heat mirage that warped her vision. This was old anger, forged over many years.

"Ah, you've fallen under the spell of Old Broken Nose," Candace said blithely. "He's quite arresting."

Can't she feel his rage? Gladys wondered, dumbfounded that Candace could move through the room without noticing the heaviness of the air and the mood, without smelling the potent tang of fresh tobacco, *real* tobacco, harvested the old way, that seemed to issue from the Face as his breath.

"He's been in our family a long time now—just over a hundred years. I don't know his story."

Well, he knows yours, Gladys thought. You really *are* Mohawk, but you don't know what that means. You don't know what you have. Gladys wanted to chide the woman for hanging the Face on her wall as if he were nothing more than a lifeless object in a collection. Something acquired. Something owned. This is a living being you've trapped in your house, but you haven't diminished his power, that's for sure. She remained still because she felt it wasn't time for lessons yet. She was dealing with a person whose eyes couldn't see and ears couldn't hear, and the advice would be useless and fall on the ground without being comprehended. We can't plant seeds until the soil is ready, she reminded herself. But she was glad she always kept some tobacco wrapped in a handkerchief in her pocket. She brought it out, and when Candace was absorbed in examining one of her paintings, she fed him some, placed it in the wide howl of his mouth. The room shifted a bit, the air rippled warmly, but his anger never abated. This is much too little, much too late, was the only response Gladys felt pumping into the shattered space.

Gladys wanted to leave. The tension of the room was so thick the pressure of it hurt her ears. But Candace was swaying with excitement, desperately eager to share each treasure. Apart from the Face that dominated an entire wall, there weren't older pieces in the room, no artifacts or heirlooms, which Gladys found refreshing. Instead, Candace had an extensive collection of contemporary paintings, and Gladys was pleased to recognize two of her own favorite artists featured there—Jim Denomie and Andrea Carlson, both of them Ojibwe.

Gladys wandered to a painting she'd seen before. "Wasn't this one at the Weisman a few years back?" she asked.

"Yes. We loaned it to them for their show. It did quite a bit of traveling for a few years, even out of the country, which is only fitting since it's titled *Migrations*."

"Is that right?" Gladys thought the painting was indeed a wonder of movement, even the sky swirled with color—white, green, purple, yellow, layered into an unquiet blue. Deep purple hills stood massively in the background, solid, yes, but alert and watchful, capable of lifting their heavy shoulders in a shrug. Buttes rose like the trunks of severed trees in the foreground. One of them no butte at all, but Minneapolis's IDS Tower, the highrise nestled among them like a spy from the city. Indians rode flying horses between these worlds, from city to reservation, from tipis to satellite dishes.

"Did you see his show at Ancient Traders?" Gladys asked.

"Oh, yes, I never miss the chance to see his work."

"One of my favorites he did is that one called *Custer's Retreat*, where the cavalry are all wearing Shriners' hats and driving golf-carts, and then that big Indian on a horse comes riding in, about to hit them with a big brown shoe."

"Priceless! I like that one, as well. But this is my crowning glory, his *Attack at Fort Snelling Bar & Grill*." The two women stood now before the large canvas and pointed out the jokes and tragic history the artist had somehow managed to bring together in one story. Fort Snelling was depicted as a White Castle restaurant and if you looked very carefully you'd see that a string of customers sitting at the counter bore a resemblance to the crew found in Hopper's *Nighthawks*.

Gladys pointed to a figure, a man whose mouth was stuffed with grass. "There's Andrew Myrick," she remarked. "The one who said of those starving Dakotas, 'Let them eat grass.'"

"Yes, Jim explained that to me. I already knew some of the history, how their treaty payments were late and they were dying of hunger even though the trader had rich stores of food he kept under lock and key."

"Well, they took care of him, didn't they? Killed him and fed him the grass he would've fed their children."

They stopped to admire *Edward Curtis, Paparazzi*, laughing to see the famous photographer of Native peoples perched on a motorbike as he chased after his reluctant subjects.

"He's funny and powerful at the same time, this one," Gladys said. Candace nodded.

They moved on to Carlson's work. "I'm so proud of her," Gladys said. "My daughter, Grace, she's an artist, too, she knows her a little. Carlson's really young, but so talented, so smart. She's got her own sense of humor, too."

Gladys was drawn to a painting she immediately thought of as "Bear Medicine." A lush brown bear was helping a woman slip into a sweater. His arm reached around her in a way that was both gentle and protective, and the winding cable design knitted into the sweater reminded Gladys of the symbol connected with medical doctors—snakes coiled around a pole. The woman looked like a mixed-blood, tall and fair, but something about the strength of her features, shape of her eyes, marked her as Native.

"It's like that story," Candace said, coming up behind her. "The Woman Who Married a Bear."

"That's right," said Gladys. "The woman's looking at us, doesn't it seem like?

Or through us, into her future. And the bear, he's tuned into her, she's his world, but see how respectful he is? He doesn't look directly in her eyes."

"I never noticed that, but it's true. Say, you're pretty good at this."

Gladys shrugged. Then she spotted Carlson's next piece. "What's this one called?" she asked Candace.

"Oh, it has a brilliant name: *I Walk All Over the Earth, Rattling*."

Gladys smiled at the curious creatures who appeared to be part animal, part spirit, playing with an exquisitely new Electrolux vacuum cleaner. It was sleek and shiny and resembled a train. They clearly didn't know how to use it, to them it was a mysterious prize, some sacred object that could never be fully understood. "This makes me think," Gladys said.

"Yes?"

"We come from people with such strong minds. Healers and philosophers. They closely observed the workings of their world, this level you can see with your eyes, but they also knew how to go deeper and see with other eyes—the vision of a strong spirit. Maybe because those early visitors were so convinced they were superior to us, everything we tried to tell them and teach them was seen as backward. No one outside our Nations saw that we had genius technologies that worked for us without causing harm to our planet, smart psychology that helped us raise our kids in a healthy way. These artists remind me of the strength of our minds, the power of our vision, when we trust it and don't let the rest of the world shut us down."

Candace was staring at Gladys as if they were just now meeting for the first time. She tucked a glossy wing of hair behind her ear and cleared her throat, then touched a hand to it as if to quiet the noise. Finally she just whispered, "Yes," and drifted on to another painting.

Take it easy, old girl, Gladys told herself. This woman isn't ready for visions. She's still collecting herself and then putting the pieces in an isolated room that's closed up tight most of the day. A rumbling from the Face caught her attention. For a brief time she heard rattles and a voice singing a song in a language she didn't recognize. The rhythm was different from Ojibwe songs. Goosebumps lifted on her arms, and she rubbed them with her warm hands. She wondered how much longer the Face would live on this wall. His patience had come to an end, and he was boiling for change.

The Glorious Mysteries

Candace was a hungry reader who hoarded books and could not feel safe or relaxed unless a visible stack of waiting volumes perched on the table beside her favorite armchair—the only disorder allowed in her domain. She favored women authors, though quite unconsciously; there was nothing political in her choices. Louise Erdrich was the reigning queen of her literary heart, but she also pounced on every Alice Munro story she could find, for each one was a world unto itself, every bit as satisfying as a novel. She'd read Byatt's *Possession* and Patchett's *The Magician's Assistant* so many times she'd had to buy replacement copies, for she'd read the originals to disintegrating rags.

She needed to hold a book in her hands, touch the pages that were warm in summer, damp in humidity, cool and slippery in frozen January. No Kindle for her. That would be like hiring a stiff robot to give one a deep massage. Plus, she liked to breathe in the book, dip her nose toward the seam where the pages met and smell the sharp spice of a new book, the dusty pepper of an old one. So when she began suffering from migraine headaches soon after she turned fifty-four, the primary tragedy for her was how much the pain interfered with her worship, for that's how she thought of her relationship to literature—religious, devotional, those cream pages filled with minor hieroglyphics her only sacred ground.

She spent more time with poetry now, which was more easily interrupted and picked up again, each poem a host to be held on the tongue until it melted and restored the soul. Recent favorites were Joy Harjo's *The Woman Who Fell from the Sky*, Heid Erdrich's *Cell Traffic*, Sophie Cabot Black's *The Misunderstanding of Nature*, and Deborah A. Miranda's *The Zen of La Llorona*, which had made her gasp and cry.

The week after Gladys moved into the carriage house behind the mansion, Candace began roaming through a small volume of poems titled *The Erotic Spirit*, which was described as "poetry celebrating the spiritual aspect of eros." She read out of order, moving from stanzas on contemporary love which was known and familiar, to verses that seemed impossibly ancient—did they really love the same way then? A brief piece by the Indian princess Mirabai, who wrote in the sixteenth century, seized her attention with the opening address to Lord Krishna:

> Dark One,
> all I request is a portion of love.
> Whatever my defects,
> you are for me an ocean of raptures.
> Let the world cast its judgments
> nothing changes my heart—a single word from your lips is sufficient—birth
>   after birth
> begging a share of that love.
> Mira says: Dark One—enter the penetralia,
> you've taken
> this girl past the limits.

She slapped the volume shut after absorbing the words and impulsively shoved it beneath her so she was sitting on the bulky mound of it. Too late, the words reverberated in her skull as if each syllable was a tiny hammer—something about "Dark One" and "limits," and her head spun a shattering storm, and the colors made her weep.

The next morning Candace awakened with a ghost headache that cobwebbed her brain. She was clutching the mattress so fiercely she'd torn through one of the sheets—they were a delicate gossamer she'd paid a fortune to sleep on, and easily damaged. She was not yet fully free of her last dream. She could still hear the high rasp of turtle rattles, but the confusion was that she was wheeling, dizzy, as if *she* were the instrument played by an unseen hand. *Shoosh-shoosh. Shoosh-shoosh.* My God, what's happening? Who's shaking me? Her thoughts screamed, though her lips remained resolutely shut.

She was alone in the bed; she could feel the breeze of emptiness at her back, from the side where Barry spent his untroubled nights. He must be showering, she thought, resentful that she had to heave herself from the dark noise of this experience all on her own. She'd been having these dreams for months, but when she tried to describe them to Barry over breakfast, while he scanned through the *New York Times* and *Wall Street Journal* in his brisk, testy way, snapping the pages as if they made him angry, he suggested she see a therapist and had nothing more to say on the subject.

All she knew for certain was that she was a turtle, and even that had taken weeks to discover since she was pulled inside her shell, operating in complete darkness. What gave it away? A feeling so new to her, so foreign, she couldn't help but note its shape and map out what it meant: She felt wholly safe in the early version of these dreams. Protected. Covered. Somehow at home in herself, by herself. When she tried to move she just rocked like a cradle and remained in place.

In recent days the dreams had become disturbing—someone, something, was trying to shake her out of her shell. Gentle nudges at first, but ultimately she was lifted high in the air, air that could not be seen, only imagined, in the terrible blind void. She was shaken, hard, her small world a cycle of quakes that left her without foundation of any kind. The gesture's message was purely physical, no words were spoken, at least none that she heard, yet it was unmistakable: *Leave your shell, leave your shell.* She would not. Dream after dream she stubbornly hid, curled into herself, blind, deaf, mute, hungry, her thirst all the dust of a desert without a single bead of moisture. No matter, she was safe in her shell, if miserable, and to poke her head from this nothingness would mean death, she was sure of it, and she preferred the death of her own making.

Gladys had made a fruit salad which Barry was eating happily when Candace joined him for breakfast.

"This is wonderful, what's in it?" he asked the older woman.

"It's different every time depending on what's at hand. This one has watermelon, nectarine, blueberries, banana, and pineapple—my secret is to shave on some fresh ginger and snip in a few fresh basil leaves."

"Just right for a humid morning like this." He helped himself to another serving and spooned a dollop of yogurt atop the colorful fruit.

Candace had never seen Barry so enthusiastic about his breakfast food. "She's a keeper," he whispered to his wife after Gladys returned to the kitchen.

"Happy you think so," she answered, sounding anything but happy.

"Another bad night?" He didn't look at her as he asked the question, he was busy forking up blueberries and juicy wedges of melon.

"Yes, you could say that. If anything, they're getting worse."

"Well," Barry paused to wipe his chin which was sticky with juice. "You could talk to someone about it, see what these dreams signify."

"I *am* talking to someone about it. I'm talking to *you*."

"I mean a professional, hon. Seriously, what do *I* know about dreams?" Barry latched on his Bluetooth mobile headset which had become such a familiar sight to Candace she thought of it as another part of his anatomy, grafted on since the market tumbles of 2008. Headset in place, Barry snapped open the *New York Times* and disappeared into its contents.

Candace sighed. The fruit salad did look good, refreshing; she nibbled at the nectarines and berries but pushed the rest to the side. Basil, she wouldn't have thought to add basil, but it was nice.

"By the way," Barry put down the paper and Candace flinched, startled to have him reappear so suddenly. "Are you okay?" He abruptly took a call from his stockbroker, and after a brief exchange, returned to his conversation with Candace as if there hadn't been a break. "Maybe this dream business is catching?" He made a face to indicate he wasn't even remotely serious. "I've been hearing strange noises in the night, completely mystifying. You sleep right through and I get up, search all over the place. Nothing." He held up empty hands. "Two nights now this has happened."

"What do the noises sound like?"

"Music. Maybe? Some kind of instruments I'm not familiar with."

"Rattles?" Candace held her breath.

"Could be. I don't know. There's some singing, too. But not like it's coming from the radio or television—not unless it's a documentary."

"What do you mean?"

"I can't really say. Just, it feels old, different. Funny how things can get to you at night that seem silly by day. This is one of those things."

Even by day, this piece of information made Candace shiver. She'd wondered if the headaches were connected to her dreams—some malfunction of the brain, some tumor blossoming like creeping vine across the landscape of her thoughts.

Yes, a cancerous wisteria that brought on visions and nightmare pain. But now Barry was involved, experiencing his own symptoms. Candace didn't know what this meant but couldn't possibly see how it was good.

"Well, I better get cracking!" Candace started again when her husband slapped down the paper and leapt to his feet in the way of a much younger man. "You take care, hon. Make it a good day," he said as he kissed her on the cheek. Then he left for work in his sporty silver Jaguar that *did* remind her of a cat—purring and graceful, muscle power kept elegantly hidden until it decided to rip across a lawn.

She knew their friends thought it was his midlife crisis baby, birthed to give him a little "zing" that apparently went missing in other areas of his life. What they didn't know is that *she* was the one who bought it to surprise *him* after her father died and left her a surprisingly large inheritance for a retired New Jersey plumber. She was the one looking for the "zing," trying to understand how she and her husband had misplaced each other in recent years, as if they were lost in different parts of the house and could barely hear the noise of the other, bumping around in the dark. At first she'd thought they were just another American cliché, wife oblivious while husband chases around with an adoring secretary or assistant half his age. She could easily believe he'd be attractive to younger women, with his thick blond curls that made him look like a marigold. (He'd cultivated their wildness after seeing William Katt in *Pippin* back in 1981, except for one brief period when he was still just an associate at his law firm, working for a balding partner who insisted that clients didn't trust attorneys with hair.) His nose was strong, almost hawk-like. She thought of it as "a statement." His cheekbones were high bright knobs that turned deep red whenever he drank his favorite Spanish red wine, and he kept himself trim with regular use of the elliptical machine at work and raging squash games—a habit he'd picked up as an undergraduate at Harvard. But his best feature, at least in her opinion, were his eyes, a rare exotic blue that reminded her how his people came from Norway—trading in that fair Northern sky for the one in Minnesota. She'd never known how to describe the color, what to call it, until they took a cruise to Alaska a few years earlier and visited the Mendenhall Glacier in Juneau. They stood on the observation deck of the visitor's center which showed how far the glacier had extended just twenty years before, how much of it had now retreated, but all Candace absorbed was its shade.

"My God, that's your eyes!" she'd nearly shouted at Barry as he stared at her, perplexed. "The glacier, you match the glacier."

He'd grinned at her then and pulled her into him. "So, the lady approves of my scandalous Scandinavian eyes," he'd teased, showing off his talent for alliteration.

Yes, she could definitely see his appeal, at least in terms of his looks. But when she'd launched a scouting expedition to test his fidelity, she'd discovered that when he said he was at work, well, he was. If he had a late night at the office and she wandered into Minneapolis to surprise him with his favorite Thai takeout, a hot red curry from Supatra's, he'd be in the office and push aside piles of books and folders to eat with her. She was nearly disappointed. She could reach him at any time of the day and night, yet could never reach him at all.

Candace checked her watch. Still some time before she had to leave for the Sweatshop, just a short drive away on Snelling. She'd been working with a personal trainer for a couple of years who had her in the best shape of her life—Pilates and weight training alternated every other day, six days a week, and recovery on Sundays. She glanced through her daily planner, a leather-bound book rather than the electronic variety. She liked the plump fullness of pages you could turn with your fingers, post-it notes in several cheerful colors attached to many of the pages, bearing her notes written in a hand so lovely and fine it looked like calligraphy. Recently, most of her days were filled with physical maintenance: workout sessions at the Sweatshop, her weekly manicure and pedicure at the Juut Salon Spa over on Grand Avenue, facials twice a month with the Dr. Hauschka aesthetician whose office was above The Yarnery on Grand, haircuts and coloring also done at the Juut Salon Spa. It kept her busy.

She'd resigned from all the boards she'd served on once the migraines started, assaulting her like a hidden enemy who'd been waiting to take her down. That's how she thought of the pain, as something malicious and personal. She wasn't sad to step down from the boards, though she still supported their efforts financially. Someone had to nurture the arts communities in a country where art was looked on as a hobby. The Loft Literary Center was her number one cause, and then a handful of theatre companies: Penumbra, Outward Spiral, Mixed Blood Theatre, Ten Thousand Things Theatre. Oh, the Twin Cities were rich with the talents of their citizens.

She'd realized once the phone calls and emails related to her board activities stopped coming in that she didn't really have any friends. Certainly there were couples she and Barry entertained now and again, mainly business colleagues of her husband's, and their wives who made polite chitchat when they were thrown together, admiring each other's houses and clothes and catered food. But no one she could confide in, no one she would trust with the information about her turtle dreams.

Friendships had been easier for her in school, back in the seventies when she was Candace Altman of West Orange, New Jersey, attending Lesley College. The young women traveled in packs, and she could follow along, perched at the periphery, chiming in with a comment, an idea, when all eyes went to her for some input that would validate her presence among them. She recalled a couple of girls who were wrestling with sexual identity (or at least their willingness to openly live their truth) confessing to her drunkenly at parties that they loved her. One even called her a "goddess." And though she couldn't return their affection beyond a mild friendliness, their admiration had been a wonderful secret she'd cherished like a bauble. For an entire year each time she'd looked in a mirror the thought had risen: "Look at you, you're a goddess!" She began carrying herself with greater confidence, let her lustrous hair grow long, and because she revealed so little about herself she was viewed as mysterious, elusive, and quickly gathered a circle of devotees who trailed along, following her life. None of this required emotional effort on her part, and apparently, when that sort of work was required to build intimacy, even simple camaraderie, she floundered, incapable of pulling it off. She didn't know where to begin.

Candace returned from Pilates workout and headed straight for her shower—a glorious space of slate and glass, with multiple shower heads positioned at different levels, and room enough for a small team to use all at once. Never baths for her. The jacuzzi tub was in Barry's bathroom, a sleek black version of his car which no amount of cajoling could induce her to enter. It wasn't modesty or shyness, they'd showered together more times than she could count, but the mouth of a bath always gave her the chills.

"My strange little wifey and her aversions," Barry once teased, which made it sound as if there were a list of phobias she carried around like a medical alert bracelet tagging her maladies. There was only the one bugaboo, as far as she knew, apart from the dream, and that would get to anybody.

Hot water worked like a massage on her muscles, and she couldn't help exulting a little in the feel of her body, lifting on her toes like a dancer, stretching each leg to show off her flexibility. She was crowding her mind with positive thoughts, pleasant items she could list to feel good about herself. She might walk through the house again to appreciate its order, stand naked before the mirror to prove what an outrageously fine specimen she was just two months away from fifty-five. She might look at her checking account to take stock of all the good money flowing from there in support of the arts and other worthy causes. There were things she could do to prop herself up, but none of them appeared to be working just now, and so it was a great luxury to be able to cry in the shower where tears would never be seen in the midst of so much water.

Candace settled into a hidden wood bench in Cochran Park, not the quaint stone shelter in the middle of the small slice of grass, but a roomier bench obscured by the dangling arms of a towering oak. From this spot she could see her house just across Western Avenue, and if she looked farther down Western, there was the old Commodore Hotel where Scott and Zelda Fitzgerald had first lived after they were married. The main reason she enjoyed this park was the statue set within a fountain. A young Native man nearly ran off his pedestal, carrying bow and arrow, eagle feather flying from his hair. The companion who charged at his side was a mixed-breed creature, part dog, part wolf, with a rich mane at his throat like a lion's. Swan-necked birds—*were* they swans, or geese?—tipped back their slender heads so sparkling threads of water could shoot from their beaks. The fountain trapped water in a blue-tiled pool protected by an iron fence covered with decorative shrubs. It was a small gem in a neighborhood full of wonders, and she liked to tuck herself into the shade and breathe in the air gusting along this hilltop so aptly named Summit.

Candace had brought her lap desk and Mac laptop to the park—the slim white computer was open and running, a fresh electronic page awaiting her words. She could see herself from a removed, omniscient perspective, see her hands poised over the keyboard, and some part of her longed to snap the machine closed, stop this nonsense before it started. But another impulse squashed the other, sensible one. She needed to write these letters, however much they disturbed her once they were sent. She began to type:

Dear Sir or Madam,

I am writing you as a satisfied customer, wholly delighted with your product. I am writing you as the perfect American consumer who doesn't make purchases on impulse, but only after considerable thought and research. I'm serious, no tongue in this cheek. I see purchasing power as a responsibility given those of us with ample resources. I want my dollars to make a statement. But I digress . . .

I've been thrilled with your product—the lavender spritz especially made for fine linens. I've been suffering from migraine headaches of late, and terrifying dreams, and I shudder to think how much worse it would all be without the gentle essence of lavender infusing my sheets and my senses with the comfort of its delicate fragrance. Perhaps it is the one ingredient that keeps me tethered to this world, rather than sinking completely into the dark abyss of whatever it is that haunts me now. So you see, the unanticipated benefits of your fine spray! To think you might be saving a life, or at the very least, the shattered sanity of a stranger.

Funny how what makes such a difference in the life of one person can be completely missed, never perceived by another. I'm referring, of course, to my husband who sleeps like a rock, with or without the advantages of your rejuvenating spritz. If only you could create a spray to revive the fallen flower of a once-vibrant relationship. Do I count my blessings? Of course. My husband is faithful, hard-working, and would never strike a blow against me. He returns every night to our wondrous home (truly it is, I've made every effort), and he changes from his business duds into comfortable clothes and drops in front of the television. He must have his *McNeil-Lehrer Report*, which he says he prefers to other news because there are no screaming debates or presentations of a false equivalence—the research of renowned experts set against the testimony of a kook. Then he must have his *Daily Show* and *Colbert Report*, which is a sight in itself to behold. I watch the watcher, and mark how the little boy in him emerges quite suddenly. He talks back to Jon Stewart and Stephen Colbert, urging them on with comments like: "Harsh!" or "Ohhh, snap!"

Yes, I can appreciate him at times when I watch him the way an anthropologist would, studying the corporate male of this century. He is more generous than most, believes in the social compact. But as my husband, he is a mystery, lost to me behind his mobile headset and stock reports, billable hours and wealthy clients. The one time I asked him not to take calls at the table while we are eating together, he snapped at me that everything he does, he does for me, and how can I complain.

We are the proverbial islands cast together in the same sea but separated by deep water. Where is the spray to restore what is lost? Where is the scent that will perfectly summon the memories we need to remind us of what is possible?

Candace felt her meagre lunch begin to rise and took several deep breaths to sooth the nausea. Sweat broke out on her forehead but the queasiness passed. This was now the sixth of her inappropriate letters, ostensibly sent to congratulate corporations on their products, yet each more horrifying than the last in its intimate revelations. My God, when she'd written the V___ Corporation to thank them for their silky, glittering hose that were like wearing a thousand kisses, she'd admitted to the humiliating phase, thankfully behind her, where she'd tried to stimulate her husband's sexual appetite by reading books with the most embarrassing titles that all but screamed to the checkout clerk in the bookstore: Yes, I have problems in the sack! She'd written how she had gone so far as to purchase an outrageously expensive, made-to-order corset set that transformed her into a Victorian fantasy, but ultimately landed on Barry with a thud. He'd walked in to find her ensconced in the outfit that gave her a wonderfully (or terribly) authentic hourglass figure, her rather small bust pushed up and out until even she found it delectable. He raised an eyebrow, said, "Wow! Does *that* look uncomfortable!" and made a beeline for the kitchen, cracking open a Guinness even before removing his tie.

Awaiting replies to these letters was both nerve-wracking and titillating, a thrumming level of excitement that purred beneath the monotony of her routine. She had yet to hear from one corporation, three responses had been dry, conventional form letters, thanking the customer for their business, but one company had generated two letters: the first a formulaic note typed on business letterhead stationery, the other a handwritten card picturing a solemn Christ pointing to His visible heart. The bland replies had been a relief but also, if she were honest, a faint disappointment. The card made her heart pound in dread, anticipation, carnival-like ebullience, all mixed together in a strange emotional soup.

I've reached out to the world and the world has answered back, Candace thought, her hands trembling so hard the thick paper shook and she closed her eyes and took a rattling breath.

Finally she read:

Dear Mrs. Jenssen,

I'm taking an awful chance here, and these are no times to compromise a person's job, but I'm a Christian and couldn't help but think of the parable of the Good Samaritan after reading your letter, which, forgive my saying so, came across like a cry for help. My superiors don't much care that you like their cosmetics, as long as you keep buying them, so letters like yours never go anywhere. For a communication to go higher you'd have to threaten a lawsuit, a boycott, or a Facebook page dedicated to bringing them down. Okay. I did what a good employee should and sent you the regular response, but I wrote down your address before shredding your correspondence and am writing you on my own time, with my own card and postage, human being to human being, hoping you're not some crazy person who'll get me in trouble.

If you're for real, and what you wrote is true, honey, I've been there. (Well, not ever wealthy.) Excuse me calling you "honey," it's not sexual harassment, I'm a grandmother now, getting ready to retire from this last job to work for the church full-time. Your husband, bless his heart, is a man. Enough said. Make your own life. I don't mean leave him, I mean, where you are. Share what he'll share and let go of the rest. There's an emptiness I hear in your words that men or money can't fill, and don't I know? I won't push religion on you, never liked it when people preached at me, but it is one way to find a deeper aspect to life so it's not so lousy. Sometimes there's even joy when you know you've done the right thing and you connect up with something so much bigger than you ever could be on your own. Just wanted you to know that some people care. I care. I've said prayers for you. We all matter some way. The suffering is terrible. It's my hope that a hug and prayer from a stranger can ease a little bit of your pain.

A person who wishes you well. God bless.

There was no name or return address included in the card, but Candace knew immediately which company the woman worked for, since she'd written in praise of only one line of cosmetics, and it was posted from Atlanta. Candace had impulsively crushed the card against her chest, the closest thing to a hug she could manage with a square bit of paper. Tears had fallen, the childhood kind that make your nose run and wreck your looks for hours. Just remembering her reaction brought tears to the rim of her eyes, which, had she been able to see them, would have shocked her, they were such an empty silver. But she pinched her eyes closed and demanded the tears to return wherever they go when they're not allowed to run their natural course. She would spare herself this one disgrace at least, the indignity of weeping in public. She'd considered sending a thank-you card to the woman, but she had no name to reference. Perhaps the woman had already left? And if not, she didn't want to get her fired or reprimanded. So she'd left well enough alone and just accepted the prayers, the kind wishes of a Good Samaritan.

The breeze picked up and blew across Candace's neck. Leaves twittered with sudden interest as if the wind brought news. The oddest sensation swept over Candace, that while she still sat on the wooden bench, could feel her thighs stick to its warm slats, she'd entered a bubble outside of ordinary time, ordinary space. She and the trees, alert together, watching the road, checking the fountain, scanning the skies. That's when she saw it. The speck that shouldn't be there, like a fleck of dirt on a postcard version of the view. Far away, as high as a plane heading for the airport. She blinked and the speck had doubled in size, and she thought of her boys, how they'd grown like this, from microscopic cells to tall strangers who called each Sunday. She was transfixed by the object, couldn't have glanced away if she'd tried. Perhaps her stare brought it down, she wondered, hazily. Is this another dream? Without looking away from the descending form, she closed her laptop computer and set it beside her on the bench. She wanted free hands. To protect herself? To do what? The form took on the shape of a woman, descending so smoothly she could have been riding an escalator. But Candace couldn't spy the means by which she traveled. She thought of Cirque du Soleil and their stunning feats, miracle acrobatics. Was this that kind of program? Some trick or show?

The woman was suddenly close enough to admire for her lovely features. Lion-like, golden eyes, a long dark braid of hair that fell past her waist, the most enviable flawless skin the color of coffee and cream. Cinnamon lips, neither smiling nor unfriendly, and a crescent scar that pierced one brow. Candace was breathless, as frozen as the park statue, and if she'd been honest with herself in that moment she would have said she knew this was real, this divine visitation. The air she couldn't breathe was scorched, smelled like incense and tobacco, and the atmosphere was charged with an electric buzz of grace which, once you've experienced it, you will never forget.

The woman landed gracefully, noiselessly, in the grass before Candace, blocking most of her view of the fountain though the streams of water rising from the throats of bronze-cast birds were still visible. Okay, the laws of the universe are still operational, Candace thought. Water flows, air circulates, I'm alive. She wanted to look away from the figure and pretend that nothing extraordinary had happened, was happening, but she couldn't, not because free will had suddenly abandoned her, but because a deeper, internal impulse compelled her to watch and listen.

The woman was the height and shape of a girl, maybe twelve? But her face was beyond age. She wore a light linen shift that fell to her toes, just visible at the hem, emerging from sturdy sandals. Her head was bare, the wind lifting tendrils of hair that framed her dusky face, but though she was physically present, her scent a warm fragrance of sun on skin, there was nothing ordinary about her. She glowed, backlit as if it was always dawn for her, the sun just beginning to rise. She was watching Candace intently, as if to inquire, Is it you? When Candace realized she was the object of scrutiny she tensed, but didn't look away. The woman unfastened a belt she was wearing, which Candace hadn't noticed before, and stepped closer until the two were only six feet apart. Candace became dizzy, overpowered by the strangeness of this unexpected encounter. You will not faint in public, she admonished herself, so she clung to the bench and remained upright, conscious.

Finally the woman broke the awful tension, speaking in a voice that was deep and warm, husky with smoke: "Dear Candace, I am Maryam, mother of Yeshua, sister to your ancestor, a woman named Jigonsaseh who gave me this belt to signify our compact, our bond of understanding." She held out a heavy wampum belt of white and purple quahog shells, and immediately Candace picked out the pattern of white figures locking hands so that two became one with that single gesture. She didn't acknowledge the woman, Maryam, but she continued to listen. Maryam looked at the belt, tenderly stroked its beads. "Your ancestor was a remarkable woman and she is still here, watching what becomes of her people, the Kanien'kehá:ka."

Candace flinched at the thought of being observed by some distant omniscient mother. She felt naked and judged, fought an impulse to run away. But where could she run and not be seen?

"Jigonsaseh was Clan Mother of the Turtles, and her son, Ayowantha, was a great spiritual leader in their Nation. You come from strong people on both sides of your family, survivors who have gifted you with everything they had to ensure that you also would continue."

What language is this? Candace wondered. It was so uncommon. Can there be such a thing as a master language that fuses the rest together, or moves beyond them altogether to reach the heart of all matters, all thoughts? She was at a loss to understand how she comprehended this woman, this stranger of all strangers.

"I didn't come to make a speech," the woman continued, "but to perform a mitzvah on behalf of the one who took me for a sister." She paused, and when Candace made no sound, Maryam smiled for the first time, revealing small white teeth. "Clearly you weren't raised Jewish by your father any more than you were raised to know what it is to be Kanien'kehá:ka. A good Jew would have challenged me or teased me—How can you mix the mitzvah with the Mohawk?"

She chuckled at her small joke, but Candace just stared, her eyes the storm gray of a wind-rocked lake.

"My girl," Maryam stepped forward, so close now to Candace she could see dew-like beads of perspiration gather above Maryam's lip, glistening brilliantly like tiny diamonds. Maryam gently tucked an errant curtain of hair behind Candace's ear so her face was exposed, nothing hidden. "Have you not heard your grandmother calling? She's been trying to reach you for so long, teach you what it is to be Kanien'kehá:ka, a member of the Haudenosaunee. What it is to be a Turtle. She's watched you thrash in agony from headaches that are no more than your own refusal to see what has always been right there before you. Refusal to hear what was always there for you to hear once you really listen. No one means to torture you or cause you harm. You torment yourself."

Maryam stroked Candace's hair, then cupped the side of her face in a tender palm. The comfort that comes from a mother's loving hands washed into Candace; she smelled the peaches her own mother had shared with her, sliced into their cereal as a summer luxury, and nearly swooned from the pressure placed upon her heart.

"You might wonder what I'm doing here," Maryam said. She removed her hand from Candace's face as if she realized the strong effect of her touch. "Jigonsaseh and I shared a council and decided that even though you weren't raised Jewish, or Christian either, I'm a kind of ancestor, too, on your father's side. Plus, I would be more familiar to you in this country, even if you're not Christian. This was a sadness between us, that on this continent which birthed your people's stories and beliefs, they would be such strangers to you. By the standards of my people and your mother's people, you are Kanien'kehá:ka, because our identity is formed by the mother's lineage, the mother's clan. I'm not here to claim you for my own, but to help you see what needs to be seen, and hear what needs to be heard. I'm here to remind you that you are a Turtle. Already you've learned a few of their tricks, how they retreat from the world when threatened. But how can they survive if they never come out? The turtle is no coward, but cautious in a smart way, careful and determined. They gather themselves within their shell and emerge, ready to lead, their armor so thick they can manage whatever is thrown at them. Come back to yourself, my girl, claim your spirit and your whole heart."

Candace was shaking now, she felt like a beetle you sometimes see fallen on its back where it wriggles, helpless, vulnerable, its soft underbelly exposed to the birds and other predators. There is nothing it can do but wait to die. No one had ever spoken to Candace this way, nakedly, openly, without niceties or pretense, no mask worn or provided. She couldn't perform what had never been practiced, so she grabbed her computer and its lightweight desk and eased past the luminous figure so that they would not touch again. She ran across Western Avenue in mad desperation, lucky there wasn't any traffic headed in either direction for she couldn't bother to check. She ran for the front door of her house and fumbled with keys, shaking like a storm-shattered sapling, clutching the earth with its shallow young roots. After opening the lock she ran to her bedroom and paused in the doorway to catch her breath. She walked inside with deliberate steps, placed her laptop on a table, and sat down in her favorite armchair. She stared straight ahead like a sightless person, closing off vision and sound, anything that contradicted the mantra developing in her mind: It's not real, it's not real, it's not real. . . . Until meaning was lost and the words were just a nonsense jumble of noise.

I'll make an appointment tomorrow and get checked for the tumor, she thought, when she'd calmed the tiniest bit. I'll get every test and cure whatever's ailing me, she decided.

She had no idea what happened to the lady in the park, if she left the way she came, riding a thermal current of air, or if she collapsed into abrupt invisibility. But we see her place the wampum belt over her shoulder and stroll from the park to the curb. She checks both ways and, no car in sight, crosses Western Avenue. She is unhurried as she walks to the front of Candace's house, then up the steps, past stone lions who stare and stare, until one snaps his jaws shut in awe.

The First Supper

Gladys heard the sweet chimes of the front doorbell, nothing like the hair-raising buzzer of her old apartment. She answered the door and looked upon a lovely woman who reminded her of Binah, when her daughter was younger and less unhappy. This isn't one of those Jehovah's Witnesses, she thought. This one is part spirit. How she knew she couldn't say, just a feeling, and her grandparents had taught her to honor those instincts so she held the door open for the woman and invited her inside.

The stranger looked familiar to her, yet she couldn't recall the reference. Then an image slid into place, a young boy in her old neighborhood who helped whenever he saw her coming down the street with groceries from the Wedge. Miguel. His eyes and forehead hidden behind a raven's wing of black hair. He wore a necklace that jangled so much you could hear him coming, his protection consisting of a crucifix, a plain silver cross, and a medal that pictured Our Lady of Guadalupe.

"You're her," Gladys blurted. "You're Our Lady. Pardon me, taking so long to figure it out, but I'm not Christian, so."

The woman touched Gladys's arm and shook her head. "No apologies are necessary between us. I'm happy you can see me at all—that's not usually the case."

"Really?" Gladys couldn't imagine why not, but she wanted to be hospitable so she didn't press the point and ushered the lady into the kitchen which had quickly become her domain in this house that was a maze of doors.

"Have a seat." She gestured toward the rattan chairs in the breakfast nook which was really another room in and of itself, set between the kitchen and sunroom. "Should I tell Candace you're here?"

The lady shook her head again, this time in sadness. "There's no point, just yet," she said. "She's pretending she has a tumor."

"Mmmm . . . I guess it's not every day you have important spirits come knocking at the door. She wasn't taught how to handle that kind of thing. Now me, I was raised by my grandparents in the old way, so I'm fortunate. They prepared me for many layers of experience."

Gladys had been puttering while she spoke, moving easily around the kitchen now she knew where everything was, not that she understood the use of even half the fancy gadgets that were stored so neatly in the drawers. She set a warm cup of coffee before the guest, with silver creamer and a small dish of sugar cubes, and offered a plate of lemon cake she'd made just that morning. The lady dropped three sugar cubes into her coffee and just a quick spill of cream. She stirred the warm liquid with fascination, completely absorbed in the task.

"I like coffee," she said dreamily, lifting the cup to her nose and breathing in the rich fragrance.

"I had a feeling you would," Gladys said. "Mothers like us, sometimes it's the only thing that keeps you going."

"But I've never had it like this, set out for me in such a nice way. I've tasted it here and there in my travels when no one is looking, when no one will miss a few sips poured from the pot."

"That's a shame," Gladys said, and she sat down to sip her own coffee which she liked black with one sugar. "I'm Gladys, by the way," she offered. "I'm new here, living out back in a mini-mansion like some kind of queen." She smiled.

"And I'm Maryam, forgive my lapse. I'm so taken with your generosity I forgot myself." Maryam drank from the cup with closed eyes, her lips turned up in pleasure. "Ahhhh," she sighed, and Gladys let her sit quietly with her enjoyment for several minutes, both of them eating the moist cake and drinking the coffee.

Maryam patted her lips with a paper napkin and broke the friendly silence. "In two thousand years you're the second person to feed me when I appeared in this form." She shook her head and Gladys wasn't sure if she was poised to laugh or cry.

"Let me guess," she said. "The other person was Native, like me?"

"Yes. A different tribe, but still."

"That's us. And that's what got us in trouble, I guess, back in the day. You need something, well, here you go. But it only works when the other side plays by the same rules or pretty soon you've got nothing left."

"That's the shame of it. People are so afraid to share what they have, thinking there won't be enough, there's never enough, when generosity is the safest kind of insurance. If you help when you can then someone will be there to help you, at least, that's how it works when people, as you say, play by those rules."

A sudden rap at the French doors behind them made the two jump. The noise was Zhigaag, thumping the pane of glass with his paw hard enough to be heard.

"He wants in," Gladys explained. She undid the latch and opened the door. "Always at your service," she teased.

"Oh, what a handsome cat!" Maryam exclaimed, and she bent over to pet him as he sauntered toward the table, but at the last moment he sidled away from her and jumped into Gladys's lap. He sniffed her fork and, disappointed, curled up to nap. She stroked his glossy fur out of habit but she was embarrassed by his behavior.

"Forgive this one," she told Maryam. "He's, to quote my granddaughter, a 'one-person person.' He doesn't give anyone else the time of day, no matter how nice they are."

"Don't give it a thought, loyalty is a wonderful thing."

The women visited, trading stories of their lives, Maryam describing the many wonders of the world she had seen, Gladys reminiscing about her earlier years up North.

"My best friend all through my girlhood was Delilah. Ho, I haven't thought of her in so long. She could *run*, beat all the boys, even some of the strong young men, when she was just a little thing. And when she sat still to listen to older ones speak, she wasn't still like anybody else. I didn't have the reference back then but now I can see what I mean by that. The way we show a film today, and pause it so the picture is frozen? That's what her stillness was like, a clenched pause before you knew she'd be off and flying again, her feet lifting so fast they blurred like hummingbird wings. She always bragged she'd never marry a man unless he could keep up with her, and it took a good while before one came along and challenged her to a race and won. He was from Mille Lacs, and you know, I always thought she threw the race because she secretly liked him. He was such a beautiful tree of a man."

"Did it work out for her?" Maryam leaned in with interest.

"For a while, and that's the good part, that she had some happy years. But he died—the drink got him and stole his looks, then stole his spirit, and she refused to follow after him since the drink would ruin her ability to run. But they never had children and eventually she started drinking, too. I was with her when she died, just thirty years old, and not making much sense she was so far gone, her liver shot. Then she had a few moments of perfect clarity at the end. I was holding her hand, singing to her. She said: 'Gladys, see what's become of me. I can't run anymore, so I might as well die. Promise me I can run in the spirit world.'

"I did. I promised her, didn't care if it was a big fat lie, though I believed for the most part what I said. I had to give her that peace. After I promised, she sighed with relief and left us. This was winter when she died, and the next day I was feeling pretty bad about her as I did some chores around our little place. Then I heard funny noises outside, a kind of squeaking and rushing, like no wind I'd heard before. I stepped out to see what was going on and I saw the snow behaving so odd. There wasn't anyone there, yet steps were punched down in the snow, making it crunch, slow at first, then picking up speed until there was a trail of flurries forming a track around my house, around and around. That was Delilah's gift to me, I think. She was showing me that she *could* run again, then she was just doing it for the joy, maybe even showing off. But I didn't care. I laughed with tears coming down and didn't even wipe them away with my apron. 'Good for you, Delilah!' I cried. And then the trail broke open and left the house, moving on, and that was that."

"You gave her a great gift, that solace at the end," Maryam said.

Gladys was embarrassed by the compliment, so she stood up and fussed around the kitchen, washing their cups and plates. Zhigaag watched her sleepily, unhappy to leave the nest of her lap. Gladys wiped her hands on a dishtowel and glanced at the ceiling.

"The one upstairs, well, I think it's going to be some time before she accepts your help."

Maryam nodded and bit her lower lip.

"So I was thinking, you might as well stay here, if you don't mind. They have so much room they won't even know there's a guest. Then you can work on her until she's ready to listen."

"That's a wonderful idea," Maryam said, and her face glowed even more than it already did, with a pure excitement that touched the older woman. "This will be my adventure," said Maryam. "Living in a house in Saint Paul. I never saw *this* coming!" she laughed, and Gladys was warmed by the rich, smoky sound of her happiness.

Gladys chose to place Maryam in a guest bedroom on the east side of the mansion, just one floor above the Indian Art Museum. She thought maybe a Sacred Being could keep a lid on the anger contained in the room. Maryam admired the view she had of Cochran Park where she'd first appeared to Candace, and then she collapsed on the king-size bed in delight, moving her arms and legs like a child making snow angels in glittering drifts.

"This is heavenly," she breathed, without a trace of irony. "I've never slept in a bed this large."

"Keep to the edge or you'll get kind of stuck in the middle. That happened to me. I'll get you some towels—what's your favorite color?"

Maryam answered immediately, "The blue-green of the Aegean Sea."

"Coming right up." Sure enough, Gladys found bright turquoise towels of a thick Egyptian cotton. Maryam held one to her cheek and shook her head.

"I'll be spoiled," she said in a sweet, wistful way. Then she looked at Gladys and watched her intently, until the woman shifted uncomfortably. "Forgive my staring, it's only that you puzzle me."

Gladys raised her eyebrows.

"Most people who see me are expecting revelations, prophecy, when usually I'm just there to encourage them in some way. You're one of the rare, most rare ones, not asking me to look into the future like a sorceress."

Gladys shrugged. "I guess I'm different from most folks in that I want to be surprised. I figure if you already know what's going to happen, what's the point of living it through? Now my girls, I wonder about them. Grace I don't worry about too much, even though she's had a hard time. Her husband was the sweetest man, a Crow artist from Montana, and they had a nice place thirty minutes south of here. A cabin and a studio surrounded by fields of trees. Then they had a bad accident, car wreck. He was killed and she hurt her head, it ruined her short-term memory though all the past was spread before her as crisp and clear as if it had just happened. Her boy, Dylan, was visiting me at the time, so he was fine. He's been such a help to her, patiently filling in the gaps when she gets like one of those old-time records that skips and snags. Something broke apart in her brain, for both good and difficult. She's always been an artist, painter, but now there's a new quality to her work where it seems almost alive. She's tapped into a vein of some kind of divine inspiration.

"But Binah, if I had questions it would be about her. She's stuck in a bad place and won't be budged. Still, if I asked you about her and you told me what would happen, maybe I'd act the wrong way and miss helping her? I'll take this life one step at a time."

Maryam smiled in approval.

"I have something to show you," Gladys said. She led Maryam to a small library—modest in floor space but abundant in books. These were not decorative books selected for the design of their covers, but well-loved volumes, the spines showing wear, dust jackets rumpled or missing. The room smelled sweet—a honey tang of pages and dreams, plot-lines that carried a reader far away from whatever world had stranded them. There were no chairs to clutter this church, just an oval table of gleaming cherrywood in the center and built-in bookcases from floor to ceiling with sturdy little ladders that slid on tracks attached to each side.

"Candace said I was welcome to borrow any of these, so I pass on my privileges to you," Gladys said.

Maryam browsed through the stacks, fingers trailing the spines. She plucked out two volumes in rather quick order. "I've been wanting to read these," she said. One was *Gilead*, by Marilynne Robinson, the other, Toni Morrison's *Song of Solomon*. Gladys found a book she wanted and pulled it out. "What have you selected?" Maryam asked politely.

The volume was *God Is Red*, by Vine Deloria Jr. Gladys held it out so Maryam could read the cover. "He was one of our great minds, a real philosopher, and in my opinion even more than that—a true prophet. I read this when it first came out, but I like to go over it again every few years, and each time I do I just admire him more."

"Ohhh, I'd like to take a look at that when you're finished," Maryam said, and the two left the library to begin reading their treasures.

For the next few days Candace was seldom home, busy with doctor appointments. She took to wearing sunglasses indoors because she said the light made her headaches worse, and while Gladys believed this was true, she also felt the dark lenses helped reduce the sunburst shimmer that surrounded Maryam. Candace steadfastly refused to acknowledge her, though Maryam delivered several kind comments to her each time they met in the hall or the sunny kitchen.

Outside the weather was a tense, hot standoff between stagnant humid air that sat upon the Cities like a leftover stew gone bad and fretful storms of cooler air that tantalized everyone, but in the end surged above or below Saint Paul, never sweeping through. Gladys thought the outside world matched the one indoors.

Gladys and Maryam went for walks in the neighborhood in the morning when it was cooler. One day they stopped by the Cathedral which had just been lovingly restored to its full glory—the granite walls pristine as the day the stone arrived from Saint Cloud, and the copper dome once again a flashing beacon. Gladys liked to sit in the pews and consider how much sorrow and joy had soaked into the kneelers over the years, just like the sacred space of her kitchen table. She wasn't Christian, raised instead with Ojibwe beliefs and prayers, but that didn't mean she couldn't appreciate someone else's place of worship, especially one as lovely as this.

She and Maryam wandered to the niche dedicated to the Virgin Mother. There were candles the faithful could light, a collection box set discreetly beside them, kneelers placed before a white marble statue of a pretty woman with a soft chin. There was a pudginess about her features that made her blandly tender. Maryam looked nothing like her. A man and woman knelt before the Virgin Mary. They didn't seem to be connected in any way beyond the fact of their praying. Maryam drifted behind them and touched the man on the shoulder. He didn't react except to drop his head to a more fervent angle. Maryam closed her eyes and seemed to be saying a prayer of her own. Then she repeated these actions with the woman. Gladys left before she saw what effect Maryam's presence had on the two, for it felt like such private, intimate business.

She sat in a pew and stared up at the star-shaped chandelier and the dove that was painted in the exact center of the dome as if its wings were what kept the vaulted ceiling aloft. When Maryam joined her they visited an area behind the altar called the Shrines of the Nations. Here there were statues of different saints representing ethnic groups who had helped build the church and the city. A saint for the Germans and Italians, the French and the Irish and Slavs. Saint Therese was there, too, for all other missions.

"This has always hurt me, some way," said Gladys.

Maryam came up behind her and touched her arm. "Because your people aren't represented?"

"Exactly. I know back then we probably weren't part of this congregation, though you never know, there were Dakota and Ojibwe converts going way back. But this place wouldn't be a place without us. This land is our closest relative, and we have cherished it, studied it, learned its ways and its stories before any other person walked this ground, hauling in their own stories that have no roots beneath the dirt." She smiled at Maryam. "I didn't mean to give a speech."

"You remind me of my Kanien'kehá:ka sister, Jigonsaseh, who spoke with passion of her home as you do now. I understand better than you may think. My people were invaded time and again. Resisted, suffered exile, fought those who found our ways offensive and strange. I am a child of my desert home as surely as you are the daughter of the lakes and the woods. I'm sorry when you are overlooked."

Gladys observed in her rambles with Maryam that she'd been right when she said most people couldn't see her. When they rode on the bus together, which Maryam entered without paying, no one glanced at her but looked straight on as if she were never there. They must sense something though, Gladys thought, for no one knocked against Maryam or sat where she was already sitting. They were riding the Number 63 bus that traveled up Grand Avenue, headed for the Whole Foods on Fairview, when someone other than Gladys finally noticed Maryam. A small boy, Somali, Gladys judged, after taking in the beautiful long oval of his mother's face and her colorful veiled dress. He sat in his mother's lap, facing the aisle, his hands folded across hers. They looked so comfortable together, such a perfect fit, they were an oasis of solemn peace. He had large chocolate-brown eyes and eyelashes long enough to brush the side of his cheek. He smiled at Maryam as she passed and lifted one small hand, which his mother gently reached for and brought back to their shared lap.

On impulse, Gladys pulled the cord before their stop. She'd noticed a tree full of waving bright clothes hanging from its branches like rare exotic flowers. She understood that this must be a shop owner's ploy to snare attention and pull in customers intrigued by the whimsy of clothes worn by a tree. And it had worked, with her at least. She was surprised by the sudden shopping urge. Oh no, maybe rich people's ways are catching, she teased herself.

"I've been thinking of jazzing myself up a little," she whispered to Maryam. "Let's take a look at these styles."

The store that caught her interest sold imported goods from India—elephants with mirror disks glued to their trunks, figures of the Buddha and Hindu deities scattered throughout, mysterious to Gladys because she didn't know their stories. She found tiered skirts made of a lightweight cotton and matching blouses you just slipped over your head, one size fits all, gauzy and simple, comfortable. She tried on a set, mixing a white top with a lilac skirt. She felt so good she actually twirled before the mirror, something she hadn't done in decades. "I'll look like an old flower child, but I don't even care!" she told Maryam, who was examining the long, jewel-colored scarves.

"Something's gotten into me, I'm not usually like this."

Maryam didn't appear troubled by Gladys's exuberance. "Sometimes we know deep inside when good things are coming."

"Maybe that's it. Out of nowhere I'm feeling gushy and silly, like my girls when they were in high school. Oh, their moods were too much to keep up with. Could this be my second childhood?"

The clerk was stationed in the front of the store, far enough away to miss what would have sounded to her like the one-sided conversation of a crazy person. But she gasped when Gladys came forward with an armful of clothes, for Gladys had shed more than her old jeans with the stretch waist and her faded, shapeless polyester blouse. She looked vibrant and youthful, as if a layer of tiredness and worry had been sloughed off to reveal a new skin of optimism. A seam of giddy happiness had opened in her, and there was nothing tidy about it, the warmth leaked and spread and lit her up like a fresh bulb.

"That outfit really suits you," the shopkeeper said, and she wasn't trying to make a sale but was wholly earnest.

"You don't think I look like a refugee from the sixties?" Gladys chuckled. "Or the 'ewe putting on the lamb'?"

"No, honest to God. You are transformed." She didn't even jump in to add that she wasn't intimating that Gladys looked poorly upon entering. There was no need. Something had shifted in the older woman, and it was plain to see.

Gladys purchased a rainbow assortment of skirt sets, which the clerk folded neatly into a shopping bag. Then she and Maryam walked up to Whole Foods. Gladys wanted to cook a special supper for Maryam and the Jenssens—she already had a stash of manoomin, her much-prized wild rice, and a bagful of morel mushrooms Binah had dropped off in a bundle, addressed to her, on the front porch of the mansion without ringing the bell. She was looking for fresh walleye to round out the simple but delectable fare. She asked Maryam if she liked fish.

"Oh, yes. I've never been fussy. When you grow up laboring so hard for every meal, you appreciate whatever's put in front of you. I was raised with dietary laws that restricted certain foods considered to be unclean, but I see now these are man's rules, and I live beyond them."

"Good, you'll be nicely surprised then." Gladys gathered what she needed, she and Maryam tasting the varieties of melon that were set out in small cubes pierced with a toothpick.

"The honeydew is best, don't you think?" Maryam asked.

So Gladys added one to her basket.

Candace approached Gladys soon after she returned from Whole Foods, and even with vision darkened by sunglasses was able to see the change in her.

"What a lovely ensemble," she enthused, "you look positively radiant!"

Gladys smiled and pinched the sides of the skirt to pull it wide. "Thank you. I went a little crazy and bought more clothes in a minute than I've bought in the last few years."

"Well, I approve," said Candace. She smiled for the first time in several days. "I've had a thought. This vile humidity is supposed to break tomorrow, and they're promising spectacular weather by Friday. What do you say we host a small dinner party together Friday night? Your family and my family. Well, it will be sparse on our side since the boys are working in New York this summer, but I could invite Jules, that's Barry's father, and of course that means Merle as well."

"Merle?"

"You'll see," Candace said mysteriously. "They come as a set."

Gladys cooked two suppers Friday evening, the first being advance portions she shared with Maryam in the kitchen. Candace was busy upstairs, enjoying the weekly visit of her masseuse, a middle-aged woman named Dottie who always wore vibrant Hawaiian-like muumuus and could only work in bare feet. Candace had a massage table permanently installed in her spacious bathroom suite, so Dottie came to her, reducing her to grateful putty.

"There'll be room for you at the dinner table," Gladys told Maryam, "but it might seem strange to have an extra setting and food disappearing before their very eyes." She burst out laughing at the image that popped into her head, a levitating forkful of walleye swallowed by a black hole.

She used a minimum of ingredients as she cooked, to allow the delicacies to speak for themselves, the wild rice flavored with a simple homemade chicken broth and browned onions, the morels and fish lightly seasoned and sautéed to release their savory juice. She'd baked biscuits and set out whipped butter and the last of the chokecherry jam she'd preserved last year. Maryam was so enthralled she could barely speak.

When Gladys passed her the biscuits she grabbed her hand and squeezed it. "Bless you," she whispered. "This is the rarest treat."

"I'm glad you like our walleye," Gladys said, awkwardly, unused to such fervent emotion. "*I* always have. But no pecan-encrusted hoo-hah for me. I want to taste the fish."

She let Candace fuss with the dining table arrangements when she emerged later, fragrant with the sage oil Dottie used to work her deep tissues.

Binah had made it clear to her mother that she and Ava would *not* be coming, but Grace and Dylan had accepted the invitation, and Gladys was pleased to get the chance to visit with them.

Jules Jenssen was the first to arrive. Barry was watching out the window, and when the wine-colored Chevy Caprice pulled up to the curb, he gave the window a quick rap with his knuckles and said to himself, "Oh, ish!"

Gladys had just walked into the room and she chuckled. "You really *are* a Minnesotan. Did you know that's an Ojibwe word?"

Barry turned. "You mean 'ish'?"

"Yes, we place it at the end of words to show we think something is not so good."

"Thank you for the language lesson," he told her. "And now I know I used the right word to describe my father's car. I offered to get him something better, something new, but he's so stubborn."

Barry moved to open the door. "Dad, welcome! Still driving that old Caprice, I see."

Jules carefully wiped his shoes on the door mat before entering the house, his arms too full to give his son the affectionate hug Gladys could see was in him, wanting to burst through. "Leave it alone, son," he said cheerfully. "Don't get in the way of a man's love for his car. She runs like a trooper, and none of this electrical system to worry about with the windows and doors—you gotta use muscle to work 'em." He barked out a laugh that was high and sharp like a coyote's. "Stop pushing those spendy little models on me."

He noticed Gladys then, lurking in the background, and he charged forward, eager to be introduced. "You must be Gladys," he practically roared. "I've heard a world of wonderful things about you. But *no* one, *no* one prepared me for the real thing and told me how beautiful you are!"

Barry stepped between them, wrapped an arm around his father's shoulder, and steered him toward the back of the house. "Let's get Merle settled in the sunroom, and you can unload the rest of whatever it is you have there."

Merle, it turned out, was an ancient toy poodle. She'd been left to wear her fur in its natural state, Gladys was relieved to see, none of those puff balls arranged on her as if she were a shrub. Her white fur was a little dingy, closer to a tea-stained ivory, and her eyes were gummy with the tears of old age. She shivered when she wasn't in Jules's arms, so he set down a soft dog bed and made a nest for her using one of his winter flannel shirts. She curled in there and tried to look up at him, though her tears were so thick he must have been no more than a watery giant.

"This is my sweetheart," he told Gladys, his voice softer now. "Named for Merle Oberon because she was so lovely, just like this one here. Aren't you, baby? The most beautiful dog that's ever lived."

Gladys didn't think he was just being kind to a dog on her last legs; he seemed to mean his words. She didn't know what to think of him. He made her nervous and stepped into her space in a way she thought of as very chimookoman. She never knew Indians to do that unless they were ready to fight you. Yet she was drawn to him, curious, maybe infected—yes, that was a good word, it denoted something that could be good or bad—infected by his rampant zest.

"Seven and seven, Dad?" Barry asked before heading to the bar.

"This might shock you, but I've discovered something else," Jules said. "Look in that sack." He pointed to a paper bag he'd placed on a table while he settled Merle.

"Vodka—horseradish flavor?" Barry sounded skeptical.

"Got it at Moscow on the Hill, just over on Selby. They make their own there, and boy, this is some good stuff. It'll knock out any bug you have, even pneumonia, I'd wager." He wriggled his eyebrows. "Why don't you put that in the freezer and get it cold again?"

Barry glanced at Gladys as if checking to make sure she could handle his father. She had relaxed some, so Barry left.

"I hope they're treating you right," Jules said. He waited nervously for her answer and she realized he was actually checking; this wasn't just one of those polite statements people make to fill in a conversation void.

"Oh, yes, they've been good to me," she assured him.

They sat opposite each other in comfortable chairs that eased the tension between them. Gladys didn't stare at the man, but took quick sidelong glances to put together a picture she could go over later, when she was alone. He was bigger than his son, though not very tall, just sturdier and darker, his skin as brown and weather-wrinkled as many of her cousins. He had a full head of white hair, thick and wavy, so silvery she thought maybe if you ran your hand through it you'd find shiny traces left behind on your skin. His eyes were a blue that reminded her of the turquoise towels she'd given Maryam to use, more shaded toward green than his son's. He was almost movie-star handsome, the way Tyrone Power might have looked in his seventies, but his eyes were close-set and deep, what would have passed for brooding in anyone else's face, anyone who wasn't bursting with so much bright energy.

Gladys was about to say something, ask him a question to hold up her end of the dialogue, but she heard a heartrending plea coming from the breakfast nook just a few steps away. "Poor Zhigaag, he wants to come in, too, and make sure I haven't forgotten him." She went over to the French doors and let him in.

"We have guests, now, so see if you can behave."

He trotted after her as she returned to the sunroom, then skidded to a halt when he saw the man and the sleeping dog. "This is Jules and Merle, and they have every right to be here, so don't get all bent out of shape."

Zhigaag blinked at her, then moved a bit closer to the small dog who looked like a dirt-smudged softball nestled in a shirt. When Merle remained still, Zhigaag went up and sniffed her, so thoroughly his inspection reminded Gladys of a doctor's exam. Then the cat did something she'd never have predicted. He leaned into the dog bed and licked Merle's tiny, sheep-like head. Merle slept on, unaware of the minor miracle developing above her.

"Look at that!" Gladys whispered in amazement. "That's something. I'm telling you. He's so unfriendly except with me."

Then Zhigaag eased cautiously in Jules's direction and in one swift motion, as if he made up his mind at the last bold second, leapt into the man's lap. Gladys fell back in her chair and fanned herself with her hand to indicate her surprise. She didn't have time to remark on this for the door chime sang its gentle notes, signaling that her daughter and grandson had arrived.

For the first time in Gladys's experience, the mansion was filled with happy noise. Her daughter grabbed her in a warm hug, then pulled back, holding her mother's hands to judge her new fashion statement.

"Mama, how beautiful you are!" she whispered in her husky voice.

"That's what I was saying," Jules roared from the sunroom, and then he was there beside them, Zhigaag slung over his shoulder like an ammunition belt. The cat appeared to enjoy the view from this unfamiliar height.

Dylan had been standing patiently behind his mother, waiting for the chance to hug Gladys (he liked to lift her a bit off the floor until she fussed over his strength), but now he tapped his mother on the shoulder and gently turned her so she could see Jules.

"Zhigaag has made a new friend," Gladys said, hoping her grandson wouldn't be hurt by this development, he'd worked so hard to win the cat's favor only to remain thoroughly ignored.

Dylan had been shy as a young boy, but his mother's injury had pushed him into a caretaking mode that built his confidence. So he strode forward in an adult way, hand stuck out. "I don't know who you are, but you must be pretty special for Zhigaag to take a liking to you." He shook hands with Jules.

Dylan was already taller than anyone in his family. He jokingly called himself "the Jolly Beige Giant," since he was a tawny golden color from his skin to his eyes and hair. He attracted the attention of girls wherever he went, but didn't seem to notice, which made him even more appealing. He didn't look much like his mother. Grace was built like Gladys, solid and strong, but her face was all her own, what she called pleasant-looking but abbreviated, her features mere suggestions; her lips a flat line, her nose a short knob, her eyebrows giving out toward the middle. Her eyes were wide-set and lovely though, dark brown with flecks of gold. She'd recently cut off her fine, wispy hair. "That's a chop, not a haircut," Dylan complained. She'd probably let it grow out again to please him.

Candace emerged from the dining room where she'd been setting and resetting the table, wanting it to be just so. Introductions were made all around. Maryam hovered at the edge of these greetings, and Gladys wanted so much to pull her into the room and include her in the festivities. Since this wasn't possible she checked on her now and again, smiled to let her know she wasn't forgotten.

At one point Gladys was certain that Jules had seen the lady—he was talking to Dylan, asking him about school, what grade he was in, favorite subjects, the usual interrogation, when the older man's gaze drifted to the corner where Maryam stood, hands clasped in front of her. He did a double-take, and then looked right at Gladys. She bustled away to get the second supper going, more confused than she had been in a very long time.

The meal was a great success; everyone applauded Gladys for her efforts and lingered for second and third helpings. Maryam watched from an extra chair tucked into a corner of the room, her eyes round with interest.

Candace asked Grace if she'd mind talking about her recent work.

Grace looked at her mother. "Did you tell them about the injury?"

Gladys nodded. "Okay, good, so you'll understand if I suddenly lose track of what I'm saying."

Dylan was carefully buttering a biscuit when he said softly, "You're almost a hundred percent, Mom. It's been forever since you got lost." He looked up and couldn't prevent the enormous grin that opened his face like a new flower. "Gold star!" he said with a dramatic flourish.

"My boy, my PR agent," Grace said warmly. "This latest painting I'm working on is a large canvas, well, large for me, and the pieces started to form before I understood the whole. So I did a lot of sketching first to find my way to the overarching image. It turns out I'm painting a turtle, our Turtle Island, this continent. But a hundred stories intertwine to bring her into focus. I started with a simple scene of an Ojibwe family out harvesting the wild rice. They're in a canoe, wielding their wooden knockers. You just know they're singing and telling jokes. The water swirls around them, the color moving from an earth-green to a blue-green until you realize it isn't water anymore but the glorious stained-glass window of a church. And four little girls in their prettiest Sunday dresses, hair lovingly arranged with barrettes and ribbons, are standing before it, their arms slung around each other. But a car approaches, the one containing a man with a bomb, ready to launch it at the sacred space."

"Oh," Candace gasped. "The little Birmingham girls."

"Yes. So it's that kind of thing, where stories meld into each other, hopefully so smoothly you can't easily find where the borders are."

"Magnificent," Candace breathed. "I *love* that."

"You'll have to come to our Art Crawl one of these Fridays when we open our studios for a few hours and talk about whatever folks want to."

"You ever get any whackos?" Barry asked.

Candace glowered at him, but he was oblivious to her reaction.

"Mom'll say, no, but *I* think we do," Dylan offered.

Grace turned to him. "Who?"

"Mom, you're too nice. There was that one guy who said he'd dreamt every one of your paintings before he ever saw them. That was weird."

"Maybe he did?"

Gladys chuckled to herself. Grace had always been her dreamy girl, one foot lightly touching the ground, the other mired in the clay of some other planet. Sometimes you had to remind her to do a chore several times, not because she was lazy or unwilling to help, but because her thoughts and visions were who knows how many light years away.

"Mom's modest, but she's been knocking people *out* with this painting, even before it's finished," Dylan said proudly. Grace put her arm around him in a sidelong hug.

"I can believe it," Candace said. "Did you notice any change in your process? I love to hear artists talk about how their creativity works. I hope you don't mind."

Dylan leaned in Candace's direction and stage-whispered, "She lives for this stuff."

"Don't be a smart guy," Grace said, but she was smiling. "Funny you should ask, I was just journaling about this the other day. Yes, something has changed. Forgive me for sounding gag-me hokey, but here it is: love." Grace paused and let the word sink into the room. No one noticed Maryam move her chair closer. "Don't get me wrong, I always adored being creative, telling a story with images—brush strokes and color. And painting is such a sensual, down and dirty kind of occupation. You have to be willing to feel, explore, make a mess of your physical self *and* your emotions. But I was always there in the process, this observer critiquing as I went, wondering what others would think. Is this good? Is this right? Heaven help me, will this sell? I'm not saying I've gone missing from the work completely, it's my hand and my sensibility, my technique and obsession laying down the paint, but part of me has slipped to the side, quieted that watcher's voice. Now I operate more on instinct, and I'm, well, this is embarrassing . . ." She playfully pretended to cover her ears. "I'm shattered with love for these subjects. *They* are front and center. *Their* stories, not mine. Sometimes I'm weeping with sympathy and joy, respect, and I don't even know it 'til Dylan walks in and wipes off my face."

He was blushing, and busied himself with another helping of mushrooms.

"I think of the injury as an actual wedge—a black chasm that opened in my brain, and thoughts and memories had to find a way to leap across it or swing around it some other way. That's the bad part. But a chasm means there's also a deep foundation that lies hidden at the dark bottom, and who knows what treasures can be accessed now that there's an opening?"

Silence fell on the table.

Jules stepped into the quiet. "I say we raise our glasses in honor of artists everywhere. Don't let the rat race get you down!"

"Here here!" said Candace, and everyone clinked glasses; even Dylan lifted his sparkling water and made sure he reached them all.

Then Dylan steered the conversation away from his mother, Gladys noticed, probably to give her a break from having to concentrate so hard. He announced: "Jules, Mr. Jenssen?—said he worked at my school for like a ton of years."

Barry cleared his throat. "That was a very long time ago."

"Did you teach?" Gladys asked.

"No," said Jules. "Never had the smarts of my boy here to do well in school. Nope, I pushed a broom, kept the halls so clean I worried sometimes that the kids, with all their horsing around, would fall and split their heads. Thank goodness for the hard heads of youth!" He barked his wild laugh.

"Did you ever tell on people, you know, when you saw them doing bad things?" Dylan asked.

"I never did. But I intervened a few times and helped folks simmer down. Told 'em stories to distract 'em. Works every time." He winked at Dylan as if they shared a secret.

"Are you retired?" Gladys asked. She wasn't usually one to ask so many questions, she'd just let people tell her what they wanted when they were ready, but she was so curious about this man who had charmed her discriminating cat.

"I am now, but after the janitor job I was a doorman at one of the fancy buildings in Minneapolis. Did that for ten years."

"They *loved* him," Candace chimed in. "You should've seen the gifts and cards they showered on him. He looked after everyone so well, knew all their stories and complaints."

Jules beamed and glanced around the table to draw everyone in to his next remark. "I love people. That's it."

"Tell them a story, Pop," Candace encouraged. "You've got fresh bait here."

"Let's see, let's see." He rubbed his hands together, the dry rasp of his work-hard palms surprisingly loud. "Since we're talking work, I'll tell you about my first job."

Barry groaned.

"We'll brook no protest from the peanut gallery," Jules said, unperturbed and happy. "This was in 1934 and I was five years old. Back then Saint Paul was known as 'the crime center of the Nation.' Can you believe it? Saint Paul? Due to some corrupt officials who'd worked out a deal with the gangsters—they could come and go as they pleased as long as they lined the pockets of the city fathers and kept their noses clean around town. For a time, John Dillinger and his girlfriend, Billie Frechette, lived over on Lexington, not far from here.

"I lived with my parents in the same little complex, the Lincoln Court Apartments, and was always hanging around outside, trying to get in the good graces of older boys. My parents were decent folks but glum, the sun never really shone for them except to beat them down. So I escaped when I could. One day I noticed this lady, she looked like she'd stepped from one of the flickers she was so gorgeous. She had black piercing eyes that could go warm or cold in a flash. She was wearing an outfit you just didn't see on many women around here, at least back then. Bright red shorts, all crisp and ironed with a nice pleat, and a red top like a horse wears. What's that called?"

"A halter," Barry sighed.

"Yes, thank you, a halter. And her lipstick matched the clothes and her fingernails, and even the paint on her pretty toes sticking out of her shoes. She was my first love."

"And she was Indian," Candace added.

"That's right. She was Menominee from Neopit. Anyhow, I was such a little nuisance, mooning around her, and not much got past Dillinger, so one day he asked me, 'You trying to steal my girl?' No sir, I said. 'Ya sure now? Good lookin' kid like you could give me a run for my money.' No, sir. He smiled at me and I knew I was fit to live another day.

"Not much happened in that complex I didn't know about, and Dillinger must've noticed that. He paid me to run errands for him, buy him a paper, some apples, but really he just wanted to pump me for information. I can see that now. Mostly he gave me nickels, but one time he gave me a silver dollar which I still have."

"Are you serious?" Dylan was beside himself with excitement.

"You bet, here you go." Jules pulled a coin from his pocket and flipped it across the table to Dylan who caught it in one satisfying snatch of the air.

"Oh, cool!"

"Dad, you know how I feel about glorifying criminals." Barry tapped the table with his fingers, as if playing a miserable drum set, the rhythm hitched and angry.

"I don't condone the killing, son, you're right there. But don't get me started on the thievery. You know my opinion of the corporatocracy running this world."

Dylan held up his hand to toss the coin back, but Jules stopped him. "You keep it, that's yours now."

"For real?"

"Sure, sure. I've used up all its luck it can spend on me, now may it bring you the luck."

"Wow! Thank you!" Dylan was doubly fascinated with the silver piece now that it was his. He passed it to his mother to admire, but didn't want it out of his hands for long.

Gladys smiled at Jules in gratitude and he pretended not to notice, but a smile crooked one corner of his clamped mouth.

"I know what story I'd like to hear," said Grace as she helped herself to another biscuit with chokecherry jam. "I'm a big romantic, a sucker for all those tearjerkers and date movies. I'm curious how you two got together." She indicated Candace and Barry.

Candace was flustered by the question, realized how precarious was her emotional balance, like a woman teetering on stilts. Barry came to the rescue and she sent him a grateful look across the table.

"That was in 1975," Barry began. "I was in my last year at Harvard Law School and Candace was a senior at Lesley, which was just down the street. I was a big-time actor wannabe back then, always in shows all through my school years. Even in law school we had a drama society that put on a big spring musical, a comedy lampooning the world of law and our professors. We advertised auditions pretty openly, and sometimes people from the community ended up in a show. That's how I met Candace. She auditioned, got a part, danced her little heart out, and the rest is history. I carried her off to Minnesota!"

Barry had rushed through the story so quickly he startled even himself. He looked at Candace in confusion. "I never did ask you why you auditioned for that show. You weren't a big theatre person as I recall."

Candace didn't know how to explain what she'd never understood herself. She remembered the moment quite vividly, though, as if it had occurred last week. How she cut through the law school's Harkness Commons on her way back from some business in Harvard Square and had seen the sign advertising auditions for the spring musical posted throughout the Hark. A voice as clear as the conversations slipping around her had announced in her head: "Do this." She'd rushed to the women's restroom, slammed herself into a stall, and leaned against the closed door. Shaking. Was she losing it? She knew she was at the age where people had their first schizophrenic breaks; she'd learned this in Psychology class.

You're not crazy, she told herself. You're just a regular girl who keeps her nose to the grindstone and gets good grades. Nothing extraordinary. Nothing off the beam. But she was spooked all the same because she recognized the voice as one she hadn't heard in fourteen years. It was her mother's. She'd washed her face then in one of the sinks, using the awful powdered soap, and dried it with paper towels. She even recalled how rough they felt on her skin, their sour brown smell. Part of her wanted to defy the order given her by the voice, but she didn't want to risk hearing it again. So she opened her notebook and wrote down the information, and though she'd never been cast in a show before she won a spot in the chorus. Just like that.

All eyes were upon her, waiting for an answer to Barry's question. She started, jogged her glass of wine so a red drop spilled and landed on the back of her hand like a spot of blood. "It was just a feeling I had," she finally said. "A feeling that good things would come of it. And they did." She managed a smile and lifted her wineglass in another toast, this time to love itself, but she forgot to wipe the spot off and the wine slid from her hand to the tablecloth, leaving a dark red stain.

Later that night when the guests had left with promises of a repeat performance soon to come, and the kitchen and dining room had been tidied, order restored, Candace realized she'd neglected to give Grace and her son a tour of the Indian Art Room. Come to think of it, each time the subject was raised Gladys had offered some distraction that made Candace forget. Why was that?

Her musings on this puzzle shifted to memories of early days with Barry—Barrett Nelson Jenssen, who stole her heart. Ugh. What a violent phrase that was if you really thought about it. Blood, she was preoccupied with blood. The color red. The red of Billie Frechette's painted toes and halter top. The red corpse of Dillinger, shot to death in an alley outside the Biograph Theater in Chicago. The red of a cherry. She smiled, half asleep, remembering how, so long ago, she'd dropped into Passim's in Harvard Square to have a cup of tea and catch up on her reading for a literature class. Edith Wharton. She'd glanced at the trinkets of jewelry and decorative items they sold on the side and impulsively purchased a gleaming red cherry made of glass—so truthful to the real thing you just wanted to pop it in your mouth and taste the burst of luscious juice. She remembered how she gave it to Barry as a present when they shared supper together at their favorite restaurant, Casablanca, tucked in a basement on Brattle Street. She'd placed it on the table, then pushed it toward him, never taking her eyes off his face. They had a telepathy back then, she didn't need to explain. He knew she wasn't a virgin when they first made love, but she'd never understood what all the fuss was about until Barry. She'd been clear on that. He grinned and covered the glass fruit with his hand, whispered, "You're getting a big reaction to this little gift. What say we blow this joint? I want you all to myself." So they'd left.

She remembered the first time they crossed the line from a flirting friendship to something more. She'd had an instant crush on Barry, the star of the show with his stunning Broadway voice and shining good looks. How had he noticed her, shuffling around with the rest of the chorus? It was incomprehensible. Unlikely. There was a dance rehearsal held in the Ames Courtroom on the second floor of Austin Hall. The entire middle was an open space useful to their purposes, with audience seating on two sides and a court bench at one end. After rehearsal she and Barry lingered, light chitchat evolving into a deeper conversation that led them to sit on the carpet. She gestured with her hands as she spoke, and Barry grabbed them playfully and held on, held on, though still watching her face as he listened. She was the one who surprised them both by leaning in and kissing his mouth. A peck, but soft because her lips were moist with the Vaseline she always wore on them, better than any gloss. Then he pulled her in for the real thing and she was falling back, onto the floor, the tie beams of the courtroom ceiling carved with the heads of wild dragons and boars, though to her they all looked like wolves, roaring above them in excitement.

For the first time in months Candace slept without dreaming of turtles. Tonight her arms were full of marigolds, more than she could hold, but still Barry kept offering another bloom and another, and she couldn't refuse, and then he was feeding her cherries and wine from his own mouth, and she threw the marigolds in the air where each became a bright sun.

Indian Confessional

Jules phoned Gladys the day after the dinner party to thank her for sharing her favorite foods and preparing them so well.

"I'd like to return the favor though you wouldn't be thanking me anytime soon for what I'd be able to put together. But I could take you out for a meal—that way you'll be safe and won't get sick." He laughed at himself, then hushed, and Gladys could hear his nerves jangling on the other end, noisy as a man playing with coins in his pocket. She found his trembling anxiety a bit endearing but couldn't resist teasing.

"I don't know. I don't usually go out with strange men unchaperoned. And to be honest, I think you're strange."

"Oh, *thank* you," he said, warmly, enthusiastically.

You see, Gladys thought, there he goes again. Unpredictable as a cat.

"I hear your worry," he continued, "and I don't make light of that. But the fact that you've thought of me at all, well, that makes me proud!"

Gladys was shaking her head, but smiling. Impossible man. Were all Norwegians like this? Then she corrected herself for generalizing. Besides, she'd always heard Norwegians were a bit stoic and reserved, nothing like this one. All she said was, "I'll make an exception this one time and have supper with you because you were so good to my grandson."

"Wonderful! Wonderful!" he said, so thrilled with her answer he accidentally pressed the telephone keypad with his cheek, disconnecting the call.

Gladys knew immediately what had happened. She set down the phone and waited. One beat. Two. The phone rang.

"I'm so sorry, so very sorry," she heard distantly through the ear piece—she was holding the phone away from her.

When his breathing calmed she said, "Okay, now I'm breaking *another* rule—I don't usually spend time with people who hang up on me. This must be your lucky day."

"It is, it is," he sang, and Gladys finally laughed. She didn't hear herself, but this was a laugh she hadn't used in several years. Brief and sweet, with flirt and innocence disarmingly joined.

Gladys said she wasn't picky about food and had no preferences when it came to restaurants, so Jules took her to his favorite spot, Moscow on the Hill. They decided to walk since it was so close, and when both of them reached the sidewalk and were about to set off, Jules suddenly held Gladys in a dancer's clinch and spun her around quite gracefully, as if he intended to waltz her all the way down Western Avenue. She made her body a rock, her face a petroglyph of disapproving lines. She crossed her arms and stood as tall as she could, though that meant she was looking at his chest.

"All right. No," she said. "I like to dance. I like to walk. These are separate things. I have the feeling you're a nice man, but behave yourself. I still have all my teeth."

"Okay, you're right, we're walking now," said Jules, though he was smiling broadly and didn't look at all chastened. He offered his arm, surprisingly strong beneath his button-down blue shirt that really brought out the ocean cast of his eyes.

"My enthusiasm has forever gotten me into trouble," Jules said. "I was the black sheep of the family, always waking up like it was the first day I'd ever seen, and even the dreary wallpaper had some new enchantment, a curled-up edge that maybe hid a treasure map behind it. I don't know where that came from—maybe my great-grandfather, Iver, who was practically excommunicated from the clan back in the day. He was the only one who claimed me. The rest said I'd been left by gypsies or mixed up at the hospital with some other child, which couldn't be since my mother never got that far but had me in the kitchen pantry of a house where she worked and was fired for the trouble.

"A few years back we had a reunion, and all these cousins my age said, DNA, let's make him get the test, DNA will tell us sure he's from somewhere else. I knew they were kidding, I looked like half the room, but that got to me. That DNA. And I thought, fine. I am my own man, my own family. So I changed my name to Jules after my favorite storyteller, Jules Verne. I think he was French. I traded Norway for France when it comes to my name."

Gladys patted his arm. "Names are important. It's how we claim ourselves, I think, and if we can't wear the one we were given, well, we need to find the right one."

They ambled the rest of the way in companionable silence, serenaded by the evening songs of birds.

When it came time to order Gladys said, "Sometimes I have such a taste for something I'd chew your arm off if you tried to order for me, but tonight I'm in your hands. Order away."

So he did. He ordered blinis and gravlax for appetizers. "What's a day without salmon?!" Then Ekaterina duck breast and beef Stroganoff for later. "So, we'll have the fish, the moo, and the quack," he said jovially.

"I wouldn't use that word if I were you," Gladys said, trying to keep her face serious.

"You can't hurt me, woman, you're here beside me and that's all it takes." Jules's ears were suddenly red and Gladys lifted a menu to hide behind. "But first," he said, his confidence already restored, "we must begin with vodka!"

They were sitting on the patio behind the restaurant, a cool breeze gently pressing Gladys's skirt against her legs in a way that tickled. She sipped a honey-flavored shot of vodka while Jules tried the ginger. They toasted their children and grandchildren, their dog and their cat, Ojibwemowin and the little bit of Norwegian Jules remembered from childhood, listening to relatives who'd been born across the water.

"And we must toast the Dakota," Jules said. Gladys dutifully clinked her shot glass against his; thank goodness they were sipping, she could barely feel her lips. She noticed his eyes glisten with tears he blinked away.

"Now why is that?" she asked. "What brought them to mind?"

Over blinis and gravlax Jules told her the story of his great-grandfather who horrified his family by marrying a Dakota woman. "Remember now, there wasn't a lot of mixing back then. Germans stayed with the Germans, Irish with the Irish. A mixed marriage was a Norwegian marrying a Swede or a Dane, certainly not a Finn. Anyway, Iver was born in 1840 and lived 'til I was seven. By that time he'd given up and married another Norwegian; she was still alive and I remember her very well. She smoked a pipe and liked to wear his clothes around the house, which he didn't mind, said she'd worked hard enough all her life to do as she pleased by the end. I come from her line, no Dakota blood in me, though I used to pretend that was what made me different from my cousins.

"His first wife was Good Road Woman. I don't know how you say it in Dakota, he didn't recall, but she'd gone over to Christian and the white folks called her Ruth. Though the way he said it was 'Root.' When war broke out he was an idealistic young man and signed on with the Third Minnesota Regiment posted at Fort Snelling. Did you know this state was the first to offer troops to the Union side? He told me this all the time. He had a love-hate feel for this state and the government and could switch sides so fast it spun you to confusion. So he left his wife and newborn boy in the care of his relatives, but that turned out to be no care at all. He wrote when he could, from Kentucky and later Tennessee, and she couldn't read but had his cousin do the reading for her. In return she sent him papers filled with pictures she drew of the boy and the chickens, and then her tears at the bottom that looked like a scatter of wild rice on the page.

"She got caught up after the Minnesota Uprising, turned over to the fort by Iver's people, though she'd had nothing to do with any killings. They said they had to, they were being threatened by their neighbors for harboring the enemy. So many Dakotas rounded up for no reason. But they were Indian, they were in the way of what the white people and the white government wanted, so to hell with promises, contracts, agreements. She and the little one died at Fort Snelling, of hunger and the measles, and no one even knew on our side 'til Iver got back from the war and went after her. They say the last piece of his mind he'd preserved whole through all he'd seen on the battlefield just went out like a candle. Whoo. Gone. They had to lock him up in a room in his cousin's house for a year or so. He was mad with the grief. Wondered what he'd fought for in the end. That much he said later to me. He told me to stay away from war if ever I could and to make my own thoughts.

"He wasn't warm too much, gruff, but he had moments when his eyes would shine and he'd say a real nice thing to me. 'Inside you're alive,' he'd say, pointing at my chest. 'The rest, dead all the time. But inside, you're alive.'"

Gladys sniffed and wiped her nose with a tissue. Took another sip of honey fire. "Očáŋku Waštéwiŋ," she said softly.

"What's that?" Jules leaned closer.

"Good Road Woman. Očáŋku Waštéwiŋ. That's the way you should say it." Then they toasted her and the Dakota one more time.

By the time the duck arrived Gladys had consumed enough water to clear her head. Jules gave her the tastiest morsels and watched over her with pleasure, wanting her to receive the best, only the best. She couldn't stop thinking of the story he'd shared with her about his Dakota connection, so she decided to offer one of her own.

"I have some Dakota blood," she told him.

"No kidding."

"Probably a lot of us do, yes, we had great battles, and more skirmishes, but we also intermarried to keep our blood-lines fresh and not too incestuous, like those crazy Royals. Here's how my little bit of blood came about: A long time ago, before the chimookoman came, or wašičuŋ, I should say since we're talking about Dakotas. Before the wašičuŋ came, there was a young Dakota man who'd grown up hearing stories of the enemy—the Ojibwe. When he was little and misbehaved, his mother told him to be careful or he'd be mistaken for Ojibwe, that sort of thing, those teasing references. He was curious about us, more curious the older he got. He wondered if there was a little Ojibwe boy being told the same things about the Dakota. He wondered if he was missing out on meeting the dearest friend of his life because of old stories that weren't even true. He wasn't afraid of the world, or of losing his life. He was afraid of dying without satisfying his curiosity, being an old man left with regrets. So he stood up one day and said goodbye to everyone, packed just a few things one needs to survive, and he set out for Ojibwe territory. His mother begged him not to go, and all the girls cried because he would have made such a good husband, but now he would never return. His heart was firm, though, and they had to let him go.

"When he arrived at an Ojibwe camp, the young warriors joked that a foolish pheasant had come for supper, so easy their warrior work would be, so easy. But older ones told them to wait and see what this young man wanted. He was alone, on foot, his hands free of weapons. What honor could there be in such a killing? We used a sign language for trade back then, so he was able to tell them his purpose. 'I want to meet you and see what you are really like,' he said.

"'That's all?' one of the elders asked. 'That's all.' At first some thought it might be a trick, but his courage intrigued them, his curiosity fueled theirs, and pretty soon he learned their language and they shared many stories, and everyone was used to him, even fond of him. He married an Ojibwe woman and had three children. He might have stayed with them forever, but when his youngest child was just beginning to talk he had a dream about his mother. She was dying without peace because she didn't know what had become of her son. The next day he told the people his dream and said he had to go back to see her before she died. He wanted to bring his wife and children, but his wife refused to go, saying she would be too homesick. Many tears were shed, but the Dakota returned to his people. His mother was so happy she lived for a few more months before she died. Eventually he married a Dakota woman and had another family, but he sent messages to his other wife through trade routes and never forgot her. I come down through her line, so I'm descended from the one who stayed put, refusing to budge, and the one who was everlasting curious. That's me, the big mishmash."

"That's the mystery of you," Jules said, so transfixed by her story he'd let his beef Stroganoff get cold. "It's all in your eyes. First they're the color of a new penny, and then they're as green as the Emerald City! Thank you for sharing that with me," he said, and resumed eating.

Later, over strong coffee served in small cups Jules barely managed with his thick fingers, he spoke of his son, Barry, how proud he was of how far he'd surpassed his old man. "I was never one for school books, for reading about things you could only hold in the mind rather than see and taste and live. I'm all about the present, I guess. Right now, right now. Even my work wasn't to stockpile cash, though I did learn frugal ways from my folks and put by enough to send Barry through school, with some loan assistance on top. I worked to be around people, doing for them, hearing them, watching them. They swirled around me in the halls like a peck of mysteries that I got little pieces of in a day.

"Barry's mother was a lovely lady, Nynah. Just another hometown girl but with so many dreams and plans. She's the only person I knew who subscribed to *The New Yorker* magazine and read it cover to cover, so carefully, like she was going to be tested. She'd display the latest issue on our wobbly little coffee table, bought secondhand, and the magazine looked to be of higher value than the wood it rested on. I was never her first choice, though she saw me mooning for her in the background. She got in trouble by her true love, you know how it was back then, beyond a scandal, it could ruin your life. The true love turned out to be a disappointment who had other plans, so I was there and she accepted me as a consolation prize. That was enough for me. I took it as a challenge, making Nynah fall in love with me. But how could she? Me, with my broom who didn't read. She lost that baby and I cried like it was my own flesh and blood—never knew was it a boy or a girl, which has always bothered me somehow, I'd like to put a name on that little lost spark. But, oh, the joy when we had Barry, and she gave him an important-sounding name like a judge on the Supreme Court might have: Barrett. How's that? He was everything she could have wanted with his straight A's and his teachers saying the sky was the limit for him. The sky was the limit.

"But poor Nynah, her life was never a match for the dreams in her head, and when she was just twenty-nine they found a mass inside her, and it killed her so fast after she got the news. The last thing she said, and I thank the stars that Barry wasn't there to hear it, he was in school, just nine years old, and it was never meant for him, of course. The last thing she said, 'It isn't cancer, it's disappointment.' I held her for so long with a young foolishness that I could put my strength in her and bring her back. But I had to let go in the end. Somehow Barry kept achieving, even without her to push him. I could only cheer him on, not knowing all it took, the ins and outs of the steps he traveled to get where he is now. He made it in spite of his old man."

Gladys was looking into her coffee cup as if she could read their futures in its scatter of grounds. "Don't sell yourself short. I taught my girls not to be fooled by people with the whole alphabet of degrees behind their name. Some are wise as well as educated, some are not. Their father never had much chimookoman schooling, yet he was the smartest man I knew, with the best counsel. Your boy had a good father."

Jules's dark skin went a shade near purple when he blushed. He sat across from Gladys, flushed to a shade of eggplant and beaming, his strong hands looking like a giant's fists as he toyed with the small cup. He couldn't speak but nodded at her. She nodded at him. It was time to get her home.

They walked through the shadows, and Gladys marveled at how awake she was. Her mind was busy going over the evening's conversation, her skin was sensitive as a baby's, each brush of the wind against her arms and neck like the teases of soft lips. *Now* she felt like dancing, twirled by wind and good feelings. Jules was quiet, his heavy hand on her light one as they strolled arm in arm. When they reached the mansion and walked to the side entrance which led to her apartment, he suddenly stopped and looked up at the lights visible in several rooms of the house.

"I meant to ask you," he began, then paused.

"Yes?"

"The other night at supper. I was sure someone else was there who somehow got away from me, wasn't introduced. Was I dreaming?"

Gladys took her time answering. She looked past him, in the direction of Cochran Park and the tireless running statue, the birds offering endless water to the sky. "No, you weren't dreaming," she finally said. "The lady who was there is a kind of relative. To Candace. They have business only they can sort out. That's all I can say."

Jules nodded, slowly. "Candace is a good girl, but she's not very happy. I can see it. I hope Barry notices pretty soon. I keep my mouth shut because it's their marriage, not mine. It's hard sometimes but, loud as I am, I can keep my trap shut, too."

He'd been holding Gladys's hand this whole time, and she didn't realize it until he lifted it to his lips and grazed the back of her hand with a kiss. "Tonight was a gift," he said. "May there be more."

"Oh, yes," she said, her voice thick with emotion before she could stop herself. "You *are* strange," she said then, to cover her shyness. "But in all the best ways."

They hugged in the dark, and Gladys's cheek was pressed against Jules's heart. He smelled of sweet tobacco, the kind she used in prayers. In one smooth motion she reached to hold his face in her hands and then kissed him firmly on the lips. She squeezed his face for emphasis, brushed a lock of hair off his forehead, and then she was moving toward the stairs so fast he'd spend the rest of the night wondering if it really happened.

The cleaning crew that came every week to scrub the Summit Hill mansion were Awakatek Mayan Indians from Guatemala, a married couple and their three daughters. They didn't speak much English or Spanish, which Gladys could speak, brokenly. But through their few shared words and much vigorous sign language on both sides, they'd established a warm camaraderie and would spend a half hour together, sharing coffee in the kitchen before the crew piled into their car to head to the next job. Gladys wondered if they might be able to glimpse Maryam, but she never got the chance to find out since Maryam had taken to trailing after Candace wherever she went. Silent, mostly, after a few rebuffed inquiries. She's more patient than I could be, Gladys thought, impressed with Maryam's perseverance.

Maryam had been living in the mansion for a week and it was now September—still summery, trees still leafing green, though the color was dusty-looking and tired. The Tepeu family came to clean as usual, and Gladys held the door open while they carried in their supplies and vacuum. They hadn't been working long when the husband came and fetched Gladys, tugging her into the Indian Art Room. He pointed to the floor. Spots of blood trailed across the room as though a wounded creature had staggered all around. In places the blood was smeared with a substance that looked suspiciously like semen. The man was horrified and kept shaking his head and swiping the air with his hands to indicate, No, no. She understood. As important as this job was to him and his family he would not clean the room. He didn't like whatever was happening here anymore than she did. She nodded and led him out, indicated with her hands and her words: Me, me, I will wash. She needed to clean the room and *clean* it. First the floor.

She used the lavender-scented Lysol Candace stocked, not caring if it harmed the glossy finish of the wood, this was such a foul mess. Once the floor was spotless, she wiped down the inside panes of the windows which were specially tinted to protect the art from direct sunlight. The room smelled fresh, but the atmosphere was still oppressively thick, unhappy. She examined the paintings one by one to look for damage. There were changes, she noticed immediately. One of Denomie's flying horses was missing a rider, the small Indian man nowhere to be found in the painting. In his Fort Snelling piece, Andrew Myrick, whose mouth was stuffed with grass, was no longer standing but lying in the painted grass, his blood soaking wetly into the ground. The other painting that showed alteration was Carlson's *Bear Medicine*. The bear looked a bit sheepish, embarrassed, and flecks of blood stained his dark muzzle. His powerful arms fell to his sides, and he no longer assisted the woman with her sweater; instead she clutched it closed around her as if to protect herself from more than the cold.

"This is *not* good," Gladys grumbled, then humphed herself. "*That's* the understatement of the year."

She brought out sage and a large abalone shell to contain it as it burned. She spoke to the Face and washed him with the pleasant smoke. "I'm Ojibwe, so forgive me not understanding what you need. I know this is disrespectful, how you've been treated, but forces are at work to turn things around. If you can just be patient a little while longer. You are so powerful, I think your anger is influencing the beings in these paintings. These are living things, too, my way of thinking, but usually they stay put once they're born because their purpose is finished. They are content with the story the artist gives them. But now you've riled them up and they're destroying each other, their purpose has been confused. I think you were made for healing, though I'm not of your Nation so I can't say for sure. It must be hard not to be allowed to do what you were created for. Maybe this is why you're angry. But healing *is* needed here. Your granddaughter needs you. Please be patient just a little bit more. Thank you for listening to me."

When she checked the next morning, Gladys was relieved to see that the bear and his woman had reconciled, he was once again helping her on with her sweater, and Andrew Myrick was back on his feet, though he didn't look happy with grass in his mouth. But the Indian rider was still missing and never did come back. She guessed he'd have to represent those Natives who get lost along the way, in the deep trenches worn between cities and ancient homelands.

Both Candace and Gladys wanted to attend a reading at Birchbark Books, an event celebrating the publication of LeAnne Howe's novel *Miko Kings: An Indian Baseball Story*. Candace offered to drive, so on a Thursday evening in early September the two buckled into her silver Lexus, Maryam gliding quietly into the backseat, and they headed for 94 West to Minneapolis and an upscale neighborhood on the west side of town near Lake of the Isles.

They left early so they could browse through the store, always a treat since the shelves were lovingly stocked with books the owner, manager, and staff had read and could warmly recommend. Candace found volumes here she might not have spotted anywhere else, gems like Tyehimba Jess's *Leadbelly*, set out on tables, catching the eye. The owner was Louise Erdrich, Candace's favorite author, and to comb through the stacks and find the notes written in Louise's elegant, slanting hand, describing the wonders of a particular volume, thrilled her. She liked to run her fingers across these notes, musing, "This is the hand of the woman who brought us Fleur and Nanapush and Agnes. Just think." There were other treasures to find as well: jewelry and hand-painted cards, sage and wild rice, a children's corner made comfortable and inviting, love birds who became excitable when poetry was read, scrawled autographs of visiting authors left on a back wall. And sitting triumphantly in the center of things, looking like a small wooden castle carved for a child to play in, was a confessional, rescued from a church scheduled for demolition. You could curl up in there amid pillows and candles, imagining the countless mistakes, some small, some terrible, that had been whispered here, haltingly, defensively, eagerly, surely spilled a thousand different ways.

Candace liked to sit inside the cloistered space and consider what errors she would confide if she believed in sin. Weren't her letters a kind of confession, an admission that somehow, somewhere, she had erred?

On the drive, all three women were silent, watching the streets pass, then the highway, then the maze of lanes to get on Hennepin Avenue. When they turned onto West 21st Street Candace noted they weren't the only ones who'd thought to arrive early.

"Isn't that your daughter?" she asked Gladys, lifting her chin in the direction of a woman stepping out of a battered little red Toyota.

"Yes, it's Binah and Ava. Uh-oh."

"What?" Candace turned to look at Gladys.

"You see that man crossing the street, headed over here? That's my son-in-law, Frank Morgan. Binah's husband."

"Oh, and that's not good?"

"Not just now."

Gladys jumped out of the car with surprising agility, and she reached Binah at the same time as Frank. Ava smoothed over the awkwardness by leaping on her father, and he swung her onto his back and danced around like a trained horse.

"Now stop," Ava ordered. He stopped. "Now speak," she commanded. He whinnied so convincingly, passersby craned their necks to look for the stampede.

Binah charged ahead anyway, "I didn't know *you* would be here," she accused.

He was bouncing again and Ava was giggling, her glasses slipping to the edge of her nose.

"Why. Wouldn't I. Come?" He spoke in a rhythm that matched his playful bounce. "I'm. A fan. Of hers."

"Oh, maybe out of respect, knowing *I'd* come and wouldn't want to see you."

"But *I* do," Ava crowed. "I miss you, Daddy."

Frank set her down so he could hold her in his arms. He covered her long face and the round knobs of her cheeks with kisses. "I miss you too, baby."

Gladys slipped her arm around Binah's waist and stood with her, not urging her toward the entrance to the shop, just offering an anchor. Candace and Maryam had slipped noiselessly into the store to give the family privacy.

Frank looked at Binah and said, "You look good, as always and forever. I'm glad to see you, even if you're not."

A shiver ran through Binah, and it was a good thing Gladys was holding her or she might have flown at him. "I have nothing to say to you. Come on, Ava." She intended to stalk off in dignified outrage but she walked straight into a thick cloud of gnats which set her coughing, spitting, and waving them out of her hair.

Ava said, "Can't I sit with Daddy?"

"Oh, fine," Binah answered, and she and her mother walked inside Birchbark Books.

Gladys liked her son-in-law, and she'd noticed that he'd shaved off his beard and mustache for the first time since she'd known him. He looked younger now, easier. She'd often wondered if he wore such a thick beard as protection, something to hide behind when Binah launched into her speeches against the white power structure. Sometimes she forgot that Frank was Frank and not all the white people who had ever let her down. Gladys wanted to greet him and see how he was doing, but first she had to care for her girl; she'd talk with Frank later.

Five months earlier, Gladys had received a distraught, late-night call from Binah, telling her Frank had left.

"He packed a bag right in front of me, his daughter sleeping in the next room, and just took off, God knows where. He wouldn't answer me when I asked him where he was going."

Binah made it sound so criminal, unreasonable and nefarious, but Gladys knew there was at least one major scene her daughter was conveniently skipping. At this late hour she didn't press, only listened and held her girl as well as she could over the phone. "You can come here," she offered.

"No, Ava is sleeping, I don't want to wake her. I'll be okay eventually, it'll take considerably more than one selfish man to bring me down." But the last three words came out in a shaky rush; she couldn't hide the lake of tears flooding her heart.

The next day Gladys heard more of the story from Frank himself when he called and asked if he could stop by. She welcomed him, made coffee, and set out plates when he arrived bearing a wax bag full of crullers dusted with cinnamon-sugar, one of her favorite indulgences. He looked as if he hadn't slept, his eyes bruised with misery, the long black hair he usually wore in a neat ponytail spilling around his shoulders. He was two years younger than his wife, but today he appeared older, his springy legs only good for a slow walk. Gladys heard him trudge up the stairs to her apartment where he usually ran them. He sat down heavily at her kitchen table and never ate the cruller before him, though he pinched one end of it apart. Later she would use a knife to cut off the shredded section and wrap the rest in cellophane to preserve for the next morning's breakfast. This is what people do who grew up during the Depression, she mused when she noticed her thrifty ways.

"I'm sure you've heard," Frank sighed.

"Yes, last night."

"It must sound terrible, what I did. I'm grateful you even let me in the door."

Gladys reached across and squeezed his hand. "There's always two sides," was all she said. She didn't tell him that now she knew she'd hear a version of the story closer to the actual events. Binah would see this position as an unforgivable betrayal, both personal and political. For Gladys to credit her son-in-law's characterization would be seen as evidence of the self-loathing mentality of a colonized people. No, Gladys argued silently in her head, it's just that he's a bit more objective, willing to take his share of the blame and not cast himself in a good or bad light. The argument quietly finished, she waited for Frank to speak.

"Where does this really start?" he asked himself. "Okay, let me go back back. You know I love your daughter. From the first time I heard her at that conference, taking on the powers that be in History, I thought, who *is* that? Why haven't I heard of her? I was an instant admirer, practically a disciple. I respected her consistency—when it comes to her principles she will not be shaken. Totally uncompromising. Even to getting her tubes tied so she wouldn't bring any children into this screwed-up world, so catastrophically out of balance. You did know that? Right?" Frank caught himself.

Gladys shook her head, no.

"Oh, shit. Chalk up another mark against me and my big mouth."

Gladys was absorbing this small earthquake. "But how . . . ?" she began.

Frank tracked her thoughts. "Ava. Yeah, Ava was just one of those unforeseen miracles. Think how much she wanted to be here, was *meant* to be born. Binah couldn't believe it when she had all the symptoms, sure it was cancer, but, no, this apparently happens sometimes. Rare, but not beyond the pale. The body is wired to repair itself, after all."

Gladys nodded to indicate she'd be fine, he could continue.

"Okay, so I was *thrilled* about Ava, I respected Binah's stand on kids but secretly wanted them. So we're a nice little family, all the love in the world. That's never been the problem. It's me, my whiteness. And sorry, but that's not something I can change. Every week I'm the stand-in representative of the power structure Binah loathes and reviles. Such a joyful part to play. Sorry, sarcasm not necessary." He slapped the back of his hand and almost smiled. Tried to. "So, did you hear my chapbook of poems won that prize? It'll be published by the University of Iowa Press next spring. That was the sign I'd been waiting for to spur me to make a change I've wanted for so long. To leave academia and focus on the creative end of things. My writing. I have plays I've been fiddling with, but never had the time to really drill in and bring them to life. I told Binah I was leaving my job at the U. *She's* the academic scholar, she thrives on that stuff, but for me, it's an artificial language and way of thinking that doesn't always care about actual communication. Real connection with the rest of the world. I *need* to connect.

"Well, she flipped. It wasn't the money, she knows I'll do my part, but I think she saw it as a rejection of her. She pounced on my talk of feeling stifled by the rules of the academy. 'But this is *your* system,' she argued. 'Your rules, your academy.' 'No, they're *not* mine. I was born into this system just like you.' Then she got me, she said, 'But it sure rains down on us differently, doesn't it? You benefit from the system. It's rigged for you. While I will always be a *Native* scholar or *Native* writer, pleasantly surprising colleagues with my abilities because their expectations are so low.' 'For some of us that designation lends a certain prestige,' I said. Oh, she glared at me then! She said, 'It's every bit as dehumanizing to place Natives on a guru-like pedestal as it is to dismiss us as ignorant savages, or drunks.' I took her point, she's right. But it was like a knife through me to hear her connect me in any way with 'dehumanizing' her.

"I suddenly *saw* our dynamic, and how we're fatally stuck. For Binah there's an argument to lose or win, and she doesn't see that sometimes you *cannot* win if it's framed as debate. I don't *want* to debate my wife. She can win, fine. She can be declared the all-time winner of every discussion or disagreement we ever have. That's not the point. I want us to *talk*. To be truthful and open and not arrange our arguments like ammunition we just shoot at each other. That's useless. That's a defeat for all concerned."

He dropped his head on his arms, and for some it might have been a dramatic gesture, a bid for sympathy, but Gladys knew Frank well enough to understand he needed to gather himself. She placed a hand on the back of his neck, didn't pat him or squeeze, just touched him. She heard a few ragged breaths and then he sat up again, quickly dashed tears from his eyes, and looked out the kitchen window to hide his embarrassment.

"I didn't want to leave. Don't want to separate. I want to live with that articulate, brilliant, peevish woman until we're so old we look like those weird wrinkly apple dolls." He chuckled weakly. "But I can't be a doormat any longer. She wouldn't respect me, I wouldn't respect myself if I kept taking it. I'm willing to get counseling, I'm willing to do whatever kind of work, but I won't do *Cross-Fire*. Heck, even that was canceled in the end."

Gladys heard him. She held his words, his intentions, in her mind and saw a spark of hope in all of it, even if he couldn't just yet.

"By the way," he sighed. "I didn't leave her exactly unscathed. The last remark I made before I started packing was pretty harsh."

Gladys waited, knew Frank would offer it up to be fair.

"I told her that if every white person in the world lined up to take her hand and offer an apology, I mean a *sincere* one, for every injustice they or their ancestors or their agents perpetrated on her and her people, she'd have nothing to live for. All joy would go out of the universe. 'Your wound matters more to you than anything. The care and maintenance of your precious wound trumps us all.'"

Silence filled the kitchen until noises from the street wafted through the open window and broke the spell. "That *is* harsh. And I know *you* know that it's never easy being society's memory, like a thorn in its side, a reminder of all the myths America stands on to function. But that's not to say there's no truth in your words. We have to walk a fine line. We must own our history and stories, correct this country's willful amnesia, yet not get so bitter we swallow the old poison every day. I don't mean to be disloyal to my girl, I love her with all my heart, but I want you to know I'm on the side of our family staying together, healing what needs to be healed. My door is open to you. You're family. I appreciate you telling me your side of things.

"We're just pitiful people. All of us. Thinking we're doing our best when, really, we can do so much better." She stood then and looked out the window, watched a Hmong woman with two small children cross the street. The little girl was wearing a bright pink dress that made her stand out like a poppy.

"I better go. I'm looking for a place in Uptown, back to graduate student type of living. Hope to hell it's temporary." Frank hugged Gladys from behind, rested his chin on the top of her head, and then left. Still taking the stairs in a slow way that hurt her heart.

Gladys offered to save Candace and Binah seats so they could explore the shop. Maryam had settled in the confessional and was reading a volume of Sherman Alexie's poetry. Shoppers seemed to sense her presence, Gladys noted. They might peek into the confessional box, but quickly backed away as if they'd overstepped a barrier. She selected a row of chairs right in front of the table where the author would make her presentation, then claimed her own chair. She looked over at Frank and Ava who were snuggled in an armchair in the children's section. Ava sat in his lap, already so tall her dangling legs nearly touched the floor. He was reading aloud to her with great drama, while she helped turn the pages, so focused on the story she had clearly forgotten the rest of the world spinning beyond them.

Gladys remembered the first time she met Frank, he and Binah had taken her to a restaurant in Uptown—La Bodega.

"Tapas, you must try tapas," Binah told her.

"I'm Ojibwe, I'll try anything once," Gladys had answered.

Binah introduced Gladys to a man with fair skin and long black hair, the strands so fine the color looked a bit dusty, faded. He had pleasant features, warm brown eyes, but then he smiled and his face lit up in a way that reminded her of the pinball machines her girls once liked to fool with—two deep dimples appeared, emphasizing his smile like exclamation marks.

"I'm Frank Morgan," he'd said, offering his hand. "Yes, like the Wizard of Oz, well, the actor who played him. But I'm from Iowa, not Kansas. Born and raised in Iowa City, the writers' mecca and home of the best bookstore in any hemisphere: Prairie Lights."

She shook his hand, kept a straight face when she asked, "Do you always introduce yourself that way? Like a tourism ad?"

He burst out laughing and she thought, yes, yes, I like this one, we'll get along just fine. Which they did. He liked to say he came from "friendly people." "They must have been pretty friendly since I'm a combination of pretty much every European tribe. Yuppers, my ancestors were busy sleeping with all the neighbors!"

Binah hadn't bothered to ask her mother what she thought of Frank when they later dissected this first meeting. She could tell Gladys liked him. Instead she bragged on him to Gladys, something new for her; she'd always been quick to list the failings of previous men in her life. Gladys listened with pleasure, happy to hear her daughter so enthused, appreciative.

"He's not like any other guy I've known," Binah said. "He can take me on in a conversation, he's read the books, knows the history, has a really good mind. But more importantly, he isn't defensive and he isn't scared. A lot of white guys, well, they're all apologetic, you know? Trying to make up for the past, feeling inadequate, that's the liberal-guilt ones, at least. They'll back down if I come on strong. I don't *want* someone who quivers at the first hint of conflict. And don't get me started on the Native guys. Did I tell you about the one who told me, actually *told* me: 'You should feel sorry for me because I'm Indian and Indian men have a hard time'? That was the end of him."

Gladys chuckled. "I'll bet. Did you leave him breathing?"

By the time the author arrived all of the seats were filled and audience members were chatting among themselves. Gladys recognized a good portion of the crowd—Jim Denomie and his wife, Diane Wilson, a writer she enjoyed reading, Andrea Carlson and her husband, Ted Cushman. Gladys liked to tease him that with the right kind of helmet he'd look just like one of those Viking invaders. He always laughed, easy around her. She heard a deep chuckle, a sexy, infectious laugh. I'll bet that's Heid, she thought. Sure enough, there was Heid Erdrich, an award-winning poet. So much talent in this room, Gladys smiled as she soaked up ribbons of talk. She couldn't help adding, privately, and much of it Native.

Heid introduced LeAnne, telling those assembled about her list of accomplishments, which they pretty much already knew since they were fans. The atmosphere was relaxed and informal. A woman no taller than Gladys stood, and Gladys marveled at her vivid energy. She was striking, ageless, supposedly a grandmother, yet you could see the excited little girl bursting through, especially in her black eyes that shone like young stars. Her hair was purple-black, like a superhero's, Gladys thought, until she realized there *were* streaks of purple threaded in the woman's hair. Neat as it was, bangs perfectly cut, the streaks were a nice touch of whimsy. LeAnne spoke with an Oklahoma accent, softened, diluted after so many years spent in the Midwest. She thanked everyone for coming and jumped right into her presentation, reading excerpts from her novel *Miko Kings*, which told the story of an all-Indian baseball team back in 1907, focusing on their Choctaw pitcher, Hope Little Leader, and Ezol Day, the town postal clerk but really a visionary, moving beyond time. The reading passed so quickly, Gladys was still caught up in the swirl of voices and images—an eye-tree, now what would an eye-tree look like?—when applause brought her back to earth.

"I'd be happy to take questions," LeAnne said, and immediately an older man toward the back of the crowd raised his hand. He looked a bit shaken.

"Am I hearing you right? You're saying that Indians invented baseball and not Abner Doubleday?"

"That's right." LeAnne went on to describe Indian stickball, base-and-ball, that was played on this continent for hundreds, if not thousands, of years.

The man spoke again. "But why wouldn't this be universally known? Why cover up the origins of a game?"

"It's not just any game, though, is it? This is the 'great American pastime.' Or, as I point out in the novel, it's 'past time.' We, Natives, have assigned roles to play, historically speaking, and we're not allowed to step beyond them, especially if it means acknowledging some contribution we made. We're the frightening, bloodthirsty savages who must be cleared out of the way, then, once we're supposedly gone, we become noble in thy sight, innocent as children, missed, longed for. Well, here we are. Deal with it!" She laughed and offered a beautiful smile to show there were no hard feelings.

Another person, a rather harried-looking professor surrounded by a number of her students, raised her hand, asked: "You said at the start you're not a baseball expert, didn't know much about the game when you launched the novel. So what inspired you to write about baseball?"

LeAnne told the story of how Hope Little Leader showed up in her dreams. "He held up his arms and from the tossing motion he made, I knew he was a ball player. Yet he had no hands. The stubs of flesh looked like sea horses, and I wondered what had happened to him? How did he lose his hands? Then I'd put him in the back of my mind, busy with conferences, papers, teaching, life. Until he'd show up again, more urgent this time as in, Why aren't you telling my story? Time's wasting, girl."

Another woman raised her hand, she looked to be part Native, and said: "This isn't a question so much as a confirmation. I have that happen to me, too, sometimes. I don't always *choose* my material so much as it chooses me. Characters find me, and pester, nudge, until I pay attention and work with them. I know it isn't everyone's process, but it's mine." She flushed suddenly, as if she'd perhaps revealed more in the excitement of the moment than she'd intended.

"Yes!" LeAnne responded. "I think some of us are open, and characters, stories, wherever it is they come from, find their way to us, knowing that we'll see them. They just walk right in and take over our lives."

Gladys could feel Binah become tense beside her. She kept shifting in her chair. She was squeezing her purse hard enough to kill it.

"It's already dead," Gladys whispered to her daughter, indicating the leather bag with her lips.

"What? Oh." Binah relaxed her grip. Then she lifted her hand.

I should've kept my mouth shut, Gladys thought.

LeAnne acknowledged Binah. "I'm not in any way disputing your points or your process, but see, here's what makes me wince. I'm Ojibwe, I have enormous respect for our spiritual traditions, our Midewiwin Society, and if it were just us talking, all Natives together, it would be fine, safe. We could be open about our connection to other levels of existence, spirits, all of that. But when we put it out there for a non-Native audience, we come across like kooks, superstitious throw-backs. We open ourselves up to condescension, disrespect, misunderstanding. I want us to *finally* be taken *seriously* in this century. It's too long in coming. Too hard-won. Do you ever think about that?"

"Of course," LeAnne said warmly. "I understand what you're saying. We're stuck between the proverbial rock and a hard place. Either we're nearly *stalked* for our beliefs, filling some void in the shallow materialism of the mainstream culture which has folks latching on to us like disciples, or we're dismissed. I've been careful about how much to reveal when it comes to my true process for similar reasons—one wants to be professional, whatever that means. But as I get older I find I have to tell the *whole* truth—it just bursts out of me whether I like it or not." She laughed. "A few of us Native authors got tired of having our work labeled as 'magical realism,' which is a pretty presumptuous designation if you really think about it, inferring the world of our books is an *other* reality, something fantastic, when we're just writing out of our ordinary experience. So I started teaching a Native Lit class called 'Real Magic, *Not* Magical Realism!' That does the trick!"

She had just started to make her point, but she must have seen the urgent look on Gladys's face. Gladys was actually pushing at her cheeks to relax them, rubbing her mouth to keep it still.

"I think you have something to offer?" LeAnne asked her.

Gladys gave up trying to restrain herself. She stood up, not to be important or the center of attention, but so she could see everyone as she spoke. She thanked LeAnne for calling on her, or, as she put it, "calling her out."

"This is my daughter," she indicated Binah, who was blinking in surprise. "I'm proud of her ability to speak, and her courage. She makes important points, so do you. I enjoy listening to the intelligent thoughts of our people. But I want to remind everyone what Vine Deloria said in his last book, that one with the long title. It always takes me a second to remember it. *The World We Used to Live In: Remembering the Power of the Medicine Men.* And he talked about this in his introduction to *God Is Red*, a note he added thirty years after the book was first published. He urges us to take our old stories as literally true. Not see them as baby stories or superstitious claptrap. He reminisces about the elders he knew who had a deep, profound understanding of the workings of our complex world. Science chases its ideas and then comes back to what we knew a long time ago. Going forward, they're finding their way back to us.

"Those early missionaries, when they saw the astonishing connection we had to the spirit world, they couldn't believe it, they couldn't respect it. It didn't come from them, so it must be bad, wrong, evil. They demonized our abilities, or dismissed them as tricks. They worked to dismantle our power, our spiritual connections, and boy, did they do a good job! We're still trying to pick up the pieces, aren't we?" She looked around at the hushed gathering; several heads were nodding, faces lit with pride and encouragement.

"Don't let them keep us from our gifts. We didn't need men to stand between us and the Creator and make introductions. We had our own experience of the one who made us; our daily lives were revelation. If we jump on the bandwagon and feel ashamed to air these things, worried how they'll be misused, misunderstood (and, yes, they will be), we're keeping ourselves lost, cut off from our greatest strength. If you don't believe me, read Vine again, our distinguished legal mind, our rational genius. Yes, we could keep all this a secret between ourselves, but we're losing our young people. Where do they go for influences? The mainstream out there. We can't hold back. We must *own* our former power to bring it roaring back to life. Unembarrassed. Unapologetic. We've spent too much time doubting ourselves. No more. No more."

She sat down, and to her great surprise, almost everyone else stood up, including her daughter. Candace rose when the others did, but looked unsure of herself. A tall Choctaw educator and hockey player, Joseph Rice, led the cheering. She waggled her hands at them, but the clapping continued, and she noticed Maryam standing in the confessional, joyfully adding her voice to the multitude of others.

As they left the bookstore Ava and Frank were making the most of their final minutes together. Now they were both horses, facing each other, doubled over, stamping their legs as if they were locked in a stall and wanted out. Stomp-stomp. Stomp-stomp. Ava tossed her head back, and her black hair flew like a wild mane. She whinnied. When she doubled over again she noticed a small tragedy she'd unwittingly set in motion.

"Oh, no!" she wailed, and the horse was suddenly a five-year-old girl again. "I killed it, Daddy. Look, I smashed it."

"What's the matter, baby?" He bent to inspect the sidewalk. Gladys wove through a clump of people still talking outside the shop.

"What is it?" she asked.

Ava was crying. "Nookomis, look what I did. I killed an ant, I didn't mean to, but now it's dead and all of its friends are upset."

The death of the ant brought a swarm of brother ants to the scene. Indeed, several of them appeared to be distraught, almost keening; they performed a peculiar combing of their faces Gladys had never noticed before.

"It was an accident, honey," Frank said soothingly. But Ava would not be comforted.

"Oh, for crying out loud," Binah exclaimed when she pushed through the crowd to see what all the fuss was about. "It's a bug. Ava, if you're going to fall apart over the death of an insect, you're going to have an awfully difficult life."

Gladys gave Binah a look that quieted her. "Noozis, come here."

Ava picked her way over to Gladys, stepping very carefully so she wouldn't trample any of the other ants who'd quickly assembled.

"What's done is done, and I'm proud of your big heart, your respect for every living thing. That means you've been raised right." She nodded fiercely at Binah and Frank, just one tip of her head for each of them. "But what can we do, now that this being is gone? We can't bring him back to life, can we?" Ava sadly shook her head, no; she was attached to Gladys's side, her face buried in the crook of an arm. "Is there anything we can do?"

Ava stopped crying, thinking. She wiped the tears from her face and adjusted her glasses. She looked up at Gladys. "We could say a prayer? I could apologize?"

"Yes, that sounds just right."

Ava turned to face the miniature drama developing on the ground. The grieving ants had lifted their fallen comrade and were carrying him away. It looks like a funeral, Gladys thought.

Ava said she'd whisper her words because the ants were so little she didn't want to hurt their ears. "We must be giants to them," she said. "Monster giants." She patted her rumpled shirt, composed her face into a solemn mask.

"Dear Ants, this is Ava. I am so so so sorry I killed your friend. It was an accident. Please forgive me. Please don't be too sad. Thank you."

Ava leaned into Gladys and reached for her father's hand. They were all together for this brief moment, collected beneath the stars. Even Binah looked relaxed, contrite. Then they split apart, Frank heading for his car, Binah and Ava toward the red Toyota, and Gladys joined Candace and Maryam who were waiting for her in the Lexus. The sidewalk was empty now, of people, of insects. There was no evidence that anything significant had happened. Another small moment in the whirl of time. But Ava would have been pleased to know that the ants were listening.

Clan Mother of the Present

Queen of the Heavens

Gladys Swan (2009)

Candace and I were working together in the kitchen, rolling out dough to bake a pizza for her husband which she says is his favorite food.

"There was this place in Cambridge, Pinocchio's Pizza, he was their best customer. They knew his name and everything, that he was from Minnesota. But he doesn't get to indulge much—clients and colleagues aren't really the pizza set." She was chopping the vegetables he favored, to layer on top, and I have to say, she's pretty skillful with that knife, quick and neat. I couldn't help but wonder how well she'd do skinning a rabbit or a beaver.

We were talking about marriage, how difficult it can be to understand the thinking of a man. Maybe seeing Binah and Frank together the night before triggered her opening up to me, just a little. Then she set down the knife all of a sudden and stared at me.

"You know, I've never even asked you about *your* husband. You lost him a while ago, I think. Is that right?"

I looked at her to see what answer she was ready for. Quick or true? I couldn't see her eyes, they were hidden behind sunglasses, so I went back to pounding the dough and just said, "Yes."

I hoped someday I could tell her what really happened.

I was born in Minigizis, when the blueberries are ripe, the month you know as July. It was 1935, the big Depression when everybody was scared and hungry. My grandfather said I came along to cheer people up, put the smile back on their faces. I got my name because of the way I came into the world. I was early, you know, I took my mother by surprise. She was all alone in our little shack doing quillwork when her water broke. And then, so soon after that, I came tumbling out. She said it felt like *I* did all the work, swam and pushed and tore away from her because I was ready to get started. I didn't cry. I sighed with satisfaction the way the Creator must have when He set this world in motion. I approved of my birth and was pleased. So they called me Ogimangeezhigikwe—Chief Woman of the Sky—because I was bossy from the first minute.

I was raised by my grandparents since I was the last baby out of ten in my family. Sometimes the older ones need a little sweetness in their life, someone to spoil, someone to make them laugh, so they had me. And they *did* spoil me, they fussed over me the way parents do today, treating their children like little kings and queens. They made me dolls and toy snares, miniature woven mats for my babies to sleep on and a cradleboard to carry them in, perfect little canoes, snow shoes I could fit on my fingers. In this way it was as if they gave me the whole world. But more than that, they gave me stories, told me all about the people who came before me, a long line of very special healers—the consolation singers. When someone lost a young husband or wife or a beloved child, any loss that seemed particularly cruel because it came too early, the singers would be asked to stay with the family and sing them funny songs, story songs, anything to distract their sad hearts. They might labor for days or weeks to cheer these grieving people, but they would keep at their work until they believed the survivors had remembered how good it is to be alive, and smell the air, and be with your relatives. So I guess that's how I came to have a pleasant nature and to see the good patch of light that's always waiting on the other side of a bad experience. Oh, I had nightmares, like anyone else, both sleeping and awake. But deep down I always knew there would be an end to the bad dream, every bad dream, so I let myself just live through the sorrow. Angry people can be jealous when they meet someone like that, someone who seems to own all the hope in the world. What they don't understand, these bitter ones, is that hope isn't anything like money; there is always plenty to go around and *anyone* can be rich.

I think my first husband was one of those angry lost people; he had a bad heart, and I don't just mean the one in his body. I mean his spirit. He must have watched me for a long time, saw me living so pleased with the world, as if the sun was my personal lamp, and grass a carpet just for my feet, and stars a messy scatter of beads I could scoop into my hand and sew on my skirt. He was greedy for that happiness he must have thought I captured and hoarded, when in truth it was always out there, around me, a warm blanket draped across my shoulders.

You might notice that as I'm telling you this I haven't used his name. I say, "My first husband," or "him," because if I speak his name, now that he is gone, it's like calling his spirit and I don't want to do that. I want his spirit to stay wherever it is. But I can tell you that he was ten years older than me, and handsome, I think, on the outside. He wore his black hair in a mean crew cut that looked knife sharp, and his skin was light, yellow pale as wood pulp, and his eyes were the dull green of paper money. He was well-formed and strong, but he walked funny, with a jerky motion, like those puppets I've seen at fairs. Something was wrong with him from birth and it made him angry at the Creator, mistrustful of everyone he met, thinking they were laughing at him behind his back.

My grandparents didn't want me to go with him when he chased after me. I was just seventeen, and so different from him we were like two people sitting across from each other on one of those seesaws, and I was always drifting up, pie in the sky, expecting miracles and grace and good news, and he was forever plunging down, down, harder and harder, the more I floated above him. But he got me, snagged me, even though deep down I didn't really want to be with him or have him touch me.

"Why? Why?" my family asked, and my curious girlfriends, and me, I asked myself that question a hundred times a day. I couldn't explain it to anyone, my love trap. I lived like that for three years, a good wife, though he wouldn't have said it. We had one little boy in that time, smaller than some of my dolls. He came out skinny and starved, furious, scratching his face. I tried to make my body a good home for him before he was born, but maybe he had his father's ways? His fears and temperament? And so he couldn't grow the right way inside me, make any use of love. He screamed at every one of us, and then he died.

My boy's father died a week later. His heart stopped while he was eating his supper, glaring at me because there wasn't any meat, just fish, trash fish, nothing tasty. He spat out the piece he had just forked into his mouth and it could be he spat out his soul, too. Because after that he tipped backwards in his chair and stayed down, become empty and heavy at the same time, the slug of his spirit crawling the floor, leaving. I finally discovered where my three years had gone when we were washing his body and dressing him in his last clothes. I was able to peek inside the medicine bag he always wore around his neck, even when he bathed. I choked when I saw what was in there—two tiny people, the size of my fingernail, crudely carved from wood. A man with his bump at the waist, and a woman with two bumps near the top. A long brown-black hair bound them together, secured in place by sticky sap. My hair. My husband was a thief, you see; he used magic to steal me, to make me his family. But even now I can see the good side of all this. He never robbed me of my heart. He was an obligation to me, not someone I cherished, and so for all that sneaky work he ended up poorer than me because the Creator made things right by taking away what he had coveted. He lost *his* heart.

I was twenty-one years old when I fell in love the right way, my heart free and choosy. Maybe because it had no practice in the past, my heart didn't fly ahead in search of anyone but stumbled over him instead, like he was a rock in the path. My Abraham was always there in our community, like the sun and the moon and Misi-zaaga'igan, our lake that is noisy with a hundred young woman emotions. The first time I saw one of those armrest pillows you can lean on to prop you up in bed, I thought of Abraham. "That's him!" I said to myself, fingering the soft corduroy. "That's my sweet man."

My heart noticed him one winter at a memorial feast—my husband's. I was the young widow dressed in all my layers of clothes to keep out the chill; cold wind outside the tribal hall, colder wind inside me, freezing my blood. I was not made to pretend, and that is all I'd been doing for one year, pretending to miss the one who trapped me until sometimes I felt more dead than he was. Then, my mind switched on like the twist of a lantern, flames leaped, awareness. Abraham sat with the other old uncles and grandfathers, all of them teasing and boasting, reminiscing. The others had children and grandchildren they could have reached for, summoned from across the room. Only Abraham was a tree without branches beyond the square tips of his fingers. I saw him as if for the first time, in a bubble of light, soft, hazy. His smooth skin was dark as a muddy river, but unlike the other Ojibwe men, he was near bald, his silver-black hair no more than the soft fuzz of a newborn. His cheekbones were bright polished knobs his smile seemed latched on. All his wrinkles framed that smile, the one that touched a match to his soul and lit him up until he shone. My fingers were laced together in my lap, but I lifted them to peek at Abraham through their design, become a net. "I will go fishing soon," I said to myself quietly, a promise.

A few days later I brought him a present, maple candy I'd made just for him, thinking sweet thoughts as I did the work.

"Uncle," I rapped on the door of his small shed of a house.

"Yes?" He opened the door and heat from his stove and his smile blasted into me, through me, a fire ghost lit me like a candle.

His world smelled delicious, a wood smoke incense that swirled around my head, making me dizzy. He helped me sit at his table, took the parcel of candy from me, and removed my gloves. He held my hands then between his own, concern showing on his face. Oh, those hands weren't skin, crude flesh. My Abraham was softer than velvet suede, smooth as satin but warmer—satin with a heartbeat.

"I want to glide you," was the only ridiculous thing I could say. And instead of laughing or pushing me out of his house, he pulled a chair beside me and sat with me, holding my hand, my new clumsy bear of love sprawling over us both. He waited. He let things develop. When I could finally speak and explain my crazy quilt of feelings, beg to look after him, be with him, he listened respectfully and didn't let my words wash him away, though they were a dangerous, unexpected flood, like a rising creek. When I was done, not finished, neat with conclusion, but tipped empty, he sighed.

"You know, I had a dream when I was little that I would be everyone's uncle, their counselor and friend, their old tree that is always there for shelter and support, no matter what else changes. But near the end of the dream it all flipped over, and instead of my arms cradling the world, the world was cradling me, and I woke up so happy I thought I must have died. Ogimangeezhigikwe, I don't know why you look at me with love eyes when you are Queen of the Sky, but I think my dream was telling me to wait for you. And I did. I listened. I am seventy years old by the chimookoman calendar, and I have never touched a woman in a way that said, 'I am a man.' I saved my touches for you."

My girlfriends snickered behind my back, looked at me cross-eyed when they heard the news that Abraham was my new husband. I didn't care. I laughed into my hands, rich with delicious secrets, love snacks. When a man has waited for you since *before* you were born, and then finds you in his bed, in his lap, wound so snug and perfect against his body you are two strands of yarn become one stitch, his desire is more than a pond or a creek or even a great lake, more than an ocean. He is the flood that kept Noah paddling the globe in his crowded boat, he is the rain poured heavy from every cloud, morning tears squeezed from every flower. His love juice is shocking, limitless, you begin to think he will populate a new planet if you give him half the chance. You forget that he is old because his manly parts have had a lifetime of rest, without recreation, and so he is a soldier down there, trained not by practice but by years of imagining. Think of it. When my Abraham touched me, he worked a magic of opposites. How could he be so gentle, the pressure of a thumb wisp-soft as the nap of a butterfly wing, and still so warmly focused, intent, packed dense with delight, that touch was penetrating as if I were no more than warm butter? Oh, he melted my shoulder with his hot mouth and busy, swiping tongue, and the brown acorns of my nipples, and the deep swirl of my navel, and the dark roses that led inside me. Was I burning wax pooling in our bed, sliding off the sheets? Was I still a woman beneath his hands and lips? He helped me lose myself, my edges, so that I opened up into him, and through him I opened to the world.

And what about Abraham, you might be wondering? Was he happy, too? Every time I kissed a section of his land, the country of his flesh, I was whispering in my head, "I love you, I love you." My thoughts worked their way into his trusting form; he heard me, all of me, and so our bodies learned to speak the same language. We created poetry good enough to last the ages. Whenever I led him to the burst-open dam of pleasure, danced and sang him there with love and vigor, he roared with laughter, showing all his teeth. Does everyone know such moments of joy? I hope so. I hope they have a treasure like mine, two fistfuls of my man's laugh, each one a diamond.

We were together for eighteen years and had two happy daughters, wine dark and round as chokecherries, spicy and sweet as those coiled sticky buns my man favored. Why do I speak of them as food? Because that's all we seemed to do together—feed each other tasty meals and stories, jokes and old songs, new songs. Our girls brought us Elvis Presley and The Beatles, live before us, wiggling and shaking, howling out of tune. They confused us with their new math, and we puzzled them with all the layers of spirits that populate our world, our Minnesota woods, more even than those ancient Greeks and Romans worshipped.

Abraham died in 1974 while he was carving out the stone bowl of a pipe and humming "Yellow Submarine." In all our years together *I* was the one who curled to him, against him, held in work-strong arms. But that final day he left his tools and pipe, nodded toward our oatmeal-lumpy couch. This time he climbed into my lap, hardly any weight at all for me to handle, twig thin as he was by then. He rested his mirror-smooth head against my chest and breathed out a long, contented sigh.

"Megwetch." His final whisper.

I didn't answer until I knew I could speak without spoiling my words with tears. "No, thank *you*," I told his retreating spirit.

Then I gave up on men altogether because what's the use of chasing tickly champagne with a cheap can of Schlitz? I'd had eighteen years of the froth cream of life skimmed right into my eager mouth. I had been given enough small miracles to pave a stone road to Venus. I traveled down to the Cities more often, for powwows and week-long visits with family and friends. Years passed that way until, at the big Minneapolis powwow they put on around Thanksgiving, I met my third husband. It was 1984 and I was almost fifty, my girls in their twenties, not yet married. I was content to be an older lady, proud of every silver hair that sprouted from my brown half braids—just long enough to point like arrows at my sleepy breasts. I danced traditional, in an old-time calico tear dress a cousin gave me, not for contests but for pleasure. There was a graceful straight dancer in simple old-style bustles, his body so stitched to the music I fancied he worked a sly magic and could direct the drum, the singers' pounding sticks, from a distance, with each movement. He started falling into step with me during intertribal numbers, so we circled the arena together like that, a tie already formed between us. He didn't speak as he danced though, and I was glad. I taught my daughters not to do that, because when you jabber and gossip over the music it is like telling those songs to be quiet and go away.

"If you're going to dance, dance," I'd been scolding them forever. "If you want to run around with your friends, then go take off your jingles." Old-fashioned, I know.

The straight dancer turned out to be Dakota, Rudy Gates. I teased him during a break: "Where's your red nose?"

He rolled his eyes at me, dark mink eyes, shadowed. "*Not* the reindeer," he said. "I'm named for an old-time star of the silent screen—Rudolph Valentino, the Sheikh of Araby." He spread his arms for drama.

I fluttered my fan, waved wings of hair off my temples. "Oh, the sex object," I said. "The dead one."

"Jeez," was all Rudy said, grinning, embarrassed. That was the best he could do, you see, because he was Dakota, and while I'm the first to admit they are an intelligent people (possibly from living alongside us for so long), they are not as quick-witted when it comes to insults. I decided to show off my verbal sparring skills. I teased him more.

"Rudolph Valentino. He sure sparked a lot of hearts in his day, ladies who are dead by now, or the grandmas of grandmas. So, do *you* have success with the white-haired gals?"

Rudy poked out his bottom lip in a pout that really was seductive. "You tell me," he finally answered.

Oh, he got me then. He didn't know it at the time because I stalked away, my thick back doing all the talking. But he'd won, he'd fished me out of the pond. For a while I pretended I wasn't interested. I called him "nephew" to point out the difference in our ages, his thirty-five years to my forty-nine. But he had fish luck, laughed about it all the time.

"Fish line up to seize my hook. I don't even need any bait. 'What an honor,' they say to one another, 'to be eaten by Rudy Gates, snagged for his supper.'"

I hated when he bragged like that, though it is a man's custom I'm used to, because fishing is the talent, the divine gift of my people; we are so clever with our lines and bait, our secret places in the lake, it annoyed me that one of the Bwaan would excel at our passion. But he did, and with that effortless touch hauled me in as well over his dark gunwales.

My Rudy kept his black hair longer than mine, and it flowed down his back or was tied with a rubber band, formed into a thick horse's tail. His eyes were a black so impossibly full of light I thought of them as black candles, strange dark flames that lit up every room he entered, every space of me he devoured with a long hot look. His face was handsome in an old-time way, dignified, but behind closed doors he could work that modest mouth in roguish, daredevil ways, like that skinny grasshopper, Mick Jagger. Kissing Rudy reminded me of my girls' favorite book they read me when they were in grade school, *Alice in Wonderland*, the passage where she falls down waboos's hole, falls and falls, because this English waboos is from a deep upside-down part of the world. Boy, my stomach would drop and my feet wouldn't feel the ground anymore, and I was so absorbed in that lovers' greedy clinch, for all I knew I might've sprouted long scarves of blonde hair, a pinafore, and shiny patent leather shoes. You could call me "Alice" and I wouldn't care, not when Rudy sucked on my lower lip as if it were a sweet bone he nursed to extract its final subtle taste, a memory of flavor.

We lived in his apartment in Minneapolis, just blocks away from the Indian Center and from the storefront office where he worked. He counseled troubled teenagers who appeared to be headed for prison if he didn't show them all the other roads they could travel if they stopped staring at the only one they knew.

"Do you have a mother fixation?" I asked him once, after I'd been learning a lot of the psychology lingo from his textbooks. "Are you with me because of a Mama complex?"

Rudy laughed so hard he choked on a forkful of chicken, and I almost had to Heimlich him. "God, no," he finally said when he could breathe easy again. "Look, there are a thousand complicated reasons why I'm with you, having to do with all the ways you're so specifically necessary to my life, and there are two plain ones. First, I'm surrounded by youth all day—young spirits, minds, and bodies. But, as you well know, it's a smashed-up world, full of the pain of beginnings. So I find it easier to be myself and relax with someone who's already discovered her good road. Second, when I saw you for the first time, I kept blinking at you like an owl because I saw *everything* in you, *more* than you, and that's a vision I've never experienced before. You wear your spirit outside your body and your clothes, and it was so strong I couldn't look away. I'll never look away."

And he didn't. We were together for fifteen years, in that same apartment, content, occupied with family and rescues and powwows, busy with pleasure. Then Rudy tried to break up a fight on the street outside his youth center, his small oasis, and someone shot him accidentally, aiming for one of his kids. He didn't come home. When we buried him I told his spirit to look out for Abraham because I thought the two of them could be friends, the kind of relative you have a joking relationship with to avoid any tension. I imagined them competing for my attention in a teasing way, once I'd joined them. Won't I be the lucky one? With two husbands, old and young, to warm my front and my back at the same time.

"I won't get married anymore," I promised them, since where would I fit another? Down by my feet where he'd have to curl like a dog? No, that's enough, I said. I'm done. So I haven't married anymore.

That doesn't mean I've given up on love, the romantic kind. Just a few years back, the spring of 2004, I found myself a boyfriend at the University of Minnesota Powwow. Rudy had been gone for a few years, but I could still feel his presence, especially at powwows. I sensed that he was dancing beside me, quiet, as was his way, solemn. I noticed an old whiskered man watching our doings with a fierce fascination. He sat forward in his chair, leaning onto a cane he held with both his hands. He rapped that cane in time to the music, matching every drum stroke if it was a slow number, and just the heavy downbeat if the song was fast. He wasn't simply an audience member settled on the edge of our celebration, our performance. He was a participant without ever rising to his feet. I came to learn that this was how Yuri lived in the world; his eyes and mouth and hands, large and hungry, latched onto everything. I don't mean to say he was greedy, just willing to eat whatever life set in front of him.

I presented myself to him at the dinner break, shook his hand, welcomed him to our gathering. Only then did I notice the young man seated beside him, pale as skim milk, his eyes as dark with rings as a raccoon's. Thin blond hair was pasted like loose threads to his skull.

"This is my grandfather," the young man explained. "He's from Russia, Saint Petersburg. He doesn't speak any English. His name is Yuri. Mine is Sergei."

The grandson turned out to be a scholarship student at the University of Saint Thomas, a cleric in training. He'd found a family to sponsor his grandfather, bring him to the States, because the two men had only each other in the world. Yuri had worked most of his life in a bottle factory, but his true vocation, the art God gave him, was blowing glass. Sergei talked and talked, about the miracle of things that were both liquid and solid, about the deaths of their relatives, about loneliness and God. I half listened, nodding at his large sunken eyes every now and then, but noticing Yuri the whole time, how he cocked his head to the side during his grandson's speech as if he understood. I later learned that Yuri *did* understand what people said. Not always the words, seldom the words, but the fruit pit, the marrow of their meaning. After I while I shooed Sergei off so I could sit with Yuri and talk to him in our private way that worked so well for us. I didn't tell him my chimookoman name, Gladys, but my *real* one, Ogimangeezhigikwe. To share the meaning I made the sign with my hands of a shapely woman, the hourglass curves. Then I pointed to the sky and opened my arms wide to indicate the vault of heaven. He nodded, growled his own words in a raw, burned voice.

Yuri was all silver hair and big teeth like those polar bears I've seen on television. He had that same quality of suspended power, terrific energy stored up and waiting for release. We became friends, we became lovers. He would speak to me with his hands and his zigzag Russian words, I would answer him with my own dramatic fingers and vivid Ojibwemowin. He was born in the Revolution year, I came to understand, and had lived a life that was like climbing and then sliding down the faces of great mountains; up and down, loving people, losing people, sharing stories, keeping secrets. Sometimes we pressed our foreheads together and spoke with our eyes, our thoughts. I never knew people could communicate in so many ways when they couldn't rely on words.

Sergei would drop Yuri off at my apartment for however long we'd arranged.

I'd feed him, and we'd talk our more-than-talk. Then we'd let our bodies bring us even closer. I never actually shared my bed with Yuri. Arthritis worked on him, turning him to stone, so it was easier to leave him sitting in an old ladder-back chair, empty of arms. And when he rested his cane on the floor and held out his hands to me, I would arrange us so that I straddled his lap and we were joined, still clothed, underwear askew to give us access. Because my plain grandma dress hid our activity, covered our yin and yang, it made our love even more exciting. We were like two kids hiding in a closet or the stall of a barn, desperate to do our business but having to be quick and sneaky. Yuri's arms were so strong, he could lift me up and down, bounce me like a baby.

"Hoopa, hoopa, hoopa," was his happy, rhythmic noise. And after our joyous, bumpy ride, better than any I'd ever tested at the fair, we would collapse against one another, breathless but smiling, locked together on that chair. We became one round body with all those arms and legs—a big love bug in my kitchen!

We relished the minutes we were able to stay connected if we held still, very still. Our old bodies merged continents, we were a testament to how much people can live through without giving up. Yuri entered me stiff with hope, I accepted him generous with need, and together we made survivor's love, smiled on by our ancestors, those tough, enduring people who had swallowed black oceans of tears and been clubbed by history.

Yuri died just eight months after we met, fiercely alive until the last minute—watching the news with his grandson and shouting at Donald Rumsfeld. Sergei brought me a gift he said his grandfather wanted me to have after his death. He handed me a small wooden box.

"Careful," he warned, as I lifted the lid and dug through old-time excelsior to find the object. My hand closed on a smooth globe, the size of my fist. I gently lifted it from its nest. The gift was a bubble of clear glass that tinkled softly, faint as the ring of spirit bells. I held up the globe to the light and saw that there were seven in all, one inside another, inside another, each smaller, just like those Russian nesting dolls. They were seven glass pearls without any flaw that I could see, no seams or bubbles.

"This was his life's work," Sergei explained. "It took him years to get it right, manage to fit them all together without breaking a single orb."

I hadn't cried when I learned my friend had died because there was nothing to grieve or regret, but now I felt tears burning my eyes, saw the glass planets as his honest spirit resting in my palm. He had somehow captured the likeness of all our spirits, the miracle artwork that is our soul, both fragile and strong, perfect and beautiful, and beautiful, and beautiful.

"Imagine," Sergei interrupted my tears and my thoughts. "Imagine a life's work being something that just exists, that can't be worn or properly exhibited or put to any use." He shook his thin skull.

What I didn't tell Sergei, because he was so young and already so tired, is that he had just perfectly described how it is with pure love, the kind the Creator wants us to learn. This truest feeling lives deep and is quiet, patient, so modest it has no need to be shown off, no requirements that it be used or returned or even recognized. But all I told that old young man was, "This is a good gift from a good man. Megwetch."

I have lived my life with open hands. When you live like that you *will* lose things, people and money and pretty objects, which you would probably lose anyway, according to the Creator's plan. But when they're open like that, new things come and fill them up, too. The world sees your need and so the next thing comes, and then the next. When I was little my Grandpa noticed this quality in me and he said, "Noozis, look at how fearless you are, even though you can't make a fist. That is *good*. That is *good*."

Stations of the Cross

A week after the reading at Birchbark Books Maryam had yet to make any headway with Candace, who was proving to be more stubborn than her slight frame suggested. Gladys didn't have to ask her friend how matters stood between them; she had only to watch Candace come and go, dark glasses dimming her view, silence answering every one of Maryam's statements. Maryam looked tired, discouraged. Late at night when the house was still the two women shared stories of their day, sweetened by one of Gladys's concoctions made of various fruit juices mixed together. Maryam's favorite so far was a blend of coconut milk and raspberry and papaya juices.

On a Thursday morning in mid-September, Gladys brought freshly laundered towels into Maryam's room. She thought Maryam was at the Sweatshop, watching as Candace stretched her long limbs on a machine that looked like a torture rack. She was startled to find her inside the room, sitting on what appeared to be a small colorful rug. Maryam had placed the mat in the center of the room and though her back was very straight, her legs crossed beneath her, she looked perfectly relaxed. Gladys nearly toppled over, so swept up in a field of, what was this? she wondered. Was this peace? She dropped the towels, hands flew to cover her face, and she sobbed into them, completely unable to restrain the emotion. She wasn't sad. This wasn't joy. She'd never felt anything like it before, which made her cry even harder.

Maryam rose, picked up the towels, and placed them on the bed. She gently tugged at Gladys's arms, trying to see her face.

"What's wrong?" she asked. She guided Gladys to a plush armchair and helped her sit, then returned to her mat and sat down as gracefully as Zhigaag when he settled himself in a tucked-in pose.

When Gladys could breathe calmly again she said, "I didn't mean to disturb you. I thought you were out with Candace."

Maryam smiled reassuringly. "Not to worry. I've been neglecting my spirit work, so I thought I'd catch up with her later."

"Whatever you were doing, it sure put out a powerful beam." Gladys didn't know what else to call the field of energy she'd entered.

"Thank you, I've had a lot of practice. I'd forgotten how shattering it is to feel true peace for the very first time. It isn't passive the way most of us are raised to believe, is it?"

Gladys could only shake her head.

"The way people usually think of 'surrender' is that it's a laziness, a giving up. For me, it's setting myself aside, the self that is small and limited, greedy and afraid, and then I *surrender*, extend, reach out, reach out, to merge with all the others, with everything. It lights me up, makes me as warm as Candace when she runs on the exercise machine." Maryam chuckled. "I guess you could say, this is *my* workout."

"Is this something your people do?" Gladys asked. Her grandfather never taught her to sit the way Maryam had arranged herself, but he'd counseled her to lie quiet some mornings so she could hear how her heartbeat moved from inside her body to outside, until it sounded as though the clouds were breathing along with her, and the wind and the trees and everything crawling through the grass.

"No, not really. My son taught me. He crowed that I was his best pupil, but I asked him to be careful and not say that anymore; it crushed the feelings of his other students. He tried to teach them these ways, the men who followed him. He took them for long retreats into the desert where they wouldn't be distracted. But they weren't successful in the practice. He scolded them for remaining stuck in their chattering heads that never stopped producing questions, instead of slipping into their hearts, that feeling space without words where all are welcome."

"What's it like when you do that? Do you see anything or is it just all feelings?"

"In the beginning I saw only the spots and indistinct shapes we all see when we close our eyes. Then I began to see a blue light, what some might call Nila Bindu, or the Blue Pearl. And everything was in that light, its intensity and beauty and inspiration, a heartbreaking sweetness. Now I no longer see the pearl. I see the blue marble of earth, spinning forever from light to shadow and light to shadow. My heart is placed here, maybe that's why. I yearn to bring the two together, the marble of earth into the luminous blue light of perfect awareness. Do you think it will ever happen?"

Gladys considered the question, and the answer came as much from her hands as her thoughts, as she watched her fists that were pinched together in her lap unfurl in a graceful way. "Yes," she said. She held up her strong hands. "Yes."

Candace was always punctual. In fact, she'd had to train herself not to get everywhere so early, what a waste of time that was, and how obsequious in a way, as if you valued everyone else's time more than your own. She cultivated a knack for arriving just a minute or two ahead of schedule, polite but not pathetic. She breezed into the Juut Salon Spa on the corner of Grand and Victoria, and was ushered upstairs, to the area where manicures and pedicures were offered. She always loved the scent of the place, a mingle of fragrant candles and aromatic oils that blended well together into a tranquil cloud. The women who worked there were lovely and calm, each wearing slinky black clothes that made them seem like priestesses of fashion. She had a standing appointment with their best manicurist, a young woman named Mia who had deep black hair threaded with bright red streaks, a colorful coif that reminded Candace of a red-winged blackbird. Her face contrasted with the drama of the hair, soft and round, a comfort, like the kindness of her hazel eyes.

Candace paid for the deluxe treatment which meant her hands and feet would be bathed in a pool of warm melted wax that soothed the joints and softened the skin. She'd even receive a brief neck and shoulder massage. She needed the pampering today; it was getting harder to ignore the hallucinations which continued even though Candace had undergone test after test, including a few that were painfully invasive. There was always another test for those with good insurance and plenty of money, but she'd reached the end of all reasonable exams. And she'd walked in on a conversation between the apparition and Gladys, and who in the world was more grounded than Gladys? So what did that mean, the sharing of a delusion? She quickly extinguished this line of thought, snuffed it by visualizing a bloom torn from its stem and thrown to the ground. Trampled. Good. Mia was pressing down her cuticles and trimming them to perfection.

"Talk to me," Candace said, the urgency in her voice making the words sound like a command. So she smiled at Mia in apology.

"I had something strange happen this morning, while I was walking to work," Mia began, only too happy to tell someone about her experience. "I don't live far from here, in a building over on Lincoln. Fun place. Cool people. So, I'm walking here like any other day, when out of the corner of my eye I see what I thought was a drab bird, maybe a cowbird, brown all over? But it's moving toward me, then it's in the center of my visual field. Bam! Hello! I'm going to be attacked by a bird? But, no, it's not a bird after all. Can you believe, it's a humongous butterfly—biggest one I've ever seen! And it decides to become my new best friend, attaches itself to my bracelet, see? This one." She indicated a silver band decorated with moonstones scattered around it like small blue eyes. "I was gripping the strap of my bag and kept walking, thinking the thing will freak out once it realizes I'm a person, and fly away. But it doesn't. Stayed with me the whole way here and then, when I reached out to open the door, it fluttered off. So bizarre. I keep thinking it's some kind of sign. But sign of what?"

The hallucination who called herself Maryam was suddenly standing behind Mia; she told Candace, "Tell her it *is* a sign. She's waking up, and beings will sense this and respond to her. Her life will be changing soon. She's called to a service different from the one she's performing now."

But Candace said nothing. She flinched a little and Mia looked at her, "Did I hurt you?"

"No," said Candace. "Not at all." The music wasn't loud enough. What was it? Loreena McKennitt. "The Mummers' Dance." She wanted to shout, "Crank that thing!" But she couldn't, of course, she was too well behaved. They knew her here. Instead she asked, "I never do color, do I? What say we change things a bit and you paint me up?" She tried for impulsive gaiety.

"Absolutely!" Mia said. "You have a ton of choices." She pulled out a tray of possibilities for Candace to consider.

"Wow, that *is* a lot."

As Candace focused on the nail color options, Mia tried not to squirm in her metal-framed chair. Her back had started to itch, well, shoulder and back, where her tattoo was. She hated being a cliché all of a sudden, a girl with a dragon tattoo. She was always quick to point out that she'd had hers made years before she ever heard of Stieg Larsson and his heroine who was similarly decorated. Six years earlier, on her eighteenth birthday, she'd gone to a parlor in Minneapolis, one on Lake Street with an excellent reputation. She worked with an artist there to design her dragon so it was personally significant, not just some flash on the wall. It was Tibetan in style, its face both fierce and wise, what she thought of as the strength of justice. The face was red and the body a complicated twining of purple, red, and gold. She had the face tattooed on her shoulder and the body trailing down the right hand side of her back, tail flicked up toward her armpit. She thought of the dragon as her protector, her guide, only violent when provoked, and her confidence level had risen as if she had secret mojo she could summon when needed. The tattoo had pained her, naturally, and itched during the healing process, but never since then. This was just another strange occurrence on a day already labeled as fatally odd.

Candace pored over the choice of nail color as if her very life, or at least her sanity, depended on it. Which was better, bold or subtle, pretty or slinky? The minutes ticked away, people died, children were born, creatures she had never heard of were suddenly extinct, the species lost. Candace was startled from her confused trance by a firm voice that boomed throughout the space, filling both upper and lower levels.

"Enough!" the voice said. It was the hallucination speaking to her more energetically than she had before, making it still harder to dismiss her words.

Maryam walked around the table to confront Candace, whipped off her sunglasses like an impetuous gust. Mia pulled back in astonishment, looking for the errant breeze.

Maryam would later tell Gladys it was the nail polish that finally ended her patience. "I have nothing against the polish itself," she said. "If she wants to decorate herself that way, what harm? What riled me was her inability to choose, to just decide on one shade over another, something that matters so little to anyone's welfare."

Maryam stood tall, diminutive as she was, her presence more potent than any aromatic oils. The air smelled like fire, tasted like incense, and though Candace was the only one who could hear the words she spoke with strong emotion, everyone felt the snap of a rubber band about the ears as if a parent were scolding.

"My girl," Maryam said, gripping the armrests of Candace's chair so she couldn't flee. "Enough of this nonsense. You waste your time. You waste your heart. If you only knew what strength resides in you, what gifts you've been given, oh, you are so blessed! You come from the ones who survived the diseases brought from Europe, the plagues and the poxes, the cruel policies. You come from the ones who survived exiles and pogroms, the Final Solution. You are supposed to be dead on both sides. Exterminated. And yet you live. I cannot see you hide like this any longer, like a seed in its egg. I crack the egg. I smash it open! Now is the time. Now!"

Candace felt a sudden heat explode within her, the physical sensations so powerful they quieted her refusing mind. Her heart felt scorched, it was melting like wax, and the warmth spread everywhere—from the very tips of each strand of hair to her unpainted toes. Her hands and feet were throbbing, was this pain, no, this was opening, barriers ripped away so there was no more separation between inside and outside. The one bled into the other. Surely her heart was running away from her, leaking through veins, spilling to the floor, nothing more now than roses of blood offered to the astonished room.

"Stigmata, it's stigmata," Mia cried, as blood poured from the center of Candace's palms. Mia pushed back her chair and knelt before Candace, removed her shoes, yes, blood splashed out of them as the wounded arches of Candace's feet were revealed. "What do we do?" Mia called. "What service do you call for this sort of thing?"

A manager appeared, holding a box filled with disposable latex gloves. "Get out of there, Mia, put on some gloves," she admonished. Paramedics were called; the manager bathed Candace's face with a wet cloth. "She's in shock," she told Mia.

Mia nodded but was suddenly aware of her own discomfort; something was happening to her back, her shoulder, it felt, crazy as it might sound, it felt like her tattoo was moving. She excused herself and ran to the closest bathroom. Once the door was locked behind her she reached to pull off her black shirt, but stopped. Afraid to look, afraid to see. She closed her eyes and took several deep breaths. She'd been thinking just recently that she wanted to be part of a spiritual community again, not her parents' church, which she found unforgiving and materialistic—Jesus as your personal ATM machine—but a Unitarian church she'd heard was warm and welcoming. No judgments. She'd made the mistake of mentioning the possibility to her parents, thinking they'd be thrilled with her return to Christianity, but her mother had cried and her father barked, "No Loony Yoonies!" before he hung up.

Her pulse had slowed; she was leaning against the counter, watching the perfect crystal flame that lifted from the scented candle. "You can do this," she told herself. She pulled off her shirt and turned to look at her dragon. The head was missing, no longer perched over her shoulder, keeping watch. She turned more, spotted the flash of color that was sewn into her skin. The tattoo was still there, still part of her, but the dragon *had* moved. She gripped the counter and focused again on breathing. Tears were falling down her face but she wasn't aware of them. This isn't a bad thing, she thought. This is just another sign. "Of what?" she asked aloud. The morning's confusion cleared away, and this time she could answer herself in a voice that was strong, confident. "This is a sign that there's *more*. There is *so* much *more*."

She smiled now, through the wash of tears, and turned to admire this new dragon, which stretched down her back, perfectly in line with her long elegant spine.

The paramedics quickly arrived, a pair of friends, Keith and Rick. They'd seen gunshot victims, the bloody aftermath of knife fights, women horribly beaten by pimps, boyfriends, husbands. But they'd never seen the equivalent of Candace's affliction, the copious, catastrophic loss of blood, yet her vitals were good. Blood pressure a bit low, but my God, why wouldn't it be? She couldn't speak, her eyes glazed with panic. When they asked her questions she just shook her head. At least she was conscious. They collected her information from the wallet handed over to them by the salon's manager. Driver's license, health insurance card.

"Do you have a preference where we take you?" Keith asked. A shake of the head. So they drove her to the second closest hospital, one that was a bit more upscale than the nearest.

Keith sat in the back with her on the ride and offered a stream of comforting conversation. He told himself it was for the lady, this strange, frightened woman, but actually he was trying to calm himself. It's not every day you witness a miracle, good or bad; he couldn't quite call this one good, it was so messy and upsetting. But the timing of it was what really shook him. Just yesterday he'd been put through a kind of intervention, ganged up on by his mother and girlfriend who were waiting for him at his apartment when he'd returned from work. They'd caught him in a web of lies, that's what his mother called his transgression, "a web of lies." What it all boiled down to is that he didn't like going to church. Never had. He supposed he did believe in God, maybe even that Jesus was some sliver of God, that complicated equation that never made sense to him. So when his mother pestered him to attend her church, a Baptist congregation in Saint Paul, he'd said, no, he couldn't, because his girlfriend wouldn't feel comfortable in an all-Black church. Then his girlfriend had begged him to go to mass with her, to solidify their relationship, she said, make it holy in the sight of God since they weren't married yet. Her church was farther away, in one of the rich suburbs where he wouldn't want to get caught after dark. Too much hassle. He told her, so sorry, no can do, I'm not comfortable being part of an all-white congregation. I'll keep going to my mother's church but I'll be thinking of you when I'm there.

Apparently his mother had phoned his girlfriend to assure her she'd be most welcome if she cared to sit in one Sunday with the Baptists, only to find Keith had bamboozled them both. That was his girlfriend's term, as in, "I do *not* like being misled, being *bamboozled*, especially about spiritual matters!" He was in the biggest doghouse of his life, and now *this*.

When the emergency vehicle pulled up to the hospital doors and Candace was lifted down, eyes still veiled with fear, blood soaking the bandages the team had wrapped around her hands and feet, Keith patted her on the arm and lowered his head to whisper in her ear: "You'll be all right, Ma'am, you hang in there. You'll be all right."

I'll pray for her, he thought, and knew that this time he would. He might even attend both churches, his mother's and his girlfriend's, since their services were at different times. Whatever you decide, you better stick to it, he told himself. It's bad enough to mess with the dearest women in your life, but you really better not disappoint the powers that be who could pull off *this* kind of stunt.

Candace was taken immediately into a private room in intensive care. She was stretched out on a cart, a pillow beneath her head, a soft white blanket covering her. But it wasn't enough, she was shivering. She was treated for shock, oxygen mask covering her nose and mouth to make sure she was getting enough air, an IV line attached to her arm since her hands were injured. The blood was soaking into the bandages, but the flow was less dramatic. She was trembling now more from nerves than her physical condition. Her purse, with the helpful wallet, was stowed somewhere beneath her on a shelf of the cart. She gestured toward it when they asked for her name, address, insurer. She wasn't ready to talk just yet. She had to get her brain under her, that's how she thought of it, some foundation of rational thought to perch on, to frame all the events of the last half hour and hopefully explain them away. But her brain didn't feel like her brain anymore, a separate entity from her heart, a different room in the mansion that was Candace Jenssen.

"I'm all of a piece," she murmured. She'd read the phrase somewhere and latched onto it now. The only coherent image she summoned to mind was a braid, a thick braid of hair like the one the apparition wore, a braid of veins, of flowers, a dancing braid of girls, their hands all locked together.

"She's coming around," a voice said, male.

Am I, she wondered. Am I coming somewhere? Am I still an I? Is this my blood? Is this my body? Or is it yours?

"Do you know your name?" the man asked.

She nodded.

"Would you care to tell me?"

Her eyes widened, she could feel them do this. They were somehow connected to her name, all part of the braid. She said, "Candace Altman Jenssen," as clearly as she could, the way she spoke more carefully when she'd had too much wine at a party.

"Altman, that's not on here. Is that a maiden name?"

"Yes."

"Good, good girl. We're glad to have you back."

Where have I been? she wondered.

"Could you tell me what happened here? It isn't every day we see a case like this."

Candace smiled, musing, Ah, isn't that the trick question. If I could answer that I wouldn't have a care in the world. She surprised herself then, heard her own voice that was part of the braid, the infamous braid, no longer controlled by a mask of propriety, blurt quite passionately: "I was given stigmata by Maryam, the Virgin Mother. She's been living in my house for two weeks, trying to get me to accept her presence. Believe me, I've had *every* test, thinking a tumor must be giving me these hallucinations, but they couldn't find anything. Perfect bill of health. I pushed her too far today, I guess, and she did this." Candace held up her hands, white bandaged paws. "She really did this. She's acting on behalf of my ancestor, we're Mohawk. Don't you think I know how crazy this sounds? The Virgin Mary is here to make me be Mohawk."

No, not again. Candace felt a swooping warmth gather her in like a glorious embrace. But this wasn't shattering, just the opposite, more of a collecting, as if all the ruptured fragments of Candace Jenssen had been brought together in one neat bundle. The bleeding stopped. She knew without even checking. That's all she wanted, Candace thought. She wanted me to tell the truth. To myself. Candace laughed, softly at first, and then the roaring, hiccupping, weeping kind of laughter that makes your diaphragm ache.

Oh dear, the doctor thought. This just gets worse and worse. He left the room to make a few phone calls but made certain to ask a nurse to remain with the patient. He couldn't predict what she'd do next and he didn't want her to harm herself on his watch.

Candace was lying on a hospital cot, you couldn't really call it a bed, she thought. It was a narrow twin bed like the ones in her old college dorm, the mattress thin. There must be a plastic slipcover beneath the sheet, she mused, since every move she made produced a sharp, crackling sound. She felt dizzy with confusion, so much had happened in such a short time. More interviews with doctors who could hear only the miracles she recounted, the ridiculous-sounding details, and never her protests that she knew this was extraordinarily bizarre, she herself had been looking for logical, pedestrian explanations. Her purse was confiscated, along with her watch and silver earrings, and she was whisked through a metal detector, then buzzed in beyond heavy metal doors that clanged shut behind her. The noise reminded her of the opening credits sequence on *Get Smart*, where barred gates keep crashing down in an ominous way.

She was in the psychiatric unit of the hospital, and a policeman (was it really a cop?) was itemizing the contents of her purse, everything she'd brought with her to the salon spa a lifetime ago, then placing them in a large envelope. She kept signing her name, nodding to everyone like a bobble-head doll, but she couldn't put the story together until she went over it all, resting on the cot. They'd walked her through a room, a lounge with a giant television set bolted into a frame connected to the ceiling. Couches were arranged around the television, and a few patients in street clothes were seated there, watching the routine of her admission. The patients' rooms surrounded the central space, creating a wheel. Candace smiled ruefully; there's probably some study that shows a psych unit without corners is more conducive to recovery. Or they just liked the look of a circle.

She had a roommate; she could hear the crinkle of movement on the other side of the small room. A soft soprano voice spoke from behind the privacy curtain. "Hi, I'm Lee. Glad to have a roommate; it was getting lonesome in here. They've locked the bathroom door, standard practice when you're new. But as long as you act stable they'll unlock it pretty soon. Another hour or so. If you need to use the facilities, just ask. They'll let you in."

"I'm sorry *you* have to be inconvenienced because of me," Candace said, relieved at how normal their conversation sounded.

"Don't think twice about it, same for all of us. Is this your first time?"

Candace's eyes filled with tears so quickly it shocked her. I'm more raw than I realized, she thought. She felt ripped open, a gazelle brought down by a tiger, flayed. I've been flayed alive. But all she told Lee was, "Yes. First time."

This seemed to impress the hidden woman. Her bed made a series of gunfire-like cracks—she must be sitting up—and then the curtain was pulled back against the wall. Candace saw a small round person and immediately thought of a snow-woman, though her complexion was very pink and smooth, like the frosting of a cake. She perched on the edge of her bed, hands twisting together in her lap.

"You're in luck . . ." she paused significantly. Candace could hear the ellipses dotting the air.

"Candace."

"Candace. You have *really* lucked out. I'm an old hand at this, wrestled with depression my whole life, I mean, *entire* life. Been in and out of places like this all over the Twin Cities and the suburbs. *This* is the best place. Top notch. They separate the major crazies—dangerous, drooling, sorry, no offense to them, not their fault—from those of us who are just sad. The sad clowns." She smiled. She didn't look very sad.

"I see," Candace said. "I'm glad then, I guess."

"I'll shut up now and let you get grounded. It's a lot to take in. Were you voluntary? I always am. That's too personal to throw at you, it'll come out later anyway, in group. Tell me if you need anything. I've got shampoo and conditioner and a bunch of magazines."

"Thank you," Candace said, barely louder than a whisper. That was all she could manage just now.

They'd given her something, some pill, and it made her feel both exhausted and wired, an odd, jittery sensation as if there was a nervous creature inside her worn-out shell who was desperately trying to claw its way out. Her neck was beginning to ache, a muscle cramp. She pulled her hands out from under the sheet and inspected them. The bandages were gone, no longer necessary. She stared at her palms, held them up to the light, expecting a starburst of scars there, evidence that the blood had a portal, it wasn't a trick, her flesh had opened like a hungry mouth and spilled the contents of her heart. Nothing. The same creases and lines, did they foretell *this* drama? The same pampered skin, expensively soft and fragrant. No wonder they thought she was nuts. Crazy, bonkers, whackadoodle. She played a game like a Monty Python skit, where she tried to recall each term, every euphemism for insanity. That took a while.

Anger blossomed so suddenly she caught her breath and had to hold herself in. She didn't want to sob or scream; she didn't want them to keep the bathroom door locked. Where's Maryam now? Her thoughts sizzled. She did this to me, made me admit she was real, and here's the result. But she knew this was unfair. She knew Maryam created a spectacle because Candace had resisted for so long. How different it would have been if she'd just let her in from the start, skipped the dark glasses and the endless medical exams.

"This is pointless," she said aloud.

"Excuse me?" Lee responded sweetly.

"Sorry, just thinking aloud." Candace laughed darkly. "Don't tell them I'm talking to myself or we'll never get the bathroom open."

"Not to worry," Lee said. "I'm not a snitch."

Candace had never felt so alone in her life. Even after her mother died when she was seven, her father, Myron Altman, was there—adoring, indulgent. She was his princess until the day, six years ago, when she lost him to lung cancer, such cruel irony since he never smoked. Her husband and sons seemed light years away; they inhabited another planet where spirits lived only in fiction and ancestors didn't take the time to reach for you from beyond the grave.

This is all my fault, she decided. I was so in love with anything fantastical, the Tolkien books, and fairy tales, films like *Portrait of Jennie*, starring Jennifer Jones of the glistening eyes who played a lovelorn ghost. When she was younger Candace tried to barge her way into Narnia, a world she *knew* existed. She didn't have an enchanted wardrobe like those fortunate Pevensie kids, but she had a houseful of closets. So every day after school she'd rummage through the lot, banging on their back walls behind mothball-scented coats and teetering boxes, knocking and knocking until her knuckles bled. She figured she'd bring her father with her once she found the entrance. If she'd learned anything growing up in New Jersey it was that plumbers were *always* in demand. He'd have no problem finding work in another world.

Was this *her* version of Narnia? Come too late in life for her to embrace? What had she been doing the past two weeks but trying to bar the door, wall herself up in a life that brought her little joy but at least was familiar, under control. Now she had none. Universe—1, Candace—0, if you could keep score of events like this. But couldn't that be liberating, too? What if she entered this world freely, excitedly, not knowing what would come of it, what it meant, but willing to make the journey as she did when she read a new book? The next page a cipher, full of potential. She loved the feeling of anticipation. What if anything *is* possible, in life as well as in fiction?

Candace rolled over on the cot, making the noise of a firing squad, and considered this last thought for an infinite hour.

By the time Barry was notified of his wife's admission to the hospital, visiting hours were over and Candace had participated in one group therapy session, where she'd kept quiet, and one arts and crafts happy hour, at least that's how she thought of it. She did *not* want to draw or paint or arrange glitter with messy glue that smelled to her like kindergarten. But she found she was still a good mother, this time to several young women, Misty, Rena, and Paris, who swarmed to her when she encouraged their efforts. It was easy to praise them, they *were* creative, and they stayed longer than usual in the activity room; they asked permission, painting and gluing so earnestly she thought her heart would break.

She was handed a message. Her husband, trying to reach her. So she went to a phone in a small niche beside the main nurses' desk in the lounge. She phoned Barry.

"Sweetheart, what's going on?" He sounded frantic. She almost didn't recognize his voice.

"I don't think I can have this conversation on the phone," she said, more coldly than she'd intended. She felt stiff, as if she were talking about intimate matters with a stranger. Or was *she* the stranger? "Just know that I'm not crazy, not at all. If you don't believe me, ask Gladys."

"Gladys, what does she have to do with anything?"

"*That's* what I can't go into right now. I have a lot to sort out. Maybe it's not such a bad thing I'm here."

"Honey, you can't be serious. Look, I've talked to the doctors, tried to convince them you're as solid as they come. Maybe, just maybe, this is a bid for attention? Married to a workaholic, it can't be easy. They said realistically you'll be in there until Monday, if you do well. There's a three-day hold to make sure you're not a danger to yourself, that takes you through Friday and the weekend. I'll be in tomorrow to see you. What should I bring?"

"No," she said. The word surprised her.

"What do you mean, no? Sweetheart, this is no time to play games."

"There you go, again. 'Bid for attention,' 'playing games.' We're not even speaking the same language. That's why it's a 'no.' I can't see you just yet."

She took a deep breath and imagined a fresh page, creamy and inviting, empty of words, deeds, no hint if what was to come was a tragedy or a comedy. Maybe both. She stepped onto the page.

"Barry, please hear me, if you can. We need to be *real*. I mean really real, as our boys might say. What's happening to me isn't invented or imagined or schemed up in my frustrated little brain. To quote one of your favorite movies, *Rosemary's Baby*: 'This is *really* happening.'"

A tense silence bloomed between them; she thought of an airbag suddenly deployed, the shocking cushion. Barry sighed. "This is serious, so I'll do as you ask. Why don't you give me a list of things you need to feel more comfortable and I'll have Gladys bring them to you tomorrow."

"Yes," she said. "Thank you. That I can do." She gave him the list as she summoned to mind items that weren't forbidden in this cautious place. Then she bid him goodnight.

"Wait!" she heard him say as she was about to replace the handset.

"What?"

"I love you. I just want you to know that. I love you."

"Thank you," she said, as kindly as she could, but she didn't offer the words in return. At this point she didn't know what she felt. All bets were off. She was standing on a fresh page, and the only thing she knew for certain was that the next chapter would be nothing like the last.

Candace soon discovered that her roommate, Lee, *was* sad. Her earlier burst of vivaciousness was short-lived, and though she continued to be kind, generous, welcoming Candace to use anything of hers, she could only bring herself to attend one of the many group activities offered throughout the day. They spoke softly together, late that night, both of them tired but jangled from sleep by their medication.

"It isn't life," Lee sighed. "I have the sweetest husband, love of my life, you'll meet him tomorrow, a large family always so concerned for me. It's just a glitch in my brain, some chemical too low or too high, I don't know. It's hard for them not to take it personally. They think if they just care for me enough they can love me out of it. Then I berate myself for letting them down. Awful. Sometimes it's so awful."

Candace listened, commiserated the best she could given that she didn't share the same experience, the same malady. She'd kept mum for the past few hours about what brought her here, opening only to one counselor, a bubbly woman named Sharlene—"Though everyone calls me Shar," she'd said. She told Shar the whole story, from top to bottom, the dreams and headaches, the visitation and her tireless quest to find a physical culprit that would place her in control again, deciding how to manage the ailment.

"Sounds like you've been through a lot," Shar said, so sympathetically, Candace had to breathe deeply for a minute or two to prevent herself from breaking down.

She observed Shar in this breathing space, thinking the woman was probably her own age, working hard to maintain herself, just in different ways. Her skin was sun-damaged yet had an attractive sheen, as if her tan were a permanent glow she'd wear forever. Her hair was a brassy red she wore in a complicated upswept twist with pieces purposely teased out here and there to make it feathery. Must take hours to arrange, Candace thought. She wore a professional jacket, almost like a lab coat, but in a soft periwinkle blue that matched her eyes. It was open, revealing a blouse with enough buttons undone to hint at cleavage. Candace liked her, a little surprised by the rush of feeling. She trusted her.

"I'm going to be honest with you," Shar said. "You've only been here one day, not even a whole day, and we need more to go on than that limited amount of time. But I'm not like the others. I believe that the things you're describing *can* happen, *do* happen. If the mystics we love to read about now, quoting and studying them so much these days, ever fell into the hands of the psychiatric community, God help them, they'd never have seen the light of day again! I can't say for sure just yet. But in case what you're telling me is one hundred percent the real deal, let me give you a piece of advice. In group, talk about your problems. Married, right? Talk about that. Issues with the parents you've never sorted out? Go there. Keep this under your hat, what you just told me. Don't give them fodder to label you as seriously ill. You impressed them enough to place you down here—more troubling cases go upstairs. Let's keep it that way." She winked at Candace. Candace nodded.

"I hear you," she said. "And I'm so grateful."

Gladys filled two shopping bags with clothes, toiletries, and books to bring Candace. The set of expensive luggage remained in the closet since Gladys wasn't sure if it would be allowed in the hospital unit, given all the metal zippers and hidden pockets. Maryam asked if she could accompany Gladys.

"Of course. And now she'll be ready to see you."

"One hopes," Maryam said. Then she asked, "Do you have a cloak?"

"A what?"

"I need to bring her something, rather large, difficult to hide. But if I'm wearing a cloak I can bring it in under that."

Gladys smiled. "Reminds me of my grandson's books—those Harry Potters. I sewed him an invisibility cloak out of old sheets when he was younger. We had to pretend we didn't see him when he wore it."

"That sort of thing would be perfect right about now."

"Well, I don't have one of those, but, me see . . ." Gladys went up to her apartment and poked around her few possessions, came back flourishing a turquoise dance shawl she'd received at a giveaway a few months earlier. She was frequently honored at powwows for being a refuge in the community, someone who would always listen to a person's troubles. The shawl was just one of the many gifts she'd been given over the years. "Will this work?" she asked Maryam as she spread the shawl across her friend's narrow shoulders.

"Oh, how beautiful!" Maryam whirled as if she knew how to fancy dance—she became a blue butterfly, the fringes waving like ripples of water. "Yes, this will be just fine," she said. "Thank you."

Jules was there to drive them to the hospital in his Chevy Caprice. "The safest ride you'll ever have," he said, patting her roof. He made a gesture like tipping his hat toward Maryam, though he wasn't wearing a hat. "Nice to finally meet you, Ma'am," he said.

"Likewise. I've heard a host of wonderful things about you." Maryam's eyes shone with pleasure.

"Oh," Jules sputtered, so pleased he was actually speechless.

"Don't say anymore," Gladys told Maryam. "It'll go to his head."

Jules ushered them into the car, all three sitting together in the spacious front.

"Buckle up, ladies," he requested, then he bent down to kiss Merle who was settled in a sling he'd rigged up that he wore across his chest like the ones he'd seen a few mothers using. "And away we go!" he said, excitedly, as if they were headed for the fairgrounds.

When Gladys went through hospital security she opened a Tupperware container filled with juicy-looking rhubarb bars she'd baked that morning, the enticing scent of cinnamon-and-brown sugar crumble that topped the fruit layer filled the hall, and the guards were only too happy to reach in and snag one of the treats.

"You're our new best friend," one of them said.

She passed through the metal detector without incident, but when Maryam walked through the alarm sounded. The guards looked at Gladys. She shrugged her shoulders and held out the bags for them to search.

"Thing must be possessed," said a guard, and he buzzed her in. Maryam slipped in behind her, unseen despite the blazing color of her shawl.

"And so it begins," Maryam said mysteriously.

Gladys was shown Candace's room, so she headed there, offering the baked goods and a paper napkin to anyone she passed along the way.

"You're like a fairy godmother," said Rena, blushing.

Gladys laughed. "Well, that's a first. But I guess it's better than being a wicked witch."

Maryam whispered in her ear, "I'll join you shortly, I have some business with my people."

Gladys nodded which Rena took to be a farewell gesture, so she drifted over to the couch and fell into one with a discontented sigh. Maryam stood behind her and gently placed a hand on the crown of the young woman's head.

"Sweet girl," Maryam breathed. "I'm sorry you've had to see so much violence. You wonder why no one was there to save your mother, no guardian angel to rescue her from harm the way they've rescued others. It would have been my honor to preserve her for you, we need our mothers so, but that wasn't her agreement in this life. We are here to learn, to teach, and sometimes the only way is through suffering. But she was surrounded by angels, or spirits, the terms don't matter. She was held at the end, though you couldn't see it, and now she holds you."

Maryam moved on and Rena stood, in search of paper and a pen. She had the urge to write a poem about her mother. Her presence was suddenly so palpable, Rena swore she could even smell her mother's favorite perfume—a light floral blend they didn't make in this country, but only back home in Sarajevo.

Maryam hovered behind Paris, smiled as she placed her hand on the girl's sturdy shoulder. "What a competitor you are, good for you. I'm proud of you for working so hard to increase your strength and the quality of your mind. I know you're missing college and you'll have to be in summer school to make up for the lost time. But you'll do well. Just remember that there's a line you must walk between performance and punishment. Move your body for the love of it, the rush of joy, study to satisfy your curiosity, not to impress people. Their good opinion is a shaky house, one you shouldn't live in. Build up your own good opinion of yourself and see how satisfying it is to shelter there."

A man of retirement age, Don, sat perfectly still, apart from the others. He faced the television but his eyes looked past its images, beyond its stories. If you stood very close to him you could see he was shaking, and Maryam sat beside him, covered a dry, reddened hand with hers.

"I remember you, Don," she said. "You've come to see me so many times. Maybe this time my message will find its way home. Eric is fine now, or he would be if he didn't see your unhappiness, how long you've blamed yourself for something that was never your fault. Yes, he was afraid to die, but you were there to hold him in the street, and later, your father took over for you and made the transition so easy for him. Easier than it's been for you. Go out with your wife tomorrow. Accept the day pass and go somewhere beautiful—walk through Como Park, maybe. Make your boy smile by smiling yourself." She gave Don's hand a squeeze and then she rose to find Candace.

Don stood with her, and everyone in the room craned to watch him, he'd been such a statue all day. He felt an impulse to call his wife, bless her patience. She'd been longing for a picnic. Perhaps he'd suggest they make a day of it at the park. Visit the zoo Eric loved so well. Why, he'd be a man now, Don realized. And here I keep seeing him as a little boy.

Maryam found Gladys and Candace visiting together like old friends. Candace was eating a rhubarb bar with appreciation, hunger. She licked the crumbs from her fingers.

Lee was sleeping, thanks to a pill she'd been given to counteract the insomnia induced by her antidepressant. The privacy curtain hid her from the others, and she slept through the events of that afternoon though she would tell her husband the next day she'd had the most fascinating dreams. She was frustrated she couldn't recall the details—they darted away from her when she reached for them.

"No matter," she said. "What's important is I woke up this morning feeling pretty darn grand!" She hugged her husband and whispered in his ear: "Something tells me it isn't for naught."

"What?" he asked, hopeful but confused.

"This." She indicated the room, but the way her hands kept moving, he took her meaning to go further than that. "Everything," she said. And he knew he'd been right.

Maryam stood quietly beside Gladys. She could have taken a seat, Lee's chair was vacant, but she didn't sit. She looked at Candace, covered her with a long look—that's what it felt like, something silk spun by invisible hands washing down her face.

"I am glad you're awake," she said.

Candace wiped her mouth, her hands, with a napkin and set it down on the bedside table. She needed free hands.

"This is a long time coming. He has been in your family for generations, dreamed to life for a future purpose he has yet to fulfill. Honor this being who has shown the patience of a saint."

Maryam withdrew the Face from inside her dance shawl, and this time Candace gasped to look upon him, for she could see how alive he was, how powerful. What had she been thinking to corral him, treat him like just another one of her many things? She heard herself speak: "He isn't art. He is life or death."

"Now you begin," Maryam said, and she smiled at Candace for the first time since the day they met. "This is not mine to wear or to explain. This sacred material does not belong to me. I am the door for you, but not the way. We will leave you now with your ancestors and return later to collect the Face."

Gladys and Maryam walked back into the lounge and settled on a couch. A group of patients had decided to watch the Disney film *Enchanted*. Their choices were limited to films with happy endings.

"I saw this one with my granddaughter," Gladys said. "It's pretty good." She passed around the Tupperware tub filled with tasty bars.

Candace held the Face in her hands and looked around the room. She didn't know what to do. She guessed she was shaken from her turtle shell after all, thrust into a story she wasn't sure she would like. She felt exposed, laid out beneath a dangling axe.

"What am I supposed to do?" she whispered. Then she heard the rattles, and they were pounding out a fast beat, quicker than her heart. A song, such an old song, that much she knew.

"This one time I allow you to see as I see and hear as I hear." The Face was speaking, and she didn't think the words were English, they were rounder, yet she understood them at once. "My Face will be your face," the mask instructed, and before she had time to think or refuse, she was lifting the basswood head until her flesh fit within its smooth contours, the rounded cheeks and full brow, and they were one.

Candace saw what the Face knew all along—the connection of beings across light, the defeat of time. This was like Grace's painting, where the small adds up, comes together to create something else, so we are never just a single lonesome story but a hundred, a thousand, a mind-boggling amount beyond numbers. She saw splinters spin together with centripetal force—Jeanne the French maid being burned in a market town while the women of Rouen watch, weeping into their aprons, the smoke the same as the haunted air above the crematoria in Auschwitz, the ashes of the beloved sifting over the living and the dead, air strikes in Iraq, the bomb in Hiroshima, the collapse of the Towers, our dust blown together, too small to identify or sort or ever separate.

Candace's tears fell from the copper eyes of a basswood face, and he showed her next her own story, the splinter that belonged to her ancestor, Jigonsaseh, who'd been speaking to her all this time and not been heard. Candace fell back on her narrow bed, and the Face looked beyond the ceiling, showed her what she was meant to see. And for the first time in a life that already exceeded half a century, this child who'd been wandering lost in the wilderness was found.

Clan Mother of Memory

Sacred Wilderness

Jigonsaseh (1626)

My people, the Kanien'kehá:ka, were placed in this territory by the Creator and here we shall remain forever. Welcome to our territory and to this story which begins and ends with the birth of my son, Ayowantha. I knew he would be different from other boys who ran through the village in packs, because already he was a leader before he was born. He came to me in dreams and directed me what to eat. He smiled a baby smile at me, his eyes full of stars, and said, "Mother, I ask you to please eat some fish every day. I need to learn how to swim, how to see under the water, how to travel through dangerous rivers. Will you do this for me?" I agreed. Later he asked me to eat deer meat and bear meat, wild turkey and pheasant, the flesh of many beings—always so he could understand their abilities. He was busy inside me with more than the growing of bones. He was learning about the world.

I kept these dreams secret from everyone, even my husband, Shasko-haro:wane, who, like his name, is my sheltering tree. He brought me whatever I asked and never complained. I wanted to tell my younger sister about these visits with my boy, but she was growing her own child, and if her baby was yet unknown to her I worried she would think I was showing off or already setting our children against each other in a race.

The night before he was born Ayowantha appeared in a final dream. He was so excited, he shook his baby fists in the air around his head and smiled at me, a baby smile empty of teeth.

"I'm coming soon!" he said. "Oh, how much I love you already!"

I woke up crying and happy, and my husband wiped the tears from my face. "He's coming today," I said, and Shaskoharo:wane nodded. He didn't ask me how I knew, simply accepted my words as truth. He is of the Bear Clan and the best example of their simple patience, never unduly curious unless the object is food.

Ayowantha slept all day as though gathering his strength and was born that night. The moon was like me, round and ripe, ready to burst in a shower of seeds. Because my boy was already a strong swimmer I knew he would come fast. I made ready to walk in the woods and receive him. But then I heard a commotion: my sister crying, others speaking all at once which was uncommon. I moved off the platform of my bed, snug against the wall, and slowly walked toward the noise, deeper into the Longhouse. My sister was standing in a small lake of blood, her eyes round with fear. I knew she was more afraid for the child than for herself; she was always concerned for everyone else before her own life.

"Too soon!" she cried. "The baby is coming too soon. Something is wrong!"

Our mother and aunts decided to attend us as we brought our children into the world, something we usually did on our own, without a fuss. They settled us side by side, and I held my sister's narrow hand—so thin and cold it was, I pressed it to pass on some of my heat.

Ayowantha was quick, as I'd expected. Smooth as a fish he emerged, and I hardly felt any pain. The women clustered around him to wash him and see his face, and I heard them breathe out in surprise.

"He's smiling," my mother said right away so I wouldn't be afraid of their reaction. "Already this one is smiling." She handed him to me and his smile opened even more, and he laughed. "He knows you're his mother."

"Yes," I agreed, and I laughed along with him until our happy noise became a song that carried him to sleep. Even dreaming, he chuckled now and then like an old man recalling the delights of his younger days. I stroked his face with a finger, caressed his plump strawberry cheeks. I dipped my head to nuzzle the black down of his hair and breathed in the scent of tobacco smoke and red cedar leaves. It was as if he had come from a place of offerings and prayers rather than his mother's cave.

A gasp from my sister brought me back to her struggle. The child was fighting to be born—we could see the Stomp Dance he performed as his terrible kicks rippled across her stomach. The teas she'd been dosed with to slow her labor dribbled out of her, and I reached over to wipe the liquid from her lips. This was my pretend daughter. A girl so patient she'd let me play the mother in our games and always accepted the powerless roles I offered her. A girl content to be in my company and walk in my shadow. She was so pale now it frightened me. I pinched her cheek to make a red flower bloom in all that gray, but I only left a chalky mark.

"I've never seen anything like this," my mother whispered. "I don't know if he's trying to be born or trying to defeat her."

The child was desperate to leave his mother but thrashed around in unhelpful ways that kept him trapped. I could sense the wild fury of him and shuddered. Eventually he made his way into the world.

"This was a war," my eldest aunt breathed.

The boy had emerged in the way of a deer, one arm thrust ahead of him as if he wanted to punch into our lives. The women had to work carefully not to injure him, and when he was free, safe in his grandmother's arms, he screamed at her and scowled, then mashed his tiny lips together and fell asleep. The women rushed to help my sister, to stop the blood from emptying her. A creek became a river, and soon what poured from my sister looked more like a thick dark soup. She died holding my hand. I felt the difference when it happened; the flesh was pliant with love and then became stiff with death. The love went somewhere else.

My nephew became my son that night, suddenly I had twins. I held him as he slept and promised I would not hold my sister's death against his small spirit. He made a sucking noise when I said this, as if he had swallowed the promise and taken it into his gullet. I tried to nuzzle his nest of stiff hair as I had Ayowantha's. But the smell made me pull back. I washed him carefully every day, yet for an entire moon he smelled of blood.

Later that summer when we ate the first green corn, both boys were given Turtle names since I am Turtle Clan and children follow their mother's lineage. But because of the way he came into our world, people called my nephew Shawiskara, after Sky Woman's grandson who killed his mother by tearing out of her side instead of being born the right way, like his brother. Sometimes the naming of a being determines its nature, and we were wrong to burden my nephew with that name and the story that pulled along behind it. We should have reminded people of his Turtle name to use instead.

Our village wasn't limited to members of a single clan as was our usual custom since we pulled together the remnants of several villages that had been decimated by wars. We had people of the Turtle, Bear, and Wolf Clans living in separate Longhouses within the same settlement. The entrance to each lodge was marked with the sign of our clan so visiting family could easily find their relatives. Ayowantha and Shawiskara spent their childhood in my people's Longhouse, beneath the sign of the Turtle.

As they grew, the boys looked more like twins than cousins. Handsome boys, whose skin was a shining darkness like night water. They were long-limbed even as babies, and I could see they would grow into tall, sturdy men. The strange thing was that while my son watched the world with pleasant interest, open-faced and welcoming, the edges of his eyes and mouth tipped downward in sadness. My nephew's expression was very different. He grinned all the time the way foxes do when you surprise them—his head tilted to one side and brows pinched together whenever anyone spoke to him, as if he couldn't believe what he was hearing. They were always together, and I understood now why Shawiskara fought his mother to release him before his time. He was determined to be his cousin's match in all things. If Ayowantha was hungry, then so was Shawiskara. If Ayowantha slept, Shawiskara followed him into the dream. When Ayowantha took his first steps, Shawiskara stomped on his shadow, and when Ayowantha spoke his first word, "Mother," Shawiskara's lips parted and he made his first speech: "Brother." Then he patted his cousin's hand. The momentary sweetness surprised me, but in the next breath my nephew launched himself at his cousin with such force their heads cracked together. The sound of it terrified me, but they sat up, rubbing their skulls and laughing as if they had a private joke.

Shawiskara was strong and intelligent and could compete with my son in all ways that were physical or required cleverness. But his spirit was different—perhaps marked by the death that accompanied his birth, perhaps shaped by the name we attached to him. Ayowantha's presence was soothing. When grumbling broke out between people his smile could restore patience, and a man grieving the death of his daughter would take heart and lift his thoughts from darkness when Ayowantha touched his hand. Early on my mother said: "This one smoothes the way." But if my son was a balm and a comfort, Shawiskara was the thorn in the flower. He brought trouble between friends with a sly comment; he unsettled a gathering with his restless, discouraged movements and sharp stares. To be watched closely by Shawiskara was violent work. His eyes could become weapons that flayed the skin and spilled a person's innards onto the ground for all to see. He was favored by no one but Ayowantha.

My boy had not yet lived three summers and already he had the calm mind of a much older being. We sat together one morning, observing Shawiskara involved in some mischief, teasing a dog until it finally marched away in disgust. Ayowantha sighed like a grandfather and said, "Oh, my brother. He tries so hard."

Then I could see it, too. My nephew's desperation. He was not Ayowantha's twin but his mirror, and how can you have the same results as your brother when you stand, always, on the other side?

This was the sweet time when my boy was only my son and not yet a story. Before he brought back a girl from the dead by whispering in her ear to wake up. "She just forgot to breathe," he explained. Before he calmed the storm that threatened our crops and our village with its wrecking winds. Before he charmed the enemy in a battle so that they put down their weapons to embrace him. When he became older he would spend more time with his uncles who would teach him how to be a man. But this baby time belonged to me.

The day I began to lose him was very beautiful. The morning was so fresh after a night rain it felt like the first morning a human being had ever seen. All of us had new eyes and marveled at the bright colors of our world. What had slept during the long winter woke up now and showed off.

"More life," my son whispered, smiling with awe.

"More life," I repeated after him.

Shawiskara scowled and dug his heels into the ground.

My boy began singing—a simple song he created as we sat there, adding to it when he noticed something else to praise. A wary rabbit. A skimming dragonfly. A group of fast-moving clouds that bumped each other along. Beneath his voice I heard a buzzing, and pretty soon I saw the arcing flight of bees. They came from different directions, drawn to Ayowantha's honey voice. One landed on his tongue, and though his eyes widened he kept humming as well as he could manage. Then another flew into his open mouth and settled beside the first. Ayowantha couldn't sing anymore, but he hummed and chuckled, unafraid of this peculiar event. I wanted to shout at him to spit them out and started to scold him in the way of a mother, yet I held back. This was a boy beyond my experience, connected to the world in a way I hadn't seen before. Who was I to tell him what to do? When he eventually quieted, the bees flew off, returned to their busy work. Not one of them had done him harm. It was Shawiskara who needed my attention, for he had trapped a bee and popped it in his mouth only to have it sting the inside of his lip.

As I moved to help him I glanced back at my boy, the singer of bees, as he sat in a patch of sun. This is a Sacred Being, I thought, in hushed wonder. Tears sprang forward and I blinked them away. I was not proud, you see, or very glad. I was afraid for him from that day on because while this world has great need of Sacred Beings, we are never ready for them.

When twelve summers had passed since the birth of Ayowantha, all the villages of the Haudenosaunee, from Kanien'kehá:ka territory at the Eastern Door to Shotinontowane'haka territory at the Western Door, had heard of my son. Visitors came to meet him and share their troubles, and no one went away unsatisfied. Sometimes he told them: "I'm sorry I can't lift your burden. What is done, is done. But we can sit together and share a smoke, and I will sing you a song." So many peaceful songs my son composed to straighten the minds of our unhappy guests, to comb the snakes from their hair.

"When we quiet the mind we can become our own best counselor," he often said.

During the long warm season between the ceremony to honor our strawberry crop and the Harvest Ceremony to honor the gifts of the Three Sisters, Ayowantha came to me and his father and told us he was called to go off on his own to seek his spirit. "To practice all these ideas the Creator has put into my head," is how he described it. I felt a pain in my chest at his words. My husband's fingers touched my back, so lightly they were barely there, but his Bear strength moved into me and stiffened my spine.

"That's good," my husband said, clapping Ayowantha on the shoulder with his heavy paw. I offered a nod, the best I could do when fear nibbled at the edges of my heart.

The next morning Ayowantha set off with nothing more than his pipe and a pouch of tobacco, the covering of his skin, and his good sense. I leaned against my husband to bear this parting, and he whispered in my ear, "Have courage. He's protected by many spirits." We watched him walk away from us, his form so dear to me, even the slanted shadow.

"He will come this way again," Shaskoharo:wane said, and this time I was the one who stiffened his spine when he drooped against me in sadness.

Ayowantha's absence had a curious effect on his cousin. Shawiskara gentled, almost as if he stood in for his brother and took on some of his qualities. He didn't comfort people in the same way as my boy, but he didn't agitate them either, as he usually did. One warm day after our work was done we sat in the sun as it began to dim its light. I scratched Shawiskara's back the way he liked, and a rare peace settled between us which gave me the nerve to ask, "You weren't called to seek your spirit like your brother?" I'd wondered about this, surprised that there was finally an activity that separated the boys. Shawiskara shook his head and rammed the knuckles of his fist into the dirt. A glimpse of his former self in that gesture.

"No. We argued about it."

"Oh?" I kept scratching his long back as if I had small interest in knowing more.

"I wanted to go, too. My own way, of course."

"Of course."

"But he said if a dream hadn't summoned me yet then I had to stay here. It wasn't my time yet."

"So the dream didn't come for you?"

Shawiskara shook his head, then peered at me so mournfully I patted his back in tender sympathy. "When he is gone, I have no purpose!" he barked. He was an injured wolf—on instinct I pulled back my hand. "We are this and this," he said, and chopped the air with hands that faced each other as opposites.

"I think I understand," I murmured, hoping to soothe my nephew. "Just one of you, alone, tips everything out of balance."

He breathed out in relief at these words. "Yes. Now there is nothing to—" He struggled for the word, raked the earth as if to find it there. "Resist." Shawiskara looked up into my face.

I hadn't caressed his cheek since he was much younger, but I did now. "Remember what Peacemaker said," I told him. "When we resist our brother and act against him, we're only resisting ourselves." The wisdom of Peacemaker rested in the air, and then, as one, my nephew and I were both seized with the image of a person trying to fight himself—punching the air, flailing in a pitiful way that made him spin like a dog that chases its tail. We fell on our backs, laughing—deep laughter that is like the relief of rain. When my husband ambled along to see what brought on this merriment, Shawiskara and I glanced at each other and fell over again, laughing away all the bad feelings in the world.

Ayowantha returned to us after being gone for two long changes of the moon. He was taller than when he left, even taller than Shawiskara, and thin as a young sapling. But that was the only youth in him. He wore the expression of a man who has lived for many generations and witnessed much to cherish and regret. He carried a heaviness across his shoulders that made me think of Sky Holder who manages to keep the earth apart from the heavens. But at least he was home, standing before us where I could embrace him and feed him. We didn't pester him for details of his journey, spirit quests are private matters, but I noticed him visiting more often with our head man and woman Faithkeepers who are so knowledgeable when it comes to dreams and visions. He must have shared his experiences with them because I noticed him setting down more and more of the unseen burden he'd brought back with him from his time alone in the woods.

Three summers later we heard news of a Huron war party moving against us—they had done some damage to a village north of ours and were still in the area. Ayowantha and Shawiskara were invited by their uncles to join our own war party which had quickly assembled to meet the threat. My husband was asked to lead a home force that would protect our village, and I secretly hoped the boys would remain here as well. But they chose to join their uncles and were excited to experience their first taste of real battle, what they had practiced for most of their lives. Even Ayowantha, whose ways were always patient and peaceful, was eager to set off on this next adventure.

I must have looked like a mother already in mourning, for Shawiskara took me aside before they left and said, "Don't worry, Mother. I'll take care of him." This promise assured me a little, stiffened my spine, because my nephew was so focused and relentless when it came to competition of any kind, especially the unmaking of a thing.

I watched them move away with their young shadows and restrained myself from crying as some of the other wives and mothers did. I comforted them and warned them not to manifest what we feared. "Our thoughts are so powerful," I reminded them. "Let's imagine them returning, and rejoice as if they're already back in our arms." So we ate a good supper to celebrate their coming victory, rather than weeping in lonesome corners of the Longhouse.

What happened on this war journey became a favorite story in our village and would quickly travel throughout our territory, as tongues move faster than running feet. When the two forces met and Ayowantha's uncles made ready to attack, one of them cried, "This is how it is done!" as he plunged forward with a cry. Another uncle tried to restrain the boys and hold them back. "Observe and learn, until you have to defend yourself," was his advice.

Shawiskara threw himself into battle, his favorite hatchet whirling above his head. Only Ayowantha was still through all this commotion. He carried a war club but never lifted it from where it dangled by his knee. He walked like a man who is dreaming, unafraid of the weapons slicing in every direction. He looked upon the enemy for the first time. Some of them very young, some of them old enough that this would be their last fight if they survived. "Like me, like my father," he later told me.

"They were such beautiful beings," he said. "They moved with a terrible grace and strength, and I marveled at how well the Creator had made them. I honored their courage, the way they faced the possibility of injury, capture, or death, and still came on without hesitation. I could see their women in their eyes, the families back home who cherished them. Oh, the stories they carried that would spill into the ground with their blood and perhaps be lost forever. Mother, I loved them. How could I not? No matter that they use different words to say the things we all say. No matter that they wanted to kill me. That was only because they did not see me."

As my famous boy drifted closer to the fighting he was recognized by the enemy. "There he is! That must be him!" one of them was heard to shout. A charge began—young warriors stampeded to become the hero who would rid this world of a boy they'd heard could not be killed, such was his power.

Oh, I can kill him, several of them were thinking as they rushed forward.

This is always a painful part of the story for me. I have to hear how my son stood, undefended, even his cousin so occupied, trading blows with another, my boy was a great target about to be destroyed. And what did he do as death approached? He smiled upon the warrior who raced toward him. Ayowantha *saw* him—the spark we all have, the spark that is unlike any other. He *saw* this man and loved him.

This first warrior watched my son's face as he raised an arm to strike a killing blow. Ayowantha beamed at him, and the man stopped short in confusion. He later said he saw acceptance there, in an enemy's eyes. Warmth, approval. "How can I kill this man who thinks so highly of me?" he wondered. So he dropped his weapon and moved to embrace my boy, then stood beside him as protector. The next warrior was angrier now to see a fellow Huron so unmanned. Oh, I shall bash in his skull, he was thinking. Until he, too, was *seen* in a way he'd never experienced before. Loved the way he imagined his father would have loved him if he'd lived long enough to know his child. He dropped his weapon and, disheartened, left the

battle. Soon the fighting ended though warriors on both sides were just getting warmed to their terrible work. Ayowantha was surrounded by the enemy, fearless men with the strength to tear him apart. But he was no longer in any danger, for he had made them into brothers.

The war parties became hunting parties that day, and together the men brought in enough game to produce a good feast. They shared the food and negotiated the end of war. Prisoners were released, wampum was offered, and six of the Huron stepped forward to replace the Kanien'kehá:ka warriors they'd injured on another day. Ayowantha suggested that foodstuffs should be given rather than their lives, but the six young warriors explained that they wanted to go with him to his village and learn his ways. This is how we adopted Huron warriors into our family.

The one we called Tailla, because that's where his people were from, is the one who told us what it was like that day from the Huron side of the story. He enjoyed remembering the surprise he felt when he changed his mind. We say that as if it's so simple, don't we? I'm hungry, no I'm not. I changed my mind. But when it is turned from killing to loving in the time it takes to sneeze, well, that makes the ground shake so hard you're knocked off your feet, and when you get up, nothing will ever look the same.

One of the people who most enjoyed telling the story of Ayowantha's first battle was my younger brother. He was the uncle who had shouted at his nephews, "This is the way it is done!" before leaping into the fight. After the strange events of that day, on the long walk back to our village, this same uncle teased my boy. "That is *not* how it's done." But, he admitted, when he glanced at their new Huron relatives following behind with their arms full of game, "Your way is better. No one dies, and we get a good feed."

Two summers later my boy was a man ready to marry. The young woman who became my daughter was of the Wolf Clan because her mother was a Wolf, yet we all thought she took more after her father's people who were Deer Clan from the Ononta'kehaka. While her mother would snap out her thoughts all day and not consider where the words fell, her father was shy and kept to himself. Like her father, my new daughter was so quiet many in our village thought she was simpleminded. They were stunned that a young man like Ayowantha would be drawn to such a girl. True, she was lovely in her silence—folding her slender legs beneath her with such grace when she settled in the grass, much like a doe. Yes, her eyes were the warm burnt brown of our maple sugar and her lips were

perfect lines like a man's bow. But how could he consult this wife and hear sense? How could she understand his talk with the spirits?

I knew my son's heart had chosen well. He saw what others failed to notice. My new daughter had a Wolf name she was given by her clan, but few of us used it. We called her simply Anokien, because she was so humble, like that first muskrat who dove to the bottom of the great water and retrieved earth for Sky Woman to stand on and mold into our Turtle Island home. Muskrat never boasted like the other, more majestic creatures who'd come up short. Often when I looked upon her, I thought of that tiny paw, stubbornly clutching a pinch of precious earth. Anokien was one who observed, loved, offered the service of her labor, and only spoke when words were truly needed. As Ayowantha liked to say, "Yes, there is power in words. But there is also great power in silence."

She herself once explained to me why she was so quiet. "When I speak, I am just one girl. When I'm silent, listening to another's conversation or to their stillness, then I connect with them and no one is alone."

It would take Shawiskara longer to find a wife. He was so insolent and contrary, discord trailed him wherever he went. Only a fearless woman with strong patience or her own stinging temper would be able to manage him. In the end he was accepted by a Bear woman, a girl so sturdy she could have carried my nephew on her back a good distance. Their match startled me at first; she was a person of great humor who crossed her tree-limb arms whenever she laughed, as if to keep from falling into the joy of a funny remark. Then I saw how her teasing soothed him, how the harmless needles they tossed back and forth was a sharpness he needed. When he moved into her people's Longhouse he was surrounded by Bears who were unimpressed with my nephew's reputation. This settled him down more than I'd expected. Shaskoharo:wane and I were pleased that our boys had married so well.

My son's wife quickly brought two daughters into the world, and I liked to tease them that they were stars I dragged down from the night sky and cooled in the creek before I could hold them the way a grandmother should. "This is why I blow gently on your foreheads," I told them, "I'm trying to turn you from burning stars into sweet girls."

Ayowantha was elected to replace the head man Faithkeeper when he died, and soon after I was chosen by my fellow Turtles to be their Clan Mother. My husband joked that now he really had to behave since his relatives were Head Turtles and he was just a simple Bear. I pinched him affectionately when he talked

this way, and he would groan as if in terrible pain and call me Snapping Turtle. These were times that will always make me smile when I remember them.

Before dawn the Thunders cracked open the sky with their warning blasts. Quickly we rose from our beds to burn tobacco and welcome them. I knew Ayowantha would be rising in the Longhouse of his wife's people, the Wolf Clan, washing before settling down to smoke a special pipe he used to greet the Thunders—a shorter pipe that would easily fit in their small hands. We went outside and he was there, singing and talking to the little grandfathers who seed the sky. The Thunder Beings brought rain and a cleansing wind that would nourish all the parched creatures of the earth, but the storm hadn't arrived yet. The air was so fat not one of us was hungry. To breathe was to eat.

This was a joyful time, the signal that new life would push up all around us, and don't we always favor beginnings? Yet my son looked serious, downcast, and I noticed Anokien gently touch his shoulder as if to support him. He glanced up at her and said, "More than rain is coming."

Later, when the showers poured on our settlement and we clustered together to receive the refreshing bath, I stood beside my boy and asked him what he'd seen. "This is truly a day for beginnings," he answered. "The storm brings guests who will be new to us in many ways." Then he patted my arm and smiled as if to comfort us both.

Rain soaked into the grateful earth and the thirsty mouths of flowers and plants, nourished the intricate arrangement of our crops. The bad air was swept out, Longhouses opened at either end to let the breeze refresh our home spaces and our minds. Water sparkled in the grass and among the leaves as if stars had fallen on our shoulders. It was a beautiful day.

Just as Ayowantha predicted, two men were spotted approaching our settlement. A quick council was assembled, which included me as Clan Mother of the Turtles. Our War Chief and his head men were ever cautious when it came to strangers and were ready to arrange a military greeting for the travelers. But Ayowantha suggested we offer them welcome. He reminded us how our Creator, Shonkwaia'tison, had disguised Himself as a humble old man and visited our people long ago, only to be turned away in village after village. "It was a woman of the Bear Clan who finally showed Him hospitality and so He gave her the gift of

His medicine. The Creator has a part in each of us, does He not? And if we turn a stranger away or meet him with violence, aren't we doing harm to our Creator?"

There was a murmur of agreement after my son spoke, and I had to pull inside my shell to conceal a mother's pride in the wisdom of her child.

We brought forth the best of our winter cache of food so we could offer our visitors a fine meal before learning what business they had with us. Cooking was well underway by the time they set foot in the village. One was a young man like us, Onkwehonwe, one of the Original People. Though he stood tall and thrust out his chest like a male bird seeking its mate, I could sense his fear in the sweat that misted his face. He introduced himself as Michael—a name we hadn't heard before. He said his father was Kanien'kehá:ka and his mother was Mahican, and so we understood that he grew up in confusion. His companion was a man he looked to at all times, as if for direction. This other man was smaller than Michael, slender as a twig. I might have mistaken him for a woman but for the nest of hair he wore on his face—a dark brown pelt of fur that hid his mouth. He wore a long black garment that covered his entire body like a blanket, though winter had been broken by the arrival of the Thunders. His black headdress was an odd shape, almost like the head of a fox, but it didn't come from any creature that had lived. He said his name was Bartholomew, and that he was sent by his Creator to tell us the news of His son, the one called Yesu. It was difficult to follow the words the men produced between them. Bartholomew was learning to make our talk, but some of the words stuck in the back of his throat like little bones. Michael assisted, but sometimes this caused them to talk over one another in a mangle of noise. I watched the hairy-faced man closely, fascinated by the pale sheen of his skin—like the underbelly of a grub worm plucked from the earth. He liked to grab our hands and squeeze them in his own as if he were going to keep them.

Our visitors came during the hungry time when winter still freezes the ground at night which then melts into a thick paste of mud once the sun is launched into the sky. It wasn't yet time to chase the fish or gather young squabs from the trees. We ate carefully to stretch what stores remained and conserved our strength for coming labors. This was a good time for stories.

We were puzzled by our guests. What were their intentions, we wondered? Our Chief finally asked what business they wanted with us. Was there something to trade? Did they have a grievance? The older man, Bartholomew, with the help of his young friend, told us he had come because he loved us and feared we were in great peril. Our War Chief and his council sat forward at this news. Bartholomew explained that the danger he predicted for us was not one of the body, threatening our lives, but the more serious matter of the spirit.

"This is your territory, I believe," he gestured at Ayowantha. My son bowed his head in response. He told us that whatever prayers we spoke to the spirits fell on empty ears because there was no one to hear us but Bartholomew's Creator, and His only son, Yesu. He said this Yesu was a loving man who cried to think of what our experience would be once we had lived out our pitiful lives and were planted in the ground. We would suffer in the spirit world, forever and ever, roasting in the hottest fires with no one to take pity on us and relieve our suffering. As he spoke, children began to cry, and one old man who was a fierce warrior in his youth spat on the ground. He didn't interrupt our guest, which would have been rude, but he muttered a few words those seated near him could hear.

He said: "We are not afraid of your fires. Pick up your terror and leave us."

The Black Coat spoke with passion of how he loved us and wanted nothing more than to rescue us, his face glowing red as if he already stood in hot coals. He didn't seem to notice how smiling faces became stern and families that had sprawled against each other with graceful ease were stiff and uncomfortable now, children clutched tightly by their parents. Michael noticed the tension that salted the air, and a dew of sweat gathered on his forehead.

The grumbling of the Black Coat's insulted audience became louder, and Ayowantha spoke up when Bartholomew sipped water to restore his voice. "These are sacred matters," my son began. "We are happy to hear your stories, after all, why should their difference cause offense?" He looked at all of us seated there, his family and friends, and smiled at us to restore a good feeling. "But we are not prepared to receive them in the right way, and so they fall on the ground. Also, important stories require a response. We must offer questions to help us move the meaning better in our minds." The people voiced their approval as my son spoke and were behind him when he proposed to formalize this talk and begin a conversation the next morning when our eyes and ears were fresh and the light of the sun could show us what was true and what was shadow. And so the next morning we began what people later called "The Conversations," where the Black Coat and his Yesu battled my son with words.

The morning was cool as we settled together in the Ceremonial Longhouse. The entire village had turned out, from the youngest infant to the oldest man.

Bartholomew looked pleased as he watched us gather before him; he stroked the leather bundle Michael had told us was a Bible—a place where all the stories important to the Black Coat's people were marked down so they would not forget them. I wondered, how precious could these stories be if the ones who followed them couldn't hold them in their minds? But I bit my tongue to prevent this impolite question from leaving my lips.

Ayowantha gestured for our guest to have the honor of opening the proceedings with a prayer of thankfulness. Bartholomew rose before us and stretched his arms wide. He looked toward the roof above our heads as he spoke these words in a song-like chant: "I thank Thee, oh, merciful Father, who has made the Heaven and the Earth and all things, including Thy children assembled here. I thank Thee for Thy blessings and ask Thee to watch over us and guide us onto the path of righteousness where we shall find our true salvation." He dropped his arms then and settled on a bench. He looked around at us, offered a smile that went crooked as if his mouth was divided in its intentions. The silence became thick as heavy smoke and even filled what chinks there were in the old Longhouse. Clearly he was finished.

Ayowantha appeared flustered, which was a surprise to all of us who knew him well. He smoothed the air before him with his hands as if to smooth his thoughts. Decided, he said to us: "When we gather at these times to produce important talk, we must begin with the Ohen:ton Karihwatekwen, where we offer our thanks for all the wonders that surround us in this life. Our list is long, from the Earth who is our Mother and the Beings that populate her, the soil itself, the plants and trees, flowers and crops, the animals and insects and birds, the Thunders and the Sun and the Moon, the winds, our fellow human beings in all their variety—grandparents and mothers, the elders and children, our leaders who guide us well, the Nations that surround us, the spirits, including Sky Woman and her grandsons, especially He Who Holds Up the Sky, the Sacred Beings, including Peacemaker who taught us the Great Law of Peace, and always the Creator, who has made us so well. As I said, our list is long because appreciation fills our hearts with happiness, and it is an honor to be able to name our many joys. But today we offer this brief prayer of thanks out of deference to our visitor whose ways are not like ours. Our hearts are larger than these few words and hold more thanks than I am speaking now. We honor the gifts we have been given, on this our minds agree."

There were sounds of astonished assent from all corners of the Longhouse. Our usual prayer of thanks could take all morning and continue even as the sun climbed high into the sky. But I understood my son's thinking—he didn't want to shame our honored guest, to show him how small was his gratitude compared to ours.

Despite the grace of my son's hospitality, the air between him and the Black Coat was thick with aggression as if they carried weapons we couldn't see with our eyes. Ayowantha tried to clear away the bad feelings by offering this reminder: "Words are trouble. Each one is medicine that can cure or kill. I tell you, there is no substance, no sinew or joint or strand of hair that can bend as many ways as a word. So let us be careful, my brother, when we set our stories against one another and expect to win. There is no true victory one way or the other with this clever noise. I ask you, who are your relatives? And how do you treat them? And if you love as much of the world as we do, then maybe we will listen. And if you treat your relatives as well as we do, then maybe we will believe you."

The Black Coat nodded through my son's speech but appeared confused when he heard the questions. "My relatives? You mean my mother and my sister?"

"Yes," Ayowantha said, "But also your trees and rivers, the wise little frogs, the crops that feed you, the Thunders that bring rain. How well do you love them? Has Yesu taught you to treat them well?"

Bartholomew's mouth hung open, and I saw the fur on his lips move with his short breaths.

"You have these beings in the world you come from?" Ayowantha pressed.

"Yes, yes, of course. But we don't think of them as relatives, though we honor everything the Lord has made in His great wisdom." Bartholomew then went on to tell us the story of Yesu's birth and life and mission, and how he suffered in his death so that all of us could be clean of the wrongdoing that is ever inside us, even as babies newly born. The warriors were most interested in the news of Yesu's death, the extent of his injuries, length of his suffering, and whether he made a good death without complaint. They understood the sacrifice of flesh and pain and were willing to lay down their lives for each of us as he had done.

"No, no," the Black Coat interrupted when the warriors approved of Yesu's death. "He didn't just die as other men do, He returned to us, risen from the very grave where His body had been placed by those who loved Him. He conquered death and won eternal life, as we all can."

Murmurs of assent flowed around the Black Coat, and he looked pleased with our reaction.

Ayowantha explained: "Many of us have seen our loved ones in dreams, the ones who have left us and live now in the village of the dead. There they wait for us and show us not to be afraid of this life's end."

Bartholomew's satisfaction did not last long; he became angry with my son's words and shook his head so hard we heard his neck crack. Michael reached to touch his hand with a warning finger to remind him of his place. He took a few careful breaths and told us in as calm a voice as he could manage: "These dreams you talk of are dangerous things. How do you know where they come from? I say they come to you from demons who wish to work sorcery on you and confuse your mind—keep you from the good path that will lead to happiness. These dreams should be ignored and forgotten."

As one, we held our breath. We were so quiet we could hear the drone of a fly circling high above us, searching for a way out of the Longhouse.

"This is your belief," Ayowantha finally said, and our lungs began to work again. "And you do well to follow the instructions your Creator has given you. But Yesu never lived in the territory of the Kanien'kehá:ka, the territory of the Haudenosaunee. His teachings never grew from this ground. Has he told you what flowers can be collected to cure a fever, which herbs make a healing tea that soothes the cough? And our Peacemaker, sent to us as a Sacred Being to teach us the ways of peace, He was never a demon. What demon plants peace and teaches us to link arms with those we once fought as enemies? I say that you honor us to share your powerful stories, but they cannot replace those that have grown from the very earth we stand on. Our stories are true for us because they are alive. We see them and hear them, and life would not be possible without them."

Tears had gathered in my son's eyes, and mine as well. He gently shook himself to clear his mind. I glanced at my husband who sat with the men on the eastern side of the Longhouse. He was always of a mild temper like a slumbering bear, never quick to take offense, but the Black Coat's words had wounded him. He slumped forward and gripped the edge of his bench with mighty fists. I knew he was quietly working to pour water on the fires of his anger. He would not lift his eyes to meet mine, yet he was aware of me and dipped his head once as if to say, "Yes, I know you are there watching over me. All will be well."

My son and Bartholomew breathed heavily as if they had just run a race. Ayowantha struggled to restrain his emotions and dissolve them into a wide lake of peace. I saw his face recover its warmth.

Then Bartholomew stood and walked before us in a stamping way, nearly panting with frustration. He stopped in front of my son, held out his hands as if to beg, but his words were no match for the gesture; they accused: "Stories may live and yet produce evil."

Without pause my son was on his feet and moved into the open space, surrounded by his people. He stretched his arms to acknowledge us all and asked: "What evil do you find in our midst? You are strangers and yet you are welcomed and looked after like beloved relatives visiting from far away. You see the love we have for one another, the generosity of those who can hunt and fish and produce the bounty of our Three Sisters—how they share what they have with the old ones and widows first, the children whose fathers are in the ground. You have heard of our ceremonies which are festivals of gratitude so that the Creator is reminded every day how much we appreciate His gifts of the relatives He sent us to populate our world. You see how we honor the creatures whose lives are taken to nourish us—they were not made for that purpose, they have their own business with the Creator, yet they abide by our compact and make sacrifices to keep the world in balance. You see us make brothers of the enemy and work to build peace. Where are the long shadows that stretch across these practices?"

A vast silence fell on us like a fog. Even babies refused to suckle or squawk. Michael was tugging at Bartholomew's coat to pull him back to the bench. Ayowantha sat and stared at his hands.

My husband rose in this emptiness, and even before he spoke his presence gathered us into protective arms. He faced the Black Coat when offering this speech: "I listen to your stories with interest and am glad your Creator has touched your heart so that you honor Him. This is unexpected news that hits me as if I've returned from the battlefield, shot full of arrows. I bleed in ways you cannot see. The blood brings questions, so many of them my tongue is confounded. But I will offer the first. Where are the women in your story? You have heard us talk of our Mother, the Earth, and Sky Woman who came down to get everything started. You have met our Clan Mothers whose wisdom is so cherished we rely on them to select our leaders, and with one word they can remove his antlers and replace him. My wife here is a Clan Mother of the Turtles, and in all our life together she's never said words without sense. She's never said words I would strike down. Oh, she sometimes expresses disgust with her husband, what man is perfect? But then she holds her tongue and speaks with a look. I tell you, her glare could scald the hairs off a dog."

The men were whooping now with the relief of a good tease. I waved my hand at Shaskoharo:wane as if he annoyed me, but had to cover the smiles of my mouth. My husband cleared his throat and continued: "When you tell us these stories empty of women, they cannot walk properly on their one leg. They sound unfinished because they ignore half the world."

The Longhouse erupted with sounds of approval. Bartholomew sat down heavily on a bench as if to organize himself. When he rose he seemed changed, subdued. He moved to the center of the floor without stamping and glanced all around him with sorrowful eyes. Hands clasped together in appeal like a man pleading for his life, he spoke again: "I am a poor servant to my Lord. I move your hearts in the wrong direction because I cannot find the words that will open the door between us. You ask about our women. In my world they are cherished, too, but differently. They are sweet flowers to be sheltered and protected, and woe unto him that does them any harm. We do not always see the strength in them that you appreciate. But our Lord came not just from His almighty Father, but from woman as well—our beloved Mary, Mother of God, who was chosen to be the Divine Womb. She loves us and intercedes on our behalf when we suffer. She is Mother to us all." His gentler words washed through the Longhouse like a soft rain, and we were more in his hands than before. "Can we not agree that my Creator, my God, created you as well?" His question took us by surprise, the humility of a question in the midst of all his certainty.

Ayowantha stood and faced him—they were ill-matched, for the Black Coat's head was no higher than my son's shoulder. His tone was tender as he addressed Bartholomew. "Perhaps the same Creator made us and talks to us differently because He knows we don't all like the same stories."

The Black Coat accepted this as a victory of some kind. He grabbed Ayowantha's hand and squeezed it like a caught fish. Michael's face relaxed, and he even allowed himself a small smile. "The Conversations" were ended for that day, but I knew they would continue, in some form or another, as long as Bartholomew's people occupied our territory.

Shawiskara's behavior was strange to me during the period of these talks. My nephew who was always so happy when conflict blossomed restrained himself now from speaking his thoughts, from showing any reaction on his face. He became friendly with Michael who seemed grateful for the protection, and I even noticed Shawiskara smile on occasion when they spoke. I did not trust that smile, it was too pleasant. I knew my nephew's honest grin was a smirk that twisted his face until he resembled a medicine mask. I whispered these thoughts to my husband one evening as we ate our supper. "He's working some mischief we cannot see," I predicted.

Shaskoharo:wane grunted in agreement, unworried. "Probably," was all he said.

We lived with our guests as well as we could. Bartholomew never offered to help us in our labors but was always trying to wet us with the water he carried in a leather jug. He said he wanted to cleanse our spirits, and I privately thought he should worry more about cleansing his flesh. We could always sense his arrival, even when our backs were turned, for the sour fragrance of his skin announced him. He argued with my boy on several occasions, pressing him to renounce our reliance on dreams and visions, insisting the direct experience we had with our Maker was not to be trusted.

Ayowantha listened patiently, his children hanging off him like ripening fruit. More than once he explained the trap that snared them. "You tell us that when we hear the voice of our Creator and other Sacred Beings they are ghost voices imagined by our brains, or, if they are real, then their source is not good, but malicious and evil. You counsel us to mistrust our ears and our eyes, our hearts and our stories, our ancestors and our dreams. Yet you see the good that comes of our ancient practices. You say you are right. I say I cannot believe you. Your story. My story. Why do they have to crack heads like antlered bucks? Why does one need to trample the other? Why can they not speak to each other in friendship?"

This left the Black Coat unsatisfied, pacing through our village like a man in a hurry, yet traveling nowhere. His dark eyes burned in his face and he was without peace. One morning he caught my son attending an old woman who would die by nightfall. Ayowantha held her hand and said something to make her laugh, an exhausted dry husk of a laugh. The Black Coat offered to wet her with his water so she would not burn in the fires, and her eyes clouded with fear.

"No," she whispered, "no."

Ayowantha ignored Bartholomew and sang her a song he composed just for her on the occasion of her dying. He sang that her spirit was a hummingbird trapped inside a shell, fluttering, fluttering, yearning to fly. "Little hummingbird, we shall release you. Beautiful One, we will cry with joy when we see you gain the sky."

The old woman had tears in her eyes when he finished the song, and with one last effort of strength she wiped them from her eyes and spread them across her forehead. "This is the only water I need to cover me," she breathed.

Several nights later the Black Coat sat down with my son at his fire and began more of his talk that reminded me of the bite of mosquitoes, how they take just a little blood each time and are never full. He said he knew that the peaceful ways of our village were not the ways of all our people. That he'd heard accounts of the savage killing, maiming, and torture that were our ancient customs. He said he wanted to save us from butchery and the brutal life of animals.

I thought my son would surely reach the limits of his patience but I was wrong. He was quiet for many breaths, taking the time to choose careful words. "Our stories and our ways are like those maps you carry that show us what paths are good, what is the pattern of the world around us. But maps can change. Deganawidah, our Peacemaker, taught us the Law of Peace and He returns to us in our dreams and visions to teach us more so we can perfect the peace. The Great White Pine that represents our Law is a living tree, and it continues to grow, its roots spreading far beyond the soil of its birth. Yes, our neighbors don't always live as we do, but they listen to the stories, and the peace will cast its seeds farther and deeper. As long as the stories live. We are not perfect, but we grope forward in effort. Let me look at you, my brother."

Ayowantha leaned forward and gazed deeply into the Black Coat's blazing face. "I have not been to your world, yet I see the suffering there, behind your eyes. The instruments you use to torture the ones who don't share your stories, the fires where you burn them when you cannot change their minds. You find here what you have left at home because that is always the way of things. We see only what we expect to see. I wish you peace and am weary of violent talk. Let us visit as friends and enjoy the children."

My son's wife plumped overnight, and I realized she was carrying another child.

"This one is a boy," Ayowantha said. "I've seen him in my dreams. His sisters will be little mothers to him, and the rest of us will rarely get to touch him."

This was already true, for my granddaughters delighted in talking to their unborn brother, their soft cheeks resting against the small mound where he was coiled. When I saw them waiting so eagerly for his arrival I thought of my own sister and how I'd played at being her little mother. The memory was a sweetness that brings the salt, my husband's term for the happiness that makes us cry.

One morning I found Anokien gnawing on a tough piece of dried fish. She worked her jaws like a starving woman, and when I walked up to her she eyed me with hungry wolf eyes and nearly growled. She came back to herself then and asked my forgiveness. "I need fish," she said, her eyes desperate.

"You're fortunate then," I told her. "The waters should be running with salmon now, and it's time for us to chase them." She calmed and returned to the work of her meal.

Ayowantha, Shawiskara, and a group of other men agreed to leave the next day to bring in the fish. They might be gone for as long as a moon, so we put on the best feast we could with our remaining stores to see them off with full stomachs and good feelings. Later that night we sat outside beneath the stars and admired the fat moon that hung over us, low in the sky, as if she wanted to hear our stories. We laughed and sang songs, and then listened to the crickets make their night music. Ayowantha addressed us just when I was ready to stand and move inside toward my bed. His voice was serious, almost sorrowful, when he said he'd like to offer us a story he'd carried in his heart most of his life.

"It is the story of my time alone in the woods when I was just a boy."

I nearly gasped in surprise to hear him willing to share such a private tale, but I trusted him. He must have good reason to speak of his experience. I settled against my husband once more and waited to hear how my son had found his spirit so long ago.

Ayowantha's Story

One night I was unhappy. I was hungry from eating nothing more than roots and mushrooms, and I was lonesome for you and our family and everyone I'm used to seeing every day. I have never fought a war, but all of a sudden my thoughts took up weapons: war clubs, arrows and knives, brands of fire. They made war on me in a terrible way and caused me to suffer.

"You will never see your family again," one hissed at me. "You are a vain fool to think you will learn anything out here on your own. You will surely die, starve to death, and your body will be eaten by wolves." The battle went on like this for a night and a day—my thoughts spearing me again and again in cruel attacks that held me prisoner and made me cry. I might as well have been tied to a tree and tortured by an enemy. I'm ashamed to say I finally howled like a mad, dying creature, howled as the sun burnt up and turned into a black night.

The world's gone blind. This thought slashed through my mind because the moon and stars had closed their eyes and hid their light from me. *None of us can see,* was my despairing idea. But then a warm breeze came visiting from the south and greeted me with an embrace that warmed my shivering body and washed my face with a soft grandfather's hand. "I may be blind but I can still feel the world," I told myself, and as soon as those whispered words flowed out of me the moon appeared from behind the blanket of a cloud and the stars opened their eyes. I could see the family that surrounded me in that place—the pine trees and birch and spruce, the mosquitoes that loved the taste of me so well, the crows and owls in their clever nests, the faithful earth.

I had the strength to sit up and smoke some tobacco, share my pipe with the breeze that had soothed me. My thoughts were still noisy, still angry, but I could feel them growing weak because I was no longer feeding them my attention. I had an idea that maybe I could get them to surrender.

"Come, join me," I said in a voice that I worked to make calm and confident. I gestured to each side of me. "There is room for you to sit and share my pipe. I have a rich tobacco, the best you've ever tasted."

My tormentors were hesitant at first, but one after the other they cautiously shuffled into view and settled beside me in a dark circle. I couldn't see their features well, but their eyes were wild with passion and they held their bodies in ways that told me who they were. Hunger was no more than a stick with shaking hands that nearly dropped my pipe whenever it was his turn to take a draw of smoke. Anger was thick and tough as a rock, and he glared at me and never looked away. Fear was small and sat at a distance from the rest, but he had long arms that could reach and grab the pipe, and he always held onto it the longest as if he might not give it up. Pain was almost formless, like a heavy fog, and the smell of him was a rotting sweetness that made me dizzy. The final being that joined us was very handsome and very tall. He had the kind of bearing any warrior would want. He was the easiest one to make out because he carried with him a kind of glow, like he was a fallen star.

"Who are you?" I asked him, and he fluttered his eyes at me, almost like a woman.

He answered, "I am Ayowantha. I am the one you could be if you carried yourself with pride." He smiled then and tilted his head, and I knew he expected me to admire him. "Oh," was all I said.

By inviting them to sit with me I stole the weapons from my tormentors and calmed them with a good smoke. I looked into their faces and was no longer afraid of them. When I was ready to sleep I told them they had better go to their own lodges because I had no room for them in my blanket, which was nothing more than the grandfather wind from the south. Hunger, Fear, and Pain slinked away, and it was hard not to pity them. Anger stamped his feet and stood above me in a threatening way, but when I ignored him he said, "Hunh!" and lurched out of view.

The gleaming Ayowantha rose gracefully but stared at me in confusion. "Do you want *me* to leave?" he asked. I knew he was insulted.

"Yes, my brother," I said as gently as I could. "I will never be as fine as you, so I might as well not even try." My words seemed to pacify him. He stepped softly past me and shimmered into the night.

I had traded unhappiness for peace, but it was the hardest work of my life. I tell you, when your thoughts attack it may be a war without blood, but the death is far more painful. Sit with your enemies and share a smoke and eventually they'll surrender their weapons. Then you will see them for what they are and have pity.

The moon had gone from a disappeared, eaten up moon to one that was round and fat as a pumpkin. Slowly it starved again, yet I was no closer to understanding my journey. I awakened one cold morning with a skin of frost covering my body. I stretched to my feet, then walked a few miles to warm myself with movement. I came across a white granite boulder blocking my path. Light from the sun poured down that rock and, oh, how I wanted to press into its side.

"Thank you, older brother, for letting me rest here," I said to the rock as I settled against him.

Gratitude is a powerful gift, and even a small gesture as the one I offered granite was enough to change the course of my life. Granite heard me and took me for a relative. He opened his fist and it was now the palm of his hand at my back, an unexpected miracle of flesh like my own. Or was I the one who changed to become stone? All I can say is that I was no longer Ayowantha, separate from that sunned-on boulder. It grew from my back like a tree, an impossible wing, another self. I was granite, with boulder strength and patience. Then I noticed an ant journeying across one of my folded legs. What courage, I thought, for him to mount a giant.

"I honor your bravery, little brother," I said. I could feel myself smile a strong boulder smile.

The ant stopped in his tracks at the warm summit of my knee and looked into my face, majestically bowed his head. Honor is a powerful gift, and by showing respect to the smallest grain of a being, I became his relative. His dutiful clan swarmed from the grass and their intricate tunnels to greet me. My legs were covered with relatives, marching soberly from one hill of leg to the next. There were so many of them they could have lifted me and carried me into another life. You see, I was beginning to learn that this man sitting before you, this Ayowantha, is not a man with edges and private thoughts that lock me up into a body. I opened my heart to all my relatives, opened my eyes so I could see how many there were, opened my ears so I could listen to their stories.

Yes, I am Ayowantha, but I am also grass and pine, and boulder and ant. I am my Huron enemy and I am even the Hairy Faces who don't recognize me. My heart is a great Longhouse with many fires—it would take a lifetime to walk from the entrance to the other side, and you are all welcome there.

I stayed in that place for several days and my body lived in a stone way, with few requirements. I had no need for food or water, the release of waste, or even movement. I closely watched the world that had absorbed me into its fellowship—a new confederacy. If a person had leaned his ear against my chest I don't think he would have heard my heart or counted any breaths. Who knows how long I would have remained like that had I not been roused, interrupted? A visitor arrived from the east—the same path I'd been traveling. He was ancient, the oldest man I've ever seen, and he leaned on a thick post as he walked in a careful, turtle way. He stopped when he saw me as if he were surprised. He blinked then, and I noticed that wrinkled as he was, he had bright, mischievous baby eyes. Wondering eyes that beheld everything as new.

"Why are you sitting there practicing your death?" he asked me. I had expected a dried up croak of a voice, but his words were wet as water, slippery like a fish that squirts from your hands when you grab it.

"I am learning patience from my brother the rock. I am learning quiet."

The old man laughed and smacked the earth with his post. "Why do you want to do that? I know who you are. I know where you come from. I've heard stories about the special boy who is growing into a remarkable young man. And here I find you—dumb as stone. Useless." He shook his head and patted the post as if it needed comfort.

I didn't answer back. He was my elder and entitled to his thoughts. Besides, I was still brother granite, capable of great endurance.

"But now that I've found you I can urge you to put an end to this foolishness.

I can see forward into parts of your story you haven't lived yet. Yours can be a glorious story that will never be forgotten." He stared at me, waiting for an answer.

"Thank you for wanting to help, Grandfather," I finally spoke. Each word was slow and heavy, a pebble that fell from my mouth. "I'm sure you are very wise and know many things I will never understand, but I must follow my own path."

"Tsah!" His tongue clicked against his teeth in irritation, and he spat on the ground. "The path you are meant to travel will bring you power. You will gain influence over many people who will gladly make war for you and conquer other tribes. The territory of the Haudenosaunee will extend to the great waters, and twenty generations from now you will still be remembered."

Perhaps Ayowantha, a lone boy far from his mother and his village, would have brightened at such words and eagerly followed the ancient man with baby eyes. But this Ayowantha sat naked in the dirt, held by the wise earth. And this Ayowantha had granite at his back, granite which is never easily moved or shaken. My answer was boulder plain: "Thank you, Grandfather, but that is not my story."

He lifted his post then with great effort and knocked me on the head—a blow that might have killed me on another day. The wood cracked and split in two, slid harmlessly from my crown.

"Rock-head!" he shouted, and tears gathered in the old man's baby eyes. He picked up one half of the post and stamped away, charging over his shoulder, "You are a disappointment and a waste!"

When he had passed and was no longer visible, the thuck of the post no longer heard, my brother ants swarmed from their tunnels and washed over the soil that bore prints of the old man's passage. Grain by grain they moved the earth until it was smooth of prints and the old man's path was scraped clean. Even a boulder can cry, for I felt tears on my cheeks when I realized their gift, their service. They offered me new ground, so that when I left I would make my own path.

The old man's visit had roused me, and I was coming back into my body, hearing the grumbling noise of a stomach that has gone too many days without food. Night was spilling its darkness into the sky when I heard a hummed song, the voice high and sweet the way a butterfly would sound if you could hear it. An old woman arrived from the east, her steps so light I couldn't hear them or see any evidence of her trail. She walked like a cloud. I knew she was old because her eyes were full of stories, and to look into them took you back more generations than a person could easily count. But her face was smooth as if she'd just been born, and her hair was a colorless fluff like the down molted from young birds.

"He-he-he," she laughed when she saw me. Her arms waved open in delight. "Hello, Grandson," she said. "Have you seen my old man come along this way?"

"Yes, I have, when the day was just beginning."

She nodded her head at me. "That old troublemaker!" she said with warm affection. "Whenever he takes off on a journey, no warning, just stands up and heads out as he pleases, he causes all kinds of problems. Gets people all worked up and confused. Then I have to follow after him and put things right again, which is a lot of hard work. Once he's back home he isn't so bad. He gets that mischief out of his heart. It doesn't look like he's done *you* any harm?" She squinted her eyes but I wasn't fooled, I knew she had clear vision, could see into me and past me, through me and around me. She was just being humble.

"No," I answered. "He offered me a different path, a different story, but I'm content to be where I am."

"Good for you!" she said, the fluff of her hair bobbing. "Nothing to clean up here. I'm so proud of you." She paused then so she could smile—a beautiful, generous, breaking-open-the-world kind of smile. Then she laughed. "He-he-he." Gave herself up to it the way a starving man falls on a stew. "He-he-he."

I laughed along with her in a coughing way, spitting gravel.

When she was finished she held her hands in front of her and watched me intently. "Ayowantha," she said, her voice kind but serious. "I have a feeling you'll be ready to get going again tomorrow. The next part of your journey won't be accomplished on foot. You'll need a canoe." The words felt true even though the message was unexpected. "You're heading into Huron country, but don't worry, Peacemaker will protect you. He wants to see you."

If my brother granite had not been at my back I would have shivered with awe. "How can this be?" I whispered.

She ignored my question. "Yes. You will travel in a stone canoe, just as He did, but this time you'll be working backward, traveling to Him rather than the land of your people. You'll see, it will come to you in the morning and you'll have the boulder strength to lift it into the water. What an adventure!" she said with excitement.

I was suddenly the most afraid I had ever been. I felt Fear's long arms reach into me. He squeezed my heart with greedy hands. "Who am I to bear such an honor?" I breathed.

"Who are you? Who are you?" The old woman turned in a full circle and though she was quick, the effect was gradual, as if that one turn had spun us into the next day. A fire built in my chest and scorched Fear's hands so he released my heart with a yelp. Courage blossomed in my chest, kindled by fire.

The old woman spoke again: "Who are you, but Ayowantha. Who are you, but rock and pine and grass and ant. Who are you, but eagle and birch, owl egg and bear. Who are you but earth?" She squinted again, and my shame made me look down. "You are everything," she concluded. "And that is enough."

All night I considered the old woman's words and the next morning moved for the first time in several days, turning my head one direction and then the other to see if a canoe had sprung up from the ground like a flower. No. I looked up and could see no boat of stone falling from the sky.

"Farewell, brother rock," I finally said, and moved to separate my human flesh from the side of the boulder that had given me shelter and strength. I was stiff, sore, and found I couldn't rise. What is this? I spoke again to my fierce relative: "Brother, I have further to go in my travels. I will miss you and honor you for the rest of my days."

I heard a sigh then, a grinding groan, and this time was able to break away from the white granite boulder at my back. I staggered under a terrible weight and nearly toppled over. Once I righted myself and found balance, I discovered that my back had formed a deep hollow in the rock and when I stood up I'd broken a piece off the side of granite's face. The canoe had been there all along—my refuge. I hoisted the canoe higher on my shoulders and tipped in such a way that I could see where I was heading.

I walked with the sun and when it was high in the sky I finally came to our lake Kaniataryo. I heaved the canoe off my shoulders, into the restless water that foamed around my legs like the sweet milk bubbles of babies. I was happy to be a boy again and stretched my limbs to shake off the last stiffness of stone. I had no paddle, no oar to help me steer the canoe, but I figured this wasn't an ordinary vessel and perhaps the flat of my hand would be enough. I stepped into the smooth white canoe and settled myself, then placed a hand in the water and pushed.

"Whaaaaaa," I cried out in wonder as the canoe shot forward with great speed. I laughed at the pleasure of skimming through waves like a water bug, chasing the wind like a man courting his one true love. It didn't take very long to reach the bay near Peacemaker's home. The canoe was a clever companion who knew just where to take me, and when we arrived it gently slowed and ground its way toward the shore until it held fast in the shallows. I stepped from the vessel and waded onto land, stood in a place I had never seen before except in stories. A head emerged from the crest of a distant hill, popped up like a ground squirrel and then vanished. I stood bewildered, uncertain of my next step. I was looking upon bright, scalded dunes that glistened in the heat of the day, the green comfort of woods on a ledge above me. A figure suddenly leapt off the nearest crumbling hill, pitched onto me so we fell in a tangle into the warm sand.

"Aaaaaahhhhh," he screamed as he pinned me on my back. Instinct made me buck him off, and so we grappled, wrestled, threw each other, grunted, and made all kinds of noise. Neither of us could best the other, and at last we paused to pant for air, wipe the sweat from our burning eyes. My opponent was a boy about my own age. Once he caught his breath he started laughing and fell on his back in the soft sand. Laughter made his entire body bounce and shake, until the ground beneath my feet rocked a little and I fell down beside him.

"Ah, that was fun!" he finally said. "That's what you get for trying to kill me that time at the Falls."

I froze then, and the sand felt to me like powdered snow. *This* was Peacemaker, the Sacred Being who brought us the Great Law of Peace. No wonder his laughter made the ground shake. He was here, in boy form to match me, teasing about the time, so many generations ago, when my people had forced him up a tree, a tall pine, then chopped it down so he would plunge to his death in the great Falls. Only after the miracle of his survival did we open our ears to hear his words of peace.

He turned onto his side, head resting on his hand, and watched me—eyes become day stars, a friendly wolf grin spread on his face. "Ayowantha, at last," he said. "You are welcome here. I've watched your life with great interest and knew that someday you would find your way to me. We have important talk to make, but are you hungry? I'll feed you first. Your ears will listen better when you've been fed."

Peacemaker led me to a campfire he'd constructed right there on the dunes beside baskets full of food that looked different from our daily fare—the fish so fresh they glistened and wriggled as though they were still swimming in water, the ears of corn like juicy strips of sun. This is spirit food, I thought. We ate roasted corn and the sweet white meat of trout, baked to a melting tenderness in its skin. I thanked these beings as I took nourishment from them and was suddenly offered visions of what their life had been.

Peacemaker smiled at me. "You will never eat the same," he said. "Now you'll know the story of every creature that offers its life to sustain yours. Come, sit with me."

We settled across from each other and I watched how Peacemaker rested so easily on folded legs. Yes, he had the features of a boy, but then he also resembled a hill of sand. He was himself, and yet he was everything else in this world.

"You are a Water Being," he told me in a hushed voice.

I closed my eyes and felt my innards melt, felt the deep heart of me open to become the lake I had so recently crossed. I was filled with a patience very different from the kind I'd learned from granite. Rock taught me to hold firm and endure, but lake taught me that I could absorb any joy, any horror, any life, and any death, take it beneath the waves and dissolve its story.

"You are an Air Being," Peacemaker said.

Water left me and I was blown empty, scoured by the wildness of wind until my heart calmed and I soared as boundless air. Breath. I was the smallest piece of life and yet most necessary. Everywhere. Everywhere. My lodge was without limits.

"You are a Fire Being," Peacemaker said.

Air gasped as it burnt away, suffocated by flames. Oh! I was filled with the courage of fire—its focused intensity, its urgent hunger. I was awed by its power to transform life; reduce us to our essence of clean ash.

"You are an Earth Being," Peacemaker said.

My mouth was filled with the taste of clay, sweet as spring. I contained roots and flowers and eggs and worms, rocks and molten fire, water streams and air pockets, ants and love and bodies and blood, unborn generations and secrets. I was heavy with life and felt the way a woman must in her final months before a son or daughter is born. I was dense with responsibility for accepting all that has died and reviving all that needs to grow again.

"You are Ayowantha, a Sacred Being." Peacemaker called me back to myself. But now I was changed.

The sky was painted in bright, going-away colors as night crept in with its dark blanket. Peacemaker said, "I will teach you a story and in the morning you'll take the canoe back across the lake, and then walk the path from west to east and return to your people. You'll teach them the story. There will be a time when some of them forget the words, but the story will live in their blood and in their hearts until they're ready to revive the teachings in order to save the world."

I settled myself more comfortably because I thought Peacemaker's story would surely be a long one—the words traveling between us from night until day. I was wrong. What Peacemaker told me took few words and might be considered simple by those of us who really like to huff and puff, talk until the mouth is dry, the tongue beaten to exhaustion. I offer a warning. What is simple to speak can be the most difficult to hear, the most difficult to live.

This is the story Peacemaker told me: "You have a good mind and I'm pleased that you and your people have accepted the Good News and made peace among yourselves to become the Haudenosaunee—the Five Nations Confederacy. Now it is time to forge a greater peace with those you consider enemies. Convince them to come to your side and lock arms in peace, not by warring against them, spilling their blood and forcing them to submit, but by loving them so well they cannot stand to live in separation any longer. You, Ayowantha, will be the best example of what I am saying.

"Our life is shaped by the twin brothers, Teharonhiawa:kon and Shawiskara—the one who gave us gifts that make the way smooth and beautiful, the one who gave gifts that make the way crooked and painful. Always their gifts go together, so your path won't be easy. Another kind of person is coming—you've already heard stories of his arrival. These men will confuse you for a while, and many of your people will be convinced that their story is superior to yours, their medicine the superior medicine. The gifts they offer will hold great power, but they are gifts that always end up taking away more than they bring. These Hairy Faces who are coming are your relatives too, no matter how different they are. Some will be good men and some will be bad, as it is with all men, but they carry themselves as conquerors. So the enemy is the arrogance of their minds.

"A great nation will be built on your shoulders, inspired by the ways of the Haudenosaunee and the Great Law of Peace, but this nation will not honor your stories or give them any credit. So it will be up to you to believe in the old stories even when the world around you says they are wrong, they are weak, they are dead. The great nation will not treat the earth as a relative, and eventually she'll be forced to make war on this and all other nations. That will be the time when your people will come forward with the old stories and offer them up again. You'll usher in the Time of the New Mind, and teach anyone who will listen about the

Great Law of Peace. You'll teach anyone who will listen how many relatives they have. Remember your stories and save them as you would your most favored child, your dearest grandmother. They are powerful medicine."

When my son finished speaking we leapt to our feet as if we were one creature. We embraced him and each other, tears flowing down our faces. His words had joined our hearts and so we smashed together as if we could move past the division of our bodies. Surely Bartholomew had been moved by this story? Surely he would see the goodness that trailed after my son, how he sewed us together and expanded our hearts? I looked around to find the Black Coat in the midst of our sudden celebration, and when I saw him, my lungs clenched, became breathless ice. He stood apart from us in a tight knot of men with sour faces. Who were they? I stepped back from my husband to have a clear view and saw them plainly: my nephew and his new friend, Michael, stood beside Bartholomew, making urgent talk. I almost pitied them, how they stood in anger when they could have embraced joy, but their unhappiness scorched me with fear. The courage my son had planted in me during his talk was shaken, and it took a great will of effort to turn my back on these men and their schemes. I opened my heart and my strong arms and held everyone who came to me.

The fishing party left at dawn when the sky was streaked with red. It looked to me like a bloody hand was reaching for the sun. Ayowantha embraced me and his father, his cheerful young girls, and finally his wife. He promised he'd return very soon so she could enjoy fish that were not long out of the water. He held the mound of her belly with an open palm and bent to bid his son farewell.

I embraced Shawiskara and asked him to return to us unharmed. He patted my back and moved away without speaking. Michael had joined the fishing party since Bartholomew was well practiced now in our talk. He seemed relieved to be rid of the Black Coat and our village, and I doubted he would return again. The men strode off with the supplies they needed to harvest fish, the tobacco they would use to appease the spirits of those who were taken. I watched until they were no longer in view and the dust that had risen with their steps was returned to earth.

Just days after the fishing party left us, my son came to me in a dream. He stood waist deep in our river, planted so firmly there the water didn't push him at all. His arms were full of bright fat salmon that were still living. They flew from his embrace in a great circle before him—up past his head then down, returning to his arms. He watched their motion with great wonder. Finally he noticed me and offered the most beautiful smile I'd ever seen. He said, "Mother, look at all the fish!" I wanted to ask when he'd return, why were the fish flying that way, where was his cousin, but I couldn't speak. I could only watch him admire the magic of the fish. Then Shaskoharo:wane woke me because I was crying.

"He will not return to us," I said, and was surprised by the words.

"What?" My husband comforted me while he slept, so he didn't hear my prediction.

As I feared, after a little less than a moon the men who chased the fish returned, weighed down by the bounty they'd hauled from the water, but Ayowantha, Shawiskara, and the Black Coat's young assistant were not with them. They said the three had disappeared one day as they each worked a different section of the river, but they hadn't thought much of it. They figured the men must have hurried back to bring a supply of fish to Ayowantha's wife. Shawiskara was an expert fisherman, so they thought it was also possible he led his cousin and friend to a secret location he didn't want to share with the others. No one worried as I did.

Moons passed and our woman Faithkeeper determined it was time for the Corn Planting Ceremony and then later for the Strawberry Festival, and still our boys had not returned. I was no longer the only one who feared we had lost Ayowantha and his cousin. The village was downhearted, and tempers became short. Bartholomew visited everywhere with his water, and though no one had accepted it yet, they were shaken by his claim that Yesu had worked this disappearance because His medicine was superior to Ayowantha's. He never said this to me or my husband, but Anokien overheard him and repeated word for word the speech he made. She told me this as she held my grandson, a sturdy boy who hooted at us like an old owl.

"This one," Anokien said, shaking her head. I was glad she had her son to distract her from worries.

After our Harvest Ceremony the trees began to change their color—the leaves painted to look like fire. I wore my heart like a heavy stone. I was polite to the Black Coat when his steps brought him near me, but now I saw him as a bird who eats the dead. I longed for him to take his water and his stories and leave us—he might have powerful medicine, yet it brought us nothing but sadness.

These were days where I could clearly see the need for good leadership. Ayowantha had inspired us with his peaceful ways, his patience and intelligence. He lifted us on his shoulders so we could have a higher view. Now our settlement had lost its great heart, and Bartholomew was trying to fill this emptiness with his fearful stories and medicine water that felt to me like a curse. How I longed to make conversation with the mothers of his clan, to move past his certainty that was the way of a child and hear his stories from measured minds—from women who understood that an open hand is more powerful than a fist.

My husband had just returned from a successful hunting trip where he'd brought down an elk. He groaned as we made ready to sleep. "My body tells me I'm no longer a young man," he whispered so only I would hear. "The elk left his mark on me."

I rubbed his back and teased him to make him feel young again, but all the while I was planning how to manifest my wishes and pull them to earth. The next day I worked with my husband to repair some mats that were beginning to wear at the edges and unravel. When we finished I grabbed my tobacco pouch and headed down the trail that led to the forest. Young ones stopped me to see if I needed their help, and each time I thanked them and told them, no, I was going to seek counsel in the woods. Their eyes widened with curiosity, but they didn't interfere or question me about these sacred matters. I was proud of them for looking after me so well, even though I had only a few gray hairs. To their young eyes I must have seemed quite old.

I never tired of walking with the trees. They stretched above me, taller than the proudest warrior, their arms filled with the nests of birds, their heads thrust into the sky where they could see more worlds than those of us who live on the ground. The trees are memory keepers who trace time in their bodies through the rings that mark their growth. They listen to us when we speak and will never forget if we are rude to them. I thanked them for letting me walk with them and asked for protection while I traveled in their world. Shoosh-shoosh, shoosh-shoosh. Their leaves answered in a gentle voice. I walked a different way than I usually did, following an urge to angle west, the direction of my heart, rather than north which is so straight ahead, like a man when he wants something. This is woman's business, I was thinking.

I came across a tall pine that had crashed to the ground, split near its base. It lay across my path like a great bench, and I patted it with my hand. I was always sad to see a pine in distress. "This is where we'll make our talk," I decided. "You have prepared our meeting ground and done us the great honor of providing a seat." I removed my tobacco and offered some to the ground, some to the tree, some to the spirits of the forest. Then I burned a rich palmful so the smoke would lift my prayer high into the sky, even beyond the heads of the tallest trees. This is what I prayed: "Mother of Yesu, the One who died to save the pitiful people of this world, please counsel with me, mother to mother, so I can hear of your powerful medicine from a woman's tongue. Men sometimes leave their hearts behind when they storm into the world, but we hold onto our hearts, and theirs, and can feel the truth of a story. Or its harm. I will not judge your medicine when I have only one man's words to tell me of it. I invite you to meet with me in this sacred place that lifts our minds above the humble lot of human beings. The trees can be trusted to protect us and keep our counsel private. I am Jigonsaseh, mother of Ayowantha. I am Clan Mother of the Turtles. I have never poked my head this far from the shell of my home but have always been content to rely on our own stories, our own medicine. Yet these are tricky times, and I am called to guide a people who are lost without their leader. I wish to guide them well, which I can only do when I have heard all sides of a story. I thank you for listening to my prayer."

I watched as the smoke rose in a straight line though a wind was humming through the trees. The shaft of it never wavered, and I knew this was good—it meant my words came from a place that was deep and true, and that the very air was determined to carry my message to the Sky World.

I thought it would be rude to expect an answer right away, so I patted the pine tree once more and said aloud that I would return the next day when the sun was high in the sky like a golden yolk. I was chided for telling the day what it would be like before it had arrived—the next morning the sun hid itself from us and never left the clouds. Late in the morning I headed for the woods anyway, since I had promised to return. The legs of trees were wrapped in a cold mist. Like the trees, I wore clouds as leggings and couldn't see the ground or my own feet. I was surrounded by mist and wondered if the woods were dreaming. I moved softly, like a spirit, and when I neared the fallen pine it was hidden by the fog. But a woman sat on its slender trunk—I could make out her face and the top part of her body. I stared, even though it was impolite. She was so lovely, like my daughter Anokien. She was smaller than our women, no taller than a girl, and her skin was a darkness that shone, without any flaw except one silver scar on her brow, shaped like a sliver of moon. Her hair was thick brown mink, so rich and full she wore it in a braid that trailed past her shoulders and was lost in the fog. She stood when I approached, and we looked into each other's eyes and found warmth there. Without hesitation we walked through the mist until we faced one another. As one, we reached across the divide between us and locked arms in greeting. We were both strong. Women who had carried burdens and babies. Women who had pulled children into the world and held the hand of the dead. We were sisters.

We sat down together in silence and waited for many breaths, listening to the excited stirring of the trees. The mist was fading into brightness, and I chuckled at the sun, thinking it finally left its wall of clouds so it could watch this meeting through the tangled branches of trees.

The woman finally spoke: "Jigonsaseh, mother of Ayowantha, I am Maryam, mother of Yeshua. I heard your prayer and was eager to meet with you. My son is blamed for the mistakes of those who tell his stories, who translate his words into meanings that satisfy them, no matter if they are true or not. I am grateful to you for the generosity of your open mind." She held up her hands then, palms open, as if to demonstrate the quality of my thoughts. She showed courage and honesty with this gesture—for when a person shows you her hands you can see they are empty of weapons, you can see they're not hiding anything.

She watched me with eyes that were golden brown like dark melted honey. They became bright with tears that never fell when she spoke with feeling: "Who are these men so sure they speak for Heaven? What have they done to my boy—my black lion? The words from his mouth become twisted, salted with judgment, and what was meant to express love becomes a snare.

"I have a test that decides for me if his follower walks truly on his path. Does his interpretation of my boy's talk bring harm? Do his words divide the people, and cause them to hate another, judge him, mistrust him? Do his words set him high above his brother? My son is union, and those who create separation do not understand him."

I trembled inside to hear her passionate words and gripped the bark of the pine to steady my emotions. What language was this she spoke, I wondered, for I could comprehend her more perfectly than the speech of my own dear husband. Then I answered myself in the same breath, This is spirit talk, and none is more eloquent.

"I thank you," I responded then, "for traveling so far to counsel with me. This is urgent talk, but it brings the salt to our eyes. Maybe we should sweeten our words with an offering of food I brought." I pulled from my pouch the tender rosy flesh of smoked salmon, treated with a rub of maple sugar. The flavor always raised pictures in my head of a powerful fish thrashing its tail as it swam through the thick blood of a tree, the two trapped between my teeth as I consumed them.

"Oh, yes," Maryam said, her voice full of wonder. She stared at my offering as if her eyes could eat, then raised the fish to her fine nose and inhaled its smoke.

We ate with appreciation, honoring the fish for the gift of its life. And as it entered us, we were fortified as if we, too, could swim against whatever currents fought us in the planting of our good seeds.

Our mouths and fingers were oiled from the meal of fish, so we stroked the pine to clean our hands.

"No one has offered me food in a long time," Maryam said. "Thank you. I will never forget the fish of this territory."

Morning passed into the middle of the day while we made our mother talk, telling stories of our sons. Bartholomew was forgotten, his words become hollow like a gourd without seeds.

I told her how Ayowantha had prevented two villages from shedding blood when desperate hunters fought over a lean bear.

"It was a time of drought," I explained, "and our crops were stunted, unable to yield much corn or squash, though the beans somehow thrived. The animals and birds were stricken, thin and wasting, and the people were hungry everywhere. Two hunting parties from different villages tracked a bear from opposite sides and met when one of the hunters killed him. He was a poor, hungry bear, who had little flesh to offer, but the men fought over him and bad feelings remained after the other village carried off the carcass for their thin soup. Our hunters felt cheated and vengeful, and it took Ayowantha a long time to soothe them. He asked them what they feared most, since fear is often to blame when we get angry.

"'That our women and children will starve before our eyes.'

"'That is a terrible vision. Anyone would be afraid,' agreed my son. 'Why were our relatives in the other settlement angry, why did they strike you?' he asked next.

"'They're afraid their people will die of hunger.'

"'Yes,' he said. 'We're all afraid together. We all want our loved ones to survive. What should we do?'

"I stepped forward then and said I had some dried corn still left in my storage basket beneath the ground. Other women came forward with wild onions and beans and dried fish, herbs and sugar and a variety of roots. What felt like meager stores soon looked like a bounty, and the eldest of us, a sweet grandfather, suggested we bring some of our wealth to share with our neighbors, to mend the bad feeling between us. So we brought gifts to the other village, and they shared with us the bear stew, and somehow, together, we made it through until the Thunders finally pitied us and brought the rain."

Tears gathered in Maryam's golden hawk eyes. "Oh, I *admire* your Ayowantha," she said. "How he meets anger with peace and wisdom and smoothes out all its snarls. That takes a rare patience."

She told me how Yeshua had also built plenty out of small stores, though time and again the people around him, even his followers, doubted it was possible. "When we see everything with fear, our vision is compromised," she explained. "We may as well be blind." She grabbed my hands after she said this and pressed them with kindness. "I know you're troubled," she told me.

"Yes. I'm afraid for my son. I think he is lost to us and will not return. I know it, even though I haven't heard the news. I must be strong for our family, our clan, our village, but how is it possible? My heart is dead."

Maryam reached for the hem of her garment and showed me the brown stains that had dried on its edge. "This is Yeshua's blood," she said, and her mouth twisted in pain, though she quickly set it straight again. "My son knew he would eventually be killed for his teachings, for sowing peace in a world that is afraid of its own magnificence, its wondrous heart. I am ashamed to say I argued with him about this possibility. I wanted him to leave the city where so many plotted against him, to save himself even if it meant he had to hide in a quiet corner. He made me a speech that gave me little comfort then, though I see the truth of it now. He said: 'I do not want to die, but I would not be content with less. Yes, my heart cries out for these limbs, this mind with its terrible, wonderful thoughts, this tongue that carries the Good News from my Father. But if I skulked away and found safety I would never sleep or smile or know a moment of peace. I must honor this path even if it crushes me. What happens to a flower when you crush it? The fragrance doubles, its spice presses into your fingers and will linger long after you have dropped the useless petals. Mother, he that crushes me shall *release* my strength. I must do what I will do, and both of us must bear it.'"

"Your strength passes into me," I said after Yeshua's words had settled on us. "I'm honored you would share this conversation with me." Maryam pressed my hand in answer.

I looked around me then. "We cannot make the Black Coat understand that this territory isn't just our home which sustains us, it is our family. This land knows us in a private way, our secrets and joys, just as we know the land. We can tell you where the bears travel in the fall to bed down for winter, which trees shelter the nests of which birds, where the deer go down to the water at night to escape the mosquitoes, which plants, and herbs, and roots can be used as medicine. The Black Coat's words separate us from our family as if we are the only beings with voices and spirits, the only beings who can forge an agreement. He says this is a wilderness place and that evil nests in every shadow. Yet we say this is a sacred place, abundantly generous and good. Our stories cannot be reconciled. But when I speak with you the stories twine together—they are different, but they don't quarrel. This adds to my peace."

"I find this a glorious place," Maryam said with feeling.

Her warm words breathed life into my stone heart. I would preserve my son by recalling his stories. I said to my new sister: "Ayowantha was filled every day with the gratitude I am feeling now. He told me once, 'Mother, we are so beautiful sometimes. Like those tiny firebugs that flicker to one another using star language. This is how I see our human spirits. We are just little pieces of light trying to find each other in the dark.'"

Maryam breathed in and her eyes flashed with excitement. "Your Ayowantha says things that remind me of a commandment that guides my people. We are here to repair the world with our good works. Spark by spark, we are mending what is torn, gathering into a form of light that is greater than a hundred suns bound up in a single orb. You spoke well, sister, when you said our stories complement each other. There are no arguments between us, on this our minds agree."

Maryam and I rose together when the trees shook with evening winds. "I could make this talk forever," I said, and she smiled, baring small white teeth. The breeze, or her own emotions, had disordered her hair—dark strands escaped her braid and curled around her ears.

"I am not ready to leave," she said, and I understood she meant our conversations weren't finished.

"Tomorrow?" I asked.

"Tomorrow, sister."

We locked arms again and turned away from one another. I didn't watch how she left my world, but I heard the trees sigh behind me as if to fill a space, a sudden absence that made them ache.

I told no one about this meeting because the story wasn't finished yet. But my husband later peered at me and brushed his hand across my cheek. "I see your heart again," he said, and he pulled me into his powerful arms and held me against his chest where I could hear the beating of his own heart that had missed me.

Five more days I met with Maryam. Five more days we ate the food I packed for us and spoke of our lives, our families, our stories. She told me about her good husband, Yusef, who stood behind her in all things, and I shared tales of my Shaskoharo:wane—the great Bear who would charge to my defense or stand patiently in my shadow, depending on my need. We laughed at our little girl dreams and shared memories of our mothers. Each day the sun moved faster across the sky and ended our conversation before we were ready.

Every good thing finally leaves us. The comfort is that suffering must leave as well, especially when we no longer open the door and invite it in. I knew there would be a last meeting with my sister, Maryam. I knew I would be sad to look upon her shining face for the last time. Something about her expression made me feel closer to my son, and my brain snagged on this question for many days—how were they similar? The answer came when I awakened on the morning of our final meeting. My son's face smiled at me behind my closed eyes. There it was, what made Maryam and Ayowantha so much alike: they glowed with hope.

The morning was cold, the air like little bites that cut the flesh. So I wrapped myself in a heavy bearskin robe given to me by my mother and headed into the woods. Trees were shedding leaves that were drab and brittle now—their noise was a death rattle. Troubled crows flapped ahead of me, forming busy clusters, then scattering in a mess of panic as if someone were throwing rocks at them. They tangled my thoughts and made me feel worried, then deeply lonesome. I pulled the bearskin robe more closely around my shoulders, gathering strength from its solid weight. "Old he-bear," I murmured to the warm skin, "help me stand up to this leave-taking. Help me to be as strong as my son—calm and accepting." Perhaps the old bear heard me and slipped some of his power into my spirit, for I noticed how the crows suddenly quieted. They watched with fascination as I passed them but kept their thoughts to themselves.

Maryam was waiting for me when I arrived, lightly seated on the fallen pine. She looked so small sitting there, her shoulders hunched against the cold, her brown bare feet glistening with frost. She was dressed for the summer world she'd described to me—her home which was a place of dry sands and hot winds. I was reminded of how far a journey she'd made to meet with me.

"You have traveled a long way to be my friend," I told her as I approached.

"Not as far as you," she said, smiling. "There are outside journeys and inside ones. The inside ones are always the hardest. You have a powerful spirit, so strong and gracious it breached the difference between us and called me here."

I dropped my head at these words, embarrassed by the compliment, and pulled out the gift I'd brought Maryam to distract us both and cover my awkwardness. The words I offered came out in white smoke when they met the chilly air, and I remembered my mother telling me the cloud of one's breath is a reminder of how much life we carry inside; on cold days we can witness the fire of our soul. Maryam's words were also white shapes in the air. We produced good smoke with our talk.

I handed her a slim belt I'd fashioned of wampum. We treasured these small shell beads of white and deep purple and used them to create designs that traced history: commemorating important events, forging a contract. The belt I made for Maryam showed two human figures with a single locked hand between them to signify their bond of understanding. Each figure stood at the narrow foot of a separate path, sister tributaries that wound their way along different routes, threading the needle of heart to spirit in ways particular to their own traditions. The separate rivers ultimately emptied into a single sea, which is where the two ends of the belt met in a great block of color—the edges merging.

"This is my compact," I told Maryam. "We will travel different paths yet find each other again in that place we walk to as spirits."

Maryam accepted the belt, and I helped her to tie the straps so it rested above her hips. "We are sisters in that place," she said. She stroked the smooth beads with a finger.

"Tell me more about your Peacemaker," Maryam said. "I like the sound of him."

A warm feeling spread from my heart at her request. This made me notice again how cold she looked in her light clothes, so I swept her up in the great bearskin robe I wore that morning. She looked like she'd been swallowed by that bear.

"Nia:wen," she said, and the word stood out from our spirit talk because it was my language, our people's way of offering thanks. Maryam smiled and bit the corner of her bottom lip, something she did when she was truly pleased.

"Peacemaker's name is Deganawidah, but we are taught not to say His name except when we teach our young ones to know Him. We don't want to call out His name too much unless it is serious business. His mother was kind, courageous, and hardworking and was raised in isolation from the people because her mother wanted to protect her from the bad ways we had fallen into. She never knew a man, and yet she learned she was going to have a child. A boy." I glanced at Maryam then, at her fawn-dark face, and was surprised to see her eyes rimmed with silver tears. I stopped my talk and wiped the tears away with my hands. For one moment she rested her cheek against my palm.

"Forgive me," she said. "But your story put me back in my own story."

"Please, tell me," I encouraged her.

"I want to hear the rest about Peacemaker," she assured me. "It's just that I vividly recall what it is to be chosen by God when you are no more than a girl. Not yet married, untouched by a man. God spears you with lightning you fear will burn the house down around you and the splinter of your body, even scorch your soul. When God's messenger arrived to tell me what I already knew deep in my heart, the room smelled like burnt feathers, and the girl I had been was dead."

I understood her, more than she knew, but I just patted her hand until she pulled in a long jagged breath and cleared her throat. "Please, go back to the story you were telling me. I'm all right now."

So I told her the strange and wonderful tale of how Peacemaker was born and crafted His stone canoe and overcame all kinds of obstacles to pull us into His peace ways. I told her how our Five Nations Confederacy was forged. She clapped her hands together and shook them when I finished, so great was her satisfaction. "That's the best story I've heard in a long time!" she said.

"I thank you for listening," was the deep answer of my heart. In that moment I thought of Bartholomew and how he expressed interest in our teachings only to dismiss them and correct them after they'd been spoken. So we felt betrayed and didn't want to tell him anymore.

Maryam watched me closely, and I wondered if she could guess my thoughts. But her next words brought us down a different trail: "You are modest, my sister, which is good. Humility is so difficult to wear in the right way. We must remind the vain spark that cares only for our own story that we share this life with equals whose stories are also rare and precious, yet we mustn't deny that we are here, that we, too, matter. This is the most difficult dance: to extend honor everywhere, even unto ourselves. We are mothers of extraordinary men, Sacred Beings sent here to remind our relatives that they are not alone, forgotten by their Creator, and that they're capable of cultivating a love in their hearts that will heal Nations. We have supported our boys and their mission—I call it the same enterprise, though differently born. We are the hands at their backs, the ear that will always listen, the arms that welcome them home, the lips that voice prayers on their behalf. We are first in line to follow them. And yet, we shouldn't forget that we are their mothers not by accident, but design. On behalf of all mothers, sometimes we need to step forward and acknowledge that we are more than vessels—we have harbored the difficult gifts of our sons, harbored them and brought them forth with devotion, because we were ready for the world to receive them. We were ready for the New Way. We should do this not with pride, but with open honest hands to show: this is what women have done; place us not in the shadows. I honor your people who are so advanced in heeding this already, recognizing the strength and wisdom of mothers, but your practice is not the way of most Nations. You talk of your son as if he were an unexpected gift, but, truly, sister, were you never prepared? Did you never feel chosen?"

Maryam's words poured into me like a boiling soup too warm to eat, that burns the tongue and the throat and doesn't satisfy. She spoke truth, which lifted the skin from my bones, the thoughts from my careful Turtle brain. My sister laid me open, there in the woods, and if I didn't restore myself I would be a meal for the crows. Always I stood behind my son, an adoring shadow, and was content to remain there in support of him. Yet my sister reminded me of my own dream that claimed me when I had lived only ten winters. I slept beside my younger sister then, awake until I heard the reassuring breaths that came when she had slipped into a dream.

"I will join you there," I sometimes whispered, and fell into a story where we played and were happy. But this night I didn't fall into a child's dream. Instead, I lay on my back in tall grass that hid me from other creatures—the sky a warm blue blanket above me, decorated with the white feathers of clouds. The plain beneath me held me like an open hand, and I was content, filled with a shade of peace we seldom feel. I never heard the Thunders approach, but a kind of lightning finger pierced me from the sky as if a being from that other world had thrown a spear into my body. The finger remained, stirred my innards in a way that was violent and frightening, yet also a deep raw comfort like the jagged sobs of a mother relieved to have found you when you are lost. Something was planted in me that night which exists even today, my eyes scorched open so they see, and then view more behind the first vision. They see and they *see*. Still pinned by that loving and terrible force, I was shown who I would be in this life—an eagle with speckled wings set upon the summit of the Great White Pine that is our Confederacy's Law of Peace. Here I would look behind to recall everything we had learned to help us plant such a magnificent tree, and I would look ahead to watch for coming dangers that threatened our peace. I was shown many stories of our past and of the generations yet to come. But these stories had remained hidden inside me until Maryam pushed to uncover what was so long buried. Trembling with the unfamiliar sense of being the first to bear news to the listeners, I told Maryam the story of my girlhood dream.

When I finished Maryam rose to embrace me, the bearskin robe slipping off one of her bare shoulders until I pulled it back to cover her. "We truly are sisters," she said, and this time the tears fell past the rim of her honey eyes and ran like swift veins of water down her cheeks. "There are difficult times ahead, as you have seen, and I cannot offer you sanctuary from what is coming. All I can give you is the strength of our friendship, a compact of my own to match the one you've given me." She removed the robe and held it out to me so I could see the soft tanned hide that had warmed her skin while we made our final talk. I noticed a flash of color that hadn't been there before, as if bright birds had flown inside and settled there. When I looked closely I saw a perfect imitation of her own face and figure somehow painted on the robe, so pressed into the old flesh the sudden dusting of snow never smudged it.

"You are one of the very few who sees me as I truly am. You see what is there rather than what you expect, what you invent. We all need to be seen sometimes, and so I offer this gift of my visage, forever shining out at you with love."

Now the tears fell for me, and we locked arms a last time. We laid our foreheads together as if our minds could talk without words. "I will remember you always," I promised as I moved away. Maryam was silent, so I turned and found nothing but the small outline of her feet in the light snow. But a voice whispered in my ear as I hoisted the robe across my shoulders: "And I, you."

I walked heavy steps back to the village, because my friend was gone and the only way I would ever see her again was to look inside my robe at the image she had left behind. The robe of the he-bear was now two ways special. To distract myself from sad thoughts I recalled its history, stroking the old fur with great respect.

This happened many generations earlier, in a time when the people did not yet have all the rules for upright behavior and were learning every day from their mistakes. This was before we understood that women on their moon time are too powerful to go about their usual business in the world. There was a young woman on her moon time who felt so filled with her own power, the strength of the life force flowing through her, senses quickened, blood pounding in her head, she was gloating. She felt like showing off. As she walked through the village, going about her chores, she would eye different people and secretly think: Ha! I could turn you to stone with one look! Of course she didn't actually wield this power against anyone—she wasn't an angry girl, or cruel. She exulted in the surge of strength in an innocent way because no one had taught her to live better. Soon, she had finished her work and decided to take this power even further into the world, showing off to the trees and the wind. She walked into the woods. Our relatives who live in that place, the foxes and deer, the squirrels and martens, immediately sensed her power. They could smell it. A she-bear with two young cubs picked up the girl's scent, which was thick with misguided aggression, and roused herself to face the threat. She moved to place her body between the strange creature and her curious children, who sniffed the air with their small muzzles. The mother bear met the girl on the path the people always used. She reared up on her hind legs, which in bear language was saying: "Shoo! Go back! I have babies behind me and I will not let you hurt them."

She startled the girl, and the two of them tangled in a way that was never supposed to be. The bears and the people live apart as distant relations who wish each other well but have little business together. The young woman's foolish behavior wrecked that balance, and she was confronted now with her mistake. The she-bear snarled a second warning that the girl was too frightened to understand. She reached for her flint dagger and stabbed the bear in the chest—straight through her mother's heart. The bear looked surprised, then sorrowful, and this blow was so unexpected and unnecessary, such a sad misuse of power, the she-bear was killed twice. She didn't merely die but also turned to stone, just as the girl had secretly imagined. When she fell from her tall height the stone bear broke into many pieces that scattered around the girl's feet. Once the bear became a field of shards, the girl could see the cubs the mother was protecting. They cowered in confusion, nosing the ground for their mother's scent, and when they found nothing but rocks, they began mewling in a pitiful way that broke the girl's heart.

"I meant no harm," she cried, and she caught them up in her arms the same way she'd comforted younger brothers and sisters. "I will feed you. I'll take care of you," she promised. She found a small den in the rotting hollow of an old tree and packed it with leaves. She settled the cubs inside and spoke to them very tenderly. "You stay here and wait for me. I'll be back with food."

She thought she could hide the wrong she had done, but the bear cubs smelled their mother's blood covering her hands, and in their trusting infant way they switched their affections to this young woman they now took as their protector. They waddled after the girl when she washed her hands in the creek, and no amount of scolding would make them turn back. They followed her all the way home. The girl arrived, crying, and confessed to everyone what she had done. The elders collected together and told her they would counsel with each other and decide what should happen next to remedy the situation. The girl nodded, comforted by her family who surrounded her and wiped away her tears. While they waited, the bear cubs played in their new mother's lap and joyfully smacked their lips when she fed them a sweet corn mush. At last the elders returned with their decision—all of them agreed that the young woman had caused a disruption in the natural order of life which tipped the world out of balance. The cubs were now her responsibility, and it was up to her to make things right again, to make them even. She would have to leave the people and the loving protection of her own mother and raise the cubs as bears, not humans. She wasn't allowed to return until the bear children were independent and could fend for themselves. The girl agreed with this decision, anxious to make amends for the harm she had caused. Still, there was great sadness when she left, and everyone wept except the playful cubs. The girl walked into the forest between them and was not seen again for several years. She grew into a sensible woman with the staunch heart of a bear. She taught her animal children as well as she could, and eventually the daughter was ready to leave and become a mother herself. The he-bear was a strong giant when it was time for the woman to return to her people; he knew how to feed himself in the warm months and bed down for winter, he knew how to stand up to danger. But he was close to his mother, still a baby in his tender heart, and he tried to follow her back the way he had so long before. She held him again, small as she was compared to him, and explained that it was time for her to become a person again. She warned him to keep his distance from the village, and from all people, otherwise they might kill him for his meat and his warm fur, or he might kill them.

The he-bear didn't listen; he lingered in his mother's territory and never completely left the trail of her scent. Eventually, what the woman most feared came to pass. A hunting party killed her son and brought back his meat to share, his skin for a robe. She recognized the pelt at once, and the hunters apologized for the mistake and gladly gave her the fur which she gathered in her arms and mourned. She carried the bearskin wherever she went, wore it on her back, and after so many years of living as a bear she walked as they did, until people wondered if she had forgotten what it was to be a woman. Her tears soaked that robe as none has been drenched before, and because her tears came from such a deep place, not just pain from the loss of a life, but regret for all the layers of sadness she set in motion, they became a powerful medicine that preserved what was left of the flesh of the bear. The woman became a teacher in the village, one who would sit with the young girls and counsel them on how to work with the extra power that descended on them every month. When she died, the bearskin robe was passed on to her daughter who told the story, and so it has been for many generations until it came to me from my mother. The robe is older than the Great Law of Peace and the Peacemaker who brought it, older than the oldest wampum belt. Yet the fur is lush and thick as it was when the young he-bear still wore it on his living body. That is the powerful medicine of regret.

When I returned to the Longhouse I folded the bearskin robe and stored it away. I would share it with the others after we'd eaten our evening meal, show them the lovely face of my friend, Maryam, who came from a Sky World of her own.

That night we shared venison and squash which even Bartholomew appeared to enjoy. Some nights when our food didn't appeal to him, he unwrapped a squashed packet of oily material that contained a white block of rank flesh he called cheese. He always offered us a piece, despite how much he treasured it, and though we are a courageous people not one of us had yet eaten a slice. It produced a stench that made people whisper against him that it was human meat gone rancid, that he was surely a cannibal. Didn't he often describe the meal he made of his God, eating the body and drinking the blood? But this night his delicacy remained hidden, and the only fragrance that spiced our lodge was the wood-smoke fire and the sweet tang of cooked dear meat.

In this dim, content hour when we rested together and told stories, I brought out the bearskin robe I had worn earlier that day on my final meeting with Maryam. For an hour I spoke about my confusion in the absence of our leader, how I went into the woods and called on the Clan Mother of Bartholomew's people to counsel with me so I could hear the news from her own lips. I told them about our meetings and the many ways she honored our medicine. How she never told me we should set aside our stories and prayers, wipe them away and replace them with her own. Just as we locked arms on that first day, in the polite grip of greeting, our dark limbs laid side by side in connection, so she saw our ways as separate teachings that could sit together in peace.

"She said her son, Yeshua, and our Ayowantha were like brothers. She wished to meet my son, and I wished to meet hers. We made good talk," I assured my family, "mother to mother."

Bartholomew was quiet this whole time, though his face looked troubled. He had learned enough to understand that contradicting me could be a dangerous thing. I knew he didn't believe me, which was the deepest insult. I was not made to foul my tongue with lies.

"The Black Coat will no doubt say I have imagined things that are not real, that are not flesh—" I offered the inner skin of my forearm. "But I have proof which even he must respect." I paused, as a good storyteller should, to draw out the suspense. Then I bundled the ancient robe over my arm and lifted the paws out of the way like a bear opening his great arms.

"My sister, Maryam, mother of Yeshua, was sad to leave me today and gave me a gift to share with all of you. I wrapped her in this blanket to warm her, and when she returned the robe it bore her image on the tanned hide." I held the blanket closer to the fire so all could see her fawn-dark face and dark honey eyes, the sliver of a scar that cut across one delicate brow.

"Ahhhh," the people breathed in approval. Fingers reached to softly brush their tips against her cheek. My husband looked at me then with a private message I could read in his eyes. He was proud of me.

Bartholomew suddenly jumped to his feet, and his face was red and sweating. He was shaking as if illness had come upon him. "Black Coat," I said in a mother's voice. "Are you well?" Still he didn't speak. "Black Coat, don't be afraid," I said. "Maryam told me you might not believe what you are seeing. She gave me a message to tell you in a language you would perfectly understand." I closed my eyes then, hands plunged deep in the bear's fur, and summoned the strange words that held no meaning for me: *"Memorare, O plissima Virgo Maria, non esse auditum—"*

Bartholomew's cry interrupted, a moan and wail that sounded like the howl of war. "The devil has done this work!" he shouted. "The devil walks these woods and possesses your heart. Stop! Before you damn us all—" He grabbed the bearskin robe from my hands and launched it into the fire, stamped it in with his feet. My husband and several of my cousins attacked him and made ready to throw him in as well on top of the destroyed robe, and I knew they would complete the act and hold him there even as their arms burned away.

"No!" I urged. My son would have made a good speech that moved their hearts, but the only words I heard myself say were: "He knows not what he does." And so they released him.

He endangered himself again when he pulled out the special water he never drank, the one he said was blessed, and tossed it in our faces. Men struggled with him and stripped him of the leather jug. I felt the wet on my cheeks and didn't know if it was the Black Coat's water or tears I found there. Maybe both.

Someone was speaking in a sorrowful voice. A woman's. I knew it was my own, and yet it was altered, thick as if there were two voices braided together. What was I saying, in a soft chant, almost like a song? It was Maryam's message, and though I didn't understand its story, I was comforted somehow: *"Memorare, O plissima Virgo Maria, non esse auditum a saeculo, quemquam ad tua currentum praesidia, tua implorantem auxilia, tua petentem suffrigia, esse derelictum."*

My relatives withdrew to their separate fires within the lodge, and Bartholomew stalked out of the Longhouse. My husband left to walk off his anger which was never easily roused, but on the rare times it burst forth was not easily quieted. I sat alone at the fire I once shared with my son and watched as white flames burned off the face of the woman who came from the sky and killed the ancient bear for the last time.

Shawiskara came back to us as suddenly as he had left, blown in behind a storm. He was the last cold whip of its tail. His hair was shorn, chopped to small uneven pieces and covered in ash. He'd been running for miles, so the gray ash had mixed with sweat and tears and painted his face in long black lines. His eyes smoldered like dying coals. Everyone stood back when he surged into the village, stunned, frightened. Our world went quiet for several moments—the birds hushed and wind held its breath. So we heard each step he made in my direction. He threw himself to his knees before me.

"Mother," he said, his voice grim and cracking. "I know what has happened to my brother."

If I weren't Turtle Clan I would have fallen down with him and shaken the story from his mouth. But I come from the Turtle, so I planted my legs where I stood and pulled my heart into its shell. I would be patient with this specter and hear whatever the truth was in an orderly way. I wished my husband were there, I wanted to feel the warmth and strength of his fingers at my back, but he was gone with a large hunting party. I stiffened my spine as if I felt his touch.

"Stand up," I said in a firm voice I tried to keep even. "Stand up when you speak of your brother." He was heavy with lean muscle but I pulled him from his knees. "Your mouth is too dry to speak clearly," I continued. "I'll get you water."

He shook his head and licked the salt rim of his lips.

"You might enjoy your suffering," I scolded, "but it doesn't help us understand you better." At that he took the water my niece had fetched and drank it slowly, carefully, spitting ash from his mouth. Then he spoke the words that entered my ears and mind but would not make sense for a long time. This is what he told us:

"All my life I have been divided. I loved my brother and yet I doubted him. I thought this was his failing. If he was really a Sacred Being, I asked myself, then why does my heart hold questions? Why can't he give me peace? Nothing he did was enough to convince me. I wanted to believe, but then I would see how everyone loved him and I thought it must be tricks to win such favor. I never once looked at my own jealous, tricky heart. I never saw that the questions I shot at him, I should have asked myself. My spirit was sick, which was my own affair. Not his. And still he loved me. Every day. He offered me peace from our first breaths together. I was the one who would not let it in.

"I didn't like the Black Coat, or the words he made against us, but I enjoyed hearing him question my brother and tell him he was wrong, his ways were empty. I licked up those insults, and to me they tasted sweet. He must have sensed my pleasure at the humiliation he offered my brother, so he courted me in secret and whispered his ideas. He knew his mission in our Confederacy would never live as long as Ayowantha was our leader. Rather than the Black Coat's stories and teachings moving from heart to heart and village to village, it was Ayowantha's influence spreading—even to our enemies. 'What can we do to push back the tide?' he asked me. And so we made our conniving, foolish talk.

"I would not see my brother dead, nor would the Black Coat. We both claimed to love him; me, through the bond of our blood, the other, through the love of his God. But we organized a plan to remove him from the people, from you, that would spare his life and open the way for the Black Coat to fill the space Ayowantha left behind. As if he could. I met his relations—men with hairy faces and skillful weapons that produce fire. They trade with our enemies and are hungry for pelts. They gave me this axe which is so sharp it can chew a small tree in two bites. The plot was for me to bring my brother to their boat on the river—they would steal him from us and sell him to other men who travel back and forth between our world and Bartholomew's. The weak one, the coward, Michael, had no part in this. He crept away from us one night as we slept. I did not care to look for him. I could manage this betrayal on my own. I told myself that a Sacred Being would never be captured, or if he was, he would surely change the hearts of the men who held him and win his release. I was pleased to put my brother through this final test.

"Sometimes when we have treacherous hopes and plot against a brother, the way is smooth and we conquer him. It should make us happy. It should make us sing in triumph. But instead our mind falls on the ground and, too late, we find that *we* are conquered. This is what I saw when the Hairy Faces bound my brother with ropes and sat him in the damp bottom of their boat. Ayowantha watched my face the whole time, his eyes wide, yet not surprised. I couldn't speak or look away. I couldn't lift my arm to save him. I was locked up inside my sick heart, and I heard my brother say, 'You look like a man who has become stone.' His captors pushed their boat away from me, into the moving water, so I didn't see Ayowantha's face when he said: 'My brother, you have done what I knew you were born to do. I will miss you.'

"He went away from us then, and I found I could not return to this village for without my brother it would no longer be home. Since that time I've been made to walk inside my spirit, down black trails where it is always night. I approved of my suffering and offered it up as a gift to my brother, though I know it is one he would have refused. This is how I would have finished my days. But I stumbled on the camp of the Hairy Faces who helped me steal Ayowantha from you. They told me a story they thought would please me.

"They said they took my brother north and handed him off to more of their people to add to a store of goods they would carry back to their home far to the east of us, across great waters. They wouldn't say what they received in exchange for his life—maybe they thought I wanted some part of these gifts. So now he was put in a bigger boat, living in its dark stomach for nearly one moon as they made ready for their journey. When they set out for those eastern lands, it was favored weather where the wind blows at your back just enough to give you greater speed but not enough to knock you over. The sun was cheerful every day, though my brother wouldn't have seen it in the belly of that boat. Maybe the winds were angry because their relative was locked up like that? They turned against the Hairy Faces three days into their travels, blew so hard the water got stirred up and boiled around the boat as if it were a single grain of corn in a great soup. The men did everything they could to keep their vessel from going over to the bottom, but the wind and the water made war against them, and we pitiful people can never win that kind of battle. Somehow, even over the wind's moaning growl, they were able to hear my brother calling from below. He asked them to bring him up to the top of the boat so he could speak to the wind and reason with the water. They understood enough of our language to make out the request, and they were so afraid of dying they let him out, though they wouldn't untie his arms.

"They fell from one end of the boat to the other, slices of water tripping them and slapping their faces. But Ayowantha was able to stand, bending this way and that way as if he were a tree. He spoke very gently, they said, so they couldn't hear his words. They only knew he was talking because his mouth moved. He was smiling the whole time, even when rain wet his hair into a drowned snake. He talked and talked, and pretty soon the wind quieted down like it wanted to hear, and the water curled around the boat in white ripples that no longer washed over the side. Now they could clearly hear Ayowantha's voice and how he thanked these beings for sparing their lives and allowing them to continue their journey in peace. They said it sounded like a kind of song that put them under a spell; they remembered being babies in their mother's arms, they remembered what it was to be loved and held and protected. When Ayowantha's work was done he sat down against the side of the boat and smiled at them. Now they were even more frightened than they'd been in the storm. The day was so still, and the pictures in their head so sweet, they knew they were being worked on by a mighty power. Since my brother is Kanien'kehá:ka, and not their Yesu who likewise calmed the water, they thought he must be the other one—the evil being who charms them and fools them until they lose their souls to his hunger. They were convinced Ayowantha was such a demon and so, as one mind, they grabbed him and threw him over the side, into the deep sea. Never trusting what he would do next, what forces would be set loose against them, they turned the boat and headed back. This is the story they have passed on to their trading partners."

All had been standing while my nephew spoke his story, but now I heard gasps and cries, and people were dropping to the ground in horrified grief. Somehow I remained on my feet. Shawiskara's expression was terrible. For a moment I thought he was the dead man among us instead of my son. The black tears had dried on his face, and these tracks were now its only color. He was gray as soot.

"I asked these men what they thought had become of my brother, and they agreed he must be dead. How can a man swim when his arms are bound behind him? And if he was a demon, well, then he never truly lived at all. They were untroubled by the story, careless of the outcome, and found it very funny that their partners had been such children in their fears. I walked away from them though I could have split them with my axe. Who is more to blame for what has passed? The Hairy Faces in their ignorance? Or me, Shawiskara, who should have known better? Still, I nourished a small flame of hope in my heart that Ayowantha yet lived. Perhaps the water had cradled him as you did, Mother, before he was born? Perhaps it bore him to our shores, and he was birthed again? I recalled what Peacemaker said to those who wanted to have news of His survival, so I found a strong birch tree and sliced its bark, into the flesh. If the wound ran with sap then I knew my brother had been given a second life. But the cut wept a dark thick blood that ran over my fingers. So I knew he was drowned and we had lost him." Shawiskara held out a shaking hand, and I saw the dried blood that stained it.

I heard the creak of hard shoes that stamp the ground—it was Bartholomew, emerging from the path that led to the woods. He carried the leather case that housed his book of silent stories, the ones you speak to yourself in the same way every time if you learn to make out the marks. When he saw Shawiskara among us, his lips opened into an odd smile. He flung his arms wide in greeting. Shawiskara's face came alive again. Everything he accomplished next was so startling, so quick, it was as if this solid, muscled man became a nimble hummingbird. He moved in unexpected flashes. Shawiskara covered the open ground without even walking it; he was there beside Bartholomew before we could blink. He embraced the Black Coat and took his space away, so their faces were nearly touching. My nephew's red eyes were weapons that stared without moving as he spoke.

"You are a fool, Black Coat! So blind you couldn't see that everything you wanted us to learn from your God, Yesu, we already learned from Ayowantha. We are brothers in our lies and our poison. We are brothers in our bloody hands. Take back the gift you gave me. Now we will be brothers in death!"

My nephew's arm twitched once, and I saw him flip his hatchet in the air so his grip could change from the lower stalk to its handle. He planted the axe in Bartholomew's heart, still holding him close. Shawiskara watched the spirit of life leave the man, and when he was dead, he stepped back from his violent work and let the body fall to the ground. Then my nephew walked in measured steps to stand before me, once again falling to his knees, his arms open and empty.

"I am ready for my death," he said.

I was shaking on the inside from everything I had learned and witnessed, but my legs were steady when I walked away from my nephew so I could separate myself from him and merge with the large circle of our people who had gathered. I said, "This is not your decision to make." I looked around me and asked the Clan Mothers from each clan, the Turtle, the Bear, and the Wolf, to confer with me. It was late in the day, when the shadows begin to collect and link arms, so we agreed to wait until the next morning for our conference to avoid the mischief spirits of twilight. When you are deciding a person's fate—what life they will continue or forfeit—you need the sun to light your thoughts and speech so you can render clean justice. Shawiskara refused to stay with us, and we let him go where his feet and his split heart would take him. We knew he would return the next day to hear our decision.

That night was the longest night I had yet lived. My mind sorted many thoughts and memories. My heart fell on the ground, and I made myself pick it up over and over so I could be the kind of Clan Mother my son would approve. Sometimes we must carve out that part of us that is weakly human. That part clutching a fist full of small angry feelings. That part wanting to give up from loneliness. If we wash ourselves with soiled water—despair, revenge—then we ruin our hearts and minds. Our spirit rushes off in the wrong direction. That night was one of unending discipline, where I sipped clear water and burned prayers and went inside my turtle shell to preserve what strength remained.

The next morning I expected the other clan leaders to call for Shawiskara's death, but the strongest part of me was ready to argue for something else. My son would not have wanted Bartholomew dead, nor his brother. He taught us peace in the face of any provocation, peace even when someone insulted us or prepared to take our precious life. I was going to request that my nephew be banished from our village, free to join some other family in our Confederacy that would take him for a relative. We had questions to ask him before we withdrew to our conversation, so we made our morning prayers and waited for Shawiskara to join us.

Early in the morning, when the grass and needles and leaves are still wet, a strange man walked into our waiting circle. I leapt to my feet, joy shaking through me. This man was Ayowantha, somehow returned to me! Yes, the edges of his eyes and mouth tipped down a little toward sadness in that familiar way, and his face showed the inner light of a sweet fire. I grabbed him to me, lifting on my toes to wrap him up in the blanket of all my love. I could smell the tobacco in his hair, and only after I made the thought did I realize how short the strands were, all hacked and messy.

"Mother, it is your nephew, Shawiskara," the man said, and pulled me off his chest with gentle hands. The tricks I'd meant to avoid by holding this conference in strong daylight had managed to find me anyway and were confusing my eyes. Shawiskara walked closer to the gathered people, and now I heard surprised noise hissing all around me. What medicine was this? I was not the only one being fooled.

"How can you wear your brother's face?" I finally asked when I could speak without crying or shouting.

"Believe me, Mother, it was not my choice," my nephew said so softly I could barely understand him.

"Something has happened to you," I accused. "Tell us what has made the change."

Shawiskara nodded and glanced all around him to acknowledge everyone, from the smallest baby to the oldest woman. In a voice that was now clear and powerful enough to reach us all he told us what the night had brought him.

"I slept on the ground at the foot of a pine, remembering how our ancestors buried their weapons beneath the Great Tree of Peace. I, Shawiskara, am a weapon now, I thought to myself. Let me be buried with everything else that causes pain and the end of what is good. I should have been cold in my bare flesh, but I wasn't. My head was cradled in a pillow of needles, and I was more comfortable than I've ever been before. I heard my brother's voice in a dream, and I was so glad he would visit me there. He said: 'See what happens when you become a man? When you take responsibility for your unhappiness? See what happens when you comb the crooked snakes from your thoughts and see all the clear paths our stories have given us from the very beginning? The Hairy Faces make maps to find their way from one territory to another, but our Maker gave us the best map of all—so easy to read, so easy to follow once we stop being afraid. I'm proud of you, my brother. Wash your face in clear water and from now on think clear thoughts. The snakes have left you because you no longer need their protection. Now you are truly a brave man.'

"My brother, Ayowantha, pointed to a creek that was laughing like a baby and somehow shining in the dark. I could see everything, even though it was full night, and I realized it was my brother's hands lighting my way, his palms burning a cold fire that did him no harm. So I got up and went over to the creek. I couldn't help but smile at how happy it was, running across stones, always laughing. I bent over the edge and plunged my hands into the stream. Oh, the water felt so good, I had to taste it before I rinsed my face. It tasted like the rain that has been too long in coming. I washed my face three times because I had made it so dirty with blood and sweat, ashes and tears.

"'Look at yourself,' my brother said, and I tried to, but I could only see his face wavering in the creek.

"'Where am *I*?' I asked, confused.

"Ayowantha chuckled, and it was just the way he did when we were boys, racing and teasing. 'Can't my brother recognize his own face?' Ayowantha said.

"I woke up then. I made my way to the creek and washed my face three times. But I kept my eyes closed. I was afraid my dream was true. I was afraid my dream was not true. In this awake moment, lost in fear, I heard my brother's voice. He told me, 'Open your eyes.' So I did. And I saw him smiling back at me. 'Now I am a part of you,' were the final words he said."

Just as my nephew had been transformed for all to see, my own heart turned over, washing out the old blood. I knew what my son wanted as surely as if he had whispered the idea in my ear. I glanced at the other Clan Mothers whose eyes were large with these surprising developments. We collected together in a small circle of gray hair and linked arms so that none of us could pull away from the other, none of us could fall down. When you have known people from your first day to the present day, when you have shared your deepest truth, sometimes you don't need words to express thoughts. All you have to do is look into each other's faces. I looked at each woman, read her eyes, and when I had made it all the way around, that is when I spoke: "Our mind is agreed?" I asked them. "Tho," they responded in unison. We let go of one another and moved as one body to encircle my nephew who waited for us with a calm, happy face. I had never seen him look like that, and I was still not used to his new expression.

"Ayowantha has decided for you," I told him, and the others nodded. "He changed your heart for all to see. From this day forward *you* are Ayowantha, my son. *You* will take his place."

For a moment my nephew looked scared in a little boy way, but he shook it off. "This is an honor I will shoulder for the rest of my days," he promised. Then each of us embraced him, and he was welcomed back into the arms of his relatives. I knew he would keep his promise because he is a Turtle, too, and we are stubborn, home creatures. So tied to our lodge we carry it with us wherever we go.

My nephew became father to Ayowantha's children as well as his own, and he taught us the peace ways that were a gift to the Peacemaker, and then to my son. It is always a brutal time on this lush earth because people are foolish creatures who refuse to believe the old stories—the map our Maker gave us. But peace lives in my heart now, and my nephew's, and that is a good start.

I should tell you, we sent out a strong canoe fitted with the supplies a person needs to begin a new life. We placed it in the water and offered tobacco, prayed that it would find its way to the sea and Ayowantha's drowned spirit. A good mother must always offer her child a way to come home. We buried Bartholomew in a bare patch of ground just outside the village, far enough away so that he would leave our ancestors alone and not talk too much to their spirits, but close enough so he could watch our lives and see what good we made of them. We buried him with his Bible and rosary and the stinky cheese that made his breath so strange. Years later, long after we'd moved our village to another site, we happened to walk through the old grounds and saw that a beech tree now grew from the Black Coat's grave. Many people stared and commented, but no one touched that tree—we weren't sure if it was good news or bad news. Some said the seed that produced its life had dropped from the beak of a passing bird, while others said it grew from the spider-like tracks inside the book we'd placed on his chest that marked down his stories about the Black Coat God named Yesu who died for every bad thing any of us has ever done.

To speak truth, I never much cared how that beech came to grow from our ground. Sometimes a tree is just a tree, and a son who was a Sacred Being, who has inspired the people and died a noble death, is just your little boy you pray will not be lost to you forever.

The Sorrowful Mysteries Become Joyful

Bartholomew went for a walk in the forest. Late in the morning, when the night chill begins to relinquish its hold. A benevolent sun washed his face and his hands, seemed to reach into his very heart and loosen what bands were fastened there. He was careful to keep to the trail a little girl had shown him. He could not recall her Mohawk name. He thought of her as Mary. She'd taken care to point out markers he could use to find his way back to the village: a tree struck by lightning and withered now on one side, another tree with natural flaws in the bark that created the illusion of a mocking face. A bearded face, like his. She'd made the connection herself—a nudge, a giggle. Then she'd quickly composed herself as if realizing her behavior was disrespectful. She was more careful the rest of the way. Chastened. A God-like child, he'd thought, as if she's been raised in a convent. Ultimately she had led him to a chair of boulders, a hidden sitting place on a cushion of rock, nestled in a tight stand of hemlock. She gestured for him to sit, and then she waved, shyly, as he had taught her to do in greeting. This was a gift, a sharing of her secret place, he understood. He had thanked her in both their languages, and she walked away. Turned suddenly, as if she'd forgotten something, and waved again. He'd been visiting this private refuge every day since then.

Bartholomew sat in the unsettling quiet. To be sure there was a breeze that set the leaves talking and whispering. He had the uneasy feeling they were gossiping about him. There was birdsong and the rustling journeys of creatures through what scant underbrush remained in this part of the woods. But he couldn't hear the comforting noise of human activity, of society and commerce. It was as if human life were only imagined here.

What is illusion? What is real? Bartholomew began to shake. He wrapped his arms around his waist and threw himself off the rock, onto his knees. He didn't pray so much as hold his body and mind together, rocking and moaning. He could have been a mother comforting her child. His intestines roused him with thunder. The noise of great hunger. He knew he was emaciated, starving, yet he could not eat. Stew dribbled from his mouth, and anything solid made him choke. He would die soon if he didn't remove the stone from his soul. He would die without confession. Decided now, Bartholomew painfully rose on his wobbling legs and sat down again on the rock.

"Here I shall tell the truth," he said aloud, and the forest hushed as if it heard him. He removed pen, ink, and paper from the leather satchel he carried with him everywhere, slung across his chest. Using the battered case as a desk settled upon his knees, he began his scratching scrawl:

> I write this for no one's eyes but mine and my beloved Savior's. I use the old code invented by my clever boyhood friend, Matthieu, which we used to compose our irreverent comedies. The private indulgence of children bent now to a serious purpose.
>
> Why write these thoughts at all? Why not harbor them in the dark castle of my brain, chained there, rebuked? My only answer a belief that whatever secret we neglect to bring forward into daylight becomes a pox more deadly than the disease that wastes the flesh. What is my secret I carry like a parasite? Can a man of faith reverse the revelation that transformed Saul into Paul on the road to Damascus? Can the scales return to the eyes? I stand in questions banked around me like fagots heaped for the burning of a heretic.

My Lord, I have loved You all my life, and yet I know You not at all. I split hairs. I split hairs. I look for You and find only the beast. I search for the beast to root him out and destroy him, and find only You in all Your strange glory. Truly I am in the New World. I cannot break Your trail. This land resists. I have maps, but they will not lie down and conform. Are you here? Or did Your story drown in the crossing? Were You here already, in this Eden before the Fall, disgusted that I bring the stink of an Old World that has spilled the blood of saints?

I am confounded by the man they call Ayowantha. Is he sent me in this wilderness to knock me from the true path of righteousness? Does he wear the horns? Or is he Thy most gracious servant speaking Thy words in another tongue, and I am Pontius Pilate, I am Caiaphas? I am just a man, the dust that rises up into form, the dust that disseminates. What perfect knowledge can belong to dust to justify his judgment, his condemnation of another?

I am humbled by this journey. It torments. I breathe for You. Yes, I offer my breath. It is all I have. My heart and mind have been pierced by the one I sought to replace, and he has compromised my faith. And he has built it up. I cannot replace him. That is certain.

I was a boy once who climbed the trees. My favorite was a beech that was quite old, and as I arranged myself in its branches I considered all it had lived through that I had not. That boy comes back to me here, I know not why. He dangles from my dreams. He laughs when I am quiet. He interrupts me when I seek to pray. God help me. I am no more than that boy.

I think what I have done is blasphemy. May You, the good Lord, have mercy on my soul.

Bartholomew didn't read what he had written but, immediately after stowing away the pen and ink, folded the intimate sheet into squares upon squares, and slid the pinch of parchment into his Bible. He made sure it rested against the opening of chapter five in the Gospel of Saint Matthew because it was a favorite section—where Jesus begins His Sermon on the Mount with a list of all the unlikeliest souls who are blessed. He stood and slung his satchel once more across his chest. Took a step, then another, still shaky with hunger but feeling more firmly the ground beneath him. Birds shrilled and other sounds he couldn't identify suddenly broke open around him, as though these creatures had held their breath in deference while he composed what he hoped was his salvation, and were now blasting him for the inconvenience.

He smiled and hallooed them all. “Make noise, my friends. And I thank you for your indulgence,” he said, and was only slightly self-conscious.

On the short walk back to the village he felt altered enough to slip his hand into the satchel and pull forth the packet of fromage he knew was too dear to him. But, oh, it reminded him of home—it was mother’s milk and boyhood pleasures brought into this unfamiliar world. He broke off a piece no larger than the shell of nail on his littlest finger. He placed it reverently on his tongue, then quickly crossed himself in apology for treating it like the sacred Host. He savored the pungent taste and swallowed. His throat accepted the food.

Bartholomew’s pace quickened as he neared the village. The closer he came, the more curious he was about the unexpected activity he could hear in the distance. Something was going on. When he emerged from the trail into the clearing he saw the reason for the uproar. Shawiskara had returned, and he stood, surrounded by his people, telling them an urgent tale. Bartholomew caught his breath when he noted the young man’s countenance—how exhausted he was, yet scalded with blistering remorse.

I can help this man, Bartholomew thought. I know what he feels.

A surge of love for this suffering brother, and for all the others gathered there, exploded within the Jesuit’s heart. Such love and connection he had never felt before in his life. The ecstasy of epiphany held him and washed through him, wave upon wave—he bobbed in its ocean.

He opened his arms when Shawiskara ran toward him. Yes, he thought. Yes, come to me, my brother. Separation is useless. Yes.

Joy prevented him from feeling the axe when it tore through his heart. Love spilled everywhere, and continued to fall even after he ceased to live.

Revelations

Candace barely noticed when Gladys and Maryam returned to her room and retrieved the Face. In the time it took them to watch the film *Enchanted* with several patients in the ward, Candace had absorbed the story of her ancestors. She was growing what felt like skin, bones, teeth, and hair, but really it was foundation, something to stand on, so when she swung her legs down to rise from her cot, when she placed her feet on the cold linoleum floor, she felt all at once like a tree—a tall, shimmering cottonwood or a graceful silver birch. A being with roots.

"I am home," she murmured, and realized this would be true for the rest of her life, for she was a Turtle and this was her island.

She stretched her fine limbs, bent and touched the palms of her hands to the floor, touched forehead to knees, flexible, strong. She lifted her arms to the ceiling, then arched each side. Stretching the body to match the mind. She stroked the closed bud of her navel and imagined a cord that extended from her body to her sons' generation and beyond. She thought of it as a rope the children could use to climb back into their history, as she had.

It was suppertime and she was hungry. Lee slept on, so Candace made her way to the dining area with a cluster of young women it was her honor to mother at least for a brief while.

■ ■ ■

Monday morning after a group therapy session, Candace met privately with Shar in a conference area. The social workers and counselors shared a couple of conference rooms, so they were impersonal spaces, no family photos arranged on a desk or art prints framed on the wall. Shar was the primary decorative piece in the room. She was once again wearing a jacket cut like a lab coat, boxy, with deep pockets, but this time the color was hot pink, with a flowery blouse beneath. She looks like a bright garden, Candace thought, fondly. A mobile one.

"You've done just great over the weekend," Shar told her. Candace couldn't help smiling, she'd always worked diligently for her good grades and this felt like another version of a report card. "The doctor will sign the release papers by this afternoon and we'll get you home before supper." Shar peered at her but Candace didn't flinch from her gaze as she might have earlier. She met the gaze and tipped her head.

"I appreciate the advice you gave me. I managed to answer questions without lying. A doctor asked, 'Do you still think the Virgin Mary is here, following you around?' And I could say, no, she isn't, in all honesty. Because she wasn't."

Shar tapped her folder bulging with patient files with the end of her pen. "But you *did* see her at some point?"

"Yes," Candace said, firmly. "I can't deny her any longer."

Shar tapped her lips with the pen, smudging her mauve lipstick. "I'll take you at your word. My mother saw things that most people wouldn't understand, even in our church, and we're Evangelical. I guess most folks think the miracle days are over and done, locked up in the Bible. But I say, open your eyes because the Bible's still being written." She flushed then. "Pardon me, wasn't *that* a bit inappropriate? I have strong feelings about these matters. But then, who doesn't? By the way, did the longtimers share their name for me?"

Candace snorted, something she hadn't done in years, snorted with laughter.

"I'll take that as a 'yes.' I don't mind one little bit. 'Shar the Cheerful Republican,' fits me just right!" She laughed along with Candace. "Most of the clients we get in here are liberal. Now, if I wanted to be ornery I could argue that says something about the mental health of progressive Americans, but to be fair, I know it's just the population we're pulling in from the Twin Cities—people who vote for Al Franken."

"*I* voted for Al Franken."

"Well, there you go."

As they stood to leave Candace surprised herself, wrapping her arms around Shar in an affectionate hug. "I don't care what you are," Candace said. "To me, you'll always be an angel."

Shar hugged her in return. "Why, thank you. And don't take this the wrong way, but I hope we don't see you again, if you know what I mean."

Jules and Gladys brought Candace home from the hospital. Barry had wanted to collect her, but she said she'd rather see him at home, after work, once she was settled. Gladys helped her carry her bags, and Candace waved to Lee and the others who were just beginning another group session. She was happy to be leaving, but she'd miss these sensitive people who treated each other so gently because they knew how easy it was to break.

Jules was standing beside his car, waiting like a chauffeur, though Merle in the sling across his chest rather ruined that image. Jules held up one of Merle's little paws and they waved to Candace which made her smile.

"Oh, Pop," she said. She grabbed him in a hug, careful not to squash the dog. "Have I told you lately that I love you?"

He rocked back on his heels and practically bounced. "A man can't hear that too many times in his life! Thank you, Candy, I love you, too."

Candace insisted that Gladys sit up front with Jules and they sped away from the hospital.

"If you don't mind, I think we should make one stop before I get you home," said Jules. He drove them over to Grand Avenue and parked in the street. The three stopped in at the Grand Ole Creamery for fresh-made ice cream in large waffle cones.

"What a good idea, Pop. I feel just like a little girl again," Candace said. "Newly minted."

They toasted each other, knocking cones, and laughed at the odd flavor combinations this created when they collided: pumpkin with peppermint and key lime pie.

Candace watched the older couple, how Gladys rarely looked at Jules directly, more often in quick glances that were admiring, shy. Jules, on the other hand, faced Gladys in every situation as if he were pulled to her, a compass bowing forever to the magnetic north. Jules was left-handed and Gladys used her right to hold the cone, and at one point their inner hands resting on the table met, and it was Gladys who raised a pinky finger and hooked it over the thick cigar of Jules's finger. A small gesture, but so full of hope and sweetness, Candace had to take a painful, cold bite of pumpkin-flavored ice cream to shock herself from tears.

When they pulled up to the mansion, Jules opened the doors for them and tipped the hat that wasn't there. "Ladies, it has been my pleasure. Now I need to get this one home for a feeding with her pill mashed up in it. Otherwise I'd beg to hang around."

Gladys pinched his wrist in a way she knew wouldn't hurt him. "Love bites!" he roared, and she shushed him, smiling. Candace thanked him, and he pulled away from the curb, his large hand thrust out of the window, fingers fluttering.

"What a character," Gladys said with warm affection.

They stood on the sidewalk, each of them holding a shopping bag full of Candace's things. They looked up at the mansion and the stone lions, which were now carved with warier expressions as if they'd seen enough strange phenomena in recent weeks to last them a lifetime.

Candace saw her home with new eyes. "It's so large," she said.

Gladys laughed. "It sure is. Maryam and I still get lost sometimes."

"Is she here?"

"Yes, she wanted the chance to get to know you a bit before she leaves, the you who talks to her and doesn't run away."

Candace shook her head. "I know, I know. I've been a putz." They laughed and carried their happy noise into the house.

The three women visited in the kitchen for a couple of hours, Candace telling Gladys the story she'd learned from the Face that was now part of her history.

"You knew Jigonsaseh," Candace said to Maryam with awe.

"Yes. And so will you."

When they heard the deep purr of Barry's Jaguar pull into the garage beneath Gladys's apartment, Gladys and Maryam seemed to melt into the walls, anxious to give the couple some privacy.

Candace wasn't so sure she was ready to be alone with Barry. She was drained, exhausted, but she knew there was no more putting him off. Usually he bounded into the house, briefcase slapped on a receiving table in the foyer, but today she barely heard him enter the front door, the kitchen. He came up behind her; she could smell his cologne, a fragrance she'd selected for him that was made for both men and women. She used it herself sometimes. He started to embrace her from behind, then stopped, his hands resting lightly on her arms.

"Is this allowed?" he asked.

She nodded, but turned so she was facing him. He gave her one of his fierce bear hugs which she hadn't received in a long time. She'd forgotten how well they fit together, how natural this felt, right. She looked into his face, they were nearly the same height, and was stunned to see a glaze of tears in his eyes. They didn't fall, just welled there as if he wasn't sure it was safe to cry.

"I'm sorry," she said then. "I'm sorry I made this harder on you."

He shook his head, unable to speak.

It's like we're foreign, Candace thought. Lovers desperately drawn to each other who share maybe three words in common. How do they do it? Where do they begin?

Barry led the way. He took her hand and guided her into a cozy den they seldom used now that the boys were gone. His destination was a mauve chenille couch that was really two chaise lounges tucked together. She followed without protest. He removed his jacket, his shoes, and his tie, tossed them to the side, not caring where they landed. He spread out cushions for them to rest their heads on and pulled her onto the couch, arranging them like puzzle pieces that make a satisfying snap when they lock into place, perfectly aligned. They were lying on their sides, knees interlaced, his and hers and his and hers. She was curled in his arms, head in his chest yet somehow able to breathe. She began to speak and he said, "Hush," very gently, not commanding, but soothing, the simplest way to let her know that words weren't needed just now. "Let's breathe," he said. And so they did.

They slept, dreamlessly, and when they awoke in the same minute of the same hour, well into the night, their breaths and bodies had restored a level of trust and goodwill that had gone missing for too long.

"I'm hungry," Barry said. "What say we whip up something and then we can talk."

He changed first, into comfortable shorts and t-shirt. Years vanished between them. This wasn't their home but someone else's, and they were guests, tiptoeing around in awe of so much splendor. She was the Lesley nerd, he was the law school star, she watched him throw together a quick spinach and feta cheese omelette with wondering, admiring eyes.

"There you go," he said, when he noticed. He folded the omelette with one hand and pulled her toward him with the other.

"There I go, what?"

"That look, I haven't seen that look since, I don't know when."

"What look is that?"

He paused to slip the omelette on a plate, one plate, she noticed. They'd share the food the way they once did. Candace was momentarily distracted by the food, she *was* hungry. She didn't wait for the omelette to cool but held a piece on her fork, blew on it, and bit down with appreciation.

"My God, this is good," she said.

"You're just hungry."

"No, you were always better at eggs than me. Than I."

Barry laughed. "Ever the English major."

"But we digress," she said. "What look did I give you? What was that all about?"

Barry made a face of joy as he wolfed his food. "Funny how things change as you get older. Some things you felt you'd rather *die* than admit; now you wonder, what was the big deal? So I can say it now, and it won't even slay me if you laugh. You had this way of looking at me like a sunflower worships the sun, growing toward the light. But here's what the sunflower doesn't know, the sun gets a big kick out of that attention, someone needing his light. There was a haunted quality about you when we first met, kind of like Estella in *Great Expectations*." Barry laughed. "There's a reference for you. I did read a few books. So I was Pip, ready to rescue you from whatever ghosts you kept in the closet. I meant to rescue you. Guess I failed."

Candace speared the last morsel of omelette with her fork and held it up to Barry.

"No, you," he said, so she finished it off.

She was quiet a moment then looked in his eyes, his glacier blue eyes, and asked, "How can you rescue someone who doesn't know they *need* saving? I think for that to work both parties have to be on the same page." Her eyes crinkled, lips curled when she heard herself. "I haven't been on *any* page until just recently. I was lost in catalogs and paint samples, and never even realized I had my own story. I am a story." She wiped her mouth with a napkin and folded it beside the plate. "I have so much to tell you about what led to my little hospital stay." She made a face and Barry laughed. "But first, since we're airing all our laundry here, could you help me understand what's been going on with you? What made you pull away?"

Barry picked up the plate about to head for the sink, but Candace stopped him, removed the plate from his grasp, pushed it to the side. She took both his hands in hers and scooted her chair to edge out a little so she faced him.

"It's me," she said. "Candace, who has loved you since the very beginning. Please talk to me." She waited while he breathed carefully, looking at the floor. This time the glaciers melted, tears ran past their icy blue lenses and fell down his cheeks. Candace plucked a tissue from her pocket and wiped them away, still holding one of his hands.

"I've been trying to hold it together for so long," he whispered raggedly. "Down to my last Band-Aid the past few days." Then he crumpled, cracked open as if a sculptor had released his form from a granite block. He cried deeply and ferociously, and Candace moved her chair beside his so she could hold him. And when he tried to apologize for soaking her blouse, being such a baby, it was her turn to hush him, remind him to breathe. When everything he'd held so tightly inside had unspooled, flooded into the soft light of dawn, Candace wet a towel and washed his face just as she would a feverish child. He blinked at her, his eyes swollen but focused again, lit.

"This was a long time coming," he said. "Thank you for holding on." Candace waited, hearing an opening. She was right. Finally, her husband came back to himself and told them a story they both needed to hear.

"This goes back to the Dark Ages, well, the Dark Ages of me." Barry's mouth pulled up at one end but you couldn't call it a proper smile. "I never liked my name, you knew that?" Barry looked at Candace. She shook her head, no. "Well, I didn't. Hated it. Barrett—in my school? You've gotta be kidding me. But I adored my mother, would have done anything to please her, so I tried to wear it as a badge of her honor, if not mine. Tried to be the golden one who brought her glory. I always knew she was unhappy, embarrassed that Dad wasn't more ambitious, couldn't help her move up the social ladder. When she died, I just redoubled my efforts so she didn't die in vain, without any of her dreams being realized. I lived her dream. But for me, it was a nightmare, always has been. Dammit, I'm an arts person. That's *all* I ever wanted—to perform, act, sing, inhabit someone else's skin and make an audience believe at least for that hour or so that I wasn't Barry, Barrett, whatever. I was whoever the hell I was tapped to play. I *know* I have it in me. I *know* I have the ability. How pathetic is this? While I'm on the elliptical machine, what do you think I'm listening to on my iPod? *Wicked. Rent.* Sondheim's musicals. Lord, even *The Music Man* once." Barry laughed. His mood was brightening.

"But what would Mother have said to her boy being, of all shaky, unpredictable things, an actor? So I tried to be sensible, though the passion leaked out here and there, in college plays and even law school productions. Then we were an item and I knew I wanted to provide well for you, later, the boys. I was on this treadmill of success, money coming in by the handfuls, this was what I was supposed to do, supposed to want, right? We've succeeded. We're the lottery winners of the American Dream. So who was I to complain, me, with all of this!" He indicated their home that rose above them like a museum, an elaborate tomb.

"But Candace," he looked her in the eyes and said the next two words so softly she read them from his lips more than heard them. "My love." He cleared his throat. "Sometimes a person can only keep up appearances and live the lie by shutting down, numbing into a hectic routine. Run, run, run, don't think, for damn sure don't feel. Just go 'til you drop."

Candace brought him a glass of water and stood behind him as he drank, her hands on his shoulders. "It doesn't have to be this way," she announced. She squeezed his arms. "That's the glory of still being alive. We get to start all over if that's what's needed."

She sat down again beside him, her voice threaded with excitement. "The boys are almost done with school, they're fine, we could walk away from this. Sell the place, our stuff, find out where your Dad got his car." Barry burst out laughing. "I've learned so much about proposals and budgets from my board work, maybe I could be a consultant for arts groups or something? I don't know. But we don't have to keep doing this. It doesn't fit anymore, does it? We've outgrown this house and this chapter."

"But with the economy so uncertain, isn't it madness to let go of a cash cow?" Barry asked. He looked both hopeful and afraid of this wild new optimism.

Candace was pleased to hear the strength in her voice when she answered him: "Isn't this the *perfect* time to make a change, risk everything? When we're being shown there is no such thing as security. Honey, it's an illusion. Banks can fail, businesses go under, investments that seemed rock solid, poof, gone! Look what happened to your alma mater's endowment fund. Let's not be a slave to unhappiness."

Barry's eyebrows shot up. "Look who's turned it all around in the blink of an eye. Good for you! You're dangerous stuff, but I kinda like a little danger in my women." He growled at her and then they both laughed in astonishment.

"Before we explore that further, and believe me, I *want* to explore," Candace said, kissing him on the mouth and gently nipping his lower lip with her teeth. "There's something I want you to see." She led him upstairs to her walk-in closet that was larger than the first apartment she and Barry had shared when they were looking for a house. The Face rested in a box, an offering of tobacco beside him. He was a fierce presence but she didn't fear him. She was grateful for all he had shown her.

"What's he doing here?" Barry asked. "Isn't he usually in the art room?"

Candace told him the story then, with the Face as a witness, his grimacing dignity making the events sound credible even to a skeptic like Barry. She didn't think he'd dare scoff in the presence of the grave basswood scowl. When she finished, Barry shook his head.

"So the old man can see her? Maryam?"

"Yes."

"How about that. He's got the goods and I don't. I clearly don't, since I'll have to chew on this a while. I'm not sure what to think."

"This isn't a competition," she admonished. "You've been shut up tight, and so have I for that matter. Your Dad, well, he's special."

"I guess I've always seen him through my mother's eyes, and that's not the kindest view."

"Or the clearest," Candace said. "Isn't it time you see things through your own eyes?" She chuckled. "Listen to me. A few days in the psych ward and I'm the expert!"

"But what about him?" Barry asked. He thrust his chin toward the mask.

"I've got to take him back eventually, back to his people. Our people. He doesn't belong here. I'll get on that, do some research. But in the meantime, can you take the day off? I'd like to hear more about your penchant for dangerous women."

Barry growled again, almost too convincingly, there was a stirring from the Face, a rustling of the tissues surrounding him. "Let's take this somewhere else," Barry suggested, and they closed the closet door so the Face would be spared the raucous noise of their reunion.

▪ ▪ ▪

The day after Candace was released from the hospital, Gladys received a surprise call from Binah, asking if she could take her out for coffee. "My class isn't 'til tonight and I'm fully prepared, so I have some free time," she said. "Ava's at a friend's house on a play date, it'll be just the two of us for once."

"Sounds good to me," Gladys said.

Binah pulled up in front of the mansion an hour later, and the two walked up Western Avenue in the direction of Nina's Cafe. The day was warm, the sky a clear blue without a single cloud Gladys could find. She pointed to it as they walked.

"It's a clean slate," she said.

"Hmm?"

"My grandfather always told me that when you get a sky like this it means you get to start over, nothing sticky to hold you back or cover you with misgivings."

"I wish such a thing were possible," Binah said, and Gladys took her arm, leaned on her a little, not because she was tired, but to show her she was needed.

"It is, my girl, it is. Maybe you can't force someone else to change with you, but that doesn't stop you from starting out fresh. And then, who knows, people around you might change to catch up?"

When they reached Nina's the side tables were all occupied by young people, their laptops open before them, plugged into the wall. They were availing themselves of the free wireless service and might camp out there for hours. But there were free tables in back, and Binah claimed the one in a private corner. The women left their bags on the table, just removing their wallets, and went to the front. They both ordered plain coffee and scones. Once they were settled, Gladys let a silence fall between them to encourage Binah to open up. She didn't want to chatter away this precious opportunity. Binah looked more rested than she had in months, and she was wearing her hair pulled off her face, clipped with a beaded barrette that was the shape and design of a butterfly, as if a radiant blue specimen had landed there to rest its wings. Binah picked at her scone much the way her husband had tortured a cruller a few months back, but Gladys didn't correct her. She waited.

Finally Binah spoke: "Mama, I'm not good at apologies. I don't know why that is. You and Dad could always take responsibility for your mistakes. Why can't I?"

Gladys held her peace, her attentive silence like soft breath on a spark when you're trying to build a fire—blow too hard and the spark dies.

"So, new slate? Well, then, here's mine. I owe you an apology. I've always respected you and Dad, glad you raised us Ojibwe but didn't discourage us from moving into other worlds as well. I've respected you, but not as much as I should have. Here I am, traveling around the country giving speeches about how Native peoples have been ignored, overlooked, condescended to, and in my own way, *I've* been a perpetrator. I set the Native scholar above, well, you, other elders. Giving lip service to your wisdom but not taking the time to *listen*, really listen. Then you stood up that night at Birchbark Books and showed us all how it's done—how to speak from the heart. Say what you mean, mean what you say. You're an example of one of our greatest gifts—clear talk, clear vision. No hidden agendas mucking everything up, no fingers crossed behind your back. I was proud of you, ashamed of myself." She shook her head as if stunned by her admission. Not the content, but the fact that she was able to speak it. Gladys reached for her hand and held it between her own.

"Thank you, I accept your apology. But I wasn't trying to shame you or outdo you, it's just that the world is in a pretty big mess, and I think it's time the powers that be take a listen to *us*. It's their failing if they choose to laugh when we mention spirits, scoff when we honor beings they consider beneath them. They can be skeptics right up until the end when the water's rising, and it's not even good enough to drink. We'll have to show them the way, how to make it through. We'll have to forgive them because, well, we're family."

Binah took back her hand and stirred her coffee. Stirred and stirred, just for something to do.

"I'll never be as forgiving as you. Once someone's failed me, betrayed me, and that can include an institution or a government, then I see it in a different light, spattered with the mud of a compromised ethic. I can't make it clean again, not in my head."

"There's your problem," Gladys said. She took a sip of coffee. "Your head's like a box, or a big trap with teeth. Snap! You have your idea, your judgment, your picture of something and it can't move, can't ever get up and change. Everything's stuck. Now me, I like to think of a healthy mind as a clothesline—sounds crazy, I know. But wait. You clip something on the line to take a look at, move around, see it from the other side. No, it doesn't work there, you take it down. Give yourself room to change your mind. No one's right all the time and nothing stays the same forever."

Binah nodded, looked as if she wanted to take notes. "I brought you something." She pulled out a book and pushed it across the table. *X-Marks: Native*

Signatures of Assent by Scott Richard Lyons. "This just came out and I think you'll like it. He's mixed like you, part Ojibwe, part Dakota. Anyway, he makes some of the points you do about how you want us to preserve our ways but not think they're set in stone, unchanging. He takes on the Native fundamentalists in a respectful way. I want to teach this in my upper-level discussion course. I realized that you are the best resource in my life, I should have you visit my class, paid for your time and trouble. You have so much to offer. So much to teach."

"Chi Megwetch," Gladys said. She felt her face grow warm with emotion. "I'll take a look at it. We're probably related some way." She put the volume in her purse. "Now, forgive me being nosy, but it's just because I care. What about Frank?"

Binah made a noise of disgust. "Don't talk to me about him. The nerve of him asking to come home. He said the romance of graduate-style living is lost on him, and the street traffic at night when the bars close in Uptown is driving him mad. So he'll deign to return for a good night's sleep."

Gladys shook her head. "Binah, do you *really* believe that, what you're saying? Do you honestly think that's why he wants to come back?" Binah opened her mouth to protest. "Wait." Gladys held up her hand like a traffic cop. "Yes, he hurt your feelings when he left, but mostly didn't he hurt your pride? Deep down you *have* to know that man loves you, adores you, and Ava is his sun, moon, and stars. If your pride is a good partner, then I say, good for you, may you live together happily ever after. But is your pride good in bed?"

"Mama!"

"Is your pride a good father? Does your pride make you laugh first thing in the morning and surprise you with breakfast in bed? Don't answer, don't argue. Just think about it?"

Binah sat like stone but creaked her head forward in a grim, barely perceptible nod.

"Good. Remember, my girl, when you and Grace were little I told you the story about the moon, how you had to be careful and not watch it too much or it might carry you away to join the little boy who's already there with his two pails. Grace just smiled and then made a drawing of the boy on the moon, but you took it to heart. I felt so bad. You were the one who hid whenever the moon was full, pulled down the shades and went under the bed. You were the one with nightmares where you'd been snatched away and could only see us from across the vast dark ocean of space. Don't make that nightmare come true in real life."

■ ■ ■

Just an hour after Binah walked her mother back to the Summit Hill mansion she was phoning her. "Mama, I thought about what you said. You're right."

Gladys covered the receiver with a hand and whispered, "Thank you." She was sitting on the suede loveseat in her apartment, Zhigaag nestled in her lap. They were listening to Bob Dylan whose distinctive voice seemed to soothe the cat—he purred contentedly. She looked down at her feet, shuffled them to do a seated soft-shoe routine of pure joy.

"So I have a favor to ask you," Binah continued. "Could you keep Ava with you at your place tomorrow night? Frank and I have a lot to discuss and, knowing me, it might get a little heated. Best if she's not here."

"Of *course*," Gladys said. "We'll have a good old time. She's been dying to see this place and now it's cleaned out, I don't have to protect her from anything."

"What?"

"Never mind, long story. I'm *so* glad you're going to talk. Talk, my girl. Listen. It doesn't have to be a war."

"Mm hmm."

Wednesday afternoon Binah brought her daughter to Summit Hill. Ava was so excited it was all she could do to wait until the car had stopped before unbuckling her seatbelt and leaping out of the vehicle. Binah left the car, grabbing a small duffle bag from the back seat. Ava ran ahead of her, up the stone steps. She wrapped her arms around one of the stone lions and then planted a kiss right on its nose.

"Whoops," she said, "I don't want to hurt the other one's feelings." So she rushed to the second lion, hugged and kissed that one as well.

"Are you finished?" Binah asked, trying to sound impatient, but smiling at her affectionate daughter.

"Yes. I need to save some for Zhigaag."

The door opened, both Candace and Gladys standing behind it, and this time Binah crossed the threshold, shook Candace's hand.

"Thank you for letting her stay here," she said.

"Oh, it'll be fun!" Candace crowed. "It has been so long since the boys were this age. A really fun age. We've got all kinds of plans."

Ava twirled in her pink polka-dotted sun dress. The top was bare and simple with thin spaghetti straps, but the skirt was full the way Ava liked.

"What a lovely dress, you look ready for a fancy party," Candace enthused. Ava smiled and adjusted her glasses.

"She's like that," Binah said. "Prefers frilly clothes, dresses, don't know where that comes from. I'm all about jeans."

"Grandma's wearing a pretty skirt," Ava pointed out.

"Yes, she is. Funny, I hadn't noticed," Binah responded. "Well, I'll let you get the party started." Binah offered a sharp smile. "Any love for Mama?" she asked, and Ava hugged her so fiercely she growled for emphasis. "Wow, that's the best one yet," Binah said. She kissed Ava on the cheek.

She hugged her mother, waved to Candace, then walked out the door and past the lions. "You'll get no sugar from me," she told them, and though she didn't turn to look, she had the distinct feeling of deflation behind her—disappointed cats.

Frank arrived bearing luggage, and Binah nearly closed the apartment door on him. "That's presumptuous," she said.

Frank entered cheerfully, deposited the bags against the wall in the entrance hall, and dropped onto their couch with a contented sigh. "I can't tell you how nice it is to be back home, looking upon your beautiful face, even if it is a bit stern." He smiled at her and Binah smiled back, despite her irritation.

"Iced tea?" she asked.

"Oh, that would be perfect. Doesn't feel like fall's anxious to get here, does it?" Frank was wearing shorts and a t-shirt advertising *The Rake* magazine. His hair was in a neat ponytail and he'd kept his face clean-shaven. "So, what do you think of my new look?" he asked Binah when she returned to the living room with the tea.

"Makes me feel like I'm robbing the cradle," she said. "You could be one of my students."

"I *am* one of your students, my dear," he said, seductively, but his grin diminished the effect.

"All right, all right." Binah sat on the couch but at the opposite end from Frank. "Good feelings all around, that's a start. But where do we go from here?"

Frank was suddenly before her, down on one knee. Good grief, but he can move quickly, she thought. "What's all this?"

"I have a speech. Well, a brief one. And all I ask is that you listen without interruption."

Binah looked nervous, but she nodded. Frank took one of her hands and brought it to his heart.

"Feel that? My Caucasian-American ticker? It's beating for you. 'Such love, such love.' Can you hear it? That's what it says in there all day, doing its two-step rhythm. I want to be with you and our amazing daughter, and live together as joyfully as we can in this unpredictable world. But, and here's the sticking point, I want us to be allies. I have your back, you have mine. Take each other as we are, right now, today. I'm not trying to mold you into Miss Congeniality, I like a little bite, and you don't turn me into a stand-in for anyone other than myself. I won't take it. You fell in love with me, Frank, not a white guy. *Me*. You're not like anyone else on this earth and neither am I. Binah and Frank, that's all we are, and in my opinion that's more than enough!

"I shall rise now. My knees aren't what they used to be." He sat beside her, put an arm around her stiff shoulders, and waited for her to relax. After a few minutes, she did.

"How was that?" he asked. "Nice speech?" She nodded. "Can we at least *try* to do this again?"

Binah was biting the inside of her mouth to keep from crying. Frank pressed her against him.

"What is it? What's going on?" She shook her head and held up a hand. A plea for time. So they sat there together, and Frank listened to his wife's shallow breathing.

"God, I feel like such a wimp!" Binah said, rising with unexpected fury. She stomped around the living room and Frank just watched, his hands pressed between his knees. "I'm not mad at *you*," she explained. "I'm frustrated with myself. Unhhhh!!" She pumped the air with clenched fists.

"Okay, now *I* have a kind of speech, but I need to move as I talk." She paced. Frank listened. "Had a round-table discussion last week. Talking about the work of Sousan Abadian on collective trauma. She argues that Natives have had a harder time recovering from historical atrocities because the main support systems a people rely on to recover were kicked out from under us. What she calls 'the violation of our socio-cultural integrity.' I won't get into that now, but what's germane is that we got into a conversation about her theories, and one guy stands up, says he's as liberal as they come, blah, blah, blah, but why do we have to rehash our past? Why pick at old scabs over and over? I was ready to throttle his skinny little chicken neck, but an elder from White Earth spoke next. She said that was just it. If the past is always swept under the rug, our stories hushed up, our claims denied, ignored, the wound stays open. Never heals. The next generation is born into that injury and carries it on. The one way to begin healing is for all of us to be honest with each other. Put our truth on the table, drag it into the light. Pain festers in the shadows. She did a good job. I didn't even start with my usual dog and pony show about how the past isn't really the past but still impacting us today. The look on that woman's face was more eloquent than I could ever be." Binah grabbed her glass of tea and took a long drink.

"That brings us to *me*. My pathetic little secret that I never wanted to speak because I thought by telling it I would give it power. Instead, by hiding it, sitting on it for so long, it's grown until it's taken me over. Like some mass that gets so tangled up with your arteries eventually no doctor wants to touch the thing, or try to remove it. Sorry, that's kind of graphic." She set down her tea, paused, staring at the wall.

"So, tell me," Frank said softly. "Tell *me* your secret and we'll hold it together and take away its power."

"I can only tell you if I'm not looking at you," Binah said. "It's too humiliating." She plunged her hands in the back pockets of her jeans and rocked back and forth on her heels. She faced the entrance hall, so Frank only saw her in profile—her strong nose and fine brow, her long hair that reached almost to her knees.

"Okay, this happened the summer of 1971. I was ten, about to start fifth grade. Where we lived, one of those border areas between the Rez and a white town, we had some white friends and some who would've liked to be friends, but their parents wouldn't let them. Then there were the prejudiced morons. That's how Grace and I thought of them, never took it as a reflection on ourselves, on our worth. Our parents did such a good job of instilling pride in us, and in our origins.

"There was this one kid, Todd, bullied everyone, white or Indian, didn't matter. Big white kid, not very bright. Always looked like his skin was peeling, flaking off on his clothes. The only thing he could lord over us was his size, so he did. I was fast though, so he never got his hands on me until this one time. Even then, it was his little henchmen who caught me. I was coming home from our library, a pitiful place, with limited selections, but I made the most of it. I skirted the town, cut through a path in the woods because I liked the smell of it, the sounds, how even on a hot day there was green shade. Todd happened along with his scared little entourage and he sicced them on me. One of them tackled me, brought me down, and then Todd told them to hold me there, spread out like some creature that's been skinned and pegged. I was more angry than scared, even at that point. Spitting angry. I howled at them to let me go, cussed them out but good. Then Todd stood over me and stuffed a nasty rag in my mouth, smelled like gasoline. And *he* talked. He spit in my face, said I was nothing, less than nothing. I wasn't a person like him. I was a toilet. To prove what he said, he pissed on me. I mean all over. From my face to my legs and back, peed like a horse until he was through. Then they all took off and there I was. Alone. Soaked. Shaking. Furious. Beyond humiliated. I went down to the little creek near our place and went in, washed the best I could. I wanted to scrub myself raw with Lysol, but I knew that smell on my skin would make Mama suspicious. So I washed there, and when Grace came looking for me I didn't tell her what happened but asked her to bring me soap, and then washed again. Over and over, every hour, until it was time for supper. Pretty lame, huh? That something so stupid could get to me? I wasn't raped, wasn't beaten. Todd's long dead—car smashup. But he got under my skin and I *hated* him. Oh God, I learned how to hate *really* well."

Frank was behind her, wrapping her in his arms. She turned to face him and he saw she was past tears. Talking had been better than crying, at least for Binah.

"It's a good thing he's gone," Frank said. "Pacifist that I am, I'd have had a bit of business with him. Thank you for telling me. I know it was hard."

"The hardest thing I've ever done," Binah said, and then she hugged him back and they rocked together until the rocking became the slowest of slow dances.

"Just think how messed up you must be to do something like that," Frank said.

"What?"

"Well, think about it. What we do, what we say, those words and actions belong to our soul. Yes, *you* were defiled, humiliated, but you washed off and went back to being a beautiful, powerful person. But this Todd, he could never wash off what he did to you, probably to others."

"I never thought of it that way," Binah said. "You and Mama, what a pair. Larger hearts than mine, that's for sure."

"Don't do it!" Frank said in a mock-angry voice. "Don't you dare malign your heart in front of me."

He stooped to kiss her heart, her left breast, her neck, her full mouth. They danced and kissed. They didn't notice the gust of wind that swept through the room, catching Binah's story by its angry tail and whipping it out the window, where, with no one else to listen, it swirled away to nothing.

Clan Mother of Regret

The Confession of Ruby Two-Axe

Ruby Two-Axe (2009)

November 4, 2009
Candace Jenssen
—— Summit Avenue
Saint Paul, MN 55——

Dear Ms. Jenssen:

I send this package with some trepidation—hoping the contents will be like a treasure coming to you from the forgotten past rather than a bombshell that upends your present life. The items contained herein: (1) a transcript of my last conversation/interview with your maternal grandmother, Ruby West, née Two-Axe, who passed away this year at the age of 105, (2) a scrap of tanned hide she handled quite reverently in her final days—the source of which becomes clear in the transcript, (3) a photograph of your great-grandfather and his lacrosse team, all of them steelworkers in the early part of the last century, and (4) a postcard of the Kanien'kehá:ka Cultural Center, much handled as you will see. On the back is a message she penned in her hand, which she asked me to convey to you.

Ruby's last years were spent in comfort at the Gellman Jewish Nursing Home on Long Island. She had listed as next of kin an attorney son of an old friend, a man neither her relative nor an intimate. He seemed pleased, actually relieved, when I offered to locate her nearest living relative, namely you, to receive these items and what little remains of her estate after all debts are settled.

Forgive me, perhaps I should have opened this missive with an identification of who I am, and how I became involved in these affairs pertaining to your family. My friendship with your grandmother came about as a result of my lifelong fascination with the Iroquois Confederacy. I grew up in Flushing, New York and was an avid Boy Scout—eventually an Eagle Scout—and hungrily read what stories I could find of your ancestors and their exploits in this, their homeland, region. No doubt I harbored fantasies of one day learning I was part Mohawk, descended from some fierce sachem or other, wince-worthy romanticizing on my part, born of the ignorance so prevalent in this country when it comes to Native American history (well, and the fact that you're not merely "history," people captured in the past, but continuing societies). Through grants and awards received in recent years (I'm a graduate student in International Studies at Columbia University), I was given the opportunity to meet and interview several Six Nations elders, your grandmother being one of them, and my clear favorite. We sort of "adopted" each other as grandmother and grandson. To be honest, I hadn't even realized I was missing that kind of relationship until it manifested so unexpectedly (my own surviving grandmother is a bit lost to me as she suffers from Alzheimer's and no longer recognizes her family).

Your grandmother was very kind to me; interested in what I was doing, supportive, teasing, insightful, and wise—everything one could wish for in an elder. I debated sending a film version of our last conversation, something I can easily make available to you in DVD form. In the end I thought it might prove a shock to see her, hear her, so vividly alive after all these years of separation. A paper text may be easier on the heart. I have injected a few of my own comments and observations, as sparingly as possible to avoid interfering with the flow of Ruby's thoughts. I hope this will assist you in gaining a fuller portrait of the exchange. I want her to live in these pages now that she is gone. I tell myself it's an offering I make to you, but perhaps it's my own selfish need to hold onto precious moments of a connection that has been important to me.

I should mention that in earlier conversations Ruby was reticent to speak of her history and deflected all probes in that direction with a question of her own—drawing *me* out instead. Then she summoned me in May 2009 and said she was ready to talk. I was touched and honored by this evidence of her trust and flew at the chance to finally hear her story. I was not disappointed. You will notice that the events she describes are not offered in chronological order. I was so often tempted to interrupt with a question, wanting to understand the story behind the story, so to speak. Instinct told me to err on the side of patience and relinquish control. A good decision. She spoke what her heart was ready to confide.

Oh, a final addition—I send along a photograph of the two of us together the last day we spoke: your grandmother and myself. I find it helps to see who is addressing us when the message is significant. I hope you're able to read from my expression how well-intended are my meddlings in your affairs.

With very best wishes,
Ari Engel
—— W. 79th Street
New York, NY 10——

Candace folded the letter and tucked it back into its envelope. She reached first for the photograph of the document's author, Ari Engel, in his last visit with her grandmother. He was younger than she'd expected, perhaps mid-twenties, and though he had the whippet-slender physique of a runner, his face was baby round, his smile deeply dimpled and sweet. This was a warm man, she could immediately sense. His sand-blond hair was an exuberant mass of curls that threatened to overwhelm the yarmulke pinned to his head. He reminded her of the fawn from the Narnia series, Mr. Tumnus. The idea made her smile. She looked next where his gaze focused. He wasn't aiming his attention or his grin at the photographer, who was probably one of the nurses, but rather at the shriveled figure nearly lost in a thicket of pillows, arranged as if her hospital bed were a throne. Ari was captured in tender profile as he leaned toward the form, and though the ancient woman faced squarely forward, her focus was similarly on him rather than the camera lens. The first detail Candace noticed was that the woman, My Grandma, she gently corrected, appeared colorless, as if her parchment flesh had lost pigment over the years and faded to a papery beige. And her eyes, which had formerly been black and sharp, were now a fuzzy brown. Once Candace looked past the collapsed scrim of wrinkles, she realized her grandmother was a beauty, the bones and lines still elegant, the bright silver hair glossy and neat in its braid. This is where that stereotype comes from, she suddenly thought. That our grandmothers were Indian princesses. Mine looks like a queen.

Without touching the inner packet containing a scrap of hide, another photograph, and a mysterious message written on a postcard, Candace pulled out the transcript and weighed it in her hands, almost as if they could tell her the difference between good news and bad news, and issue fair warning. The hands gave nothing away. To understand her grandmother, and perhaps a bit more about her mother, she would have to read.

TRANSCRIPT

[I arrived with a sack containing Ruby's favorite meal: hot pastrami on rye, pickle on the side, and a wedge of halva for dessert. Hardly healthy fare, but the nurses looked the other way due to her advanced age. I think they felt she deserved some small pleasures. She was proud to still have her "choppers" and a good appetite.]

RUBY: Why did I change my name from Two-Axe to West? It was a bland word I grabbed from the air. Safe, because it didn't mean anything to me, it didn't tie me to anyone. Later I saw it wasn't just accident, that choice. The Six Nations Confederacy, the Haudenosaunee, is a league of six tribes: the Mohawk, Seneca, Oneida, Cayuga, Onondaga, and Tuscarora. My people, the Mohawk, lived on the eastern edge of Six Nations territory. We are the Keepers of the Eastern Door. So when I left my home in Kahnawà:ke, left my family, my language, the ways of lifelong training, even my old God, I slammed a door shut between the past and the present, turned my back on everything I loved. I faced west. I was no longer Mohawk. I dragged my poor girl with me, my Mavis, who was just a toddler with chubby legs and a little round stomach. Folks at home called her Junebug. I tore her away from all her aunts and uncles and cousins, a beloved Grandma, and it was so sudden she turned into a quiet, shocked baby. Always wide-eyed and afraid. Nothing was familiar. I made my way to Brooklyn because I'd heard of it from the steelworkers and their families who sometimes lived there. Eventually a whole community of us settled in the North Gowanus neighborhood—you know all about that if you've read Joseph Mitchell's old piece. But I didn't head for Gowanus. I wandered into a different part of Brooklyn, moved into a tiny place above a kosher delicatessen. That's why I need my fix now and then.

[She gestured toward the remains of her pastrami sandwich.]

RUBY: This, to me, is New York.

Folks were curious about us at first and shuttled all their questions through Ruth Plotsky who lived across the hall. "You're Indian, and the little one, too? Did you live in the woods? Did you live in a house? Will your husband stay here? Is he coming soon?" All I said was yes, or no, or if I didn't want to say even that much I'd shrug the question away. Finally, after about a week of this, I looked right into Ruth's eyes—they were a soft pearl gray that seemed so kind—and I said real firm: "My people are dead." She sucked in a little piece of air between us and held it, and I remember thinking it was a generous thing to do, like she had breathed in some of my sadness and accepted it. She protected me from all other busybodies from that day on. This was before World War II, you see. After the war everyone was more careful about the questions, about how far to press, because so many people had lost relatives back home to the Nazis.

What little money I had was quickly running out, so I took in mending and later beading, but not the Indian kind. I decorated fancy wedding dresses and veils—although that sort of fine sewing came much later, after I had connections in the garment business. From schmattas to dos khupe kleyd!

The main way I made money at first was by helping out on Shabbat. I never lived with the real strict Orthodox Jews, but the families around me kept kosher and observed Shabbat. They were struggling families from places like Poland and Romania, Hungary and Ukraine. No extra pennies to lose or fool around with, but always there was some forgotten business in one or two households, some little errand or chore that couldn't wait, and here I was, the Indian goy lady ready to lend a hand. Maybe because I lived so light at the edge of things, people seemed to trust me pretty quick. I was never pushy or nosy, invisible most of the time. Come to think of it, my neighbors would probably be more suspicious of you than they were of me—a German Jew with all your fellowships!

[She smiled at me and patted my hand as if to say she *trusted me. Her touch was a silk scarf, so soft and weightless. Then her face changed, clouded over. I waited for her to share the memory that had wrecked her smile.]*

RUBY: We can walk away from our history but that doesn't mean it lets us go. Maybe I thought I was one little bead sewn to a piece of fabric, set apart from the rest. But always there's a design, and we find ourselves connected no matter how much empty ground we've staked out around our hearts and our lives. I was fooling myself to think I'd get away scot free. A few months after I moved to Brooklyn my brothers found me.

My older, taller, beautiful pine tree brothers who had always been my shelter growing up. Like a gypsy caravan they came in their beat-up reservation cars, my brothers, their wives and kids, some cousins. I guess they thought they were a rescue party come to support me and bear me on home. I lived in a dark old tenement building—all the light and air was used up in the deli downstairs. The upper floors were squat and crowded, always too hot or too cold, noisy with a baby crying or sometimes a goat, couples arguing with each other in a half dozen languages. Into this nest of confusion my people climbed, a quiet group that barely set the stairs groaning. So many of them, they filled the hall outside my door in a tight bunch like a clutch of dark eggs. That's my impression at least, when I think how I stuck my head out the door to answer their knock, expecting Ruth or some other neighbor, never my past.

"Ruby, what are you doing here?" my eldest brother said in a low voice, smoky with tears. I was struck dumb, death itself in the doorway, frozen for several long moments until I felt my Mavis poke forward from behind my legs. She was peering into the dim hall, and when she saw the figures she cried out a sound of joy. "Junebug, I missed you!" Now my brother's voice was husky with delight, and Mavis opened her arms to him. Time doesn't always move the same amount of breaths and beats; it can speed up and it can slow down until everyone's caught in a sticky pudding almost impossible to move through. That moment was slowed down. I'll remember it forever. I glanced at the faces of my family and didn't register them separately or think their names; they looked to me like hungry ghosts, ready to wail and rattle their shells, launch some terrible haunting. My brother leaned forward to catch up his niece in a fierce hug, set her on the branch of his shoulder. Her face was already thrilled as if she were flying through the air in the safety of his arms. I broke the spell and sped up time with a quick snatch of my hand. I yanked Mavis behind me so quickly I knocked her off her feet and she sat down hard on her bottom. She stayed down, too stunned to cry. Then I spoke to my brother these words, the last he'd ever hear from me: "No one is here." I slammed the door in his face.

[After this revelation, Ruby put her hands over her eyes as if to press away the old visions. Gradually her hands slipped from their position and I saw that she'd fallen into a hard sleep, no doubt a healing sleep that pulled her in like a refuge. I went for a walk and returned an hour later to find her restored again, ready to resume her narrative.]

RUBY: I say I lived invisible, at the edge of my neighbors' world, but that was more in the beginning. Humans beings are creeping ivy. We can shut up our heart and intend to keep our business strictly to ourselves, but we just keep growing over each other, one tendril at a time, so puny at first you're fooled to think it doesn't count. I started out a stranger and ended up an honorary yenta. My talent was escape. I didn't want to live the story I'd lived before so I took my girl to the flickers whenever I had a few extra coins. Such movies were coming out then! Top Hat, *with Fred and Ginger dancing as if no one was hungry anymore,* Captain Blood, *featuring that swashbuckler, Errol Flynn, with his snarling good looks,* China Seas *starring the platinum goddess, Jean Harlow, who died so young and tragic. And I picked up the film rags now and then, too, fascinated by the scandals, all the complicated love lives of America's royalty—the Hollywood stars. That was when Shirley Temple was in her heyday, raised pretty right, it seemed to me. She won an Oscar in 1935 and it didn't impress her one little bit. She was a real kid, nothing phony. To the housewives in my building I was like Hedda Hopper. I brought that whole glistening world they couldn't afford right to their kitchen table. I'd read them the stories and show them the pictures. I'd act out the latest film I just saw, and carry us away from the pile of dishes in the sink, the laundry drying on the line that had to be brought in. We all need a little glamor in our lives, and that's what I delivered, like the ambassador to glitz.*

Then pretty soon I'd be hearing their stories, coming to know their kids, their talents and flaws, how they worried their parents. Everyone fussed over Mavis and her curious shocked hair. One woman, Bsora, was real good with hair and she twisted Mavis's locks up in rags to make ringlets, and that finally calmed it down. Mavis loved having thick curls like that, and would wind them around her fingers until it looked like she was wearing black sausages. We had our spats, of course, and could get competitive in the sly way of mothers. Where you complain about your kid but it's really a way of showing off some ability they have that others envy. We borrowed back and forth, the flour and the eggs, and pretty soon I was keeping kosher, too, without even trying. I could be frugal when there was a reason, but when you're living from day to day, and the future is nothing more to you than a hammer, it's hard to save for tomorrow. It was my neighbors and their connections what helped me grow the little I had, taught me where to invest and when, so that eventually we moved out of the tenement into nice houses in Queens. But that took years.

Mavis grew up in Brooklyn and went to public school there. She was smart and liked her homework—I never had to scold her for leaving it go. She'd finish it up first thing after class, then go out to jump rope and chase around with the other girls. I can see now that the way I left the reservation, the way I stormed to Brooklyn and banished our relatives, must have been a mystery to Mavis. She soon learned that questioning me was useless, so as she got older she simply worked things out her own way. Mavis thought there was something wrong with being Mohawk. I picked this up when I heard her telling stories to the other kids about who we really were, where we really came from. According to her our people were Spanish royalty in old times, shipwrecked in the Americas and stolen by Indians. "If I want it," she said, "there is a crown waiting for me in Europe." Such nonsense, and at first her friends teased about it. But Mavis could wear you down with how determined she was, and she clung to her story like it was the single thing that kept her from drowning. I could have told her the truth to give her something to stand on—that she came from people who loved her and were good to her, that our folks were always so proud to be Mohawk, Kanien'kehá:ka, the real Founding Fathers of this country with our complex system of government that proved so inspiring to old Ben Franklin. I should have taught her these things, told her her Mohawk name, which is buried with her now. But I was afraid to even start because one piece of history connected to another and another, like a magician's chain of scarves pulled from his sleeve, and the telling would get closer to home than I was ready to go. So I let her grow up in an orphan way, ignorant of all that came down to her in the blood, in the stories, in the spirit. It's like planting a seed without giving it the light or the water, and expecting it to turn into a flower. She looked *like a flower, like an Indian version of Anne Baxter who steamed it up with Charlton Heston in* The Ten Commandments. *She had boys coming and going from the time she was twelve, kept the trinkets they offered her in a shoebox she treasured like it contained the crown jewels. She told me once, "Mama, look how many admirers I have. The numbers are important. The more you have, the more you are." So wise and so foolish. Wise to know what it took to make her feel she mattered, foolish to think this was the way to go about it. I knew this was the wrong path, but I kept quiet, pretending it was schoolgirl talk she'd outgrow. But it was more serious than that. I'd given birth to a whole child and then tipped her over like a jug and poured her out. All she was trying to do was fill herself up again with whatever came to hand.*

She was so comfortable with Jewish boys she dated them the most. She got a lot of her friends in trouble that way, since their Mamas wanted them to marry a nice Jewish girl rather than the exotic shiksa. Despite my daughter's misguided ways, she chose the right boy when it came to marrying: Myron Altman, who was just her age but seemed a little older. There was a patience about him, he listened well and chose his words with care. I complimented him once, the first time Mavis brought him up to our apartment to meet me. I said he reminded me of old-time Mohawks who placed such importance on open ears and respectful tongue. We were consensus-builders, after all, and you can't pull people together if you talk over one another and don't really hear. He blushed and explained that he'd had a speech impediment as a kid, and it took a lot of practice to tame it so he could be understood. That made me think of Peacemaker, the one who brought us the Great Law of Peace and helped us forge the Confederacy. They say He was born with a double row of teeth which made it hard for Him to speak clear. Maybe He was given those extra teeth as a gift more than a problem, like He was marked from the beginning as someone whose speech would matter, and He had to be held back from careless talking. I said all this to Myron and then asked: "So, what's the Good News you *bring?" He blushed again, but it was more pleasure than shame, and we crossed over into friendship at that moment. Mavis changed the subject, snapping her eyes at me in warning. That look said: Keep this up, Mama, and we're outta here! She always hated it the rare times I mentioned we were Mohawk. What she'd yearned for in her earliest years she now rejected. I'd missed my chance.*

The two of them got married right out of high school in May of 1951. I feel bad I don't recall the date. Myron's folks were the most secular of Jews, I think they'd have tackled him if he tried to set foot in a Temple, so the kids went through one of those dusty ceremonies in a courthouse. He went right into his father's plumbing business and helped expand it to New Jersey. He and Mavis ended up living in a smart little bungalow in West Orange. One time I asked Mavis how Myron beat out all the other suitors who'd been courting her since the seventh grade. Myron didn't seem as exciting as some, and Mavis was all about excitement! "Oh, Myron," she sighed, but her forehead smoothed to contentment. "Others came and went, enthusiasms up and down, but Myron was steady. The flame might be lower, but it's always burning."

"Good answer," I said, then knew I'd blundered. Mavis looked upset, like the last thing she wanted was to please me.

"Hmp," was all she said. If anyone could have made my girl happy it would have been Myron. He tried. Oh, that man tried. Whenever I think of him I see him with a shovel, and he's chucking all he's got into the great maw of emptiness that is my Mavis. Trying to fill that hole. But when we got nothing to stand on, we leak, and no one else can fix that for us. I should know.

They had a nice house, nice furniture, money in the bank. Trips to Manhattan to see the shows my daughter loved, and to go to nightclubs. They had their own little girl, Candace, born in 1954, and nothing was too good for that one. Every toy and every book, and her closet full of fancy clothes, those party dresses with the net underneath to make the skirt stand out. Myron watched my daughter like an attendant butler, ready to pounce on her least little wish.

"She's married a genie," I joked with the yentas, but then Devorah Lemberg made some remark about Mavis rubbing his lamp, and I closed the topic.

I seldom saw my daughter after they moved to New Jersey. I knew Mavis had reinvented herself again in West Orange and didn't want a mother around to ruin her stories. Contradict. I saw my granddaughter on rare occasions when the whole family came to the city, and I don't know what Mavis told her about me—that I was some wild Indian? Something to scare her. She cried when I tried to hold her and would spend most of a visit in the cave under my dining table. "She's just sensitive to change, a new environment," Mavis said, dismissive of this behavior, and I wondered if that was a backhand slap at me who'd changed her whole life in a single day. Then I didn't see them for a couple of years, just cards sent back and forth, and a monthly call was the only contact. So I didn't know that Mavis was struggling with what we called back then "the blues." Only later I heard from Myron how hard he tried to help her, cheer her, find her a therapist. He said she insisted she could muscle through.

"I come from strong women who never cracked," she told him. I wondered where she'd gotten that. Yes, there were strong women before us, but I broke that tradition and kept my girl from knowing the rest.

When I closed my heart on the past, on the good mother and good wife I'd once been, I never felt a profound connection to my daughter as some mothers describe—where they know when their child is in trouble in some psychic way. But I have to say, on the morning of November 11, 1961, I woke up in a panic and looked at my clock. Just 4 A.M. My heart was racing, and at first I thought it was a heart attack coming to claim me. I got up and took an aspirin, but my health seemed okay. I was scared, really scared, the way people must feel when the enemy is at the door and you know you're all going to be dragged off and killed. When I couldn't stand it anymore I called New Jersey and learned that this fear had come too late to be of any use. Mavis was dead. She'd cut her wrists in the night when everyone was asleep, and a neighbor woman was over there looking after Candace. Who was just seven. You would've thought I'd crumple and dissolve into the tears that were building up like breakers against the shore of my heart. But you'd be wrong. I stood in my kitchen, gripping the table before me and held on, held on, warding off a first tear that would bring on the ocean.

Myron wasn't raised Jewish but he had the impulse to go by Jewish custom now and bury my girl before the night was out. I don't know how he managed it, given the circumstances of her death, but he did. A friend drove me out there for the burial, worried I'd wreck myself on the way, so when I saw Myron and Candace the three of us were still in grim shock, wrapped tight like mummies. I think I pressed my granddaughter's hand and said, "Be good," or something else ridiculous. Inadequate. Myron was just twenty-eight years old but he stooped like an old man and his hands kept shaking. He never had a tremor before. He showed me something that managed to lift one corner of my numb grief into a trace of surprise. The week before he'd been insulating the attic and went through some old boxes that were laying around. He found a medicine mask, what some call a false face mask, wrapped in a flour sack.

"She wouldn't tell me about this," he said. "But I figured it must have come from you." He touched one of its copper eyes, set in a wooden face that was squashed in a twist on one side. That was when he broke and his whole body shuddered like it was going to fly to pieces. I wrapped him in my arms. "The night before, we went to a party," he sobbed. "We both had too much to drink which was a bad idea, given her mood. It's a depressive." I nodded my head and held him up. "When we got home she told me she was nothing. Nothing. I'd married a nothing. And I tried to make her see how wrong she was. I must've told her 'I love you' a hundred times that night, and it never came out the same way twice. I didn't even know I loved her so many ways."

I comforted my son-in-law the best I could and so I never had the chance to tell him about the mask, that it was made because my father had a dream, and he crafted the metal eyes himself, though the rest he left to a carver who sculpted it from a living tree. I didn't tell Myron that this mask had a way of bringing itself along even though we tried to ignore it. When I stormed from Kahnawà:ke, that mask was a secret stowaway my fingers grabbed and couldn't leave behind. I'd thought it was still in my possession. My girl who pretended she was Spanish royalty, who denied the Mohawk heritage I'd snatched her from, had carried away some piece of it despite herself. Locked away, yes. Hidden and forgotten, yes. But still there, waiting. Still alive.

[Ruby fell silent at this point, and when I stood, she didn't react—lost in reverie. So I left her for twenty minutes or so, went for another walk on the blooming grounds. Upon my return she picked up the story again as if she'd never stopped.]

RUBY: When I was a little girl I thought my parents were the sun and the moon. I mean I really thought my father got up before the day and hoisted that fiery red star into the sky with his huge hands, welded it in place so it could warm and light the world until he hauled it in for the night. Then I thought my Mama took over—singing and coaxing the milky pearl marble of the moon from its hiding place in the yard, urging it to fly into position so I could have a night light up there keep an eye on me. They were that big to me, that special, the first mother and father in all of creation.

The reservation where I was born, Kahnawà:ke, began as a settlement made up of Mohawks who'd converted to Christianity back in the 1600s. But my folks, they were more Mohawk than Catholic, and I grew up speaking our language and attending dances and ceremonies we had to make in secret because they were illegal. I had three older brothers who treated me like the best gift our parents ever gave them. I was happy. Those words are easy little words, aren't they? But they contain everything.

My father liked to tell me the story of where I came from—like a legend it became in the family. Here he was, a papa with three sons; wonderful brave boys, but, alas, only boys. He wanted a little girl to sweeten his life, oh, he wanted this so bad he had to chew his lip to keep from crying. No use, a long tear spilled over and sl-o-o-o-wly moved down his face and took with it a drop of blood from his lip. Then it fell onto the earth, the very dust at his feet. Because the tear came from such a deep place in his heart, from the marrow of his "bonesies, bonesies," he liked to sing at me, and from deep in his "toesies, toesies" (he'd be tickling me, too, by this point), the substance became a ruby teardrop—glistening and beautiful. He picked it up and brought it to his wife, telling her the story, and she swallowed the jewel the way the ground swallows a new seed. Months later, the long-cherished daughter, Ruby, was born. My father would ask then, "And who is she?"

"Me!" I would shout. "Me, that's me!" So you see, there was a time when I knew who I was.

My father was nine years old when they built that railroad bridge to cross the Saint Lawrence River onto our reservation—the Black Bridge in 1886. He was fascinated by the work of raising such a structure, he said steelworkers must be strong magicians—they could take a pile of dead steel and breathe it to life where it would become something out of nothing, a bridge or a skyscraper. It looked to him like they were trying to build their way back into the sky, that other world above us where the Original People come from. No one could keep him from going into that line of work when he was older—he joined an all-Mohawk raising gang and became a connecter. He always wanted to be the first one climbing the air, he said. Sky-walking. My mother worried about him and didn't worry. I think she believed in his magic steel as much as he did, and I seldom saw her nervous. He was such a big presence, my father, he dwarfed fear and bad temper. If you were standing beside him you couldn't help but feel good, feel like everything would be all right.

When I was four years old the whole family joined him when he worked to build a bridge near Quebec City. Of all the steelworkers working on the Quebec Bridge in 1907, about forty of them were Mohawks from our reservation. My father was excited to be part of this particular project because it was so challenging and would be one for the history books—the longest cantilever bridge in the world. The men worked long, hard days, but on Sundays we got to visit with our father and watch him and the others from home play lacrosse. He was a smiling player—the more fierce the combat, the harder he'd smile, the farther he'd stretch, the faster he'd run. They were all as graceful as dancers on the playing field, light on their feet in that panther way. No wonder they could skim across a narrow beam without losing their balance. Their skill as lacrosse players showed their skill on the job.

By August I sensed a change in the air, in everyone's mood. I was too young to be privy to much grown up talk, but I nibbled at the edges like a hovering ghost because I didn't like the feeling that clouds were chasing us. I guess there was some trouble with construction, things not lining up the right way they should, but more than that, the bridge felt to my father like a crooked thing, a being worked on by Shawiskara who unmakes the good work of his twin brother, Teharonhiawa:kon, by throwing some kink in the mix, some snarl. "It just doesn't feel *right," I remember him saying. My brothers told me years later that the morning of August 29, 1907, I woke earlier than usual, when it was still dark and my father was making ready to leave for the bridge. They said I cried like a banshee and kept clinging to our father, but when he asked me what was wrong I couldn't say, and just shook my head and howled some more. He was gentle with me, and it was my mother who had to pry me off so he could leave. All my fuss prevented him from hugging her the way he always did, whispering some love talk into the shell of her ear.*

I guess you know what happened after that. Near the end of the day, less than an hour before quitting time, that bridge came down, collapsed into the river. We heard the terrible noise and felt the ground shake like it was the end of the world. It became an ugly dead creature whose innards were torn open and twisted. A greedy death. The bridge killed seventy-five steelworkers, thirty-three of them Mohawk, and carried most of them down with it. Twenty-five of our friends and relatives from Kahnawà:ke, including my father, were never recovered from the disaster site. We didn't see him again, alive or dead, after that day.

We returned home and our community condoled with us in our grief. The Mohawk way and the Catholic way. I suppose it was all the support that got my mother through and held her up so she could keep going for us kids. She was a strong woman. That summer didn't break her, though she lost a lot of her laughter, and it became harder to make her smile beyond a small pinch of her lips. But me, I was a different story. I became like that bridge right before it broke—still standing, but in such a way that things weren't lined up right. Now when I looked at the sky it was only air. The sun was no longer a magic star pulled into place by my father, and the moon was nothing more than a cold white stone thrown at the sky.

I kept on living until suddenly I was a woman. People said I was pretty, like my mother, but the boys never sparked after me. Too sad, I guess. I had one good friend, a boy named Ab who had one of those minds that sees a story in everything. He could make the dullest day seem exciting once he started inventing a yarn. He mixed in just enough truth to confound us, and to this day I don't know all the pieces of his past—how much really happened and how much was created in his clever brain? Maybe he fell in love with me because of a story he told himself one day, making me mysterious and special? We grew up together, comfortable in each other's company and kindly in our dealings, and then the sweetness got cooked somehow and boiled over into steamy love soup. That woke me up, for sure, and brought me out of my gray days. Can you imagine living in black and white and then having loud color turned on without warning? That was how Ab changed my life. I'm calling him Ab the way folks did back then, sometimes Abby if they were real close. But his actual name was Absolom—how peculiar is that? His Mama had a fondness for the Bible and looked for those rare selections when naming her ten kids. After I crossed over into my love fog I didn't call him Ab anymore, but his full name—drawn out in a soft breath like I was kissing the word just to say it. Who knew I had so much romance squirreled away in my heart? I surprised even myself.

We got married in 1929 and liked to joke that just as the rest of the country was going to hell in a handbasket with the stock market crash and the start of the Depression, our fortunes were on the rise because now we had each other. And what did Absolom do for a living? He was a steelworker, too, like my father. Yet different in that he worked a decking gang, laying out the sheet metal floor. He wasn't a sky-climber so much as a company man—and I'm not talking about business. Absolom was part of a tight-knit group of boys who grew up to be the closest friends; buddies who had your back in any situation, who you could trust with your life. When a few of them started hankering to be steelworker cowboys (or warriors, I should say, since that's more how they thought of it on the reservation), the ones like Ab who might have gone on to something else followed along, just to keep the group together. Things had changed since my father's day. After the tragedy of 1907 the Clan Mothers decided that we couldn't afford to lose so many men on one job, so there were never more than a couple of Mohawk crews working the same project. Once we got married we did pretty well for ourselves. Despite the crash of the market a slew of buildings contracted in boom times were too far along to cancel, and bridges were still going up in the boroughs, so Absolom had steady work. He'd spend the week in Manhattan, then with a car-full of friends he'd head home to Kahnawà:ke for the weekend. I stayed on the reservation so we could save our money. If we'd gotten our own little place in the city it would've cost more than the crash pad the boys all shared. For me, the week was a sweet torture. I'd go about my work, tending the garden, canning, doing beadwork we could sell at fairs and to the tourists, but my mind would be tracing through each word and touch we'd shared the previous days. To have love doled out in precious bites like a rare candy, well, maybe that's what keeps it everlasting sweet. When you find your bashert, may your own union be like this.

I got married kind of late for those days, twenty-six, and when I didn't get pregnant right away, why, I thought my eggs were no longer fresh. What did I know? Now these actresses are having babies with forty-five-year-old eggs! My Mavis came along eventually, in 1933. She took her time. Maybe she was waiting for the Depression to be over and finally gave up. Maybe she sensed all the sadness to come and didn't want to get started. But her first two years were real happy at least. She was so lovely always, from the first to the last, her face like a little brown heart, her eyes black pools like they'd been painted with the richest dark ink. And she had her father's wild hair—thick black tufts that never wanted to lie down. My pileated woodpeckers, both of them. Absolom could sing, something he only did in private, croon to his girls. He sang us awake on Sundays, show tunes that were popular at the time like, "You're Getting to Be a Habit With Me." He was better than Dick Powell!

He told me once that our life together was finer than any stories he ever made up. I remember when he said this, our Mavis had just turned a year old that day so it was the night of May 4, 1934, and he'd pulled in in the wee hours, so glad to be home. Those were such good days I haven't been able to take them out and look at them until recently. Sometimes you can't bear the shine of old happiness—it will only remind you of the hole in your heart and maybe tear it open even more. These memories have been stored up in mothballs and buried underground. It's a shame. Absolom and my girl deserve to be remembered.

It was shortly after Mavis turned two that I was mocked for all the joy I'd been collecting. You know, because I lost my father such a bad way he became a talisman to me against further harm. I felt that the Creator would say, okay, you're paid up now and we'll leave well enough alone. Absolom was working on a building in Rockefeller Center, one of the last in that complex to be erected. The International Building at 630 Fifth Avenue, just forty-one stories tall which might have been impressive in former times but was overshadowed by more famous skyscrapers like the Empire State and Chrysler Buildings, or the RCA Building only a catty-corner angle away.

His best friend, Jonas, who worked the same gang, told me later what happened the afternoon Absolom died. He said my husband had just laid out another deck on an upper floor—a piece of corrugated metal for follow-up crews to stand on. He took off his work cap and used it to scrub the sweat off his forehead, swiped it back on, examined his work, clapped his hands together as though to indicate he was ready for the next job, then took a step back into empty air. He didn't fall to the sidewalk far below, but another deck thirty feet down. Some men have survived a drop like that, but Absolom fell backward and hit his head; he wasn't able to turn like a cat in the air.

I could not accept my husband's death even when his gray body was before me. My mind ran a loop of thought over and over, where I played through the events that led to his fall, each step, and then adjusted them to change the outcome. Now I *was the storyteller, saving him in the frozen vault of my brain. Saving him. Saving him. We'll all take a breath and step back from the edge and return him to me. Anything less than that was simply unimaginable. It was not possible that I would never hold him in my arms again. It was not possible that the scent of him would fade from the sheets and his clothes. It was not possible that he'd never again croon me a saucy love song. It was not possible.*

I lived in that strange place for several weeks, led around by my family who reminded me to wash and eat and comb my hair, reminded me that I had a little girl who needed me. When Absolom remained in his death and did not return, fury began to rise in me unlike anything I'd felt before. If I'd been a God, or a Sacred Being, I would have torn down the sky and ripped it to shaggy pieces. I would have pounded the earth into a fine powder. One morning I went deep into the woods, and when I thought there was no one near to listen I screamed and screamed and screamed until I damaged my voice and no more sound would come. And still I was screaming in my mind. Such anger is a kind of madness. What I did next I cannot excuse. I was so angry at the Creator for blasting my world not once, but twice, angry at my family because they could not work the miracle I needed and return my husband to me. The hurt and rage twisted me into my father's lost bridge, and now I would imitate its cruel revenge, how it got the last word on us all. I would disappear from the face of the earth as much as I could manage, walk away from the ones who would miss me. Powerful emotions leave a trail, and I wanted mine to shatter, so that anyone foolish enough to love me would be demolished by that mistake. I didn't care that I was condemning my own future and that of my daughter. As far as I was concerned we were already dead and just going through the motions. I did to my girl the opposite of what Absolom did for me. I snatched her from a world of rich color and locked her up in black and white. Took her from fragrant woods to a city apartment so small it was like a coffin.

[Ruby never cried during this—I want to call it—confession. She confessed to herself, to the powers she believed in, to you. The spark of her had always been so bright I was forgetful of her great age—but now I saw it. She was dim and small, diminished by memories. She stared at her hands as they fiddled and fiddled, plucked at the sheets. When she found what she'd been scrabbling for, she drew the thing from the tangle of her bedclothes and gently smoothed it across her lap.]

RUBY: Remember I said my pastrami sandwich, the gorgeous smell of it, was New York to me? Well, this is New York to me, too.

[She held out the fabric, and I saw it was a rectangle of leather hide, just a flap, really, tanned in a way that produced a rich, smoky fragrance.]

RUBY: Nice, isn't it? This was a gift from the spirits. They've been visiting me for weeks now, luring me back into my old skin. They had a heck of a time finding me, I'll bet! I wasn't in any of the usual places you might look for an old Mohawk lady. I wasn't in the kitchen or the woods, I wasn't in a Longhouse, or a church either. I wasn't in a condo, or a cabin on the reservation. Here I was in a Jewish rest home, playing Mahjongg with Mrs. Rabinsky, who cheats. Just goes to show, you can't generalize about Indians—we'll surprise you with our lives.

I know you're wondering about the spirits, though you're too polite to say so. Is this some kind of dementia talking, or what? Absolutely not. And I'm not one of those preachy people, trying to convert you to something or tell you what to believe. I don't have answers for you, just for myself. My answers came right in the door, sat down on my bed and filled my chairs, gave me no choice but to hear them out. I'm too old to storm around, you see, and that's how they got me.

Some of these spirits I know, and some of them I don't, but even the strange ones are connected. They're my ancestors, or my people's friends, and they're respectful about being in this place. They never raise their voices or make too much noise. Just talk to me real gently, tossing in a word of Mohawk here and there, like kanakta (that's "bed") and owira (that's "baby"), which is probably what I look like to them, an ancient baby in her crib. They never scold me for my mistakes, for living most of my life with a stony heart. They don't chide me for speaking English and a speck of Yiddish (or should I say, bisseleh?), but they offer me the old language in small sweet bites, like spoon-feeding. I think maybe my roommate, Mrs. Blum, must hear them as well. They barely talk above a whisper, but she's got those ear implants what make her hear when a bug lands on the window. I'm guessing this because the other day I forgot myself, and instead of greeting her in English, I said, "Sekoh, skennen ken." And she answered, "Hene, skennen kowa," just the way a person should. She didn't even notice she was talking Mohawk, just kept right on moving her arms in slow motion, doing her morning Tai Chi.

Different ones show up on different days. It isn't the same group every time. I've seen my parents and my brothers. Finally my husband came, and it was a shock because he looked like he did back when he died—so young and handsome. A lifetime ago. I was a little ashamed to have him see me this way, but maybe spirit eyes are different than these ones we have? He looked at me, and looked at me, like he was sucking on some kind of nectar and didn't want to pause even a second from the taste of the juice. We held hands and he reminded me what love talk sounds like in Mohawk—water rippling across stones is the best way I can describe it. Before he left he pulled something out of his back pocket and it was this, this beautiful hide. He held it to my nose and smiled, and all the joy came back to me as I smelled that sweet smoke.

I know what they're doing. It's a kind of healing ceremony to bring me back into my body after a lifetime of running away. So when I die I'll be at peace and make a good death. There was one spirit I never saw, and I was too afraid to ask about her. I worried that maybe she didn't find her way home since I'd done such a good job of spinning her around until she lost all sense of direction. And then, finally, she came. I saw my daughter last night. She sat on the edge of my bed and smiled at me. At first I couldn't look at her more than just a blink-look, fast, fast, that's how sad and ashamed I was of all what I did to her. I can't even cry properly anymore—these old eyes make sticky tears that won't fall. I wanted to cry then. I peeked the best I could and she kept smiling, which gave me courage. Then she held up her hands and I saw that the scars were gone—the ones on her wrists where she slashed herself. That told me she's done being injured. Being lost and angry and ashamed. That showed me better than any words. You see, it's forgiveness time, and if I don't forgive myself, all that love and generosity is just wasted. Hearts open and love pours at you, but you gotta let it in. Forgiveness is a door. All these spirits have been picking my locks, trying to get in, trying to reach my angry heart, my lonesome, ridiculous heart.

You know, I wondered at first what gave these spirits the courage to look for me in the first place? Several of them were ones I'd slammed the door on back in 1935. Why did they think they'd reach me now? More than seventy years I've been perfecting my escape. The answer hit me like someone threw a brick at my head. I laughed then, embarrassed. For all my dramatic retreat, worthy of an Oscar nomination, if not the prize, how far had I really gotten? I changed my name to West, sure, to turn my back on my people and the life that brought such heartbreak, only because it had also brought such joy. But I never moved *west, did I? I never left New York state, the homeland of my people. Hnh!*

[Your grandmother passed away a day after telling me this story. She appeared filled rather than drained once she'd finished, perhaps similar to the pleasing lightness one feels when we set down heavy luggage. It was my honor to know her and to be the bearer of this message which I never doubted was always meant for you.]

Candace Altman Jenssen was trembling the way her father had the day they buried her mother. All she remembered of that day was the dirty sky, spoiled by smears of soot-colored clouds she'd longed to reach up and clear away. Shakily she opened the packet Ari Engel had tucked in the larger mailer. She glanced at the photograph first—thirteen men holding lacrosse sticks posed in the tragic summer of 1907. Eight of them would be dead within the month. Their names were neatly labeled on the back so she quickly found her great-grandfather, a striking young man with smiling eyes. She handled the tanned hide next, brought it to her nose and breathed in the scent of smoky woods. So this was what home smelled like. She left the postcard for last. The dog-eared front pictured an unexceptional building with a painted sign in front reading: Kanien'kehá:ka Cultural Center. She took a breath, held it, and turned the card over. A single sentence was scrawled there in a slanted hand, surprisingly legible and robust. Ruby had written simply: I was wrong.

The past now littered her table, and Candace grabbed onto its edge to steady herself. "I am a Two-Axe woman," she said aloud. The violence of the name hit her then, how apt it was to put weapons in the hands of these Mohawk women—her mother and *her* mother—who had sliced themselves away from her. The thought made her shiver. She knew her life would not be the same. The contents of the package were, come to think of it, like the drop of an axe so swift and astonishing your life becomes a snake hacked in two, the pieces wriggling on either side of the cut, trying to remember how they once fit together. Yes, Candace mused. But this axe is sweet.

The Time of the New Mind

Candace stood in her private library before the shelf containing all of the photo albums she'd carefully put together over the years. No loose pictures in a shoebox for her; she'd typed and, in recent years, printed captions for each snap—what year, event, person. An entire life as methodically labeled as an archeological find. She pulled out the first in the series, its faux leather cover cracked and peeling, and carried it to her favorite armchair in the bedroom. She sat, holding the album on her knees. She tucked wings of hair that fell across her cheeks behind her ears, then flexed her arms and hands the way a concert pianist might before stroking the keys. Deep breath, open the book, her mother there on the very first page.

Mavis Two-Axe. So stunning, the one her father called "My dark Gypsy beauty," but only after she was gone; she wouldn't have stood for it in life. No reference to her "otherness" allowed beyond her own fancies.

"Just twenty-eight years old," Candace whispered. "Oh, Mother, you were so young. Five years older than my boys are now. I am so sorry."

Her mother was wearing a dark red dress, tight velvet that stretched across her voluptuous figure in a way that made you think, Va-va-voom! Shoulders bare, plunging neckline, but tasteful, old Hollywood style. Her dark hair permed into neat waves, her brows plucked into perfect arches. Lush red lips, painted in lipstick to match the dress. The red swirled before Candace's eyes and she covered them, but couldn't banish that final image, when she'd awakened in the night, frightened, and gone to the bathroom in the upstairs hall, the only one on that floor, for a drink of water. Finding her lovely, mysterious mother neck deep in cold water that looked to the seven-year-old like Kool-Aid—red as it was, sticky. She'd touched her mother, shaken her, and some of the red water had lapped over the rim of the tub and fallen on Candace's bare toes. She tried to pull her mother by the arm, and that's when she saw the slices; her mother had extra mouths where she shouldn't. Candace screamed and screamed, and then her father was there, howling beside her.

When Barry came home from work—it was his last month, he would be leaving the firm by Thanksgiving, "Then I'll *really* have something to be thankful for," he'd quipped—Candace was still sitting in the chair. She was reading a letter she'd tucked between pages in the album, uncharacteristically sloppy of her; she'd forgotten about it altogether. It was from her father, the last one he wrote before he went into hospice and she flew to New Jersey to be with him. The letter had accompanied the Iroquois Mask, she remembered now.

> Sweetheart, I've been going through some old boxes and came across this piece—something that belonged to your mother. He gave me a fright. Pretty funny, huh? A big galoof like me scared of some wood and hair? I'm not one to be superstitious, don't believe in more than I know, and that's mainly drains and pipes, but something came over me when I held this face. I knew beyond a shadow of a doubt that he belonged with you. That you might have need of him. Isn't that strange? Maybe it's all the chemicals they've pumped into me making me squirrelly at the end? But just in case there's more to this than I'll ever understand, I send him on to you, wanting you to always have everything you need in this life.
>
> You'll always be my Princess. I love you like crazy. If there's something on the other side of death, which I'm not holding my breath there is, don't you know I'll be watching your doings and rooting for you all the way!
>
> Love and kisses to my one and only. Your Dad.

Candace handed the letter to Barry. "We really lucked out when it came to our fathers," she said, wiping her eyes. "He didn't know but he *knew*—he sent me what I was going to eventually need."

"May I read this?" Barry asked, one hand curved around her head, stroking her hair.

"Please, and there's more downstairs. I'll get it for you." Candace retrieved the packet Ari Engel had so kindly sent her. She placed it on the arm of the chair. "Why don't you change and I'll finish supper. It'll take me a while. Would you mind looking at that, once you're more comfortable?" She indicated the packet.

"Of course," Barry said.

Candace was just setting out plates on the breakfast table when Barry joined her. He hugged her from behind and whispered in her ear, "My God, baby, I had no idea."

She turned and held him.

"Please forgive me those asinine jokes," he said, his voice husky with emotion.

"What?"

"You, your thing about bathtubs. Well, no wonder!"

"Can you believe, I didn't put it together, until you just said it? Our brains are amazing, aren't they? What they refuse to remember when we can't handle it."

All night memories of her mother washed through Candace like a ticker-tape running through her head. Many quite wonderful—the way her mother read aloud to her most nights to help her fall asleep, with great feeling and drama so the characters came alive and seemed to move around Candace's pretty room. Her father tried to read to her now and again, but it wasn't as satisfying. He had a flat, earnest delivery that made every moment sound the same. She recalled baking with her mother, crescent pecan cookies dusted with powdered sugar that just melted in your mouth in a miraculous way. More sophisticated than the sugar cookies her friends made with their mothers.

But some of the emerging stories were painful. One episode in particular would haunt Candace for days, perhaps because it happened just the week before her mother's death. It was early November, the trees looking lonesome without their leaves, or so Candace had thought as her mother walked her the few blocks to a meeting at a friend's house. They were Camp Fire Girls that year, their uniforms still new enough to be a novelty, their booklets and badges treated like treasures. Her mother wasn't going to stay, as some mothers did, just drop her off. But Candace didn't mind, she was used to her mother's elusiveness. That meeting had been particularly gratifying. The troop leader was telling them stories about Indians in preparation for Thanksgiving a few weeks away. She held up a book with pictures, and one page depicted a woman dressed in buckskins and feathers who looked just like Candace's mother. Candace raised her hand at some point and said, importantly, "I'm part Indian."

"You are?"

"Yes, Mohawk."

The troop leader was excited, said maybe she could ask her mother—it *was* her mother who was Mohawk?—to come and talk to the girls next time. Share some of her stories. Maybe teach them to bead?

This was when Candace realized her mistake, but it was too late. And when her mother fetched her after meeting's end, the leader fussed over her, asked her enthusiastic questions. Mavis was holding Candace's hand as the woman spoke, and she could feel the anger through that grasp. Her mother's fingernails pressed into Candace's palm, squeezed and cut. But all her mother said was, "I'm sorry to disappoint you, but it's just another one of my daughter's stories. She has *such* an imagination! She doesn't mean to *lie*." Then she'd turned and walked them down the steps, long silent blocks home. Candace was chewing her lip because the pain from her mother's nails was exquisite, a small torture, but she knew better than to cry.

Once they were home it was her mother who said, "Let me take a look," and caught her breath when she saw the angry smiles she'd carved into her girl's hand. "I'm sorry, Candy," she said, and she got out the bottle of mercurochrome and painted the wounds, which to Candace's way of thinking just made it that much worse.

"I forgive you, Mother," Candace whispered aloud each morning after receiving the illuminating packet from New York. She whispered the words until one day they were true, and the long horror of blood had drained away.

Maryam had told Candace that she would see her ancestor, Jigonsaseh, but when she asked how, when, Maryam shook her head and smiled. Didn't say. Then Maryam was gone and Candace's link to her ancestors seemed lost, except for the connections she'd made with living relatives in Kahnawà:ke. She planned to visit there in the spring, returning the basswood Face to his true home.

But one night as Candace slept, her ancestor walked into a silly dream she was having about attending a bowling party at the White House, she who had never bowled even once in her life. The bowling balls kept turning into birds that flew away before they reached the pins, and the handsome young president said, "See, this is why I prefer basketball."

Jigonsaseh stepped across the lanes until she stood before Candace. She removed the bowling ball from Candace's hands and rubbed it as if to dust it off. The ball became an eagle, and it flew to a corner of the room and, with a loud screech, clawed at the air until the place dissolved in tatters—nothing more than a painted backdrop. Now they stood in a forest, and tall trees rose around them, forming long alleys like the narrow vaulted aisles of a Gothic church.

"This is *my* church," Jigonsaseh said, as if she could hear Candace's thoughts. She led her to a fallen pine, and they sat there, staring at one another. Jigonsaseh had an oval face the color of gleaming cherrywood, her eyebrows long and straight above silver-black eyes. Her features were narrow, all lines and planes, yet the whole added up to a face Candace wanted to gaze at forever. Jigonsaseh held out her hand, and Candace offered hers. The older woman accepted it and stroked the palm with her strong fingers.

"My flesh is your flesh. My blood, your blood. Now my story is your story. I give it to you so you have something to stand on. We all need something to stand on in difficult times. I am glad you've left your shell and are back among the living. Your life is just beginning. I have a message I would like to share with you if you care to listen."

Candace said, "Yes, I'm listening."

"This is for you and all your relations who are starting to wake. We all come from tribal peoples at one time or another, each of us belongs to a clan, even if we've forgotten what it was. Remember your ancestors with respect, and don't let the invader schools and invader mind fool you. Some of you believe our old stories are simple children's tales told to amuse them and help them sleep, or dull things that go around and around in useless repetition you don't care to hear. Don't be fooled. You don't remember how a single word had fifty meanings behind it, each one with a story like a hidden seed. What you see as repetition is another version and still another version—each of them older and deeper, each of them taking you closer to the truth. You don't know how many of your ancestors were people of large spirits and minds who could hear the voice of the Creator as clearly as Yeshua did. But we are here now to remind you, to push you, because it's time to remember and wake up.

"Haven't you wondered why your generation is so unhappy? Your minds nervous and twitchy as a squirrel's? Or ground down in gray clouds of sadness? They are feeding you more and more medicines, but it doesn't heal you, it only makes you sicker. You are unhappy because you've lost the old trails and yet you know you've been chosen—the generation with the weight of the world's survival on your shoulders. Once you accept this responsibility and listen to us, your grandmothers of the clans, you won't be sick any longer. You won't feel so alone. We surround you. We see you. It's time for your spirits to grow and fit the shape of your new life. This will be a larger life than your mother's or father's. A bigger story. We will help you grow your spirit to fit the shape of your new life. I know it will happen. It's beginning. Now."

When Candace awakened the next morning she wrote down Jigonsaseh's message, astonished that she remembered it word for word. She would share it with Barry, and Gladys and Jules, her sons who would be home for the holidays. Maybe she'd share it with her extended family in Kahnawà:ke, though that was presumptuous, wasn't it? The lost sheep carrying teachings from the past? No matter, she would risk appearing foolish, pushy, because if she'd learned anything in the past weeks it was that you should always listen to your dreams.

A week before Thanksgiving the University of Minnesota hosted a Tlingit dance group from Juneau, Alaska—a visit Binah worked hard to manifest. She'd heard the group was traveling around the Midwest, performing in Chicago, Milwaukee, Madison, and Iowa City, and she arranged for them to make the detour to Minneapolis. There weren't funds in the department budget for hotel rooms, just an honorarium, so Candace offered to put them up in her house; there would be more than enough room, especially now that Gladys had moved into Jules's condominium just blocks away on Laurel Avenue. The presentation was for one night only at the university's Bell Auditorium, free and open to the public.

When Gladys and Jules arrived they were pleased to see a line of people snaking out of the building, waiting to find a seat inside. Merle had been left at home in Zhigaag's care, since the cat had taken a protective interest in the frail poodle. She was never clean enough to suit his immaculate standards.

"Gaawiin!" Gladys admonished when she thought his washing of Merle was excessive. He would blink at her and walk away for an hour, then join the dog in her bed, curl beside her to offer some of his warmth.

Jules was beaming as he viewed the young crowd before them and behind them. He told Gladys in a voice meant to be a whisper, only heard by half the assembled crowd: "I wish you'd let me wear a sign that says, 'Can you believe this woman is with me?!'" He kissed her hand and wouldn't let her have it back when she tugged. Gladys heard a smattering of kind laughter.

A woman about Binah's age said, "You give us all hope! Good for you."

Gladys leaned into him and gave him an example of a true whisper, hissing in his ear: "I didn't sign on to be a spectacle. Behave yourself." But she kissed him hard on the cheek to remove the sting of her words.

They spotted Grace and Dylan and waved them over. "My man!" Dylan said when he noticed Jules, and for the next five minutes tried to teach him a complicated handshake.

Grace kissed her mother on the cheek, saying, "You look radiant! Young love must agree with you."

Gladys shushed her, but couldn't stop smiling. She looked up at Jules and patted his face with her hand. "He's my Saint Paul surprise, this one. Aren't I lucky?"

Dylan lifted his grandmother in a hug and pretended nonchalance when she grabbed his upper arm, proclaiming: "Look at this! What are you feeding him? Spinach all day. We'll have to call him Popeye if he gets any stronger."

Suddenly Binah was waving at them from the door of the building. "I think she wants us to come over there," said Dylan, so the small group wove in and around the crowd to reach her.

"I've got seats reserved for you up front," she said. "Frank and Ava are already there, and Candace and Barry. Just look for them, and I'll join you once I've got the dancers settled."

Ava was standing on a seat to watch for them and waved so vigorously when she spotted Dylan she would have toppled over if Frank's hands hadn't been poised to catch her. "Over here, over here!" she called.

A small reunion took place in the aisle, Ava leaping into Dylan's arms. She latched a thin arm around his neck and told everyone, "I'm his pet howler monkey."

"Where'd you get that?" Dylan asked, and when she shrugged, her forehead wrinkled with the effort of remembering, everyone roared with laughter.

"Why do they do that?" she asked her cousin in a quiet voice.

"They think you're cute. Eat it up, it doesn't last long," he advised sagely. Then he called for attention, saying he had "momentous news."

"Not now," Grace murmured.

"Don't be modest. She's being modest," he argued. "Mom just learned that her proposal's been accepted, she'll have a show at the Minneapolis Institute of Art next year—a whole room to herself."

There were cheers all around, and Candace actually hopped up and down a couple of times. She didn't notice Barry's reaction to her enthusiasm, how he seemed lit by the warm joy in her face.

Candace said, "And Frank has his poetry book out this spring, and Barry was accepted into an acting class at the Guthrie. I'm surrounded by such talent!"

Splinters of conversation developed as they settled themselves in the old-fashioned leather seats that snapped and creaked in a cross way when they were made to open. Then Binah arrived and clambered over Grace and Dylan to sit between Ava and Frank.

"This will be good," she said, to the air, to everyone. "There's just something about them. You'll see, Mama," she turned to Gladys. "I bet you'll want to adopt them all after the performance."

The lights flickered twice, signaling everyone to find a seat. The audience quieted, and the house lights dimmed. A college student walked from the wings into the spotlight and nervously introduced the group, saying she was thrilled to get to hear the songs and see the dances of another tribe from such a different region. She, herself, was Dakota, she said. She spoke welcoming words in her own language and then told the audience the name of the Tlingit dance group was Woosh.ji.een, which meant "Hands Working Together." Then she hurried off the stage, nearly tripping down the black side stairs.

A young man stepped into the spotlight, and something about the intensity of his presence, the way he wielded a tall carved post and stood so simply, with great dignity, caused the audience to hold its breath in anticipation. He was barefoot, bare-chested, but wore a black vest intricately decorated with buttons along the edges and an appliquéd design of the eagle on its back. He gazed across the audience from one end of the hall to the other, as if he could see every face, as if each one mattered. When he finally spoke his voice was passionate, the way a person speaks when he believes with his whole heart what he is saying. He spoke in his ancestors' language, Tlingit, and then translated, honoring his people, his teachers, and the assembled crowd—offering gratitude. Young dancers joined him on the stage for an opening song, wearing button robes in red and black wool, appliquéd with images of coho and killer whales, ravens and eagles. They were carrying carved dance paddles, and some of them wore hats woven of cedar bark. The women danced together, turning from side to side, while the young men danced scenes of hunting and chasing the fish, paddling long miles in their boats.

After two numbers the group invited people from the audience to join them, and Ava was out of her seat in an instant, dragging Dylan behind her. Scores of students ran up the steps and followed the best they could. The dancers smiled at them all for their courage.

Gladys leaned over Frank to tell Binah, "You were right. There's something magic about them—it's the sincerity, I think. They're dancing with such open hearts." She pointed to either side of the room. "Can you feel it? There are more of us here than we can see with our eyes—they've brought out so many good spirits. Our ancestors are watching and they're proud."

Gladys rose to her feet and bobbed in place, dancing for her grandfather, her beloved husbands, and the strange man beside her who had won her heart. Then Jules stood, followed by Candace, Frank, and Barry, last of all the reluctant Binah, looking self-conscious, but allowing Frank to take her by the hand. People rose behind them, stomping and swaying, moved by old songs that had traveled such a distance of miles and years and interrupted history.

Too soon the evening was coming to a close, and the young leader of the group announced a closing song written by his wife, a tall, striking woman who had what Gladys called "Cleopatra eyes." The song was written in honor of her cousin who had been lost at sea—a farewell they sang to his spirit, wishing him a good journey, and to all the people who had come together to hear them. The women's voices were plaintive, you could hear the thick sorrow, and the rhythm was like the pounding of waves.

Dancers paddled the air and moved toward the edge of the stage, then danced down the steps and across the aisles of the hall. The audience fell in behind them, and the line moved out the door, into the cold night air. The song continued, singers following the young man who carried a hand drum. The drummer quickened the tempo, and the haunting farewell became hopeful and joyous—the unexpected reconciliation after all was thought to be lost. A song of the ocean, with rhythms unfamiliar to this territory, rang out beside the Mississippi River and was accepted, carried into its dark waves to merge with the first songs the river learned at the time of its beginning.

Clan Mother of Hope

The Gospel of Maryam

Maryam (2009)

Maryam left a gift for her friends when she moved out of the mansion—a micro-cassette tape, containing pieces of her story she wanted to share with Gladys and Candace. As she explained in an introductory statement, in her rich smoky voice that made Candace think of night-blooming flowers like jasmine, fragrant and mysterious, she had been circumspect about sharing too much of her own story when she was with them. She said this territory was not hers; she belonged to other soil, other hills and rivers, as did her tales. But to leave like a cipher when there had been such connection felt wrong as well.

"Each night I speak a few words into this device so you will know me better, as I know you," she told them. They listened eagerly, hearing the scratch of the reel, the water hiss of recorded air. And then:

. . . In the beginning were my mother's hands, beautiful to me though marked with nicks and burns from a life of service. I kissed each scar when she let me hold them. I traced the deep lines of her palms with my finger as if I had made those tracks, walking her hands with mine. She taught me songs to make our work a joyful prayer, and when I climbed steep hills to mind the goats I sang to them, and they flicked their ears at me in pleasure and bleated when I stopped. I longed to live with her forever, in the

shadow of her love and guidance, and the shy smile that was so difficult to win. She would cover her mouth to hide an overlapping tooth.

How she cried when I was chosen by the kind Yusef, and clutched me to her body as if she could bring me once more inside the nest of her womb. In the end she didn't lose me to my husband but to God, the one we didn't name. I think He was always standing there, outside our house, ready at the threshold to claim me before anyone. She would have cried even harder if she knew what it was to be chosen, for God does not enter you like a man. . . .

. . . Yusef, the one who waited. He told me that my honor was his honor, and he believed me. He looked into my eyes just once when we made the talk about my child, and I did not look away. His eyes were brown and green like the hills I knew so well. They were a comfort, and every chance I had to look in them was like coming home somewhere you are wanted.

When jealous women whose daughters were quiet and forgotten made noise about my shame, claimed my tale was nonsense, worse, was blasphemy, I was caught in their circle. They looked to me like mad crows about to eat my flesh, their tongues screeching whips that lashed and made me stumble. Then someone raised the stone and threw it at my head, struck me on the brow. I didn't guard my face but my unborn child instead. I tried to turn my back and blink away the dark blood, but they were all around me, so I turned and turned and turned. A cousin ran for Yusef, and he was suddenly there, making the crows scatter, shouting at them to respect our house. And that's when I knew, yes, he was my house, and when no one could see we held each other. We built a tower as we stood like that, our bodies leaned together, the child safe in his room between us. . . .

. . . All my life I favored salty olives except during the months my son built his strength inside me and I felt what he felt, I craved what he craved. Anything sweet he saw with my eyes was desired—a date, a fig, a cone of honey. Yusef never complained, but doubled his work to bring me fruits for my appetite, treats that were hard to come by. My son was not greedy, I tell you, but aware of the vinegar his life would be. And so in this rare time of peace before struggle he gathered enough sweetness to sustain him in all the savage days ahead. . . .

. . . Some say the birth of my son was painless—he was magicked from inside me in a way that circumvented my woman's channel, that narrow road to life. But they are wrong. They weren't there to hold my hand as Yusef did, when I near cracked his fingerbones as my child and I battled in my body. Why was it a war, my labor? Because of all I sensed, and my precocious infant feared. We knew, in our deepest

memory of promises made to God before we were created that this life would be a strange and difficult journey. My son didn't want to leave the safety of my womb that held him, shielded him from the waiting world. And I? I longed to keep him there as well, a cherished promise to hold for myself, unharmed, unchallenged. But I was God's disciple, fierce with faith, and so I crushed my husband's hand in mine, and chewed my lip to a shred of skin, and expelled my boy, pushed him, screaming and bloody, into his fate. . . .

. . . I kept his umbilical cord, dried it and wore it beneath my shift. I knew he would belong to the world, but this flesh was my selfish reminder that he was mine first. . . .

. . . Sometimes I had to remind my boy to be humble. When he was small he summoned all the butterflies until they covered him—not one inch of his flesh or garments showed. He stood like that in the courtyard, motionless and aquiver at the same time. A statue rippling with wings. Later, he would chide me when my belief in his abilities, my motherly pride, spurred me to ask miracles of him at every opportunity. Now he was humbled by the gifts and responsibilities his Father apportioned him. . . .

. . . Many days I longed to be a scatter of dust on a table. But we are, none of us, insignificant. I had to reconcile myself to that. We are all seen. What we do is remembered and collected, and not a single grain is ever lost. The hardest thing I ever did was not pray to God to release my son from his fate. Not ask to take his place, which I would gladly have done, because when you are a mother your child's pain is double what you yourself would suffer alone.

Instead I begged for strength to support him in his mission, his suffering. To endure what should not be endured, what is unnatural to accept. If I am a saint, then let me be Our Lady of Restraint, the one who lashed tight Our Lady of Tears, banished her, the emotional one, to a single chamber of my heart. Don't think she's dead, the keeper of my sorrows. I feel the cruel hook of her grief even today. Celebrate the things I never did, the absence of everything I would have done if I had been a natural mother. . . .

. . . I thought I would be prepared for my boy's sacrifice, the termination of flesh as I had known it and bathed it and kissed it. But when at last his suffering was done and I held him in my arms, I was not proud or reassured, I was not grateful, nor did I feel blessed. I was a creature so tormented I would gladly have eaten my own heart to end its pain. "Woman, I am risen, be glad," he told me in a dream even before the stone outside his crypt had rolled away to reveal its emptiness. But in truth my heart did not rejoice. And I would have forfeited the rest of the world entire to save this single child. . . .

. . . Oh, how they argue me, so much that even I become confused and see myself as a broken pane of glass, all splintered. Which shard is me? Which truth, my truth? Which story?

Some say I was conceived and born without sin, a stainless vessel made perfect by God. And yet I remember hiding from my mother when I was little, peeking from my sanctuary as she called and searched: "Maryam, where are you?" Her voice eventually threaded with fear and worry. I returned to her before her tears fell because I didn't want to cause her pain, merely exult in this show of love, to see how she missed me. And I remember the small cruelties of childhood, envy, impatience, selfishness, rebellion. Were these not sins?

I tell those scholars who would make my soul unblemished that they underestimate me and God's love for me. How easy it would have been if I were perfect, a saint from the first seed. I would never struggle, never doubt, never test my powerful faith. How unworthy a vessel is she who never suffers, never does battle with the weak snake of fear that coils in the gut. I believe God chose me for sacred duties because He trusted I would overcome my human frailties. I would never stop fighting the lower demon self that rides us all, twins us like a shadow.

God triumphs when we accept hard work and apply ourselves to the yoke. When we toil out of love and pinch our lazy hatreds to a speck—a bitter crystal. To become a pure vessel is salty work, why else is that substance found in our blood and tears and sweat? We are not given sweetness from the start, but work it in, bit by bit, until we brim with honey and love becomes our skin. . . .

. . . I close with an offering your ancestor neglected to share with you. She didn't want her vision to compete with her son's, but they belong together in the same story, how the son echoes the mother, and the mother echoes the son. She told me what she saw in a dream when she was still a girl:

I dreamt that I was an eagle with broad, speckled wings, perched on the topmost branch of a great white pine that grew on the summit of the tallest mountain in the world. From that place I could see everything. I could see our present world below me and the Sky World above me. I could see into the past where everyone who is now dead was yet living, and I could see into the future where the seeds of seeds had taken root and bloomed into new life.

The air where I stood was cold and thin; I realized as I breathed those scraping slices of air that what I was seeing was true. How I trembled in that tree, and if I didn't have great wings to pulse a little this way or that way when I leaned too far in one direction, I would have fallen. I prayed to the Creator, asked Him: Why am I here at the top of the world? Tell me what You want me to see. The answer, to face east where the future comes from. I was annoyed at first because I wanted to search west and watch the great histories of my ancestors play out as if I were living those days alongside them. But my will bowed down and my spirit took over.

I faced east where the sun was drumming its noisy light onto every field and object and creature, but where ordinarily the sun would scorch my vision with its brightness, in this dream I was able to look through the sun and witness behind it the days ahead where each picture was more complicated than the last. How quickly the people multiplied, like ferocious ants, building lodges in every corner and finally high into the sky. More people all the time but fewer of our relatives, the trees, and the Three Sisters who feed us so generously with their tender flesh were torn from one another and made to grow in separate lots where they withered in their grief. I shuddered at the next sight and called what I beheld the Time of the Woodtick—for some people had hoarded so much of what the earth offers they became bloated with tight, round bellies, and might as well have fed directly on their brother's blood, for other people fell like dry sticks in terrible, neglected piles of dead brush.

And where are we? I wondered, as I searched for my people. Relieved to find we were there, still there beyond the sun. But faded, like the soup you make in starvation times, stretching the flavor with water and more water to fill the pot. Our former strength hammered into dust. Ah, but then I smiled, for I saw the sense of our survival, our patience. How cunning is the fluff and down that floats from wild weeds; how harmless, insubstantial it seems as it drifts in the air, compliant, unnoticed, only to seed new life. For you see, we were now forgotten, overlooked by all the others who glanced past our faces as if we were nothing but ghosts, as if we had all been dispatched to the Village of the Dead where we would trouble them no longer. Our stories lost, and our means of telling them. Yet there I was, on the white pine that is our promise of peace—the Good News that is our gift to the world—still the foundation from which I balanced.

What I looked upon next would have cut me down if I hadn't been taught to look straight into what I most fear and welcome it with a smile. For I witnessed the Time When the Turtle Wakes! I will call it a crazy time since so much of what I saw did not make sense to me. This truly was a new world, bent to a new shape, led by people who were at war with the very earth they stood on—their arrows of ignorance shooting into the air, into the seas, into the soil, the stories on their lips and in their thoughts the empty vapors of dying men who cannot feed themselves in a desperate winter and so are forced to eat their moccasins. Just as a greedy bear tears open a hornets' nest so he can lick the ripe larvae from his paws, so did the people of the future tear everything they could from the earth atop the Turtle's back. Until she waked and protested and painted her face for war. It is a terrible thing to see a mother fight her children, but I was made to watch this kind of battle. The mother's anger flared from her thoughts and blazed across the land in hungry fires. The mother's sorrow wept from the sky and rained floods that covered villages. She huffed with impatience and unleashed great storms of wind, she shivered in pain, injured as she was, and shook the people with her. I could not harden my heart against these foolish people, or chide them for their mistakes. I cried like the mother and wanted to close my eyes against their suffering. *Have courage,* I heard my heart speak, and so I continued watching, glad now that I did. For every foolishness there is a remedy, and the mother's laws always tip toward balance. I saw how the people had fallen together in their extremity so that now they were a comfort to one another and cherished each other. I saw how my own descendants stepped forward to break trail in the new snow, in the ashes, planting the Good News, sowing peace. And so my dream ended with the Time of the New Mind.

When your ancestor finished reciting her dream her features were pleasant with relief. She held my hand like a sister before she left, and we placed our foreheads together for a moment to acknowledge how much our thoughts ran together in sympathy. And what did I make of her dream, her prophecy? It settled upon me like the truth. Do you know these words in Ecclesiastes?

The thing that hath been, it is that which shall be;
and that which is done is that which shall be done;
and there is no new thing under the sun.
Is there anything whereof it may be said, see, this is new?
It hath been already of old time, which was before us.
There is no remembrance of former things;
neither shall there be any remembrance of things that are
to come with those that shall come after.

The phrases have a kind of weary sense that holds me down in my spirit, persuasive on days when the rain never ceases but cries with the grim determination of old women who will not stop grieving. Yes, an industrious man must resent the yoke of a circle, how what is born must necessarily die—his efforts, his children, his pleasures, his life, all lost to him in the end. But, I would argue, this is the bleak perspective of a man, not a mother's. For when your blood has divided itself into new blood, and a mind that will never produce thoughts like yours grows miraculously within the vessel containing your own mind, when bones fragile as the skeleton of a fish knit themselves into a boy's strength and your child cries for the first time in a voice you recognize as unique from all others—you realize this is surely new life you have nourished in the planet of your womb and none like him has ever lived before, nor shall ever live again. And, I would offer, that these words are the conviction of a man sensitive to ambition, and never the view of his grandmother whose memory is long, her sacks and pockets lined with stories, memorializing all that has come before, which she will gladly tell you if only you are willing to hear. Jigonsaseh told me that her people, like the author of Ecclesiastes, believe in the circle, the repetition of cycles and lessons, the wheel of time, but to her way of thinking it is never flat, never a single trench running over and over itself like the tracks of deer in deep snow. It is my thought, also, that the circle I believe in is more like the spiraling chambers of a nautilus shell that repeat a curling pattern without ever covering the same ground, rather coiling tighter and tighter, until you find yourself at the perfect center of all things.

It has been my honor to speak on behalf of your grandmother, who came so long before you but is never gone. Remember, all knowledge of the past is still available if you are only willing to ask for it with a humble and open heart. Ask, and it shall be given you; seek, and ye shall find; knock, and it shall be opened unto you. *These things are now matters between you and your ancestors.* Ye are the light of the world. A city that is set on a hill cannot be hid. *At least, not forever. As for my part, think of me as just another grandmother whose apron is bunched tight with stories—some of them comical, some of them so pathetic they can break your heart, and some of them powerful enough to save the world.*

Assumption

The day Maryam left was a bright cold morning in early October, the wind not chilly enough to make the average Minnesotan shiver yet carrying a crystal-blue edge that sharpens the mind. Gladys and Candace walked with Maryam through Crocus Hill, up and down tree-shaded streets, their progress watched by rabbits and woodpeckers and the shy albino squirrels who peeked from bushes.

"This is the one," Maryam indicated with a gentle lift of her chin. The three women stopped on Goodrich Street before a roomy lemon-yellow house decorated with wood lace trim. A tall pine reigned over the front lawn, its generous branches reaching impossibly high like a ladder to heaven. "This is how I want to return," Maryam said, the smallest glint of mischief sparked her eyes. "How often can we be a girl again?"

Gladys smiled broadly and clapped her hands together. "I'd follow you up there if I thought I'd make it down again. Knowing me, I'd get trapped like an old cat. Then you'd have to call the fire department."

Candace laughed, nervously, and looked all around to be certain they weren't observed by neighbors. Gladys noticed her apprehension.

"Don't worry," she offered. "We'll be out of here before we get in trouble. And maybe what my Grandpa told me years ago might be of help to you. He said:

'Noozis, what do you care what people think of you as long as you know what you're doing is right?' That's stayed with me all this time."

"Good advice," Candace said. She squared her shoulders and stopped checking for watchers.

Maryam looked uncertain how to begin so Gladys said, "Here, we'll give you a boost." Maryam tied her sandals to her belt, and Gladys and Candace joined hands to create a step for her small bare foot. She was so light they barely felt the nudge of toes that gripped their palms as she sprang onto the lower branches of the fragrant giant.

Suddenly, unexpectedly, the women left standing on the ground began to cry. Silent tears rolled down their cheeks. Maryam was already halfway to the summit of the pine when she paused to peer down.

"Chi Megwetch," she said, and, "Nia:wen, Pidamaya, Toda, Tusen Takk." All the many ways there are to express gratitude.

Gladys replied, "And also with you."

The women waved to Maryam as she climbed, admiring her swift grace, and gasped when her pocket overturned to shower them with the sunflower seeds she liked to crack with her little teeth. Some of the seeds burrowed into a clump of loose soil and later sprouted in abundance in the middle of the yard to the owner's astonishment. But none of us should be surprised. For the soil of the Americas is unembarrassed ground, determined to bring forth miracles.

Acknowledgments

This novel was a seven-year odyssey, and I could not have completed it without the support of many people.

Thank you to my mother, Susan K. Power, for being the first enthralled audience to these pages, and for the spiritual journey she took with me as I covered so much sacred ground on behalf of my characters. I'm grateful as well for her activism and community involvement—what a rich upbringing I had meeting Native peoples from so many different regions.

I offer gratitude to the many dear friends and family members whose support has made my creative life possible: Irene Connelly, Louise LeBourgeois, Cheri LeBeau, Alyssa Haywoode and Malcolm Robinson, Reuben Auspitz and Dawn Good Elk, Rosemary Fei and Gary Harrington, Brenna Daugherty Gerhardt, Susan and Michael Howe, Sharmagne Leland-St. John, Rachel Kadish, Bradley Pritchett, Erika Wurth, Jim Denomie and Diane Wilson, Joy Harjo, Marguerite Anderson.

I am profoundly grateful to early readers who offered encouragement and insight: Nancy Linnerooth, Galway McCullough, Elizabeth Fletcher, Patti Sloan, Denise Breton, Karen Straus, Lisa Brooks, Brianna Burke, Laura Livrone, Carter Meland, Julie Hart, Heidi Mastrud, Mimi Goodwin, Elizabeth Diamond Gabriel, and Ernestine Hayes.

Thank you to my Choctaw sister, LeAnne Howe, for championing my writing and for all the terrific advice which helped me find the right home for this labor of love.

For generous friendship and encouragement, I am enormously grateful to my colleagues in the American Indian Studies Department at the University of Minnesota and my fellow writers at Hamline University's Graduate Writing Program, in particular Brenda Child, Jeani O'Brien, Sheila O'Connor, and Mary Rockcastle.

I have been blessed to find a group of people in my adopted home of the Twin Cities who have become family, in particular Andrea Carlson and Ted Cushman, Paula Anderson, Elizabeth Fletcher, Patti Sloan, Julie Hart, Shannon Scott, Renée Copeland, Heather Johnson, and Katherine Kline. Thank you for the many ways you inspire me and sustain me.

I offer much gratitude to the many Native communities, including my own Dakota Nation, that taught me so much when I was growing up, conferring more wisdom than any institution of higher learning. In particular I'd like to acknowledge the Ho-Chunk people (and my Ho-Chunk Godmother, Angeline DeCorah) who always treated my family with such warm generosity, especially during difficult times. I'm enormously grateful as well to the Kanien'kehá:ka community of Akwesasne where my family stayed on several memorable occasions. Our connection to this powerful place was the remarkable Tom Porter, and while it was an honor to attend his traditional Longhouse wedding back in 1971, I recall being devastated that he hadn't waited for me to grow up so I could marry him (I was ten years old and just adored him). I will never forget the profound words given to us by Rarihokwats (Jerry Gambill) of *Akwesasne Notes* upon my father's death and the histories Ray Fadden shared with us. (And thank you Lisa Brooks for putting Tom Porter's important book into my hands at the perfect time!) Finally, I extend my appreciation to the Ojibwe friends who welcomed me upon my move to the Twin Cities, in particular the Erdrich family who immediately invited me into their homes and lives.

This novel could not have been completed without assistance from the United States Artists organization which is working tirelessly on behalf of American artists. I was blessed to receive one of their fellowship awards in 2006 which bought me writing time free of financial stress, as well as another grant in 2010 which gave me the opportunity to spend a month in Sitka, Alaska as part of the Island Institute. Walking in the Sitka woods every day worked on me like a balm and helped me finally hear Jigonsaseh's voice which had been eluding me for so long. I am grateful to Carolyn Servid and Dorik Mechau for making my stay in Sitka such a joy. Toward the end of the trip I was fortunate to be able to visit Juneau and spend time with Tlingit author Ernestine Hayes whose writing and vision give me hope for the future of our troubled world. My gratitude to her and her family for hosting me so graciously and introducing me to the terrific young people at University of Alaska Southeast. What an honor it was to dance with Woosh.ji.een!

I am enormously grateful to Gordon Henry and Julie Loehr at Michigan State University Press for championing this book and giving it a home! Without you these characters would not be heard. I would also like to thank the editors at *Natural Bridge* and *Yellow Medicine Review* for publishing chapters of the novel in their literary journals, in particular Drucilla Wall and Chip Livingston.

While I have thanked some of them already given specific contributions they have made to the completion of this book, it is my pleasure to offer my love, respect, and eternal appreciation to those friends who make this strange journey possible—sharing their lives and joys and struggles, reminding me I am never alone: Andrea Carlson, Irene Connelly, Nancy Linnerooth, Louise LeBourgeois, Elizabeth Fletcher, Paula Anderson, Tasha Harmon, and Patti Sloan.

Finally, a resounding Megwetch to Galway Krishna McCullough for generous-hearted love and support, patience and mischief, guidance and laughter, for introducing me to the original, unforgettable Zhigaag, and for bringing the beloved fire.